An Introduction to Literature of English

Reading, Explicating, & Responding Critically

英语文学概论

邓绪新 编著

武汉大学出版社

图书在版编目(CIP)数据

英语文学概论=An Introduction to Literature of English/邓绪新编著.—武汉:武汉大学出版社,2002.7(2024.1重印)
ISBN 978-7-307-03496-9

Ⅰ.英… Ⅱ.邓… Ⅲ.英语—文学—文学评论 Ⅳ.I106

中国版本图书馆CIP数据核字(2002)第008868号

责任编辑:黄朝昉　　责任校对:王　健　　版式设计:支　笛

出版发行:**武汉大学出版社**　(430072　武昌　珞珈山)
(电子邮箱:cbs22@whu.edu.cn 网址:www.wdp.com.cn)
印刷:湖北金海印务有限公司
开本:850×1168　1/32　印张:13.5　字数:337千字
版次:2002年7月第1版　　2024年1月第9次印刷
ISBN 978-7-307-03496-9/I·254　　定价:49.00元

Contents

Drama

Critical Approaches to Literature

Glossary of Literary Terms

Preface

Introduction to literature of English*: *Reading*, *Explicating*, *and Responding Critically is a unique book . Not only of selected readings, the book is also a comprehensive guide to explicating and responding to literature. From my own experience of teaching literature, I have found that almost everybody who studies literature experiences the same problem: how to explicate and respond to the text. It is perfectly possible for students of English and of literature to read a story or a poem over and over again and yet still to feel baffled and at loss as to what to say about it. One way of solving this problem, of course, is to go to the library, look it up in some reference books and be ready to accept someone else's view of the text. But how much rewarding it would be if they could work out their own critical response to any work they choose or are required to study.

The aim of this book is to help them develop their critical skills by offering a variety of original texts, explaining some basic elements of literature, and providing some practical models and advice to read, understand, analyze and respond to literature critically. The mastery of this skill can teach them never to take for granted; it can also develop within their critical skills, incisive thinking, and a sense of judgement. Learning the complexities expressed in the brief form of a poem, for instance, can teach them to look for the details in simple things. Each chapter provides them with a major subject and a clear method of study so that they can see how to set about tackling texts on their own. It also attempts to provide them with some broad ideas about the kind of texts they are likely to be studying and some ideas about how to think about literature. It then shows them how to apply these ideas in helping them construct their own analysis and interpretation.

The book is not an exhaustive one , and is not intended to the student a general coverage of major authors; rather, it is designed to expose them to the major literary genre—fiction, poetry and drama—and to some masters of language. The usual topics and terms of literary scholarship are discussed, such as plot, character, point of view, figurative language, symbolism, irony, form and style, and so forth. In addition, the book also pays some attention to representative, basic sub - genres (the sonnet and the tragedy, as examples) in order better to understand the demands of artistic form. My hope is that although this book is, on the whole, intended to serve a practical purpose, it may also enrich their enjoyment of literature by making them more confident readers, alert to the interest and pleasure to be derived from literary texts.

Xuxin Deng

2002. 1

Fiction

Chapter 1 Plot

Although an independent part of all fiction and drama, whether in prose or verse, plot is a concept about which there has been much disagreement. Aristotle called it "the first principle" and "the soul of a tragedy." He called it "the imitation of an action" and also "the arrangement of the incidents." The action imitated should be "a whole"—that is, it should have a beginning, a middle and an end. A plot, Aristotle maintained, should have unity, that is, imitating one whole action. He disliked episodic plots, "in which the acts succeed one another without probable or necessary sequence."

E. M. Forster made a helpful distinction between **story** and plot. A story is "a narrative of events in their time-sequence. A **plot** is also a narrative of events, the emphasis falling on causality." A story arouses only curiosity; a **plot** demands intelligence and memory. Thus plotting is the process of converting story into plot, of changing a chronological arrangement of incidents into a causal and inevitable arrangement. Thus functioning of some kind of intelligent overview of ACTION, which establishes principles of selection and relationship among EPISODES, make a plot. Clearly there must be more than one episode, and equally clearly the relation among the episodes must be close. Out of the welter of experience, a selection of episodes is made that in itself constitutes a "whole" action.

Critics, particularly in the nineteenth and twentieth centuries, have quarreled with Aristotle's assigning plot the chief place in a dramatic composition, and have insisted that CHARACTER and CHARACTERIZATION are more important, the plot being merely a "mechanical means" by which a STRUCTURE designed to display CHARACTERS is arranged. Based on their arguments, we might tentatively formulate a definition like this: **Plot** is an intellectual formulation about the relations among the incidents of a DRAMA or a NARRATIVE, for EPISODES do not in themselves make a plot, the plot lies in relations among episodes. To define plot as an intellectual formulation is to define it as formulation of incidents—CHARACTERS and ACTIONS—and how they relate.

Since the plot consists of CHARACTERS performing actions in incidents that comprise a "single, whole, and complete" ACTION, this relation involves CONFLICT between opposing forces. CONFLICT is the struggle that grows out of the interplay of the two opposing forces in a plot. CONFLICT provides interest, suspense, and tension. At least one of the opposing forces is usually a person, or, if an animal or an inanimate object, is treated as though it were a person. This person, usually the PROTAGONIST, may be involved in CONFLICTS of four different kinds: (1) a struggle against nature, as in Jack London's "*To Build a Fire*"; (2) a struggle against another person, usually the ANTAGONIST, as in Stevenson's "*Treasure Island*"; (3) a struggle against society, as in the novels of Dickens and George Eliot; or (4) the struggle against fate or destiny. However, we seldom find a simple, single CONFLICT in a Plot, but rather a complex one involving two or more of the preceding elements. For example, the basic CONFLICT in Hamlet may be interpreted as a struggle within Hamlet himself, but it is certainly also a struggle against his uncle as ANTAGONIST and even a struggle against nature and destiny. Dreiser's *Sister Carrie* records a girl's struggle against society, as represented by the city, and yet it is also a struggle against her animal nature and even partly with herself. CONFLICT, in short, is the raw material out of which Plot is constructed. Without conflict, without composition, plot does not exist. This opposing force knits one incident to another and develops the struggle. This struggle between the forces, moreover, comes to a high tension in some one incident—the CRISIS; and then comes to the highest tension in that incident—the CLIMAX—that forms the turning point of the STORY. In this climactic EPISODE the RISING ACTION comes to an end and the FALLING ACTION begins; and as a result of this incident some DENOUEMENT or CATASTROPHE is bound to follow.

In brief, the **Plot** of a story usually has this structure:

1. **Exposition**—setting forth of the initial situation or setting the scene, including the introduction of the main characters and any other background information.

2. **Conflict**—a complication that moves to a climax.

3. **Denouement**—the outcome of the conflict or the resolution or "the untying of the knot".

This structure might be demonstrated as follows:

Let us look at the Grimm brothers' tale "*Godfather Death*". The tale has a beginning, a middle, and an end. It begins with an EXPOSITION. The exposition is brief—all in the opening

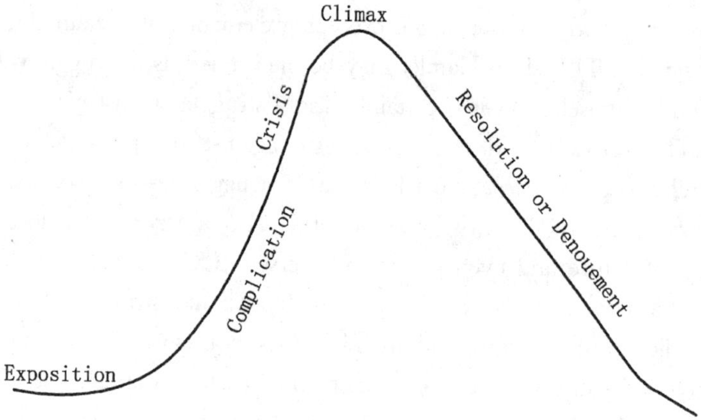

paragraph: the unfolding of a dramatic situation (a poor man with many children to feed), the introduction of the main characters (besides the poor man, we have God, Devil and Death) and some other background information that we need in order to understand and care about the events to follow. The middle section of the story begins with the second paragraph in which Death gives the herb to the boy and warns the boy not to defy him and ends with the fourth paragraph in which the doctor defies his godfather for a second time. This section is a COMPLICATION in which the son and not the father is to be central human character of the story (the son as the protagonist and the godfather as the antagonist). It provides some basic elements of the RISING ACTION before the action moves to the CLIMAX. The statement "But take care not to use the herb against my will or it could be the worst for you" (see the second paragraph) may serve both as a WARNING and a FORESHADOWING. In the third paragraph, SUSPENSE is created among the readers (Will the doctor triumphs over Death? Does the doctor stand any chance against such a superman? What will be the outcome of his defiance?) When SUSPENSE goes, a CRISIS comes (The doctor defies his godfather for the first time) and at the end of this paragraph another WARNING or FORESHADOWING appears ("... but if you ever dare do such a thing again, you put your own head in the noose and it is you I shall carry away with me.") In the fourth paragraph, another CRISIS is produced (The doctor cheats his godfather for a second time.) CLIMAX comes with the last paragraph, which is the moment of greatest tension at which the OUTCOME is to be decided and finally comes DENOUEMENT in which Death allows the little candle to go out and "the doctor sank to the ground and had himself fallen into the hands of death." And the story ends with Death's triumphing over the doctor.

Jakob Grimm (1785—1863) and ***Wilhelm Grimm*** (1786—1859)

Godfather Death

Translated by Lore Segal

A poor man had twelve children and worked night and day just to get enough bread for them to eat. Now when the thirteenth came into the world, he did not know what to do and in his misery ran out onto the great highway to ask the first person he met to be godfather. The first to come along was God, and he already knew what it was that weighed on the man's mind and said, "Poor man, I pity you. I will hold your child at the font and I will look after it and make it happy upon earth." "Who are you?" asked the man. "I am God." "Then I don't want you for a godfather," the man said. "You give to the rich and let the poor go hungry." That was how the man talked because he did not understand how wisely God shares out wealth and poverty, and thus he turned from the Lord and walked on. Next came the Devil and said, "What is it you want? If you let me be godfather to your child, I will give him gold as much as he can use, and all the pleasures of the world besides." "Who are you?" asked the man. "I am the Devil." "Then I don't want you for a godfather," said the man. "You deceive and mislead mankind." He walked on and along came spindle-legged Death striding toward him and said, "Take me as godfather." The man asked, "Who are you?" "I am Death who makes all men equal." Said the man, "Then you're the one for me; you take rich and poor without distinction. You shall be godfather." Answered Death: "I will make your child rich and famous, because the one who has me for a friend shall want for nothing." The man said, "Next Sunday is the baptism. Be there in good time." Death appeared as he had promised and made a perfectly fine godfather.

When the boy was of age, the godfather walked in one day, told him to come along, and led him out into the woods. He showed him an herb which grew there and said, "This is your christening gift. I shall make you into a famous doctor. When you are called to a patient's bedside I will appear and if I stand at the sick man's head you can boldly say that you will cure him and if you give him some of this herb he will recover. But if I stand at the sick man's feet, then he is mine, and you must say there is no help for him and no doctor on this earth could save him. But take care not to use the herb against my will or it could be the worse for you."

It wasn't long before the young man had become the most famous doctor in the whole world. "He looks at a patient and right away he knows how things stand, whether he will get better or if he's going to die." That is what they said about him, and from near and far the people came, took him to see the sick, and gave him so much money he became a rich man. Now it happened! that the king fell ill. The doctor was summoned to say if he was going to get well. When he came to the bed, there stood Death at the feet of the sick man, so that no herb on earth could have done him any good. If I could only just this once outwit Death! thought the doctor. He'll be annoyed, I know, but I am his godchild and he's sure to turn a blind eye. I'll take my chance. And so he lifted the sick man and laid him the other way around so that Death was standing at his head. Then he gave him some of the herb and the king began to feel better and was soon in pesfect health. But Death came toward the doctor, his face dark and angry, threatened him with raised forefinger, and said, "You have tricked me. This time I will let it pass because you are my godchild, but if you ever dare do such a thing again, you put your own head in the noose and it is you I shall carry away with me."

Soon after that, the king's daughter lapsed into a deep illness. She was his only child, he wept day and night until his eyes failed him and he let it be known that whoever saved the princess from death should become her husband and inherit the crown. When the doctor came to the sick girl's bed, he saw Death at her feet. He ought to have remembered his godfather's warning, but the great beauty of the princess and the happiness of becoming her husband so bedazzled him that he threw caution to the winds, nor did he see Death's angry glances and how he lifted his hand in the air and threatened him with his bony fist. He picked the sick girl up and laid her head where her feet had lain, then he gave her some of the herb and at once her cheeks reddened and life stirred anew.

When Death saw himself cheated of his property the second time, he strode toward the doctor on his long legs and said, "It is all up with you, and now it is your turn," grasped him harshly with his ice-cold hand so that the doctor could not resist, and led him to an underground cave, and here he saw thousands upon thousands of lights burning in rows without end, some big, some middle-sized, others small. Every moment some went out and others lit up so that the little flames seemed to be jumping here and there in perpetual exchange. "Look," said Death, "these are the life lights of mankind. The big ones belong to children, the middle-sized ones to married couples in their best years, the little ones belong to very old people. Yet children and the young often have only little lights." "Show me my life light", said the doctor, imagining that it must be one of the big ones. Death pointed to a little stub threatening to go out and said, "Here it is." "Ah, dear godfather," said the terrified doctor, "light me a new one, do it, for my sake, so that I may enjoy my life and become king and marry the beautiful princess." "I cannot," answered Death. "A light must go out before a new one lights up." "Then set the old on top of a new one so it can go on burning when the first is finished," begged the doctor. Death made as if to grant his wish, reached for a tall new taper, but because he wanted revenge he purposely fumbled and the little stub fell over and went out. Thereupon the doctor sank to the ground and had himself fallen into the hands of death.

John Updike (1932—)

A & P*

In walks three girls in nothing but bathing suits. I'm in the third check-out slot, with my back to the door, so I don't see them until they're over by the bread. The one that caught my eye first was the one in the plaid green two-piece. She was a chunky kid, with a good tan and a sweet broad soft-looking can with those two crescents of white just under it, where the sun never seems to hit, at the top of the backs of her legs. I stood there with my hand on a box of HiHo crackers trying to remember if I rang it up or not. I ring it up again and the customer starts giving me hell. She's one of these cash-register-watchers, a witch about fifty with rougc on her cheekbones and no eyebrows, and I know it made her day to trip me up. She'd been watching cash registers for fifty years and probably never seen a mistake before.

---

* *A & P*: "The Great Atlantic and Pacific Tea Company," a large grocery chain still operating in many states of America.

By the time I got her feathers smoothed and her goodies into a bag—she gives me a little snort in passing, if she'd been born at the right time they would have burned her over in Salem— by the time I get her on her way the girls had circled around the bread and were coming back, without a pushcart, back my way along the counters, in the aisle between the check-outs and the special bins. They didn't even have shoes on. There was this chunky one, with the two-piece—it was bright green and the seams on the bra were still sharp and her belly was still pretty pale so I guessed she just got it (the suit)—there was this one, with one of those chubby berry-faces, the lips all bunched together under her nose, this one, and a tall one, with black hair that hadn't quite frizzed right, and one of these sunburns right across under the eyes, and a chin that was too long—you know, the kind of girl other girls think is very "striking" and "attractive" but never quite makes it, as they very well know, which is why they like her so much—and then the third one, that wasn't quite so tall. She was the queen. She kind of led them, the other two peeking around and making their shoulders round. She didn't look around, not this queen, she just walked straight on slowly, on these long white prima-donna legs. She came down a little hard on her heels, as if she didn't walk in her bare feet that much, putting down her heels and then letting the weight move along to her toes as if she was testing the floor with every step, putting a little deliberate extra action into it. You never know for sure how girls' minds work (do you really think it's a mind in there or just a little buzz like a bee in a glass jar?) but you got the idea she had talked the other two into coming in here with her, and now she was showing them how to do it, walk slow and hold yourself straight.

She had on a kind of dirty-pink—beige maybe, I don't know—bathing suit with a little nubble all over it and, what got me, the straps were down. They were off her shoulders looped loose around the cool tops of her arms, and I guess as a result the suit had slipped a little on her, so all around the top of the cloth there was this shining rim. If it hadn't been there you wouldn't have known there could have been anything whiter than those shoulders. With the straps pushed off, there was nothing between the top of the suit and the top of her head except just *her*, this clean bare plane of the top of her chest down from the shoulder bones like a dented sheet of metal tilted in the light. I mean, it was more than pretty.

She had sort of oaky hair that the sun and salt had bleached, done up in a bun that was unraveling, and a kind of prim face. Walking into the A & P with your straps down, I suppose it's the only kind of face you *can* have. She held her head so high her neck, coming up out of those white shoulders, looked kind of stretched, but I didn't mind. The longer her neck was, the more of her there was.

She must have felt in the corner of her eye me and over my 5
shoulder Stokesie in the second slot watching, but she didn't tip. Not this queen. She kept her eyes moving across the racks, and stopped, and turned so slow it made my stomach rub the inside of my apron, and buzzed to the other two, who kind of huddled against her for relief, and they all three of them went up the cat-and-dog-food-breakfast-cereal-macaroni-rice-raisins-seasonings-spreads-spaghetti-soft-drinks-crackers-and-cookies aisle. From the third slot I look straight up this aisle to the meat counter, and I watched them all the way. The fat one with the tan sort of fumbled with the cookies, but on second thought she put the packages back. The

sheep pushing their carts down the aisle—the girls were walking against the usual traffic (not that we have one-way signs or anything)—were pretty hilarious. You could see them, when Queenie's white shoulders dawned on them, kind of jerk, or hop, or hiccup, but their eyes snapped back to their own baskets and on they pushed. I bet you could set off dynamite in an A & P and the people would by and large keep reaching and checking oatmeal off their lists and muttering "Let me see, there was a third thing, began with A, asparagus, no ah, yes, applesauce!" or whatever it is they do mutter. But there was no doubt, this jiggled them. A few houseslaves in pin curlers even looked around after pushing their carts past to make sure what they had seen was correct.

You know, it's one thing to have a girl in a bathing suit down on the beach, where what with the glare nobody can look at each other much anyway, and another thing in the cool of the A & P, under the fluorescent lights, against all those stacked packages, with her feet padding along naked over our checkerboard green-and-cream rubber-tile floor.

"Oh Daddy," Stokesie said beside me. "I feel so faint."

"Darling," I said. "Hold me tight." Stokesie's married, with two babies chalked up on his fuselage already, but as far as I can tell that's the only difference. He's twenty-two, and I was nineteen this April.

"Is it done?" he asks, the responsible married man finding his voice. I forgot to say he thinks he's going to be manager some sunny day, maybe in 1990 when it's called the Great Alexandrov *

---

* *Great Alexandrov and Petrooshki*: Apparently a reference to the possibility that someday Russia might rule the United States.

and Petrooshki Tea Company or something.

What he meant was , our town is five miles from a beach , with a big summer colony out on the point, but we're right in the middle of town, and the women generally put on a shirt or shorts or something before they get out of the car into the street. And anyway these are usually women with six children and varicose veins mapping their legs and nobody, including them, could care less. As I say, we're right in the middle of town, and if you stand at our front doors you can see two banks and the Congregational church and the newspaper store and three real-estate offices and about twenty-seven old freeloaders tearing up Central Street because the sewer broke again. It's not as if we're on the Cape * ; we're north of Boston and there's people in this town haven't seen the ocean for twenty years. The girls had reached the meat counter and were asking McMahon something. He pointed, they pointed, and they shuffled out of sight behind a pyramid of Diet Delight peaches. All that was left for us to see was old McMahon patting his mouth and looking after them sizing up their joints. Poor kids, I began to feel sorry for them, they couldn't help it.

Now here comes the sad part of the story, at least my family says it's sad but I don't think it's sad myself. The store's pretty empty, it being Thursday afternoon, so there was nothing much to

---

* *the Cape*: Cape Cod, the southeastern area of Massachusetts, a place of many resorts and beaches.

do except lean on the register and wait for the girls to show up again. The whole store was like a pinball machine and I didn't know which tunnel they'd come out of. After a while they come around out of the far aisle, around the light bulbs, records at discount of the Caribbean Six or Tony Martin Sings or some such gunk you wonder they waste the wax on, six-packs of candy bars, and plastic toys done up in cellophane that fall apart when a kid looks at them anyway. Around they come, Queenie still leading the way, and holding a little gray jar in her hand. Slots Three through Seven are unmanned and I could see her wondering between Stokes and me, but Stokesie with his usual luck draws an old party in baggy gray pants who stumbles up with four giant cans of pineapple juice (what do these bums *do* with all that pineapple juice? I've often asked myself) so the girls come to me. Queenie puts down the jar and I take it into my fingers icy cold. Kingfish Fancy Herring Snacks in Pure Sour Cream: 49¢. Now her hands are empty, not a ring or a bracelet, bare as God made them, and I wonder where the money's coming from. Still with that prim look she lifts a folded dollar bill out of the hollow at the center of her nubbled pink top. The jar went heavy in my hand. Really, I thought that was so cute.

Then everybody's luck begins to run out. Lengel comes in from haggling with a truck full of cabbages on the lot and is about to scuttle into that door marked MANAGER behind which he hides all day when the girls touch his eye. Lengel's pretty dreary, teaches Sunday school and the rest, but he doesn't miss that much. He comes over and says, "Girls, this isn't the beach."

Queenie blushes, though maybe it's just a brush of sunburn I was noticing for the first time, now that she was so close. "My mother asked me to pick up a jar of herring snacks." Her voice kind of startled me, the way voices do when you see the people first, coming out so flat and dumb yet kind of tony, too, the way it ticked over "pick up" and "snacks." All of a sudden I slid right down her voice into her living room. Her father and the other men were standing around in ice-cream coats and bow ties and the women were in sandals picking up herring snacks on toothpicks off a big plate and they were all holding drinks the color of water with olives and sprigs of mint in them. When my parents have somebody over they get lemonade and if it's a real racy affair Schlitz in tall glasses with "They'll Do It Every Time" cartoons stencilled on.

"That's all right," Lengel said. "But this isn't the beach." His repeating this struck me as funny, as if it had just occurred to him, and he had been thinking all these years the A & P was a great big dune and he was the head lifeguard. He didn't like my smiling—as I say he doesn't miss much—but he concentrates on giving the girls that sad Sunday-school-superintendent stare.

Queenie's blush is no sunburn now, and the plump one in 15
plaid, that I liked better from the back—a really sweet can—pipes up, "We weren't doing any shopping. We just came in for the one thing."

"That makes no difference," Lengel tells her, and I could see from the way his eyes went that he hadn't noticed she was wearing a two-piece before. "We want you decently dressed when you come in here."

"We *are* decent," Queenie says suddenly, her lower lip

pushing, getting sore now that she remembers her place, a place from which the crowd that runs the A & P must look pretty crummy. Fancy Herring Snacks flashed in her very blue eyes.

"Girls, I don't want to argue with you. After this come in here with your shoulders covered. It's our policy." He turns his back. That's policy for you. Policy is what the kingpins want. What the others want is juvenile delinquency.

All this while, the customers had been showing up with their carts but, you know, sheep, seeing a scene, they had all bunched up on Stokesie, who shook open a paper bag as gently as peeling a peach, not wanting to miss a word. I could feel in the silence everybody getting nervous, most of all Lengel, who asks me, "Sammy, have you rung up this purchase?"

I thought and said " No " but it wasn't about that I was 20
thinking. I go through the punches, 4, 9, GROC, TOT—it's more complicated than you think, and after you do it often enough, it begins to make a little song, that you hear words to, in my case "Hello (*bing*) there, you (*gung*) hap-py *pee*-pul (*splat*)!" — the *splat* being the drawer flying out. I uncrease the bill, tenderly as you may imagine, it just having come from between the two smoothest scoops of vanilla I had ever known were there, and pass a half and a penny into her narrow pink palm, and nestle the herrings in a bag and twist its neck and hand it over, all the time thinking.

The girls, and who'd blame them, are in a hurry to get out, so I say "I quit" to Lengel quick enough for them to hear, hoping they'll stop and watch me, their unsuspected hero. They keep right on going, into the electric eye; the door flies open and they flicker across the lot to their car, Queenie and Plaid and Big Tall Goony-Goony (not that as raw material she was so bad), leaving me with Lengel and a kink in his eyebrow.

"Did you say something, Sammy?"

"I said I quit."

"I thought you did."

"You didn't have to embarrass them." 25

"It was they who were embarrassing us."

I started to say something that came out "Fiddle-de-doo." It's a saying of my grandmother's, and I know she would have been pleased.

"I don't think you know what you're saying," Lengel said.

"I know you don't," I said. "But I do." I pull the bow at the back of my apron and start shrugging it off my shoulders. A couple customers that had been heading for my slot begin to knock against each other, like scared pigs in a chute.

Lengel sighs and begins to look very patient and old and gray. 30
He's been a friend of my parents for years. "Sammy, you don't want to do this to your Mom and Dad," he tells me. It's true, I don't. But it seems to me that once you begin a gesture it's fatal not to go through with it. I fold the apron, "Sammy" stitched in red on the pocket, and put it on the counter, and drop the bow tie on top of it. The bow tie is theirs, if you've ever wondered. "You'll feel this for the rest of your life," Lengel says, and I know that's true, too, but remembering how he made that pretty girl blush makes me so scrunchy inside I punch the No Sale tab and the machine whirs "pee-pul" and the drawer splats out. One advantage to this scene taking place in summer, I can follow this up with a

clean exit, there's no fumbling around getting your coat and galoshes, I just saunter into the electric eye in my white shirt that my mother ironed the night before, and the door heaves itself open, and outside the sunshine is skating around on the asphalt.

I look around for my girls, but they're gone, of course. There wasn't anybody but some young married screaming with her children about some candy they didn't get by the door of a powder-blue Falcon station wagon. Looking back in the big windows, over the bags of peat moss and aluminum lawn furniture stacked on the pavement, I could see Lengel in my place in the slot, checking the sheep through. His face was dark gray and his back stiff, as if he'd just had an injection of iron, and my stomach kind of fell as I felt how hard the world was going to be to me hereafter.

Questions:

1. What part of the story seems like the exposition? How does Updike set the story in an ordinary supermarket?
2. Where in "A & P" does the dramatic conflict become apparent? What moment in the story brings the crisis? What is the climax of the story?
3. Does anything lead you to expect Sammy to make some gesture of sympathy for the three girls? What incident earlier in the story seems a foreshadowing?
4. How fully does Updike draw the character Sammy? What traits does Sammy show? To what extent is he more thoroughly and fully portrayed than the doctor in "Godfather Death"?
5. What comment does Updike—through Sammy—make on supermarket society?

Anton Chekhov (1860—1904)

Misery

Translated by Constance Garnett

"To Whom Shall I Tell My Grief?"

The twilight of evening. Big flakes of wet snow are whirling lazily about the street lamps, which have just been lighted, and lying in a thin soft layer on roofs, horses'backs, shoulders, caps. Iona Potapov, the sledge-driver, is all white like a ghost. He sits on the box without stirring, bent as double as the living body can be bent. If a regular snowdrift fell on him it seems as though even then he would not think it necessary to shake it off.... His little mare is white and motionless too. Her stillness, the angularity of her lines, and the stick-like straightness of her legs make her look like a halfpenny gingerbread horse. She is probably lost in thought. Anyone who has been torn away from the plough , from the familiar gray landscapes, and cast into this slough, full of monstrous lights, of unceasing uproar and hurrying people, is bound to think.

It is a long time since Iona and his nag have budged. They came out of the yard before dinner-time and not a single fare yet. But now the shades of evening are falling on the town. The pale light of the street lamps changes to a vivid color, and the bustle of the street grows noisier.

"Sledge to Vyborgskaya!" Iona hears. "Sledge!"

Iona starts, and through his snow-plastered eyelashes sees an officer in a military overcoat with a hood over his head.

"To Vyborgskaya," repeats the officer. "Are you asleep? To 5
Vyborgskaya!"

In token of assent Iona gives a tug at the reins which sends cakes of snow flying from the horse's back and shoulders. The officer gets into the sledge. The sledge-driver clicks to the horse, cranes his neck like a swan, rises in his seat, and more from habit than necessity brandishes his whip. The mare cranes her neck, too, crooks her stick-like legs, and hesitatingly sets off...

"Where are you shoving, you devil?" Iona immediately hears shouts from the dark mass shifting to and fro before him. "Where the devil are you going? Keep to the right!"

"You don't know how to drive! Keep to the right," says the officer angrily.

A coachman driving a carriage swears at him; a pedestrian crossing the road and brushing the horse's nose with his shoulder looks at him angrily and shakes the snow off his sleeve. Iona fidgets on the box as though he were sitting on thorns, jerks his elbows, and turns his eyes about like one possessed, as though he did not know where he was or why he was there.

"What rascals they all are!" says the officer jocosely. "They are 10
simply doing their best to run up against you or fall under the horse's feet. They must be doing it on purpose."

Iona looks at his fare and moves his lips... Apparently he means to say something, but nothing comes out but a sniff.

"What?" inquires the officer.

Iona gives a wry smile, and straining his throat, brings out huskily: "My son..., er... my son died this week, sir."

"H'm! What did he die of?"

Iona turns his whole body round to his fare, and says:

"Who can tell! It must have been from fever... He lay three days in the hospital and then he died... God's will."

"Turn round, you devil!" comes out of the darkness. "Have you gone cracked, you old dog? Look where you are going!"

"Drive on! drive on!..." says the officer. "We shan't get there till tomorrow going on like this. Hurry up!"

The sledge-driver cranes his neck again, rises in his seat, and with heavy grace swings his whip. Several times he looks round at the officer, but the latter keeps his eyes shut and is apparently disinclined to listen. Putting his fare down at Vyborgskaya, Iona stops by a restaurant, and again sits huddled up on the box... Again the wet snow paints him and his horse white. One hour passes, and then another...

Three young men, two tall and thin, one short and hunchbacked, come up, railing at each other and loudly stamping on the pavement with their galoshes.

"Cabby, to the Police Bridge!" the hunchback cries in a cracked voice. "The three of us,... twenty kopecks!"

Iona tugs at the reins and clicks to his horse. Twenty kopecks is not a fair price, but he has no thoughts for that. Whether it is a rouble or whether it is five kopecks does not matter to him now so long as he has a fare... The three young men, shoving each other and using bad language, go up to the sledge, and all three try to sit down at once. The question remains to be settled: Which are to sit down and which one is to stand? After a long altercation, ill-temper, and abuse, they come to the conclusion that the hunchback must stand because he is the shortest.

"Well, drive on," says the hunchback in his cracked voice, settling himself and breathing down Iona's neck. "Cut along! What a cap you've got, my friend! You wouldn't find a worse one in all Petersburg...."

"He-he!... he-he!..." laughs Iona. "It's nothing to boast of!"

"Well, then, nothing to boast of, drive on! Are you going to drive like this all the way? Eh? Shall I give you one in the neck?"

"My head aches," says one of the tall ones. "At the Dukmasovs' yesterday Vaska and I drank four bottles of brandy between us."

"I can't make out why you talk such stuff," says the other tall one angrily. "You lie like a brute."

"Strike me dead, it's the truth!..."

"It's about as true as that a louse coughs."

"He-he!" grins Iona. "Me-er-ry gentlemen!"

"Tfoo! the devil take you!" cries the hunchback indignantly. "Will you get on, you old plague, or won't you? Is that the way to drive? Give her one with the whip. Hang it all, give it her well."

Iona feels behind his back the jolting person and quivering voice of the hunchback. He hears abuse addressed to him, he sees people, and the feeling of loneliness begins little by little to be less heavy on his heart. The hunchback swears at him, till he chokes over some elaborately whimsical string of epithets and is overpowered by his cough. His tall companions begin talking of a certain Nadyezhda Petrovna. Iona looks round at them. Waiting till there is a brief pause, he looks round once more and says:

"This week... er... my... er... son died!"

"We shall all die,..." says the hunchback with a sigh, wiping his lips after coughing. "Come, drive on! drive on! My friends. I simply cannot stand crawling like this! When will he get us there?"

"Well, you give him a little encouragement... one in the neck!"

"Do you hear, you old plague? I'll make you smart. If one stands on ceremony with fellows like you one may as well walk. Do you hear, you old dragon? Or don't you care a hang what we say?"

And Iona hears rather than feels a slap on the back of his neck.

"He-he!..." he laughs. "Merry gentlemen... God give you health!"

"Cabman, are you married?" asks one of the tall ones.

"I? He-he! Me-er-ry gentlemen. The only wife for me now is the damp earth.... He-ho-ho!... The grave that is!... Here my son's dead and I am alive.... It's a strange thing, death has come in at the wrong door.... Instead of coming for me it went for my son...."

And Iona turns round to tell them how his son died, but at that point the hunchback gives a faint sigh and announces that, thank God! they have arrived at last. After taking his twenty kopecks, Iona gazes for a long while after the revelers, who disappear into a dark entry. Again he is alone and again there is silence for him.... The misery which has been for a brief space eased comes back again and tears his heart more cruelly than ever. With a look of anxiety and suffering Iona's eyes stray restlessly among the crowds moving to and fro on both sides of the street: can he not find among those thousands someone who will listen to him? But the crowds flit by heedless of him and his misery.... His misery is immense, beyond all bounds. If Iona's heart were to burst and his misery to flow out, it would flood the whole world, it seems, but yet it is not seen. It has found a hiding-place in such an insignificant shell that one would not have found it with a candle by daylight....

Iona sees a house-porter with a parcel and makes up his mind to address him.

"What time will it be, friend?" he asks.

"Going on for ten.... Why have you stopped here? Drive on!"

Iona drives a few paces away, bends himself double, and gives himself up to his misery: He feels it is no good to appeal to people. But before five minutes have passed he draws himself up, shakes his head as though he feels a sharp pain, and tugs at the reins.... He can bear it no longer.

"Back to the yard!" He thinks. "To the yard!"

And his little mare, as though she knew his thoughts, falls to trotting. An hour and a half later Iona is sitting by a big dirty stove. On the stove, on the floor, and on the benches are people snoring. The air is full of smells and stuffiness. Iona looks at the sleeping figures, scratches himself, and regrets that he has come home so early....

"I have not earned enough to pay for the oats, even," he thinks. "That's why I am so miserable. A man who knows how to do his work,... who has had enough to eat, and whose horse has had enough to eat, is always at ease...."

In one of the corners a young cabman gets up, clears his throat sleepily, and makes for the waterbucket.

"Want a drink?" Iona asks him. 50

"Seems so."

"May it do you good.... But my son is dead, mate.... Do you hear? This week in the hospital.... It's queer business...."

Iona looks to see the effect produced by his words, but he sees nothing. The young man has covered his head over and is already asleep. The old man sighs and scratches himself.... Just as the young man had been thirsty for water, he thirsts for speech. His son will soon have been dead a week, and he has not really talked to anybody yet.... He wants to talk of it properly, with deliberation.... He wants to tell how his son was taken ill, how he suffered, what he said before he died, how he died.... He wants to describe the funeral, and how he went to the hospital to get his son's clothes. He still has his daughter Anisya in the country.... And he wants to talk about her too.... Yes. he has plenty to talk about now. His listener ought to sigh and exclaim and lament.... It would be even better to talk to women. Though they are silly creatures, they blubber at the first word.

"Let's go out and have a look at the mare," Iona thinks. "There is always time for sleep.... You'll have sleep enough, no fear...."

He puts on his coat and goes into the stables where his mare is 55
standing. He thinks about oats, about hay, about the weather.... He cannot think about his son when he is alone.... To talk about him with someone is possible, but to think of him and picture him is

insufferable anguish....

"Are you munching?" Iona asks his mare, seeing her shining eyes. "There, munch away, munch away.... Since we have not earned enough for oats, we will eat hay.... Yes,.... I have grown too old to drive.... My son ought to be driving, not I.... He was a real coachman.... He ought to have lived...."

Iona is silent for a while, and then he goes on:

"That's how it is, old girl.... Kuzma Ionitch is gone.... He said goodbye to me .... He went and died for no reason.... Now, suppose you had a little colt, and you were mother to that little colt.... And all at once that same little colt went and died.... You'd be sorry, wouldn't you?..."

The little mare munches , listens , and breathes on her master's hands. Iona is carried away and tells her all about it.

Questions:

1. What can we know from the first paragraph of the story?
2. What do you think is the theme of "Misery"?
3. Do you think the ending is, in a way, a happy ending?

Chapter 2 Point of View

Every story is told by someone. Mark Twain wrote "*Adventures of Huckleberry Finn*," but he does not tell the story; Huck is the speaker, and he begins to tell his own story:

> You don't know about me without you have read a book by the name of *The Adventures of Tom Sawyer*, but that ain't no matter. That book was made by Mr. Mark Twain, and he told the truth, mainly. There was things which he stretched, but mainly he told the truth.

The above passage gives a reader a very strong sense of the narrator—of the invented person who tells the story, and the work is expected to be chiefly about the speaker. Now compare that opening page with this one from Hawthorne's "*Young Goodman Brown*":

> Young Goodman Brown came forth at sunset into the street at Salem village; but put his head back, after crossing the threshold, to exchange a parting kiss with his young wife. And Faith, as the wife was aptly named, thrust her own pretty head into the street, letting the wind play with the pink ribbons of her cap while she called to Goodman Brown.

In this passage, a reader is scarcely aware of the personality of the narrator; our interest is almost entirely in the scene that the speaker reveals, not in the speaker's response to the scene.

To identify the narrator of a story, describing any part he or she plays in the events and any limits placed upon his knowledge, is to identify the story's **Point of View. Point of View** is the standpoint from which a story is told or the angle from which a fictional work is narrated or the perspective from which a story is presented to the reader. Theoretically, a great many points of view are possible. But in reading fiction, again and again we encounter familiar and recognizable points of view. Here is a list of them that may provide a few terms with which to discuss the stories that you read and to describe their points of view:

Participant (or First-Person) Point of View:

1. a major character.
2. a minor character.

Nonparticipant (or Third-Person) Point of View:

3. all knowing (seeing into any of the characters).
4. seeing into one major character.
5. seeing into one minor character.
6. objective (not seeing into any characters).

In a first person narrative, the story is told by "I," one of the characters involved in the story. Such a narrator may be the protagonist as in Charlotte Bronte's "*Jane Eyre*" and in Mark Twain's "*Adventures of Huckleberry Finn*" or may be an observer—a minor character standing a little to one side, watching a story unfold that mainly involves someone else.

First person narrators may be reliable, in which case the reader can pretty much accept what they say or they may be **unreliable narrators**. An unreliable narrator is one who does not understand the full implications of what he reports or one who makes incorrect conclusions and assumptions about events witnessed, or perhaps one who is mentally impaired, even insane; this type is exemplified by the narrator of Edgar Allen Poe's "*The Tell-Tale Heart.*" As the author has kept showing us in the story, the narrator's view of things is untrustworthy. You don't kill someone just because you dislike the look in his eyes.

The attitudes and opinions of a narrator aren't necessarily those of the author; in fact, we may notice a lively conflict between what we are told and what we are meant to believe. This is the result of a related device—the **naive narrator**, that is, a story may be told by an **innocent narrator**, a character who does not have the sophistication to understand the full implications of the story's events, though the reader understands. In this case, the narrator is usually a child (as in "Huckleberry Finn" in which Huck accepts without questioning the morality and lawfulness of slavery and feels guilty about helping Jim, a runaway slave) or a not-too-bright adult (as in William Faulkner's novel "*Sound and Fury*," the idiot Benjy, a grown man with the intellect of a child). Such a story, in which the reader understands more than the teller himself does, is Ring Larder's "*Haircut*," a story told by a garrulous barber who does not perceive that the "accident" he is describing is in fact a murder. The tension between the limited comprehension of the narrator and the wider vision shared by the author and reader usually creates the Dramaic Irony that is an important part of the effect in such works.

In a non-participant (or third-person) point of view, the teller of the story is not a character in the story. The narrator has receded from the story. If the point of view is omniscient (**all-knowing**), the teller can at any time enter the mind of any or all of the characters and is capable of knowing, seeing, and telling whatever he or she wishes. This is the point of view in "*Godfather Death*," whose narrator knows the feelings and motives of the father, of the doctor, and even of Death himself.

Furthermore, a distinction can be made between **neutral** or **impartial omniscience** (the narrator recounts the thoughts and actions of the characters, but does not judge them or comment on them) and **editorial omniscience** (the narrator not only recounts, but also judges). The narrator in Hawthorne's "*Young Goodman Brown*", for example, knows what goes on in the mind of Brown, and he comments approvingly or disapprovingly: "With this excellent resolve for the future, Goodman Brown felt himself justified in making mare haste on his present evil purpose."

Because a short story can scarcely hope to develop effectively a picture of several minds, an author may prefer to limit his or her omniscience to the minds of only a few of the characters, or even to that of one of the characters, whether a major character or a minor one. This point of view is sometimes called **limited** (or **selective**) **omniscience.** Limited omniscience provides a focus, especially if it is limited to a single character. When thus limited, the author sees one of the characters from outside and from inside and sees other characters only from the outside and from the impact they make on the mind of this selected receptor. In "*Young Goodman Brown*" the reader sees things mostly as they make their impact on the protagonist's mind.

He could have well-nigh sworn that the shape of his own dead father beckoned him to advance, looking downward from a smoke wreath, while a woman, with dim features of despair, threw out her hand to warn him back. Was it his mother? But he had no power to retreat one step, nor to resist, even in thought, when the minister and good old Deacon Gookin seized his arms and led him to the blazing rock.

When selective omniscience attempts to record mental activity or presents thoughts and sense impressions in a lifelike fashion, it is sometimes called **stream-of-consciousness** point of view. In the 20th century, some writers attempted to capture the total flow of their characters' consciousness, rather than limit themselves to rational thoughts. To represent the full richness, speed, and subtlety of the mind at work, the writer may incorporate snatches of incoherent thought, ungrammatical constructions, and free association of ideas and images. When in his novel "*Ulysses*" James Joyce takes us into the mind of Leopold Bloom, an ordinary Dublin mind well-stocked with trivia and fragments of odd learning, the reader may have an impression not of a smoothly flowing stream but of an ocean of miscellaneous things, all crowded and jostling.

> As he set foot on O'Connell bridge a puffball of smoke plumed up from the parapet. Brewery barge with export stout. England. Sea air sours it, I heard. Be interesting some day to get a pass through Hancock to see the brewery. Regular world in itself. Vats of porter, wonderful. Rats get in too. Drink themselves bloated as big as a collie floating.

Perceptions—such as the smoke from the brewery barge—trigger Bloom's reflections. A moment later, as he casts a crumpled paper ball off the bridge, he recalls a bit of science he learned in school, the rate of speed of a falling body: "thirty-two feet per sec." The stream-of-consciousness novel commonly uses the narrative techniques of Interior Monologue. In addition to James Joyce's "*Ulysses*", another masterpiece of stream-of-consciousness is William Faulkner's "*The Sound and Fury.*"

Finally, sometimes a third-person narrator does not enter even a single mind, but describes events from the outside. Telling us what people say and how their faces look, he leaves us to infer their thoughts and feelings. Such a point of view is **objective** (sometimes called **the camera** or **fly-on-the-wall** [This metaphor assumes the existence of a fly with a highly discriminating gaze, who knows which details to look for to communicate the deepest meaning.]). Since the absence of comment and of dissection of the mind often produces the effect of a play, this method is sometimes called **the scenic method**, because it unfolds the story in scenes like a play. By any name, the method, a form of the objective method, is characterized by complete objectivity in description of characters and scenes and in reporting of action and speech. Much of Hemingway's "*Cat in the Rain*" is objective, consisting of bits of dialogue that make the story look like a play:

> "I'm going down and get the kitty," the American wife said.
>
> "I'll do it," her husband offered from the bed.
>
> "No, I'll get it. The poor kitty out trying to keep dry under a table."
>
> The husband went on reading, lying propped up with the two pillows at the foot of the bed.
>
> "Don't get wet," he said.

The absence of comment on the happenings forces readers to make their own evaluations of the happenings. In the passage just quoted, when Hemingway writes "'Don't get wet,' he said," readers probably are forced to think that the husband is indifferent to his wife. Above all, how can she go out into the rain and not get wet? The writer uses an objective point of view, and yet, still controls the feelings of the reader.

Ernest Hemingway (1899—1961)

Cat in the Rain

There were only two Americans stopping at the hotel. They did not know any of the people they passed on the stairs on their way to and from their room. Their room was on the second floor facing the sea. It also faced the public garden and the war monument. There were big palms and green benches in the public garden. In the good weather there was always an artist with his easel. Artists liked the way the palms grew and the bright colors of the hotels facing the gardens and the sea. Italians came from a long way off to look up at the war monument. It was made of bronze and glistened in the rain. It was raining. The rain dripped from the palm trees. Water stood in pools on the gravel paths. The sea broke in a long line in the rain and slipped back down the beach to come up and break again in a long line in the rain. The motor cars were gone from the square by the war monument. Across the square in the doorway of the café a waiter stood looking out at the empty square.

The American wife stood at the window looking out. Outside right under their window a cat was crouched under one of the dripping green tables. The cat was trying to make herself so compact that she would not be dripped on.

"I'm going down and get that kitty," the American wife said.

"I'll do it," her husband offered from the bed.

" No , I'll get it . The poor kitty out trying to keep dry under a table."

The husband went on reading, lying propped up with the two pillows at the foot of the bed.

"Don't get wet," he said.

The wife went downstairs and the hotel owner stood up and bowed to her as she passed the office. His desk was at the far end of the office. He was an old man and very tall.

"Il piove," * the wife said. She liked the hotel-keeper.

"Si, si, Signora, brutto tempo. It is very bad weather."

He stood behind his desk in the far end of the dim room. The wife liked him. She liked the deadly serious way he received any complaints. She liked his dignity. She liked the way he wanted to serve her. She liked the way he felt about being a hotel-keeper. She liked his old, heavy face and big hands.

Liking him she opened the door and looked out. It was raining harder. A man in a rubber cape was crossing the empty square to the café. The cat would be around to the right. Perhaps she could go along under the eaves. As she stood in the doorway an umbrella

---

* *Il Piove*: It's raining (Italian).

opened behind her. It was the maid who looked after their room.

"You must not get wet," she smiled, speaking Italian. Of course, the hotel-keeper had sent her.

With the maid holding the umbrella over her, she walked along the gravel path until she was under their window. The table was there, washed bright green in the rain, but the cat was gone. She was suddenly disappointed. The maid looked up at her.

"Ha perduto qualque cosa, Signora?" *

"There was a cat," said the American girl.

"A cat?"

"Si, il gatto."

"A cat?" the maid laughed. "A cat in the rain?"

"Yes," she said, "under the table." Then, "Oh, I wanted it so much. I wanted a kitty."

When she talked English the maid's face tightened.

"Come, Signora," she said, "We must get back inside. You will be wet."

"I suppose so," said the American girl.

They went back along the gravel path and passed in the door. The maid stayed outside to close the umbrella. As the American girl passed the office, the padrone bowed from his desk. Something felt very small and tight inside the girl. The padrone made her feel very small and at the same time really important. She had a momentary feeling of being of supreme importance. She went on up the stairs. She opened the door of the room. George was on

---

* *Ha... Signora*: Have you lost something, Madam?

the bed, reading.

"Did you get the cat?" he asked, putting the book down.

"It was gone."

"Wonder where it went to," he said, resting his eyes from reading.

She sat down on the bed.

"I wanted it so much," she said. "I don't know why I wanted it so much. I wanted that poor kitty. It isn't any fun to be a poor kitty out in the rain."

George was reading again.

She went over and sat in front of the mirror of the dressing table looking at herself with the hand glass. She studied her profile, first one side and then the other. Then she studied the back of her head and her neck.

"Don't you think it would be a good idea if I let my hair grow out?" she asked, looking at her profile again.

George looked up and saw the back of her neck, clipped close like a boy's.

"I like it the way it is."

"I get so tired of it," she said. "I get so tired of looking like a boy."

George shifted his position in the bed. He hadn't looked away from her since she started to speak.

"You look pretty darn nice," he said.

She laid the mirror down on the dresser and went over to the window and looked out. It was getting dark.

"I want to pull my hair back tight and smooth and make a big knot at the back that I can feel," she said. "I want to have a kitty to sit on my lap and purr when I stroke her."

"Yeah?" George said from the bed.

"And I want to eat at a table with my own silver and I want candles. And I want it to be spring and I want to brush my hair out in front of a mirror and I want a kitty and I want some new clothes."

"Oh, shut up and get something to read," George said. He was reading again.

His wife was looking out of the window. It was quite dark now and still raining in the palm trees.

"Anyway, I want a cat," she said, "I want a cat. I want a cat now. If I can't have long hair or any fun, I can have a cat."

George was not listening. He was reading his book. His wife looked out of the window where the light had come on in the square.

Someone knocked at the door.

"Avanti," * George said. He looked up from his book.

In the doorway stood the maid. She held a big tortoise-shell cat pressed tight against her and swung down against her body.

"Excuse me," she said, "the padrone asked me to bring this for the Signora."

Questions:

1. From what point of view is Hemingway's story told? Is it effective?

---

* *Avanti*: Come in.

2. In this story the chief characters are George, George's wife, and the innkeeper (the padrone). What traits does each of them seem to possess?
3. Do you find the end satisfying? Why or why not?
4. Do you have any thoughts about the title? If so, what are they?

Edgar Allan Poe (1809—1849)

The Tell-Tale Heart

True! —nervous—very, very dreadfully nervous I had been and am; but why *will* you say that I am mad? The disease had sharpened my senses—not destroyed—not dulled them. Above all was the sense of hearing acute. I heard all things in the heaven and in the earth. I heard many things in hell. How, then, am I mad? Hearken! and observe how healthily—how calmly I can tell you the whole story.

It is impossible to say how first the idea entered my brain; but once conceived, it haunted me day and night. Object there was none. Passion there was none. I loved the old man. He had never wronged me. He had never given me insult. For his gold I had no desire. I think it was his eye! yes, it was this! One of his eyes resembled that of a vulture—a pale blue eye, with a film over it. When-ever it fell upon me, my blood ran cold; and so by degrees—very gradually—I made up my mind to take the life of the old man, and thus rid myself of the eye for ever.

Now this is the point. You fancy me mad. Madmen know

nothing. But you should have seen *me.* You should have seen how wisely I proceeded—with what caution—with what foresight—with what dissimulation I went to work! I was never kinder to the old man than during the whole week before I killed him. And every night, about midnight, I turned the latch of his door and opened it—oh, so gently! And then, when I had made an opening sufficient for my head, I put in a dark lantern, all closed, closed, so that no light shone out, and then I thrust in my head. Oh, you would have laughed to see how cunningly I thrust it in! I moved it slowly—very, very slowly, so that I might not disturb the old man's sleep. It took me an hour to place my whole head within the opening so far that I could see him as he lay upon his bed. Ha! — would a madman have been so wise as this? And then, when my head was well in the room, I undid the lantern cautiously—oh, so cautiously—cautiously (for the hinges creaked)—I undid it just so much that a single thin ray fell upon the vulture eye. And this I did for seven long nights—every night just at midnight—but I found the eye always closed; and so it was impossible to do the work; for it was not the old man who vexed me, but his Evil Eye. And every morning, when the day broke, I went boldly into the chamber, and spoke courageously to him, calling him by name in a hearty tone, and inquiring how he had passed the night. So you see he would have been a very profound old man, indeed, to suspect that every night, just at twelve, I looked in upon him while he slept.

Upon the eighth night I was more than usually cautious in opening the door. A watch's minute hand moves more quickly than did mine. Never before that night had I *felt* the extent of my own powers—of my sagacity. I could scarcely contain my feelings of triumph. To think that there I was, opening the door, little by little, and he not even to dream of my secret deeds or thoughts. I fairly chuckled at the idea; and perhaps he heard me; for he moved on the bed suddenly, as if startled. Now you may think that I drew back—but no. His room was as black as pitch with the thick darkness (for the shutters were close fastened, through fear of robbers), and so I knew that he could not see the opening of the door, and I kept pushing it on steadily, steadily.

I had my head in, and was about to open the lantern, when my 5
thumb slipped upon the tin fastening, and the old man sprang up in the bed, crying out—"Who's there?"

I kept quite still and said nothing. For a whole hour I did not move a muscle, and in the meantime I did not hear him lie down. He was still sitting up in the bed listening; —just as I have done, night after night, hearkening to the death watches in the wall.

Presently I heard a slight groan, and I knew it was the groan of mortal terror. It was not a groan of pain or of grief—oh, no! — it was the low stifled sound that arises from the bottom of the soul when overcharged with awe. I knew the sound very well. Many a night, just at midnight, when all the world slept, it has welled up from my own bosom, deepening, with its dreadful echo, the terrors that distracted me. I say I knew it well. I knew what the old man felt, and pitied him, although I chuckled at heart I knew that he had been lying awake ever since the first slight noise, when he had turned in the bed. His fears had been ever since growing upon him. He had been trying to fancy them causeless, but could not. He had been saying to himself—"It is nothing but the wind in the chimney—it is only a mouse crossing the floor," or "it is merely a cricket which has made a single chirp." Yes, he had been trying to comfort himself with these suppositions; but he had found all in vain. *All in vain*; because Death, in approaching him, had stalked with his black shadow before him, and enveloped the victim. And it was the mournful influence of the unperceived shadow that caused him to feel—although he neither saw nor heard—to *feel* the presence of my head within the room.

When I had waited a long time, very patiently, without hearing him lie down, I resolved to open a little—a very, very little crevice in the lantern. So I opened it—you cannot imagine how stealthily, stealthily—until, at length, a single dim ray, like the thread of the spider, shot from out the crevice and full upon the vulture eye.

It was open—wide, wide open—and I grew furious as I gazed upon it. I saw it with perfect distinctness—all a dull blue, with a hideous veil over it that chilled the very marrow in my bones; but I could see nothing else of the old man's face or person: for I had directed the ray as if by instinct, precisely upon the damned spot.

And now have I not told you that what you mistake for madness 10
is but over-acuteness of the senses? —now, I say, there came to my ears a low, dull, quick sound, such as a watch makes when enveloped in cotton. I knew *that* sound well too. It was the beating of the old man's heart. It increased my fury, as the beating of a drum stimulates the soldier into courage.

But even yet I refrained and kept still. I scarcely breathed. I held the lantern motionless. I tried how steadily I could maintain the ray upon the eye. Meantime the hellish tattoo of the heart increased. It grew quicker and quicker, and louder and louder every instant. The old man's terror *must* have been extreme! It grew louder, I say, louder every moment! —do you mark me well? I have told you that I am nervous: so I am. And now at the dead hour of the night, amid the dreadful silence of that old house, so strange a noise as this excited me to uncontrollable terror. Yet, for some minutes longer I refrained and stood still. But the beating grew louder, louder! I thought the heart must burst. And now a new anxiety seized me—the sound would be heard by a neighbor! The old man's hour had come! With a loud yell, I threw open the lantern and leaped into the room. He shrieked once—once only. In an instant I dragged him to the floor, and pulled the heavy bed over him. I then smiled gaily, to find the deed so far done. But, for many minutes, the heart beat on with a muffled sound. This, however, did not vex me; it would not be heard through the wall. At length it ceased. The old man was dead. I removed the bed and examined the corpse. Yes, he was stone, stone dead. I placed my hand upon the heart and held it there many minutes. There was no pulsation. He was stone dead. His eye would trouble me no more.

If still you think me mad, you will think so no longer when I describe the wise precautions I took for the concealment of the body. The night waned, and I worked hastily, but in silence. First of all I dismembered the corpse. I cut off the head and the arms and the legs.

I then took up three planks from the flooring of the chamber, and deposited all between the scantlings. I then replaced the boards so cleverly, so cunningly, that no human eye—not even *his*—could have detected anything wrong. There was nothing to wash out—no stain of any kind—no bloodspot whatever. I had been too wary for that. A tub had caught all—ha! ha!

When I had made an end of these labors, it was four o'clock—still dark as midnight. As the bell sounded the hour, there came a knocking at the street door. I went down to open it with a light heart, —for what had I *now* to fear? There entered three men, who introduced themselves, with perfect suavity, as officers of the police. A shriek had been heard by a neighbor during the night; suspicion of foul play had been aroused; information had been lodged at the police office, and they (the officers) had been deputed to search the premises.

I smiled, —for *what* had I to fear? I bade the gentlemen welcome. The shriek, I said, was my own in a dream. The old man, I mentioned, was absent in the country. I took my visitors all over the house. I bade them search—search *well.* I led them, at length, to *his* chamber. I showed them his treasures, secure, undisturbed. In the enthusiasm of my confidence, I brought chairs into the room, and desired them *here* to rest from their fatigues, while I myself, in the wild audacity of my perfect triumph, placed my own seat upon the very spot beneath which reposed the corpse of the victim.

The officers were satisfied. My *manner* had convinced them. I was singularly at ease. They sat, and while I answered cheerily, they chatted familiar things. But, ere long, I felt myself getting pale and wished them gone. My head ached, and I fancied a ringing in my ears: but still they sat and still chatted. The ringing became more distinct: —it continued and became more distinct: I talked more freely to get rid of the feeling: but it continued and gained definitiveness—until, at length, I found that the noise was *not* within my ears.

No doubt I now grew *very* pale: —but I talked more fluently, and with a heightened voice. Yet the sound increased—and what could I do? It was *a low, dull, quick sound—much such a sound as a watch makes when enveloped in cotton.* I gasped for breath—and yet the officers heard it not. I talked more quickly—more vehemently; but the noise steadily increased. I arose and argued about trifles, in a high key and with violent gesticulations, but the noise steadily increased. Why *would* they not be gone? I paced the floor to and fro with heavy strides, as if excited to fury by the observation of the men—but the noise steadily increased. Oh God! what *could* I do? I foamed—I raved—I swore! I swung the chair upon which I had been sitting, and grated it upon the boards, but the noise arose over all and continually increased. It grew louder—louder—*louder*! And still the men chatted pleasantly, and smiled. Was it possible they heard not? Almighty God! —no, no! They heard! —they suspected! —they *knew*! —they were making a mockery of my horror! —this I thought, and this I think. But any thing was better than this agony! Any thing was more tolerable than this derision! I could bear those hypocritical smiles no longer! I felt that I must scream or die! —and now—again! —hark! louder! louder! louder! *louder*! —

"Villains!" I shrieked, "dissemble no more! I admit the deed! —tear up the planks! —here, here! —it is the beating of his hideous heart!"

Questions:

1. From what point of view is Poe's story told? Why is this point

of view particularly effective for "*The Tell-Tale Heart*"?

2. Do you think the speaker is a reliable narrator? Point to details to support your argument?
3. How do you explain the police officers' chatting calmly with the murderer instead of reacting to the sound that stirs the murderer into frenzy?

Chapter 3 Character and Characterization

Before talking about the characters, we should point out that the word "**character**" has two chief meanings:

1. A person in a work of fiction or a figure in a literary work (thus in Chekhov's "*Misery*," Iona is a character, the officer who hires the cab is another character, and the drunks are additional characters).

2. The moral qualities, personality traits, or other distinctive attributes of a real or fictional figure, as when we say that Iona's character is described only briefly, or that Hamlet's character is complex. Usually the context makes clear the sense in which the word is used, but in your own writing, make sure that there is no confusion.

Characters in literature, whether based on history or original with the author, may be classified by function in a number of ways. First of all, literary characters may be classified by the degree or quality of their resemblance to real people. The English novelist E. M.Forster distinguishes the **flat** from the **round**. Flat characters, often vivid in outline, are striking and interesting two-dimensional characters that like cardboard cutouts holding up signs saying "jealous lover," "cruel landlord," "kind mother," and so forth. They lack the depth and complexity of living humans (figures with simple personalities). **Round characters**, however, are three-dimensional, having the depths and complexities of real life. Round characters are complex and undergo development, sometimes sufficiently to surprise the reader. Flat characters are sometimes called black and white, as opposed to grayed for more rounded characters. Yet, such a distinction is not to damn a flat character as an inferior work of art. As a rule, the major characters in a fiction need three-dimensional treatment, while minor characters are often handled two-dimensionally. This is because rounding those minor characters would cost time and space; and so enlarged, they might only distract us from the main characters. And in fact, many good stories do not give even their central characters much complexity. In "*Misery*," for instance, Iona is shown chiefly as a grieving father aching to speak of the death of his son. We don't know what sort of food he likes, whether he ever gets drunk, what he thinks of the Czar, or whether he belongs to the church. But it is hard to imagine that knowing any of these things would be relevant and would increase our interest in him.

On the other hand, Iona is not quite so flat as we have perhaps implied. A careful reader notices, for instance, that Iona reveals other things about himself in addition to his need to express his grief. For example, he treats his horse as kindly as possible. When the officer gets into the cab, Iona is "more from the habit than necessity brandishes his whip,"—but he gets the horse moving by making a clicking sound, and he actually whips the horse only when the officer tells him to hurry. Later the hunchback will say of the mare, "Give her one with the whip. Hang it all, give it her well," but we feel that Iona uses his horse as gently as is possible.

It should be noted, however, that the drunks, though they are not much more than drunks, are not less than drunks either. They are quarrelsome and they even display touches of cruelty, but we cannot call them villains. In some degree, the fact that they are drunk excuses their "bad language," their "ill-tempers," and even their displays of cruelty.

Furthermore, the characters in a story help to characterize other characters, by their resemblances or their differences. How Iona might behave if he were an officer, or if he were drunk, we do not know, but he is in some degree contrasted with the other characters and thus gains some complexity, or quarrelsome.

Finally, literary characters are usefully classified as either **static** or **dynamic**. **Static characters** retain essentially the same qualities throughout a work. They may respond superficially to the passing time, sprouting white hairs or putting on spectacles, but they retain in age the personalities they had in youth. Again, the reader may come to understand them differently as the work progresses, but discovers on reflection that it is not they who have changed, but only the reader's knowledge of them: Gilbert Osmond of "*The Portrait of a Lady*" is an example. Some characters do change, however, in response to their experiences. The Pip who narrates Great Expectations is much less shallow than the young Pip he describes, and the reader can see the change coming as the work progresses. Moll Flanders says at the end that she has changed, but her argument fails to convince. Emma Woodhouse clearly changes in that she makes some sophisticated mistakes in the last two books of "*Emma*" than she does in the first, but it is questionable how deeply the change goes; she is still fundamentally Emma.

Dynamic characters, on the other hand, are those who are modified by actions and appearances, and one objective of the work in which the character appears is to reveal the consequences of these actions. In general, most great dramas and novels have dynamic characters as protagonists. Short stories are more likely to reveal static characters through action than to show changes in dynamic characters resulting from actions.

In addition to the above classifications of characters, we will have to get acquainted with stock characters. **Stock characters** are type characters repeated in literature to become the stock in trade of a particular genre, like the *bragging* soldier of Greek and Roman tragedy, the *mad* scientist of horror movies, the *strong*, *silent* hero and the *loyal* sidekick of Westerns, the *greedy* explorer of Tarzan films, the *brilliant* but *alcoholic* brain surgeon of medical thrillers on television or the *hard-boiled* hero of the detective story. Although stock characters tend to have single dominant virtues and vices, characters in the finest contemporary short stories tend to have many facets, like people we meet.

One more term that has much to do with character is characterization. **Characterization** is commonly defined as the delineation of a real person or the creation of an imaginary one. In the **Lyric** and the **Autobiography**, the author reveals aspects of his or her own character; in the **Biography** and the **Historical** Novel, the author presents the characters of actual persons; and in **Fiction** (the **Drama**, the **Novel**, the **Short Story**, and the **Narrative Poem**), the author reveals the characters of imaginary persons so that they exist for the reader as lifelike is called characterization. The character of a fictional creation—Hamlet, Emma Woodhouse, Huckleberry Finn, Willy Loman—is fixed forever in the words of the creator, though it is open to differing interpretations by readers. The ability to characterize is a primary attribute of a good writer.

There are three fundamental methods of **characterization** in fiction: (1) the explicit presentation by the author of the character through direct EXPOSITION, either in an introductory block or more often bit by bit throughout the work, illustrated by action; (2) the presentation of the character in action, with little or no explicit comment by the author, in the expectation that the reader will be able to deduce the attributes of the actor from the actions; and (3) the representation from within a CHARACTER, without comment on the character by the author, of the impact of actions and emotions on the character's inner self, with the expectation that the reader will come to a clear understanding of the attributes of the character.

It is difficult to distinguish among these methods of characterization without discussing them in terms of narrative POINT OF VIEW (see Chapter 2). Usually the explicit method results when the story is told by a first-person NARRATOR, such as Dickens's "*David Copperfield*" or by an OMNISCIENT AUTHOR, such as Thackery in "*Vanity Fair.*" The success of the explicit method of CHARACTERIZATION rests at least in part on the nature of the NARRATOR. The presentation of characters through actions is essentially the dramatic method. It is the traditional way of establishing character in the DRAMA. For example, we know Hamlet through what he says and what he does, yet the riddle of what Shakespeare intended his true character to be is forever unanswerable. The NOVEL and the SHORT STORY in the twentieth century have frequently adopted the dramatic technique by making objective presentations of characters in action without authorial comment, to such an extent that the SELF-EFFACING AUTHOR has become a commonplace. Writers of the REALISTIC NOVEL such as

Galesworthy and Howells, usually employ this method of character presentation. The presentation of the impact of external events and emotions on the PROTAGONIST'S inward self begins with the novels of Henry James, whose "*The Ambassadors*" is an excellent example, and continues into the STREAM OF CONSCIOUSNESS NOVEL where, through Interior Monologue, the subconscious or unconscious mind of the character is presented, as in Joyce's "*Ulysses*" or Faulkner's "*The Sound and the Fury.*"

Katherine Anne Porter (1890—1980)

The Jilting of Granny Weatherall

She flicked her wrist neatly out of Doctor Harry's pudgy careful fingers and pulled the sheet up to her chin. The brat ought to be in knee breeches. Doctoring around the country with spectacles on his nose! "Get along now, take your schoolbooks and go. There's nothing wrong with me."

Doctor Harry spread a warm paw like a cushion on her forehead where the forked green vein danced and made her eyelids twitch. "Now, now, be a good girl, and we'll have you up in no time."

"That's no way to speak to a woman nearly eighty years old just because she's down. I'd have you respect your elders, young man."

"Well, Missy, excuse me." Doctor Harry patted her cheek. "But I've got to warn you, haven't I? You're a marvel, but you must be careful or you're going to be good and sorry."

"Don't tell me what I'm going to be. I'm on my feet now, morally speaking. It's Cornelia. I had to go to bed to get rid of her."

Her bones felt loose, and floated around in her skin, and Doctor Harry floated like a balloon around the foot of the bed. He floated and pulled down his waistcoat and swung his glasses on a cord. "Well, stay where you are, it certainly can't hurt you."

"Get along and doctor your sick," said Granny Weatherall. "Leave a well woman alone. I'll call for you when I want you.... Where were you forty years ago when I pulled through milk-leg and double pneumonia? You weren't even born. Don't let Cornelia lead you on," she shouted, because Doctor Harry appeared to float up to the ceiling and out. "I pay my own bills, and I don't throw my money away on nonsense!"

She meant to wave goodby, but it was too much trouble. Her eyes closed of themselves, it was like a dark curtain drawn around the bed. The pillow rose and floated under her, pleasant as a hammock in a light wind. She listened to the leaves rustling outside the window. No, somebody was swishing newspapers; no, Cornelia and Doctor Harry were whispering together. She leaped broad awake, thinking they whispered in her ear.

"She was never like this, *never* like this!" "Well, what can we expect?" "Yes, eighty years old...."

Well, and what if she was? She still had ears. It was like Cornelia to whisper around doors. She always kept things secret in such a public way. She was always being tactful and kind. Cornelia was dutiful; that was the trouble with her. Dutiful and good: "So good and dutiful," said Granny, "that I'd like to spank her." She saw herself spanking Cornelia and making a fine job of it.

"What'd you say, Mother?"

Granny felt her face tying up in hard knots.

"Can't a body think, I'd like to know?"

"I thought you might want something."

" I do. I want a lot of things. First off , go away and don't whisper."

She lay and drowsed, hoping in her sleep that the children would keep out and let her rest a minute. It had been a long day. Not that she was tired. It was always pleasant to snatch a minute now and then. There was always so much to be done, let me see: tomorrow.

Tomorrow was far away and there was nothing to trouble about. Things were finished somehow when the time came; thank God there was always a little margin over for peace: then a person could spread out the plan of life and tuck in the edges orderly. It was good to have everything clean and folded away, with the hair brushes and tonic bottles sitting straight on the white embroidered linen: the day started without fuss and the pantry shelves laid out with rows of jelly glasses and brown jugs and white stone-china jars with blue whirligigs and words painted on them: coffee, tea, sugar, ginger, cinnamon, allspice: and the bronze clock with the lion on top nicely dusted off. The dust that lion could collect in twenty-four hours! The box in the attic with all those letters tied up, well, she'd have to go through that tomorrow. All those letters—George's letters and John's letters and her letters to them both—lying around for the children to find afterwards made her uneasy. Yes, that would be tomorrow's business. No use to let them know how silly she had been once.

While she was rummaging around she found death in her mind and it felt clammy and unfamiliar. She had spent so much time preparing for death there was no need for bringing it up again. Let it take care of itself now. When she was sixty she had felt very old, finished, and went around making farewell trips to see her children and grandchildren, with a secret in her mind: This is the very last of your mother, children! Then she made her will and came down with a long fever. That was all just a notion like a lot of other things, but it was lucky too, for she had once for all got over the idea of dying for a long time. Now she couldn't be worried. She hoped she had better sense now. Her father had lived to be one hundred and two years old and had drunk a noggin of strong hot toddy on his last birthday. He told the reporters it was his daily habit, and he owed his long life to that. He had made quite a scandal and was very pleased about it. She believed she'd just plague Cornelia a little.

"Cornelia! Cornelia!" No footsteps, but a sudden hand on her cheek. "Bless you, where have you been?"

"Here, Mother." 20

"Well, Cornelia, I want a noggin of hot toddy."

"Are you cold, darling?"

"I'm chilly, Cornelia. Lying in bed stops the circulation. I must have told you that a thousand times."

Well, she could just hear Cornelia telling her husband that Mother was getting a little childish and they'd have to humor her. The thing that most annoyed her was that Gornelia thought she was deaf, dumb, and blind. Little hasty glances and tiny gestures tossed around her and over her head saying, "Don't cross her, let her have her way, she's eighty years old," and she sitting there as if she lived in a thin glass cage. Sometimes Granny almost made up her mind to pack up and move back to her own house where nobody could remind her every minute that she was old. Wait, wait, Cornelia, till your own children whisper behind your back!

In her day she had kept a better house and had got more work done. She wasn't too old yet for Lydia to be driving eighty miles for advice when one of the children jumped the track, and Jimmy still dropped in and talked things over: "Now, Mammy, you've a good business head, I want to know what you think of this? ..." Old. Cornelia couldn't change the furniture around without asking. Little things, little things! They had been so sweet when they were little. Granny wished the old days were back again with the children young and everything to be done over. It had been a hard pull, but not too much for her. When she thought of all the food she had cooked, and all the clothes she had cut and sewed, and all the gardens she had made—well, the children showed it. There they were, made out of her, and they couldn't get away from that. Sometimes she wanted to see John again and point to them and say, Well, I didn't do so badly, did I? But that would have to wait. That was for tomorrow. She used to think of him as a man. but now all the children were older than their father, and he would be a child beside her if she saw him now. It seemed strange and there was something wrong in the idea. Why, he couldn't possibly recognize her. She had fenced in a hundred acres once, digging the post holes herself and clamping the wires with just a negro boy to help. That changed a woman. John would be looking for a young woman with the peaked Spanish comb in her hair and the painted fan. Digging post holes changed a woman. Riding country roads in the winter when women had their babies was another thing: sitting up nights with sick horses and sick negroes and sick children and hardly ever losing one. John, I hardly ever lost one of them! John would see that in a minute, that would be something he could understand, she wouldn't have to explain anything!

It made her feel like rolling up her sleeves and putting the whole place to rights again. No matter if Cornelia was determined to be everywhere at once, there were a great many things left undone on this place. She would start tomorrow and do them. It was good to be strong enough for everything, even if all you made melted and changed and slipped under your hands, so that by the time you finished you almost forgot what you were working for. What was it I set out to do? she asked herself intently, but she could not remember. A fog rose over the valley, she saw it marching across the creek swallowing the trees and moving up the hill like an army of ghosts. Soon it would be at the near edge of the orchard, and then it was time to go in and light the lamps. Come in, children, don't stay out in the night air.

Lighting the lamps had been beautiful. The children huddled up to her and breathed like little calves waiting at the bars in the twilight. Their eyes followed the match and watched the flame rise and settle in a blue curve, then they moved away from her. The lamp was lit, they didn't have to be scared and hang on to mother any more. Never, never, never more. God, for all my life I thank Thee. Without Thee, my God, I could never have done it.

Hail, Mary, full of grace.

I want you to pick all the fruit this year and see that nothing is wasted. There's always someone who can use it. Don't let good things rot for want of using. You waste life when you waste good food. Don't let things get lost. It's bitter to lose things. Now, don't let me get to thinking, not when I am tired and taking a little nap before supper....

The pillow rose about her shoulders and pressed against her heart and the memory was being squeezed out of it: oh, push down the pillow, somebody: it would smother her if she tried to hold it. Such a fresh breeze blowing and such a green day with no threats in it. But he had not come, just the same. What does a woman do when she has put on the white veil and set out the white cake for a man and he doesn't come? She tried to remember. No, I swear he never harmed me but in that. He never harmed me but in that... and what if he did? There was the day, the day, but a whirl of dark smoke rose and covered it, crept up and over into the bright field where everything was planted so carefully in orderly rows. That was hell, she knew hell when she saw it. For sixty years she had prayed against remembering him and against losing her soul in the deep pit of hell, and now the two things were mingled in one and the thought of him was a smoky cloud from hell that moved and crept in her head when she had just got rid of Doctor Harry and was trying to rest a minute. Wounded vanity, Ellen, said a sharp voice in the top of her mind. Don't let your wounded vanity get the upper hand of you. Plenty of girls get jilted. You were jilted, weren't you? Then stand up to it. Her eyelids wavered and let in streamers of blue-gray light like tissue paper over her eyes.

She must get up and pull the shades down or she'd never sleep. She was in bed again and the shades were not down. How could that happen? Better turn over, hide from the light, sleeping in the light gave you nightmares. "Mother, how do you feel now?" and a stinging wetness on her forehead. But I don't like having my face washed in cold water!

Hapsy? George? Lydia? Jimmy? No, Cornelia, and her features were swollen and full of little puddles. "They're coming, darling, they'll all be here soon." Go wash your face, child, you look funny.

Instead of obeying, Cornelia knelt down and put her head on the pillow. She seemed to be talking but there was no sound. "Well, are you tongue-tied? Whose birthday is it? Are you going to give a party?"

Cornelia's mouth moved urgently in strange shapes. "Don't do that, you bother me, daughter."

"Oh, no, Mother, Oh, no...."

Nonsense. It was strange about children. They disputed your every word. "No what, Cornelia?"

"Here's Doctor Harry."

"I won't see that boy again. He just left five minutes ago."

"That was this morning, Mother. It's night now. Here's the nurse."

"This is Doctor Harry, Mrs. Weatherall. I never saw you look so young and happy!"

"Ah, I'll never be young again—but I'd be happy if they'd let me lie in peace and get rested."

She thought she spoke up loudly, but no one answered. A 40
warm weight on her forehead, a warm bracelet on her wrist, and a breeze went on whispering, trying to tell her something. A shuffle of leaves in the everlasting hand of God, He blew on them and they danced and rattled. "Mother, don't mind, we're going to give you a little hypodermic." "Look here, daughter, how do ants get in this bed? I saw sugar ants yesterday." Did you send for Hapsy too?

It was Hapsy she really wanted. She had to go a long way back through a great many rooms to find Hapsy standing with a baby on her arm. She seemed to herself to be Hapsy also, and the baby on Hapsy's arm was Hapsy and himself and herself, all at once, and there was no surprise in the meeting. Then Hapsy melted from within and turned flimsy as gray gauze and the baby was a gauzy shadow, and Hapsy came up close and said, "I thought you'd never come," and looked at her very searchingly and said, "You haven't changed a bit!" They leaned forward to kiss, when Cornelia began whispering from a long way off, "Oh, is there anything you want to tell me? Is there anything I can do for you?"

Yes, she had changed her mind after sixty years and she would like to see George. I want you to find George. Find him and be sure to tell him I forgot him. I want him to know I had my husband just the same and my children and my house like any other woman. A good house too and a good husband that I loved and fine children out of him. Better than I hoped for even. Tell him I was given back everything he took away and more. Oh, no, oh, God, no, there was something else besides the house and the man and the children. Oh, surely they were not all? What was it?

Something not given back.... Her breath crowded down under her ribs and grew into a monstrous frightening shape with cutting edges; it bored up into her head, and the agony was unbelievable: Yes, John, get the Doctor now, no more talk, my time has come.

When this one was born it should be the last. The last. It should have been born first, for it was the one she had truly wanted.Everything came in good time. Nothing left out, left over. She was strong, in three days she would be as well as ever. Better. A woman needed milk in her to have her full health.

"Mother, do you hear me?"

"I've been telling you—" 45

"Mother, Father Connolly's here."

"I went to Holy Communion only last week. Tell him I'm not so sinful as all that."

"Father just wants to speak to you."

He could speak as much as he pleased. It was like him to drop in and inquire about her soul as if it were a teething baby, and then stay on for a cup of tea and a round of cards and gossip. He always had a funny story of some sort, usually about an Irishman who made his little mistakes and confessed them, and the point lay in some absurd thing he would blurt out in the confessional showing his struggles between native piety and original sin. Granny felt easy about her soul. Cornelia, where are your manners? Give Father Connolly a chair. She had her secret comfortable understanding with a few favorite saints who cleared a straight road to God for her. All as surely signed and sealed as the papers for the new Forty Acres. Forever... heirs and assigns forever. Since the day the wedding cake was not cut, but thrown out and wasted. The whole bottom dropped out of the world, and there she was blind and sweating with nothing under her feet and the walls falling away. His hand had caught her under the breast, she had not fallen, there was the freshly polished floor with the green rug on it, just as before. He had cursed like a sailor's parrot and said, "I'll kill him for you." Don't lay a hand on him, for my sake leave something to God. "Now, Ellen, you must believe what I tell you...."

So there was nothing, nothing to worry about any more, ex- 50
cept sometimes in the night one of the children screamed in a nightmare, and they both hustled out shaking and hunting for the matches and calling, "There, wait a minute, here we are!" John, get the doctor now, Hapsy's time has come. But there was Hapsy standing by the bed in a white cap. "Cornelia, tell Hapsy to take off her cap, I can't see her plain."

Her eyes opened very wide and the room stood out like a picture she had seen somewhere. Dark colors with the shadows rising towards the ceiling in long angles. The tall black dresser gleamed with nothing on it but John's picture, enlarged from a little one, with John's eyes very black when they should have been blue. You never saw him, so how do you know how he looked? But the man insisted the copy was perfect, it was very rich and handsome. For a picture, yes, but it's not my husband. The table by the bed had a linen cover and a candle and a crucifix. The light was blue from Cornelia's silk lampshades. No sort of light at all, just frippery. You had to live forty years with kerosene lamps to appreciate honest electricity. She felt very strong and she saw Doctor Harry with a rosy nimbus around him.

"You look like a saint, Doctor Harry, and I vow that's as near as you'll ever come to it."

"She's saying something."

"I heard you, Cornelia. What's all this carrying-on?"

"Father Connolly's saying—" 55

Cornelia's voice staggered and bumped like a cart in a bad road. It rounded corners and turned back again and arrived nowhere. Granny stepped up in the cart very lightly and reached for the reins, but a man sat beside her and she knew him by his hands, driving the cart. She did not look in his face, for she knew without seeing, but looked instead down the road where the trees leaned over and bowed to each other and a thousand birds were singing a Mass. She felt like singing too, but she put her hand in the bosom of her dress and pulled out a rosary, and Father Connolly murmured Latin in a very solemn voice and tickled her feet. My God, will you stop that nonsense? I'm a married woman. What if he did run away and leave me to face the priest by myself? I found another a whole world better. I wouldn't have exchanged my husband for anybody except St. Michael himself, and you may tell him that for me with a thank you in the bargain.

Light flashed on her closed eyelids, and a deep roaring shook her. Cornelia, is that lightning? I hear thunder. There's going to be a storm. Close all the windows. Call the children in.... "Mother, here we are, all of us." "Is that you, Hapsy?" "Oh, no, I'm Lydia. We drove as fast as we could." Their faces drifted above her, drifted away. The rosary fell out of her hands and Lydia put it back. Jimmy tried to help, their hands fumbled together, and Granny closed two fingers around Jimmy's thumb. Beads wouldn't do, it must be something alive. She was so amazed her thoughts ran round and round. So, my dear Lord, this is my death and I wasn't even thinking about it. My children have come to see me die. But I can't, it's not time. Oh, I always hated surprises. I wanted to give Cornelia the amethyst set—Cornelia, you're to have the amethyst set, but Hapsy's to wear it when she wants, and Doctor Harry, do shut up. Nobody sent for you. Oh, my dear Lord, do wait a minute. I meant to do something about the Forty Acres, Jimmy doesn't need it and Lydia will later on, with that worthless husband of hers. I meant to finish the altar cloth and send six bottles of wine to Sister Borgia for her dyspepsia. I want to send six bottles of wine to Sister Borgia, Father Connolly, now don't let me forget.

Cornelia's voice made short turns and tilted over and crashed. "Oh, Mother, oh, Mother, oh, Mother...."

"I'm not going, Cornelia. I'm taken by surprise. I can't go."

You'll see Hapsy again. What about her ? "I thought you'd never come." Granny made a long journey outward, looking for Hapsy. What if I don't find her? What then? Her heart sank down and down, there was no bottom to death, she couldn't come to the end of it. The blue light from Cornelia's lampshade drew into a tiny point in the center of her brain, it flickered and winked like an eye, quietly it fluttered and dwindled. Granny lay curled down within herself, amazed and watchful, staring at the point of light that was herself; her body was now only a deeper mass of shadow in an endless darkness and this darkness would curl around the light and swallow it up. God, give a sign!

For the second time there was no sign. Again no bridegroom and the priest in the house. She could not remember any other sorrow because this grief wiped them all away. Oh, no, there's nothing more cruel than this—I'll never forgive it. She stretched herself with a deep breath and blew out the light.

Questions:

1. What does the name of Weatherall have to do with Granny's nature (or her life story)? Is the character of Granny Weatherall round or flat, static or dynamic? What changes has she undergone throughout her life? What strengths has she developed? What weaknesses does she retain?
2. By what specific means (e. g., recollection, reflection, conversation, stream of consciousness) do we learn the specific details that make up the story? How accurate are her recollections of the things going through her consciousness?
3. How is this the story of another "jilting"? What is similar between that fateful day of sixty years ago and the moment when Granny is dying? Contrast her disappointments at having been "jilted" twice.
4. References to light and darkness are made in the story. What do these references indicate about the character of Granny?

Edith Wharton (1862—1937)

Roman Fever

I

From the table at which they had been lunching two American

ladies of ripe but well-cared-for middle age moved across the lofty terrace of the Roman restaurant and, leaning on its parapet, looked first at each other, and then down on the outspread glories of the Palatine and the Forum,* with the same expression of vague but benevolent approval.

As they leaned there a girlish voice echoed up gaily from the stairs leading to the court below. "Well, come along, then," it cried, not to them but to an invisible companion, "and let's leave the young things to their knitting"; and a voice as fresh laughed back: "Oh, look here, Babs, not actually *knitting*—" "Well, I mean figuratively," rejoined the first. "After all, we haven't left our poor parents much else to do..." and at that point the turn of the stairs engulfed the dialogue.

The two ladies looked at each other again, this time with a tinge of smiling embarrassment, and the smaller and paler one shook her head and coloured slightly.

"Barbara!" she murmured, sending an unheard rebuke after the mocking voice in the stairway.

5 The other lady, who was fuller, and higher in colour, with a small determined nose supported by vigorous black eyebrows, gave a good-humoured laugh. "That's what our daughters think of us!"

Her companion replied by a deprecating gesture. "Not of us individually. We must remember that. It's just the collective modern idea of Mothers. And you see—" Half guiltily she drew from her

---

* Palatine: one of the seven hills of Rome, with ruins of ancient palaces built by the Caesars; Forum: the ruins of the Roman Forum, the political, religious, and business center of ancient Rome.

handsomely mounted black hand-bag a twist of crimson silk run through by two fine knitting needles. "One never knows," she murmured. "The new system has certainly given us a good deal of time to kill; and sometimes I get tired just looking—even at this." Her gesture was now addressed to the stupendous scene at their feet.

The dark lady laughed again, and they both relapsed upon the view, contemplating it in silence, with a sort of diffused serenity which might have been borrowed from the spring effulgence of the Roman skies. The luncheon-hour was long past, and the two had their end of the vast terrace to themselves. At its opposite extremity a few groups, detained by a lingering look at the outspread city, were gathering up guide-books and fumbling for tips. The last of them scattered, and the two ladies were alone on the air-washed height.

"Well, I don't see why we shouldn't just stay here," said Mrs. Slade, the lady of the high colour and energetic brows. Two derelict basket-chairs stood near, and she pushed them into the angle of the parapet, and settled herself in one, her gaze upon the Palatine. "After all, it's still the most beautiful view in the world."

"It always will be, to me," assented her friend Mrs. Ansley, with so slight a stress on the "me" that Mrs. Slade, though she noticed it, wondered if it were not merely accidental, like the random underlinings of old-fashioned letter-writers.

"Grace Ansley was always old-fashioned," she thought; and 10
added aloud, with a retrospective smile: "It's a view we've both been familiar with for a good many years. When we first met here we were younger than our girls are now. You remember?"

"Oh, yes, I remember," murmured Mrs. Ansley, with the same undefinable stress. —"There's that head-waiter wondering," she interpolated. She was evidently far less sure than her companion of herself and of her rights in the world.

"I'll cure him of wondering," said Mrs. Slade, stretching her hand toward a bag as discretely opulent-looking as Mrs. Ansley's. Signing to the head-waiter, she explained that she and her friend were old lovers of Rome, and would like to spend the end of the afternoon looking down on the view—that is, if it did not disturb the service? The head-waiter, bowing over her gratuity, assured her that the ladies were most welcome, and would be still more so if they would condescend to remain for dinner. A full moon night, they would remember....

Mrs. Slade's black brows drew together, as though references to the moon were out-of-place and even unwelcome. But she smiled away her frown as the head-waiter retreated. "Well, why not? We might do worse. There's no knowing, I suppose, when the girls will be back. Do you even know back from *where*? I don't!"

Mrs. Ansley again coloured slightly. "I think those young Italian aviators we met at the Embassy invited them to fly to Tarquinia for tea. I suppose they'll want to wait and fly back by moonlight."

"Moonlight —moonlight! What a part it still plays. Do you suppose they're as sentimental as we were?"

"I've come to the conclusion that I don't in the least know what they are," said Mrs. Ansley. "And perhaps we didn't know much more about each other."

"No: perhaps we didn't."

Her friend gave her a shy glance. "I never should have supposed you were sentimental, Alida."

"Well, perhaps I wasn't." Mrs. Slade drew her lids together in retrospect; and for a few moments the two ladies, who had been intimate since childhood, reflected how little they knew each other. Each one, of course, had a label ready to attach to the other's name; Mrs. Delphin Slade, for instance, would have told herself, or any one who asked her, that Mrs. Horace Ansley, twenty-five years ago, had been exquisitely lovely—no, you wouldn't believe it, would you?... though, of course, still charming, distinguished.... Well, as a girl she had been exquisite; far more beautiful than her daughter Barbara, though certainly Babs, according to the new standards at any rate, was more effective—had more *edge*, as they say. Funny where she got it, with those two nullities as parents. Yes; Horace Ansley was—well, just the duplicate of his wife. Museum specimens of old New York. Good-looking, irreproachable, exemplary. Mrs. Slade and Mrs. Ansley had lived opposite each other—actually as well as figuratively—for years. When the drawing-room curtains in No. 20 East 73rd Street* were renewed, No. 23, across the way, was always aware of it. And of all the movings, buyings, travels, anniversaries, illnesses—the tame chronicle of an estimable pair. Little of it escaped Mrs. Slade. But she had grown bored with it by the time her husband made his big *coup* in Wall Street, and when they bought in upper Park Avenue had already begun to think: "I'd rather live opposite a speak-easy for a change; at least one might see

---

* *No. 20 East 73rd Street*: Fashionable street in New York City.

it raided." The idea of seeing Grace raided was so amusing that (before the move) she launched it at a woman's lunch. It made a hit, and went the rounds—she sometimes wondered if it had crossed the street, and reached Mrs. Ansley. She hoped not, but didn't much mind. Those were the days when respectability was at a discount, and it did the irreproachable no harm to laugh at them a little.

A few years later, and not many months apart, both ladies lost their husbands. There was an appropriate exchange of wreaths and condolences, and a brief renewal of intimacy in the half-shadow of their mourning; and now, after another interval, they had run across each other in Rome, at the same hotel, each of them the modest appendage of a salient daughter. The similarity of their lot had again drawn them together, lending itself to mild jokes, and the mutual confession that, if in old days it must have been tiring to "keep up" with daughters, it was now, at times, a little dull not to.

No doubt, Mrs. Slade reflected, she felt her unemployment more than poor Grace ever would. It was a big drop from being the wife of Delphin Slade to being his widow. She had always regarded herself (with a certain conjugal pride) as his equal in social gifts, as contributing her full share to the making of the exceptional couple they were: but the difference after his death was irremediable. As the wife of the famous corporation lawyer, always with an international case or two on hand, every day brought its exciting and unexpected obligation: the impromptu entertaining of eminent colleagues from abroad, the hurried dashes on legal business to London, Paris or Rome, where the entertaining was so handsomely reciprocated; the amusement of hearing in her wake: "What, that handsome woman with the good clothes and the eyes is Mrs. Slade—*the* Slade's wife? Really? Generally the wives of celebrities are such frumps."

Yes; being *the* Slade's widow was a dullish business after that. In living up to such a husband all her faculties had been engaged; now she had only her daughter to live up to, for the son who seemed to have inherited his father's gifts had died suddenly in boyhood. She had fought through that agony because her husband was there, to be helped and to help; now, after the father's death, the thought of the boy had become unbearable. There was nothing left but to mother her daughter; and dear Jenny was such a perfect daughter that she needed no excessive mothering. "Now with Babs Ansley I don't know that I *should* be so quiet," Mrs. Slade sometimes half-enviously reflected; but Jenny, who was younger than her brilliant friend, was that rare accident, an extremely pretty girl who somehow made youth and prettiness seem as safe as their absence. It was all perplexing—and to Mrs. Slade a little boring. She wished that Jenny would fall in love—with the wrong man, even; that she might have to be watched, out-maneuvered, rescued. And instead, it was Jenny who watched her mother, kept her out of draughts, made sure that she had taken her tonic....

Mrs. Ansley was much less articulate than her friend, and her mental portrait of Mrs. Slade was slighter, and drawn with fainter touches. "Alida Slade's awfully brilliant; but not as brilliant as she thinks," would have summed it up; though she would have added, for the enlightenment of strangers, that Mrs. Slade had been an extremely dashing girl; much more so that her daughter, who was pretty, of course, and clever in a way, but had none of her mother's—well, "vividness," some one had once called it. Mrs. Ansley would take up current words like this, and cite them in quotation marks, as unheard-of audacities. No; Jenny was not like her mother. Sometimes Mrs. Ansley thought Alida Slade was disappointed; on the whole she had had a sad life. Full of failures and mistakes; Mrs. Ansley had always been rather sorry for her....

So these two ladies visualized each other, each through the wrong end of her little telescope.

II

For a long time they continued to sit side by side without speaking. It seemed as though, to both, there was a relief in laying down their somewhat futile activities in the presence of the vast Memento Mori* which faced them. Mrs. Slade sat quite still, her eyes fixed on the golden slope of the Palace of the Caesars, and after a while Mrs. Ansley ceased to fidget with her bag, and she too sank into meditation. Like many intimate friends, the two ladies had never before had occasion to be silent together, and Mrs. Ansley was slightly embarrassed by what seemed, after so many years, a new stage in their intimacy, and one with which she did not yet know how to deal.

Suddenly the air was full of that deep clangour of bells which periodically covers Rome with a roof of silver. Mrs. Slade glanced at her wrist-watch. "Five o'clock already," she said, as though surprised.

---

* *Memento Mori*: Reminder of mortality.

Mrs. Ansley suggested interrogatively: "There's bridge at the Embassy at five." For a long time Mrs. Slade did not answer. She appeared to be lost in contemplation, and Mrs. Ansley thought the remark had escaped her. But after a while she said, as if speaking out of a dream: "Bridge, did you say? Not unless you want to.... But I don't think I will, you know."

"Oh, no," Mrs. Ansley hastened to assure her. "I don't care to at all. It's so lovely here; and so full of old memories, as you say." She settled herself in her chair, and almost furtively drew forth her knitting. Mrs. Slade took sideway note of this activity, but her own beautifully cared-for hands remained motionless on her knee.

"I was just thinking," she said slowly, "what different things Rome stands for to each generation of travellers. To our grandmothers, Roman fever;[*] to our mothers, sentimental dangers—how we used to be guarded! —to our daughters, no more dangers than the middle of Main Street. They don't know it—but how much they're missing!"

The long golden light was beginning to pale, and Mrs. Ansley lifted her knitting a little closer to her eyes. "Yes; how we were guarded!"

"I always used to think," Mrs. Slade continued, "that our mothers had a much more difficult job than our grandmothers. When Roman fever stalked the streets it must have been comparatively easy to gather in the girls at the danger hour;[**] but

---

* *Roman fever*: Malaria.

** *the danger hour*: Malaria was thought to be most easily contracted during the night hours.

when you and I were young, with such beauty calling us, and the spice of disobedience thrown in, and no worse risk than catching cold during the cool hour after sunset, the mothers used to be put to it to keep us in—didn't they?"

She turned again toward Mrs. Ansley, but the latter had reached a delicate point in her knitting. "One, two three—slip two; yes, they must have been," she assented, without looking up.

Mrs. Slade's eyes rested on her with a deepened attention. "She can knit—in the face of *this*! How like her...."

Mrs. Slade leaned back, brooding, her eyes ranging from the ruins which faced her to the long green hollow of the Forum, the fading glow of the church fronts beyond it, and the outlying immensity of the Colosseum.* Suddenly she thought: "It's all very well to say that our girls have done away with sentiment and moonlight. But if Babs Ansley isn't out to catch that young aviator—the one who's a Marchese—then I don't know anything. And Jenny has no chance beside her. I know that too. I wonder if that's why Grace Ansley likes the two girls to go everywhere together? My poor Jenny as a foil —!" Mrs. Slade gave a hardly audible laugh, and at the sound Mrs. Ansley dropped her knitting.

"Yes—?"

"I—oh, nothing. I was only thinking how your Babs carries everything before her. That Campolieri boy is one of the best matches in Rome. Don't look so innocent, my dear—you know he is. And I was wondering, ever so respectfully you understand...

---

* *the Colosseum*: vast amphitheater of ancient Rome.

wondering how two such exemplary characters as you and Horace had managed to produce anything quite so dynamic." Mrs. Slade laughed again, with a touch of asperity.

Mrs. Ansley's hands lay inert across her needles. She looked straight out at the great accumulated wreckage of passion and splendour at her feet. But her small profile was almost expressionless. At length she said: "I think you overrate Babs, my dear."

Mrs. Slade's tone grew easier. "No, I don't. I appreciate her. And perhaps envy you. Oh, my girl's perfect; if I were a chronic invalid I'd—well, I think I'd rather be in Jenny's hands. There must be times... but there! I always wanted a brilliant daughter... and never quite understood why I got an angel instead."

Mrs. Ansley echoed her laugh in a faint murmur. "Babs is an angel too."

"Of course — of course! But she's got rainbow wings. Well, they're wandering by the sea with their young men; and here we sit... and it all brings back the past a little too acutely."

Mrs. Ansley had resumed her knitting. One might almost have imagined (if one had known her less well, Mrs. Slade reflected) that, for her also, too many memories rose from the lengthening shadows of those august ruins. But no; she was simply absorbed in her work. What was there for her to worry about? She knew that Babs would almost certainly come back engaged to the extremely eligible Campolieri. "And she'll sell the New York house, and settle down near them in Rome, and never be in their way... she's much too tactful. But she'll have an excellent cook, and just the right people in for bridge and cocktails... and a perfectly peaceful old age among her grandchildren."

Mrs. Slade broke off this prophetic flight with a recoil of self-disgust. There was no one of whom she had less right to think unkindly than of Grace Ansley. Would she never cure herself of envying her? Perhaps she had begun too long ago.

She stood up and leaned against the parapet, filling her troubled eyes with the tranquillizing magic of the hour. But instead of tranquillizing her the sight seemed to increase her exasperation. Her gaze turned toward the Colosseum. Already its golden flank was drowned in purple shadow, and above it the sky curved crystal clear, without light or colour. It was the moment when afternoon and evening hang balanced in mid-heaven.

Mrs. Slade turned back and laid her hand on her friend's arm. The gesture was so abrupt that Mrs. Ansley looked up, startled.

"The sun's set. You're not afraid, my dear?"

"Afraid—?"

"Of Roman fever or pneumonia? I remember how ill you were that winter. As a girl you had a very delicate throat, hadn't you?"

"Oh, we're all right up here. Down below, in the Forum, it does get deathly cold, all of a sudden... but not here."

"Ah, of course you know because you had to be so careful." Mrs. Slade turned back to the parapet. She thought: "I must make one more effort not to hate her." Aloud she said: "Whenever I look at the Forum from up here, I remember that story about a great-aunt of yours, wasn't she? A dreadfully wicked great-aunt?"

"Oh, yes; Great-aunt Harriet. The one who was supposed to have sent her young sister out to the Forum after sunset to gather a night-blooming flower for her album. All our great-aunts and grandmothers used to have albums of dried flowers."

Mrs. Slade nodded. "But she really sent her because they were in love with the same man—"

"Well, that was the family tradition. They said Aunt Harriet confessed it years afterward. At any rate, the poor little sister caught the fever and died. Mother used to frighten us with the story when we were children."

"And you frightened *me* with it, that winter when you and I were here as girls. The winter I was engaged to Delphin."

Mrs. Ansley gave a faint laugh. "Oh, did I? Really frightened you? I don't believe you're easily frightened."

"Not often; but I was then. I was easily frightened because I 55
was too happy. I wonder if you know what that means?"

"I—yes..." Mrs. Ansley faltered.

"Well, I suppose that was why the story of your wicked aunt made such an impression on me. And I thought: 'There's no more Roman fever, but the Forum is deathly cold after sunset—especially after a hot day. And the Colosseum's even colder and damper'."

"The Colosseum—?"

"Yes. It wasn't easy to get in, after the gates were locked for the night. Far from easy. Still, in those days it could be managed; it *was* managed, often. Lovers met there who couldn't meet elsewhere. You knew that?"

"I—I daresay. I don't remember." 60

"You don't remember? You don't remember going to visit

some ruins or other one evening, just after dark, and catching a bad chill? You were supposed to have gone to see the moon rise. People always said that expedition was what caused your illness."

There was a moment's silence; then Mrs. Ansley rejoined: "Did they? It was all so long ago."

"Yes. And you got well again—so it didn't matter. But I suppose it struck your friends—the reason given for your illness, I mean—because everybody knew you were so prudent on account of your throat, and your mother took such care of you.... You *had* been out late sight-seeing, hadn't you, that night?"

"Perhaps I had. The most prudent girls aren't always prudent. What made you think of it now?"

Mrs. Slade seemed to have no answer ready. But after a moment she broke out: "Because I simply can't bear it any longer—!"

Mrs. Ansley lifted her head quickly. Her eyes were wide and very pale. "Can't bear what?"

"Why—your not knowing that I've always known why you went."

"Why I went—?"

"Yes. You think I'm bluffing, don't you? Well, you went to meet the man I was engaged to—and I can repeat every word of the letter that took you there."

While Mrs. Slade spoke Mrs . Ansley had risen unsteadily to her feet. Her bag, her knitting and gloves, slid in a panic-stricken heap to the ground. She looked at Mrs. Slade as though she were looking at a ghost.

"No, no—don't," she faltered out.

"Why not? Listen, if you don't believe me. 'My one darling, things can't go on like this. I must see you alone. Come to the Colosseum immediately after dark tomorrow. There will be somebody to let you in. No one whom you need fear will suspect'—but perhaps you've forgotten what the letter said?"

Mrs. Ansley met the challenge with an unexpected composure. Steadying herself against the chair she looked at her friend, and replied: "No; I know it by heart too."

"And the signature? 'Only *your* D. S.' Was that it? I'm right, am I? That was the letter that took you out that evening after dark?"

Mrs. Ansley was still looking at her. It seemed to Mrs. Slade that a slow struggle was going on behind the voluntarily controlled mask of her small quiet face. "I shouldn't have thought she had herself so well in hand," Mrs. Slade reflected, almost resentfully. But at this moment Mrs. Ansley spoke. "I don't know how you knew. I burnt that letter at once."

"Yes; you would, naturally—you're so prudent!" The sneer was open now. "And if you burnt the letter you're wondering how on earth I know what was in it. That's it, isn't it?"

Mrs. Slade waited, but Mrs. Ansley did not speak.

"Well, my dear, I know what was in that letter because I wrote it!"

"You wrote it?"

"Yes."

The two women stood for a minute staring at each other in the last golden light. Then Mrs. Ansley dropped back into her chair.

"Oh," she murmured, and covered her face with her hands.

Mrs. Slade waited nervously for another word or movement. None came, and at length she broke out: "I horrify you."

Mrs. Ansley's hands dropped to her knee. The face they uncovered was streaked with tears. "I wasn't thinking of you. I was thinking—it was the only letter I ever had from him!"

"And I wrote it. Yes; I wrote it! But I was the girl he was engaged to. Did you happen to remember that?"

Mrs. Ansley's head drooped again. "I'm not trying to excuse myself... I remembered..."

"And still you went?"

"Still I went."

Mrs. Slade stood looking down on the small bowed figure at her side. The flame of her wrath had already sunk, and she wondered why she had ever thought there would be any satisfaction in inflicting so purposeless a wound on her friend. But she had to justify herself.

"You do understand? I'd found out—and I hated you, hated you. I knew you were in love with Delphin—and I was afraid; afraid of you, of your quiet ways, your sweetness... your... well, I wanted you out of the way, that's all. Just for a few weeks; just till I was sure of him. So in a blind fury I wrote that letter... I don't know why I'm telling you now."

"I suppose," said Mrs . Ansley slowly, "it's because you've always gone on hating me."

"Perhaps. Or because I wanted to get the whole thing off my mind." She paused. "I'm glad you destroyed the letter. Of course I never thought you'd die."

Mrs. Ansley relapsed into silence, and Mrs. Slade, leaning above her, was conscious of a strange sense of isolation, of being cut off from the warm current of human communion. "You think me a monster!"

"I don't know.... It was the only letter I had, and you say he didn't write it?"

"Ah, how you care for him still!"

"I cared for that memory," said Mrs. Ansley. 95

Mrs. Slade continued to look down on her. She seemed physically reduced by the blow—as if, when she got up, the wind might scatter her like a puff of dust. Mrs. Slade's jealousy suddenly leapt up again at the sight. All these years the woman had been living on that letter. How she must have loved him, to treasure the mere memory of its ashes! The letter of the man her friend was engaged to. Wasn't it she who was the monster?

"You tried your best to get away from me, didn't you? But you failed; and I kept him. That's all."

"Yes. That's all."

"I wish now I hadn't told you. I'd no idea you'd feel about it as you do; I thought you'd be amused. It all happened so long ago, as you say; and you must do me the justice to remember that I had no reason to think you'd ever taken it seriously. How could I, when you were married to Horace Ansley two months afterward? As soon as you could get out of bed your mother rushed you off to Florence and married you. People were rather surprised—they wondered at its being done so quickly, but I thought I knew. I had an idea you did it out of *pique*—to be able to say you'd got ahead of Delphin and me. Girls have such silly reasons for doing the most serious things. And you marrying so soon convinced me that you'd never really cared."

"Yes. I suppose it would," Mrs. Ansley assented.

The clear heaven overhead was emptied of all its gold. Dusk spread over it, abruptly darkening the Seven Hills. Here and there lights began to twinkle through the foliage at their feet. Steps were coming and going on the deserted terrace—waiters looking out of the doorway at the head of the stairs, then reappearing with trays and napkins and flasks of wine. Tables were moved, chairs straightened. A feeble string of electric lights flickered out. Some vases of faded flowers were carried away, and brought back replenished. A stout lady in a dust-coat suddenly appeared, asking in broken Italian if any one had seen the elastic band which held together her tattered Baedeker.* She poked with her stick under the table at which she had lunched, the waiters assisting.

The corner where Mrs. Slade and Mrs. Ansley sat was still shadowy and deserted. For a long time neither of them spoke. At length Mrs. Slade began again: "I suppose I did it as a sort of joke—"

"A joke?"

"Well, girls are ferocious sometimes, you know. Girls in love especially. And I remember laughing to myself all that evening at the idea that you were waiting around there in the dark, dodging out of sight, listening for every sound, trying to get in—. Of

---

* *Baedeker*: A tourist's guidebook.

course I was upset when I heard you were so ill afterward."

Mrs . Ansley had not moved for a long time . But now she turned slowly toward her companion. "But I didn't wait. He'd arranged everything. He was there. We were let in at once," she said.

Mrs. Slade sprang up from her leaning position. "Delphin there? They let you in? —Ah, now you're lying!" she burst out with violence.

Mrs. Ansley's voice grew clearer, and full of surprise. "But of course he was there. Naturally he came—"

"Came? How did he know he'd find you there? You must be raving!"

Mrs. Ansley hesitated, as though reflecting. "But I answered the letter. I told him I'd be there. So he came."

Mrs. Slade flung her hands up to her face. "Oh, God — you answered! I never thought of your answering...."

"It's odd you never thought of it, if you wrote the letter."

"Yes. I was blind with rage."

Mrs. Ansley rose, and drew her fur scarf about her. "It is cold here. We'd better go.... I'm sorry for you," she said, as she clasped the fur about her throat.

The unexpected words sent a pang through Mrs. Slade. "Yes; we'd better go." She gathered up her bag and cloak. "I don't know why you should be sorry for me," she muttered.

Mrs. Ansley stood looking away from her toward the dusky secret mass of the Colosseum. "Well—because I didn't have to wait that night."

Mrs. Slade gave an unquiet laugh. "Yes; I was beaten there.

But I oughtn't to begrudge it to you, I suppose. At the end of all these years. After all, I had everything; I had him for twenty-five years. And you had nothing but that one letter that he didn't write."

Mrs. Ansley was again silent. At length she turned toward the door of the terrace. She took a step, and turned back, facing her companion.

"I had Barbara," she said, and began to move ahead of Mrs. Slade toward the stairway.

Questions:

1. How would you characterize Grace and Alida? Who do you think might be more ruthless?
2. How accurate are the judgements the two women have made about each other?
3. Do you happen to think about the narrowness of the lives of Grace and Alida?
4. How is the title "*Roman Fever*" related and contributed to the story as a whole? Or why is the story called "*Roman Fever*"?

Chapter 4 Setting

By the **setting** of a story, we mean the location and time frame in which the action of a narrative (novel, drama, short story, poem) takes place.

The makeup and behavior of fictional characters often depend on their environment quite as much as on other personal characteristics. **Setting** is of great importance for Emily Zola, for example, because he believed that environment determined character. In some cases the entire action of a story or a novel is determined by the locale in which it is set. Gustave Flaubert's "*Madame Bovary*" could hardly have been placed in Paris, because the tragic life and death of the heroine have a great deal to do with the circumscriptions of her provincial surroundings.

The elements making up a **setting** are: (1) the physical environment; (2) the time or period in which the ACTION takes place; (3) the general environment of the characters, for example, religious, mental, moral, social and emotional conditions through which the people in the NARRATIVE move; and (4) the occupations and daily manner of living of characters.

The idea of the physical environment includes the actual geographical location, its topography, scenery, a street, a city, a region, a house, even the location of the windows and doors in a room. It is said that physical places mattered so greatly to French novelist Honore de Balzac that sometimes, before writing a story set in a town, he would visit that town, select a few houses, and describe them in detail, down to their very smells. Henry James once admiringly said of him, "the place in which an event occurred was in his view of equal moment with the event itself.... It had a part to play; it needed to be made as definite as anything else."

Physical place is especially vital to a REGIONAL WRITER, who usually sets stories in one geographical area. William Faulkner, a distinguished regional writer, almost always sets his novels and stories in his native Mississippi. Though born in St. Louis, Kate Chopin writes about Louisiana in many of her short stories. Willa Cather, another outstanding regionalist, sets most of her novels in frontier Nebraska. Sarah Orne Jewett writes of New England and O. Henry chronicled both the Texas frontier and the streets of New York City.

As such writers show, a place can profoundly affect the character who grew up in it. Willa Cather is fond of portraying strong-minded, independent women, such as the heroine of her novel "*My Antonia*," strengthened in part by years of coping with the hardships of life on the wind-lashed prairie. Physical place is equally important to a naturalist writer, who tends to draw the characters as helpless puppets of their environment and to see them as the products and victims of environment of heredity. Stephen Crane, a noted naturalist, sets the heroine of "*Maggie: A Girl of the Street*" in a slum, which helps to strengthen Maggie's descent into prostitution and eventual suicide. Theodore Dresser's "*Sister Carrie*" is often looked upon as the first masterpiece of the American naturalistic movement. Its physical place is set in a pretty small town (where the heroine was born and grown up) and the big city (where she was used by men and used them in turn to become a successful Broadway actress).

Often, **setting** and **character** will reveal each other. Recall how Faulkner, at the start of "*A Rose for Emily*," depicts Emily Grierson's house, once handsome but now "an eyesore among eyesore" surrounded by gas stations. Still standing, refusing to yield its old-time horse-and-buggy splendor to the age of the automobile, the house in "its stubborn and coquettish decay" embodies the character of its owner. In some fiction, setting is closely bound with theme, as you will find in John Steinbeck's "*The Chrysanthemums*," a story beginning with a fog that has sealed off a valley from the rest of the world—a fog like the lid on a pot. In "*The Scarlet Letter*," Hawthrone introduces to us a colonial jailhouse with a grass-plot at the beginning of the story. Apparently, Hawthrone wishes to show us that Puritan Boston, a town of rutted streets and an ugly jail with a grass-plot, may be rough but still has some beauty in it. As the story unfolds, we know what he will suggest is that secret sin and a beautiful child may go together just like pigweed and wild roses. In his artfully crafted novel, setting is organically connected with characters, theme and symbols.

In some stories, a writer will seem to draw a setting in order to evoke a certain atmosphere. In such a story, setting starts us feeling whatever the storyteller would have us feel. In "*The Tell-Tale Heart*," Poe sets the action in an old, dark, lantern-lit house, which greatly contributes to our sense of unease and helps the story's effectiveness. (Old, dark mansions are favorite settings for the Gothic story.) Again, Faulkner's story "*A Rose for Emily*" portrays an aristocratic who refuses to admit that her world has vanished. Yet, a rundown mansion, together with a mysterious servant, a mad woman and a hideous secret, helps to create a mysterious atmosphere. That is why when

Miss Emily Grierson died, the women mostly out of curiosity went to see the inside of her house.

Besides place, **setting** may involve the time of the story, for example, epoch in history, season of the year, or even at dawn of the day. In "*The Scarlet Letter*," nineteenth-century author Nathaniel Hawthrone, by a long introduction and a vivid opening scene at a prison door, prepares us to witness events in the Puritan community of Boston in the earlier seventeenth century. This setting, together with scenes of Puritan times, helps us understand what happens in the novel. We can appreciate the shocked agitation in town when Hester is accused of adultery: she has borne an illegitimate child. Such an event might seem commonly today, but in the stern, God-fearing New England Puritan community, it was a flagrant defiance of church, which was all-powerful. That Hawthrone's novel takes place in a time remote from our own leads us to expect different customs and different attitudes.

In addition to time and space, **setting** may also include the weather—which indeed, in some stories, may be crucial. Take Chekhov's "*Misery*" for example. In the first paragraph, we have been given a brief but entirely adequate view of the setting: a Russian city (place) in the days of horse-drawn sleighs (time—most probably in the late nineteenth century), and lots of snow (wea-ther). "Big flakes of wet snow" make the sledgedriver "all white like a ghost." In a way, coldness of weather suggested by snow (external coldness), and coldness of people who refuse to listen to the cabdriver's story of his son's death (internal coldness) help to formulate the theme: This world is filled with coldness and human beings in it have become indifferent to the sufferings of others.

Besides, that "the wet snow paints him and his horse white" further suggests that the sledgedriver and his horse are bound to be fellow suffers and to commiserate with each other. He will express his grief to no one else except his mare.

Kate Chopin (1851—1904)

The Storm

I

The leaves were so still that even Bibi thought it was going to rain. Bobinôt, who was accustomed to converse on terms of perfect equality with his little son, called the child's attention to certain somber clouds that were rolling with sinister intention from the west, accompanied by a sullen, threatening roar. They were at Friedheimer's store and decided to remain there till the storm had passed. They sat within the door on two empty kegs. Bibi was four years old and looked very wise.

"Mama'll be' fraid, yes," he suggested with blinking eyes.

"She'll shut the house. Maybe she got Sylvie helpin' her this evenin'," Bobinôt responded reassuringly.

"No; she ent got Sylvie. Sylvie was helpin' her yistiday," piped Bibi.

Bobinôt arose and going across to the counter purchased a can of 5
shrimps, of which Calixta was very fond. Then he returned to his perch on the keg and sat stolidly holding the can of shrimps while the storm burst. It shook the wooden store and seemed to be

ripping great furrows in the distant field. Bibi laid his little hand on his father's knee and was not afraid.

II

Calixta, at home, felt no uneasiness for their safety. She sat at a side window sewing furiously on a sewing machine. She was greatly occupied and did not notice the approaching storm. But she felt very warm and often stopped to mop her face on which the perspiration gathered in beads. She unfastened her white sacque at the throat. It began to grow dark, and suddenly realizing the situation she got up hurriedly and went about closing windows and doors.

Out on the small front gallery she had hung Bobinôt's Sunday clothes to air and she hastened out to gather them before the rain fell. As she stepped outside, Alcée Laballière rode in at the gate. She has not seen him very often since her marriage, and never alone. She stood there with Bobinôt's coat in her hands, and the big rain drops began to fall. Alcée rode his horse under the shelter of a side projection where the chickens had huddled and there were plows and a harrow piled up in the corner.

"May I come and wait on your gallery till the storm is over, Calixta?" he asked.

"Come 'long in, M'sieur Alcée."

His voice and her own startled her as if from a trance, and she seized Bobinôt's vest. Alcée, mounting to the porch, grabbed the trousers and snatched Bibi's braided jacket that was about to be carried away by a sudden gust of wind. He expressed an intention to remain outside, but it was soon apparent that he might as well have been out in the open: the water beat in upon the boards in driving sheets, and he went inside, closing the door after him. It was even necessary to put something beneath the door to keep the water out.

"My! what a rain! It's good two years since it rain like that," exclaimed Calixta as she rolled up a piece of bagging and Alcée helped her to thrust it beneath the crack.

She was a little fuller of figure than five years before when she married; but she had lost nothing of her vivacity. Her blue eyes still retained their melting quality; and her yellow hair, dishevelled by the wind and rain, kinked more stubbornly than ever about her ears and temples.

The rain beat upon the low, shingled roof with a force and clatter that threatened to break an entrance and deluge them there. They were in the dining room—the sitting room—the general utility room. Adjoining was her bed room, with Bibi's couch along side her own. The door stood open, and the room with its white, monumental bed, its closed shutters, looked dim and mysterious.

Alcée flung himself into a rocker and Calixta nervously began to gather up from the floor the lengths of a cotton sheet which she had been sewing.

"If this keeps up, *Dieu sait*[*] if the levees goin' to stan'it!" she exclaimed.

"What have you got to do with the levees?"

"I got enough to do! An' there's Bobinôt with Bibi out in that storm—if he only didn't left Friedheimer's!"

---

* *Dieu sait*: God only knows.

"Let us hope, Calixta, that Bobinôt's got sense enough to come in out of a cyclone."

She went and stood at the window with a greatly disturbed look on her face. She wiped the frame that was clouded with moisture. It was stiflingly hot. Alcée got up and joined her at the window, looking over her shoulder. The rain was coming down in sheets obscuring the view of far-off cabins and enveloping the distant wood in a gray mist. The playing of the lightning was incessant. A bolt struck a tall chinaberry tree at the edge of the field. It filled all visible space with a blinding glare and the crash seemed to invade the very boards they stood upon.

Calixta put her hands to her eyes, and with a cry, staggered backward. Alcée's arm encircled her, and for an instant he drew her close and spasmodically to him.

"*Bonte*!*" she cried, releasing herself from his encircling arm and retreating from the window, "the house'll go next! If I only knew w'ere Bibi was!" She would not compose herself; she would not be seated. Alcée clasped her shoulders and looked into her face. The contact of her warm, palpitating body when he had unthinkingly drawn her into his arms, had aroused all the old-time infatuation and desire for her flesh.

"Calixta," he said, "don't be frightened. Nothing can happen. The house is too low to be struck, with so many tall trees standing about. There! aren't you going to be quiet? say, aren't you?" He pushed her hair back from her face that was warm and

---

* *Bonte*!: Heavens!

steaming. Her lips were as red and moist as pomegranate seed. Her white neck and a glimpse of her full, firm bosom disturbed him powerfully. As she glanced up at him the fear in her liquid blue eyes had given place to a drowsy gleam that unconsciously betrayed a sensuous desire. He looked down into her eyes and there was nothing for him to do but gather her lips in a kiss. It reminded him of Assumption.[*]

"Do you remember—in Assumption, Calixta?" he asked in a low voice broken by passion. Oh! she remembered; for in Assumption he had kissed her and kissed and kissed her; until his senses would well nigh fail, and to save her he would resort to a desperate flight. If she was not an immaculate dove in those days, she was still inviolate; a passionate creature whose very defenselessness had made her defense, against which his honor forbade him to prevail. Now—well, now—her lips seemed in a manner free to be tasted, as well as her round, white throat and her whiter breasts.

They did not heed the crashing torrents, and the roar of the elements made her laugh as she lay in his arms. She was a revelation in that dim, mysterious chamber; as white as the couch she lay upon. Her firm, elastic flesh that was knowing for the first time its birthright, was like a creamy lily that the sun invites to contribute its breath and perfume to the undying life of the world.

The generous abundance of her passion, without guile or trickery, was like a white flame which penetrated and found response

---

* *Assumption*: a parish west of New Orleans.

in depths of his own sensuous nature that had never yet been reached.

When he touched her breasts they gave themselves up in quivering ecstasy, inviting his lips. Her mouth was a fountain of delight. And when he possessed her, they seemed to swoon together at the very borderland of life's mystery.

He stayed cushioned upon her, breathless, dazed, enervated, with his heart beating like a hammer upon her. With one hand she clasped his head, her lips lightly touching his forehead. The other hand stroked with a soothing rhythm his muscular shoulders.

The growl of the thunder was distant and passing away. The rain beat softly upon the shingles, inviting them to drowsiness and sleep. But they dared not yield.

The rain was over; and the sun was turning the glistening green world into a palace of gems. Calixta, on the gallery, watched Alcée ride away. He turned and smiled at her with a beaming face; and she lifted her pretty chin in the air and laughed aloud.

III

Bobinôt and Bibi, trudging home, stopped without at the cistern 30
to make themselves presentable.

"My! Bibi, w'at will yo' mama say! You ought to be ashame'. You oughtn' put on those good pants. Look at 'em! An' that mud on yo' collar! How you got that mud on yo'collar, Bibi? I never saw such a boy!" Bibi was the picture of pathetic resignation. Bobinôt was the embodiment of serious solicitude as he strove to remove from his own person and his son's the signs of their tramp over heavy roads and through wet fields. He scraped the mud off Bibi's bare legs and feet with a stick and carefully removed all traces from his heavy brogans. Then, prepared for the worst—the meeting with an overscrupulous housewife, they entered cautiously at the back door.

Calixta was preparing supper. She had set the table and was dripping coffee at the hearth. She sprang up as they came in.

"Oh, Bobinôt! You back! My! but I was uneasy. W'ere you been during the rain? An'Bibi? he ain't wet? he ain't hurt?" She had clasped Bibi and was kissing him effusively. Bobinôt's explanations and apologies which he had been composing all along the way, died on his lips as Calixta felt him to see if he were dry, and seemed to express nothing but satisfaction at their safe return.

"I brought you some shrimps, Calixta," offered Bobinôt, hauling the can from his ample side pocket and laying it on the table.

"Shrimps! Oh, Bobinôt! you too good fo' anything!" and she gave him a smacking kiss on the cheek that resounded. "*J'vous reponds*,* we'll have feas' to night! umph-umph!"

Bobinôt and Bibi began to relax and enjoy themselves, and when the three seated themselves at table they laughed much and so loud that anyone might have heard them as far away as Laballière's.

IV

Alcée Laballière wrote to his wife, Clarisse, that night. It was a loving letter, full of tender solicitude. He told her not to hurry back, but if she and the babies liked it at Biloxi, to stay a month

---

* *J'vous reponds*: Let me tell you.

longer. He was getting on nicely; and though he missed them, he was willing to bear the separation a while longer—realizing that their health and pleasure were the first things to be considered.

V

As for Clarisse, she was charmed upon receiving her husband's letter. She and the babies were doing well. The society was agreeable; many of her old friends and acquaintances were at the bay. And the first free breath since her marriage seemed to restore the pleasant liberty of her maiden days. Devoted as she was to her husband, their intimate conjugal life was something which she was more than willing to forego for a while.

So the storm passed and everyone was happy.

Questions:

1. In the story as a whole, how do setting and plot reinforce each other?
2. In Part Ⅲ do you think Calixta is insincere in her expressions of solicitude for Bobinôt? Why or why not?
3. Why does Chopin bother, in Part Ⅴ, to tell us about Clarisse? And what do you make of the last line of the story? What meanings do you find in the title "*The Storm*"?
4. Do you think the story is immoral?
5. What general attitudes towards sex, love, and marriage does Chopin imply? Cite evidence to support your argument.

John Steinbeck (1902—1968)

Chrysanthemums

The high grey-flannel fog of winter closed off the Salinas Valley * from the sky and from all the rest of the world. On every side it sat like a lid on the mountains and made of the great valley a closed pot. On the broad, level land floor the gang plows bit deep and left the black earth shining like metal where the shares had cut. On the foothill ranches across the Salinas River, the yellow stubble fields seemed to be bathed in pale cold sunshine, but there was no sunshine in the valley now in December. The thick willow scrub along the river flamed with sharp and positive yellow leaves.

It was a time of quiet and of waiting. The air was cold and tender. A light wind blew up from the southwest so that the farmers were mildly hopeful of a good rain before long; but fog and rain do not go together.

Across the river, on Henry Allen's foothill ranch there was little work to be done, for the hay was cut and stored and the orchards were plowed up to receive the rain deeply when it should come. The cattle on the higher slopes were becoming shaggy and rough-coated.

---

* *the Salinas Valley*: south of San Francisco in the Coast Ranges region of California.

Elisa Allen, working in her flower garden, looked down across the yard and saw Henry, her husband, talking to two men in business suits. The three of them stood by the tractor shed, each man with one foot on the side of the little Fordson. They smoked cigarettes and studied the machine as they talked.

Elisa watched them for a moment and then went back to her work. She was thirty-five. Her face was lean and strong and her eyes were as clear as water. Her figure looked blocked and heavy in her gardening costume, a man's black hat pulled low down over her eyes, clod-hopper shoes, a figured print dress almost completely covered by a big corduroy apron with four big. pockets to hold the snips, the trowel and scratcher, the seeds and the knife she worked with. She wore heavy leather gloves to protect her hands while she worked.

She was cutting down the old year's chrysanthemum stalks with a pair of short and powerful scissors. She looked down toward the men by the tractor shed now and then. Her face was eager and mature and handsome; even her work with the scissors was over-eager, over-powerful. The chrysanthemum stems seemed too small and easy for her energy.

She brushed a cloud of hair out of her eyes with the back of her glove, and left a smudge of earth on her cheek in doing it. Behind her stood the neat white farm house with red geraniums close-banked around it as high as the windows. It was a hard-swept looking little house with hard-polished windows, and a clean mud-mat on the front steps.

Elisa cast another glance toward the tractor shed. The strangers were getting into their Ford coupe. She took off a glove and put her strong fingers down into the forest of new green chrysanthemum sprouts that were growing around the old roots. She spread the leaves and looked down among the close-growing stems. No aphids were there, no sowbugs or snails or cutworms. Her terrier fingers destroyed such pests before they could get started.

Elisa started at the sound of her husband's voice. He had come near quietly, and he leaned over the wire fence that protected her flower garden from cattle and dogs and chickens.

"At it again," he said. "You've got a strong new crop coming." 10

Elisa straightened her back and pulled on the gardening glove again. "Yes. They'll be strong this coming year." In her tone and on her face there was a little smugness.

"You've got a gift with things." Henry observed. "Some of those yellow chrysanthemums you had this year were ten inches across. I wish you'd work out in the orchard and raise some apples that big."

Her eyes sharpened. "Maybe I could do it, too. I've a gift with things, all right. My mother had it. She could stick anything in the ground and make it grow. She said it was having planters' hands that knew how to do it."

"Well, it sure works with flowers," he said.

"Henry, who were those men you were talking to?" 15

"Why, sure, that's what I came to tell you. They were from the Western Meat Company. I sold those thirty head of three-year-old steers. Got nearly my own price, too."

"Good," she said. "Good for you."

"And I thought," he continued, "I thought how it's Saturday afternoon, and we might go into Salinas for dinner at a restaurant, and then to a picture show—to celebrate, you see."

"Good," she repeated. "Oh, yes. That will be good."

Henry put on his joking tone. "There's fights tonight. How'd you like to go to the fights?"

"Oh, no," she said breathlessly. "No, I wouldn't like fights."

"Just fooling, Elisa. We'll go to a movie. Let's see. It's two now. I'm going to take Scotty and bring down those steers from the hill. It'll take us maybe two hours. We'll go in town about five and have dinner at the Cominos Hotel. Like that?"

"Of course I'll like it. It's good to eat away from home."

"All right, then. I'll go get up a couple of horses."

She said, "I'll have plenty of time to transplant some of these sets, I guess."

She heard her husband calling Scotty down by the barn. And a little later she saw the two men ride up the pale yellow hillside in search of the steers.

There was a little square sandy bed kept for rooting the chrysanthemums. With her trowel she turned the soil over and over, and smoothed it and patted it firm. Then she dug ten parallel trenches to receive the sets. Back at the chrysanthemum bed she pulled out the little crisp shoots, trimmed off the leaves of each one with her scissors and laid it on a small orderly pile.

A squeak of wheels and plod of hoofs came from the road. Elisa looked up. The country road ran along the dense bank of willows and cottonwoods that bordered the river, and up this road came a curious vehicle, curiously drawn. It was an old spring-wagon, with a round canvas top on it like the cover of a prairie schooner. It was drawn by an old bay horse and a little grey-and-white burro. A big stubble-bearded man sat between the cover flaps and drove the crawling team. Underneath the wagon, between the hind wheels, a lean and rangy mongrel dog walked sedately. Words were painted on the canvas, in clumsy, crooked letters. "Pots, pans, knives, scissors, lawn mores, Fixed." Two rows of articles, and the triumphantly definitive "Fixed" below. The black paint had run down in little sharp points beneath each letter.

Elisa, squatting on the ground, watched to see the crazy, loose-jointed wagon pass by. But it didn't pass. It turned into the farm road in front of her house, crooked old wheels skirling and squeaking. The rangy dog darted from between the wheels and ran ahead. Instantly the two ranch shepherds flew out at him. Then all three stopped, and with stiff and quivering tails, with taut straight legs, with ambassadorial dignity, they slowly circled, sniffing daintily. The caravan pulled up to Elisa's wire fence and stopped. Now the newcomer dog, feeling outnumbered, lowered his tail and retired under the wagon with raised hackles and bared teeth.

The man on the wagon seat called out, "That's a bad dog in a fight when he gets started."

Elisa laughed. "I see he is. How soon does he generally get started?"

The man caught up her laughter and echoed it heartily. "Sometimes not for weeks and weeks," he said. He climbed stiffly down, over the wheel. The horse and the donkey drooped like unwatered flowers.

Elisa saw that he was a very big man. Although his hair and

beard were greying, he did not look old. His worn black suit was wrinkled and spotted with grease. The laughter had disappeared from his face and eyes the moment his laughing voice ceased. His eyes were dark, and they were full of the brooding that gets in the eyes of teamsters and of sailors. The calloused hands he rested on the wire fence were cracked, and every crack was a black line. He took off his battered hat.

"I'm off my general road, ma'am," he said. "Does this dirt road cut over across the river to the Los Angeles highway?"

Elisa stood up and shoved the thick scissors in her apron pocket. "Well, yes, it does, but it winds around and then fords the river. I don't think your team could pull through the sand."

He replied with some asperity. "It might surprise you what them beasts can pull through."

"When they get started?" she asked.

He smiled for a second. "Yes. When they get started."

"Well," said Elisa, "I think you'll save time if you go back to the Salinas road and pick up the highway there."

He drew a big finger down the chicken wire and made it sing. "I ain't in any hurry, ma'am. I go from Seattle to San Diego and back every year. Takes all my time. About six months each way. I aim to follow nice weather."

Elisa took off her gloves and stuffed them in the apron pocket with the scissors. She touched the under edge of her man's hat, searching for fugitive hairs. "That sounds like a nice kind of a way to live," she said.

He leaned confidentially over the fence. "Maybe you noticed

the writing on my wagon. I mend pots and sharpen knives and scissors. You got any of them things to do?"

"Oh, no," she said quickly. "Nothing like that." Her eyes hardened with resistance.

"Scissors is the worst thing," he explained. "Most people just ruin scissors trying to sharpen'em, but I know how. I got a special tool. It's a little bobbin kind of thing, and patented. But it sure does the trick."

"No. My scissors are all sharp." 45

"All right, then. Take a pot," he continued earnestly, "a bent pot, or a pot with a hole. I can make it like new so you don't have to buy no new ones. That's a saving for you."

"No," she said shortly. "I tell you I have nothing like that for you to do."

His face fell to an exaggerated sadness. His voice took on a whining undertone. "I ain't had a thing to do today. Maybe I won't have no supper tonight. You see I'm off my regular road. I know folks on the highway clear from Seattle to San Diego. They save their things for me to sharpen up because they know I do it so good and save them money."

"I'm sorry," Elisa said irritably. "I haven't anything for you to do."

His eyes left her face and fell to searching the ground. They 50
roamed about until they came to the chrysanthemum bed where she had been working. "What's them plants, ma'am?"

The irritation and resistance melted from Elisa's face. "Oh, those are chrysanthemums, giant whites and yellows. I raise them every year, bigger than anybody around here."

"Kind of a long-stemmed flower? Looks like a quick puff of colored smoke?" he asked.

"That's it. What a nice way to describe them."

"They smell kind of nasty till you get used to them," he said.

"It's a good bitter smell," she retorted, "not nasty at all." 55

He changed his tone quickly. "I like the smell myself."

"I had ten-inch blooms this year," she said.

The man leaned farther over the fence. "Look. I know a lady down the road a piece, has got the nicest garden you ever seen. Got nearly every kind of flower but no chrysanthemums. Last time I was mending a copper-bottom washtub for her (that's a hard job but I do it good), she said to me, 'If you ever run across some nice chrysanthemums I wish you'd try to get me a few seeds.' That's what she told me."

Elisa's eyes grew alert and eager. "She couldn't have known much about chrysanthemums. You *can* raise them from seed, but it's much easier to root the little sprouts you see there."

"Oh," he said. "I s'pose I can't take none to her, then." 60

"Why yes you can," Elisa cried. "I can put some in damp sand, and you can carry them right along with you. They'll take root in the pot if you keep them damp. And then she can transplant them."

"She'd sure like to have some, ma'am. You say they're nice ones?"

"Beautiful," she said. "Oh, beautiful." Her eyes shone. She tore off the battered hat and shook out her dark pretty hair. "I'll put them in a flower pot, and you can take them right with you. Come into the yard."

While the man came through the picket gate Elisa ran excitedly along the geranium-bordered path to the back of the house. And she returned carrying a big red flower pot. The gloves were forgotten now. She kneeled on the ground by the starting bed and dug up the sandy soil with her fingers and scooped it into the bright new flower pot. Then she picked up the little pile of shoots she had prepared. With her strong fingers she pressed them in the sand and tamped around them with her knuckles. The man stood over her. "I'll tell you what to do," she said. "You remember so you can tell the lady."

"Yes, I'll try to remember."

"Well, look. These will take root in about a month. Then she must set them out, about a foot apart in good rich earth like this, see?" She lifted a handful of dark soil for him to look at. "They'll grow fast and tall. Now remember this: In July tell her to cut them down, about eight inches from the ground."

"Before they bloom?" he asked.

"Yes, before they bloom." Her face was tight with eagerness. "They'll grow right up again. About the last of September the buds will start."

She stopped and seemed perplexed. "It's the budding that takes the most care," she said hesitantly. "I don't know how to tell you." She looked deep into his eyes, searchingly. Her mouth opened a little, and she seemed to be listening. "I'll try to tell you," she said. "Did you ever hear of planting hands?"

"Can't say I have, ma'am."

"Well, I can only tell you what it feels like. It's when you're picking off the buds you don't want. Everything goes right down into your fingertips. You watch your fingers work. They do it themselves. You can feel how it is. They pick and pick the buds. They never make a mistake. They're with the plant. Do you see? Your fingers and the plant. You can feel that, right up your arm. They know. They never make a mistake. You can feel it. When you're like that you can't do anything wrong. Do you see that? Can you understand that?"

She was kneeling on the ground looking up at him. Her breast swelled passionately.

The man's eyes narrowed. He looked away self-consciously. "Maybe I know," he said. "Sometimes in the night in the wagon there—"

Elisa's voice grew husky. She broke in on him. "I've never lived as you do, but I know what you mean. When the night is dark—why, the stars are sharp-pointed, and there's quiet. Why, you rise up and up! Every pointed star gets driven into your body. It's like that. Hot and sharp and—lovely."

Kneeling there, her hand went out toward his legs in the greasy black trousers. Her hesitant fingers almost touched the cloth. Then her hand dropped to the ground. She crouched low like a fawning dog.

He said. "It's nice, just like you say. Only when you don't have no dinner, it ain't."

She stood up then, very straight, and her face was ashamed. She held the flower pot out to him and placed it gently in his arms. "Here. Put it in your wagon, on the seat, where you can watch it. Maybe I can find something for you to do."

At the back of the house she dug in the can pile and found two old and battered aluminum saucepans. She carried them back and gave them to him. "Here, maybe you can fix these."

His manner changed. He became professional. "Good as new I can fix them." At the back of his wagon he set a little anvil, and out of an oily tool box dug a small machine hammer. Elisa came through the gate to watch him while he pounded out the dents in the kettles. His mouth grew sure and knowing. At a difficult part of the work he sucked his under-lip.

"You sleep right in the wagon?" Elisa asked.

"Right in the wagon, ma'am. Rain or shine I'm dry as a cow in there."

"It must be nice," she said. "It must be very nice. I wish women could do such things."

"It ain't the right kind of a life for a woman."

Her upper lip raised a little, showing her teeth. "How do you know? How can you tell?" she said.

"I don't know, ma'am," he protested. "Of course I don't know. Now here's your kettles, done. You don't have to buy no new ones."

"How much?"

"Oh, fifty cents'll do. I keep my prices down and my work good. That's why I have all them satisfied customers up and down the highway."

Elisa brought him a fifty-cent piece from the house and dropped it in his hand. "You might be surprised to have a rival some time. I can sharpen scissors, too. And I can beat the dents out of little pots. I could show you what a woman might do."

He put his hammer back in the oily box and shoved the little anvil out of sight. "It would be a lonely life for a woman, ma'am, and a scarey life, too, with animals creeping under the wagon all night." He climbed over the single-tree, steadying himself with a hand on the burro's white rump. He settled himself in the seat, picked up the lines. "Thank you kindly, ma'am," he said. "I'll do like you told me; I'll go back and catch the Salinas road."

"Mind," she called, "if you're long in getting there, keep the 90
sand damp."

"Sand, ma'am?... Sand? Oh, sure. You mean around the chrysanthemums. Sure I will." He clucked his tongue. The beasts leaned luxuriously into their collars. The mongrel dog took his place between the back wheels. The wagon turned and crawled out the entrance road and back the way it had come, along the river.

Elisa stood in front of her wire fence watching the slow progress of the caravan. Her shoulders were straight, her head thrown back, her eyes half-closed, so that the scene came vaguely into them. Her lips moved silently, forming the words "Good-bye—good-bye." Then she whispered, "That's a bright direction. There's a glowing there." The sound of her whisper startled her. She shook herself free and looked about to see whether anyone had been listening. Only the dogs had heard. They lifted their heads toward her from their sleeping in the dust, and then stretched out their chins and settled asleep again. Elisa turned and ran hurriedly into the house.

In the kitchen she reached behind the stove and felt the water tank. It was full of hot water from the noonday cooking. In the bathroom she tore off her soiled clothes and flung them into the corner. And then she scrubbed herself with a little block of pumice, legs and thighs, loins and chest and arms, until her skin was scratched and red. When she had dried herself she stood in front of a mirror in her bedroom and looked at her body. She tightened her stomach and threw out her chest. She turned and looked over her shoulder at her back.

After a while she began to dress, slowly. She put on her newest under-clothing and her nicest stockings and the dress which was the symbol of her prettiness. She worked carefully on her hair, penciled her eyebrows and rouged her lips.

Before she was finished she heard the little thunder of hoofs 95
and the shouts of Henry and his helper as they drove the red steers into the corral. She heard the gate bang shut and set herself for Henry's arrival.

His step sounded on the porch. He entered the house calling, "Elisa, where are you?"

"In my room, dressing. I'm not ready. There's hot water for your bath. Hurry up. It's getting late."

When she heard him splashing in the tub, Elisa laid his dark suit on the bed, and shirt and socks and tie beside it. She stood his polished shoes on the floor beside the bed. Then she went to the porch and sat primly and stiffly down. She looked toward the river road where the willow-line was still yellow with frosted leaves so that under the high grey fog they seemed a thin band of sunshine. This was the only color in the grey afternoon. She sat unmoving for a long time. Her eyes blinked rarely.

Henry came banging out of the door, shoving his tie inside his vest as he came. Elisa stiffened and her face grew tight. Henry stopped short and looked at her. "Why—why, Elisa. You look so nice!"

"Nice? You think I look nice? What do you mean by 'nice'?"

Henry blundered on. "I don't know. I mean you look different, strong and happy."

"I am strong? Yes, strong. What do you mean 'strong'?"

He looked bewildered. "You're playing some kind of a game," he said helplessly. "It's a kind of a play. You look strong enough to break a calf over your knee, happy enough to eat it like a watermelon."

For a second she lost her rigidity. "Henry! Don't talk like that. You didn't know what you said." She grew complete again. "I'm strong," she boasted. "I never knew before how strong."

Henry looked down toward the tractor shed, and when he brought his eyes back to her, they were his own again. "I'll get out the car. You can put on your coat while I'm starting."

Elisa went into the house. She heard him drive to the gate and idle down his motor, and then she took a long time to put on her hat. She pulled it here and pressed it there. When Henry turned the motor off she slipped into her coat and went out.

The little roadster bounced along on the dirt road by the river, raising the birds and driving the rabbits into the brush. Two cranes flapped heavily over the willow-line and dropped into the river-bed.

Far ahead on the road Elisa saw a dark speck. She knew.

She tried not to look as they passed it, but her eyes would not obey. She whispered to herself sadly, "He might have thrown them off the road. That wouldn't have been much trouble, not very much. But he kept the pot," she explained. "He had to keep the pot. That's why he couldn't get them off the road."

The roadster turned a bend and she saw the caravan ahead. She 110
swung full around toward her husband so she could not see the little covered wagon and the mismatched team as the car passed them.

In a moment it was over. The thing was done. She did not look back.

She said loudly, to be heard above the motor, "It will be good, tonight, a good dinner."

"Now you're changed again," Henry complained. He took one hand from the wheel and patted her knee. "I ought to take you in to dinner oftener. It would be good for both of us. We get so heavy out on the ranch."

"Henry," she asked, "could we have wine at dinner?"

"Sure we could. Say! That will be fine." 115

She was silent for a while; then she said, "Henry, at those prize fights, do the men hurt each other very much?"

"Sometimes a little, not often. Why?"

"Well, I've read how they break noses, and blood runs down their chests. I've read how the fighting gloves get heavy and soggy with blood."

He looked around at her. "What's the matter, Elisa? I didn't know you read things like that." He brought the car to a stop, then turned to the right over the Salinas River bridge.

"Do any women ever go to the fights?" she asked. 120

"Oh, sure, some. What's the matter, Elisa? Do you want to go? I don't think you'd like it, but I'll take you if you really want to go."

She relaxed **limply** in the seat. "Oh, no. No. I don't want to go. I'm sure I don't." Her face was turned away from him. "It will be enough if we can have wine. It will be plenty." She turned up her coat collar so he could not see that she was crying weakly—like an old woman.

Questions:

1. Elisa works inside a "wire fence that protected her flower garden from cattle and dogs and chickens." What does this wire fence suggest?
2. For what motive does the traveling salesman take an interest in Elisa's chrysanthemums? What immediate effect does his interest have on Elisa?
3. Of what importance to Elisa is the sight of the contents of the flower pot discarded in the road?
4. Why are Elisa Allen's chrysanthemums so important to the story?
5. In a sentence, try to state this story's theme. How does the setting contribute to the theme?

Chapter 5 Tone and Style

Tone has been used in modern CRITICISM, following I. A. Richard, as a term designating the author's attitudes toward the subject and the audience implied in a literary work. In such a usage a work may have a tone that is playful, serious, formal, informal, intimate, solemn, affectionate, angry, ironic, condescending, or any of many other possible attitudes. Clearly, tone in this sense contributes in a major way to the effect and the effectiveness of a literary work.

Take Chekhov's "*In Exile*" for example. The author begins the short story with a description of a young man:

> The Tartar was worn out and ill, and wrapping himself in his rags, he talked about how good it was in the province of Simbirsk, and what a beautiful and clever wife he had left at home. He was not more than twenty-five, and in the firelight his pale, sickly face and woebegone expression made him seem like a boy.

Other than the comparison of the Tartar to a child, the details in this passage seem mostly factual: the young man's illness, ragged clothes, and facial expression. But these details form a portrait that stirs pity. By his selection of these imaginary details, Chekhov firmly directs our feelings about the Tartar and the description arouses out sympathy for the young man who is physically sick and mentally homesick. We readers share the compassion and tenderness of the narrator. Contrast this episode with the following famous scene from Emily Bronte's "*Wuthering Heights.*" The narrator has been dreaming and has just woken up to find that the cause of his bad dream was "merely the branch of a fir-tree that touched my lattice, as the blast wailed by, and rattled its dry cones against the panes." Here is how the narration resumes:

I listened doubtingly an instant; detected the disturber, then turned and dozed, and dreamt again; if possible, still more disagreeably than before.

This time, I remembered I was lying in the oak closet, and I heard distinctly the gusty wind, and the driving of the snow; I heard, also, the fir-bough repeat its teasing sound, and ascribed it to the right cause; but it annoyed me so much, that I resolved to silence it, if possible; and, I thought, I rose and endeavored to unhasp the casement. The hook was soldered into the staple, a circumstance observed by me when awake, but forgotten.

"I must stop it, nevertheless!" I muttered, knocking my knuckles through the glass, and stretching an arm out to seize the importunate branch: instead of which, my fingers closed on the fingers of a little, ice-cold hand!

The intense horror of nightmare came over me; I tried to draw back my arm, but the hand clung to it, and a most melancholy voice sobbed,

"Let me in—let me in!"

"Who are you?" I asked, struggling, meanwhile, to disengage myself.

"Catherine Linton," it replied shiveringly... "I'll come home,

I'd lost my way on the moor!"

As I spoke, I discerned, obscurely, a child's face looking through the window—terror made me cruel; and, finding it useless to attempt shaking the creature off, I pulled its wrist on to the broken pane, and rubbed it to and fro till the blood ran down and soaked the bed clothes: still it wailed, "Let me in!" and maintained its tenacious gripe, almost maddening me with fear.

Surely every reader will share the narrator's feeling of horror here. Although we have been told that it is only a dream, we know how horrifying some dreams can be: we seem to experience this one directly. Of course, here the story is told directly by the narrator. The experience begins with reality—the branch of the fir-tree—and turns into terror—the icy hand of the child. But there is more to the effect of the episode than sheer experience: notice how the author prepares us for the strange transformations of branch to arm by referring to how the fir-tree "touched" the window-pane, how its sound was "teasing". The branch is "importunate", as if it were already a hand stretched out for help. And as the narrator touches the branch, it is changed to the fingers of "a little, ice-cold hand." A further horror is that what seems to be human fails to behave in a human way: despite its loss of blood, it maintains a tenacious hold on the narrator's arm. In this passage we are not aware of any authorial voice which comments on the narrator's story. The tone of the writing directs our attention to the honesty of the narration.

In another sense **tone** is used to designate the MOOD of the work itself and the various devices that create that mood. Rather than the author's projecting a mood, Willa Cather saw the work's mood as dominating the author: the "language, the stresses, the very structure of the sentences are imposed upon the writer by the special mood of the piece." MOOD and **tone** are virtually synonymous, though some critics distinguish MOOD—the author's attitude toward the subject—from **tone**, the writer's attitude toward the audience. It is safe to say that tone results from combinations and variations of such things as choice of characters, events, and situations and choice of words (diction). Besides, METER, ALLITERATION, ASSONANCE, CONSONANCE, SENTENCE STRUCTURE, REPETITION, IMAGERY, SYMBOLISM, and so forth may also lead us to infer the author's attitude. In short, whatever leads us to infer the author's attitude is commonly called **tone**.

One of the clearest indications of the tone of a story is the **style** in which it is written. In general, **style** refers to the individual traits of characteristics of a piece of writing: to an author's personal manner or expression. This may be highly individualistic or idiosyncratic, so that we understand rather quickly by the manner, without much consideration, that we have come upon a passage, say by Faulkner or Hemingway.

Style is a combination of two elements: the idea to be expressed and the individuality of the author. It is the result of the choices an author makes, with respect not to subject matter but to its presentation. A **style** may be ABSTRACT or CONCRETE, heavy with CONNOTATION or essentially denotative, characterized by particular uses of FIGURATIVE LANGUAGE or largely free of them. Indeed, all elements of diction (word choice), sentence structure, paragraph construction, and organization are proper subjects for stylistic analysis in prose, as are, in verse, such elements as METER and RHYME.

To see what **style** means, compare the stories by William Faulkner "*Barn Burning*" and by Ernest Hemingway "*A Clean, Well-Lighted Place*." Faulkner frequently falls into a style in which a statement is followed by another statement expressing the idea in a more emphatic way. Sentences are interrupted with parenthetical elements thrust into them unexpectedly. Besides, Faulkner is fond of long sentences.

Hemingway's famous style includes simple words and short sentences. He also uses long sentences, but when the sentences are long they tend to be relatively simple in construction and they are usually long compound sentences (clause plus clause plus clause), sometimes joined with "ands." In addition to those mentioned above, Hemingway is a master of swift, terse dialogue, and often casts whole scenes in the form of conversation. The narrator of a Hemingway story often addresses us in understatement, implying greater depths of feeling than he puts into words. Read Hemingway's "*A Clean Well-Lighted Place*" and you will see that its style and tone cannot be separated.

Furthermore, the **tone** of a story may be ironic. Whenever we sense a sharp distinction between the narrator of a story and the author, **irony** is likely to occur. In general, irony is the perception of a clash between appearance and reality. It seems to fall into three categories: (1) verbal, (2) situational, and (3) dramatic.

Verbal irony—saying something contrary to what it means. The appearance is what the words say; the reality, their contrary meaning. Jonathan Swift is an archironist—his "*Modest Proposal*" for saving a starving Ireland, by suggesting that the Irish sell their babies to the English landlords to be eaten—is perhaps the most savagely sustained ironic writing in English literature. Antony's insistence, in his oration over the dead Caesar, that "Brutus is an honorable man" bears a similar ironic imprint.

Situational irony—events turning to the opposite of what is expected or what should be (also called **circumstantial** irony and the **irony of fate** or in some circumstances, COSMIC IRONY).

Kate Chopin (1851—1904)

The Story of an Hour

Knowing that Mrs. Mallard was afflicted with a heart trouble, great care was taken to break to her as gently as possible the news of her husband's death.

It was her sister Josephine who told her, in broken sentences, veiled hints that revealed in half concealing. Her husband's friend Richards was there, too, near her. It was he who had been in the newspaper office when intelligence of the railroad disaster was received, with Brently Mallard's name leading the list of "killed". He had only taken the time to assure himself of its truth by a second telegram, and had hastened to forestall any less careful, less tender friend in bearing the sad message.

She did not hear the story as many women have heard the same, with a paralyzed inability to accept its significance. She wept at once, with sudden, wild abandonment, in her sister's arms. When the storm of grief had spent itself she went away to her room alone. She would have no one to follow her.

There stood, facing the open window, a comfortable, roomy armchair. Into this she sank, pressed down by a physical exhaustion that haunted her body and seemed to reach into her soul.

She could see in the open square before her house the tops of trees that were all aquiver with the new spring life. The delicious breath of rain was in the air. In the street below a peddler was crying his wares. The notes of a distant song which some one was singing reached her faintly, and countless sparrows were twittering in the eaves.

There were patches of blue sky showing here and there through the clouds that had met and piled above the other in the west facing her window.

She sat with her head thrown back upon the cushion of the chair quite motionless, except when a sob came up into her throat and shook her, as a child who has cried itself to sleep continues to sob in its dreams.

She was young, with a fair, calm face, whose lines bespoke repression and even a certain strength. But now there was a dull stare in her eyes, whose gaze was fixed away off yonder on one of those patches of blue sky. It was not a glance of reflection, but rather indicated a suspension of intelligent thought.

There was something coming to her and she was waiting for it, fearfully. What was it? She did not know; it was too subtle and elusive to name. But she felt it, creeping out of the sky, reaching toward her through the sounds, the scents, the color that filled the air.

Now her bosom rose and fell tumultuously. She was beginning to recognize this thing that was approaching to possess her, and she was striving to beat it back with her will—as powerless as her two white slender hands would have been. 10

When she abandoned herself a little whispered word escaped her slightly parted lips. She said it over and over under her breath: "Free, free, free!" The vacant stare and the look of terror that had followed it went from her eyes. They stayed keen and bright. Her pulses beat fast, and the coursing blood warmed and relaxed every inch of her body.

She did not stop to ask if it were not a monstrous joy that held her. A clear and exalted perception enabled her to dismiss the suggestion as trivial.

She knew that she would weep again when she saw the kind, tender hands folded in death; the face that had never looked save with love upon her, fixed and gray and dead. But she saw beyond that bitter moment a long procession of years to come that would belong to her absolutely. And she opened and spread her arms out to them in welcome.

There would be no one to live for her during those coming years; she would live for herself. There would be no powerful will bending her in that blind persistence with which men and women believe they have a right to impose a private will upon a fellow creature. A kind intention or a cruel intention made the act seem no less a crime as she looked upon it in that brief moment of illumination.

And yet she had loved him — sometimes. Often she had not. What 15 did it matter! What could love, the unsolved mystery, count for in face of this possession of self-assertion which she suddenly recognized as the strongest impulse of her being.

"Free! Body and soul free!" she kept whispering.

Josephine was kneeling before the closed door with her lips to the key-hole, imploring for admission. "Louise, open the door! I beg; open the door—you will make yourself ill. What are you doing, Louise? For heaven's sake open the door."

"Go away. I am not making myself ill." No; she was drinking in a very elixir of life through that open window.

Her fancy was running riot along those days ahead of her. Spring days, and summer days, and all sorts of days that would be her own. She breathed a quick prayer that life might be long. It was only yesterday she had thought with a shudder that life might be long.

She arose at length and opened the door to her sister's importunities. There was a feverish triumph in her eyes, and she carried herself unwittingly like a goddess of Victory. She clasped her sister's waist, and together they descended the stairs. Richards stood waiting for them at the bottom.

Some one was opening the front door with a latchkey. It was Brently Mallard who entered, a little travel-stained, composedly carrying his gripsack and umbrella. He had been far from the scene of accident, and did not even know there had been one. He stood amazed at Josephine's piercing cry; at Richards' quick motion to screen him from the view of his wife.

But Richards was too late.

When the doctors came they said she had died of heart

disease—of joy that kills.

Questions:

1. Analyze the tone of paragraph 5. How does the imagery here contradict the grief she should be feeling? How does it seem appropriate for her developing mood? How may this paragraph be interpreted ironically?
2. What is the apparent attitude of the narrator toward the institution of marriage, and what elements of tone make this apparent?
3. What do Louise's sister and Richards have in common? How are your attitudes toward her affected by their understanding of her feelings? How do their attitudes contribute to the irony of the story?
4. Consider the tone of the last paragraph, in which we learn the judgment by the doctors about the cause of Louise's death.

Ernest Hemingway (1899—1961)

A Clean, Well-Lighted Place

It was late and every one had left the café except an old man who sat in the shadow the leaves of the tree made against the electric light. In the day time the street was dusty, but at night the dew settled the dust and the old man liked to sit late because he was deaf and now at night it was quiet and he felt the difference. The two waiters inside the café knew that the old man was a little drunk, and while he was a good client they knew that if he became too drunk he would leave without paying, so they kept watch on him.

"Last week he tried to commit suicide," one waiter said.

"Why?"

"He was in despair."

"What about?"

"Nothing."

"How do you know it was nothing?"

"He has plenty of money."

They sat together at a table that was close against the wall near the door of the café and looked at the terrace where the tables were all empty except where the old man sat in the shadow of the leaves of the tree that moved slightly in the wind. A girl and a soldier went by in the street. The street light shone on the brass number on his collar. The girl wore no head covering and hurried beside him.

"The guard will pick him up," one waiter said.

"What does it matter if he gets what he's after?"

"He had better get off the street now. The guard will get him. They went by five minutes ago."

The old man sitting in the shadow rapped on his saucer with his glass. The younger waiter went over to him.

"What do you want?"

The old man looked at him. "Another brandy," he said.

"You'll be drunk," the waiter said. The old man looked at him. The waiter went away.

"He'll stay all night," he said to his colleague. "I'm sleepy now. I never get into bed before three o'clock. He should have killed himself last week."

The waiter took the brandy bottle and another saucer from the counter inside the café and marched out to the old man's table. He put down the saucer and poured the glass full of brandy.

"You should have killed yourself last week," he said to the deaf man. The old man motioned with his finger. "A little more," he said. The waiter poured on into the glass so that the brandy slopped over and ran down the stem into the top saucer of the pile. "Thank you," the old man said. The waiter took the bottle back inside the café. He sat down at the table with his colleague again.

"He's drunk now," he said.

"He's drunk every night."

"What did he want to kill himself for?"

"How should I know?"

"How did he do it?"

"He hung himself with a rope."

"Who cut him down?"

"His niece."

"Why did they do it?"

"Fear for his soul."

"How much money has he got?"

"He's got plenty."

"He must be eighty years old."

"Anyway I should say he was eighty."

"I wish he would go home. I never get to bed before three o'clock. What kind of hour is that to go to bed?"

"He stays up because he likes it."

"He's lonely. I'm not lonely. I have a wife waiting in bed for me."

"He had a wife once too."

"A wife would be no good to him now."

"You can't tell. He might be better with a wife."

"His niece looks after him."

"I know. You said she cut him down."

"I wouldn't want to be that old. An old man is a nasty thing."

"Not always. This old man is clean. He drinks without spilling. Even now, drunk. Look at him."

"I don't want to look at him. I wish he would go home. He has no regard for those who must work."

The old man looked from his glass across the square, then over at the waiters.

"Another brandy," he said, pointing to his glass. The waiter who was in a hurry came over.

"Finished," he said, speaking with that omission of syntax stupid people employ when talking to drunken people or foreigners. "No more tonight. Close now."

"Another," said the old man.

"No. Finished." The waiter wiped the edge of the table with a towel and shook his head.

The old man stood up, slowly counted the saucers, took a leather coin purse from his pocket and paid for the drinks, leaving half a peseta tip.

The waiter watched him go down the street, a very old man walking unsteadily but with dignity.

"Why didn't you let him stay and drink?" the unhurried waiter asked. They were putting up the shutters. "It is not half-past two."

"I want to go home to bed."

"What is an hour?"

"More to me than to him."

"An hour is the same."

"You talk like an old man yourself. He can buy a bottle and drink at home."

"It's not the same."

"No, it is not," agreed the waiter with a wife. He did not wish to be unjust. He was only in a hurry.

"And you? You have no fear of going home before the usual hour?"

"Are you trying to insult me?"

"No, hombre, only to make a joke."

"No," the waiter who was in a hurry said, rising from pulling down the metal shutters. "I have confidence. I am all confidence."

"You have youth, confidence, and a job," the older waiter said, "You have everything."

"And what do you lack?"

"Everything but work."

"You have everything I have."

"No. I have never had confidence and I am not young."

"Come on. Stop talking nonsense and lock up."

"I am of those who like to stay late at the café," the older waiter said. "With all those who do not want to go to bed. With all those who need a light for the night."

"I want to go home and into bed."

"We are of two different kinds," the older waiter said. He was not dressed to go home. "It is not only a question of youth and confidencc although those things are very beautiful. Each night I am reluctant to close up because there may be some one who needs the café."

"Hombre, there are bodegas open all night long."

"You do not understand. This is a clean and pleasant café. It is well lighted. The light is very good and also, now, there are shadows of the leaves."

"Good night," said the younger waiter. 75

"Good night," the other said. Turning off the electric light he continued the conversation with himself. It is the light of course but it is necessary that the place be clean and pleasant. You do not want music. Certainly you do not want music. Nor can you stand before a bar with dignity although that is all that is provided for these hours. What did he fear? It was not fear or dread. It was a nothing that he knew too well. It was all a nothing and a man was nothing too. It was only that and light was all it needed and a certain cleanness and order. Some lived in it and never felt it but he knew it all was nada y pues nada y nada y pues nada. Our nada who art in nada, nada be thy name thy kingdom nada thy will be nada in nada as it is in nada. Give us this nada our daily nada and nada us our nada as we nada our nadas and nada us not into nada but deliver us from nada; pues nada. Hail nothing full of nothing, nothing is with thee. He smiled and stood before a bar with a shining steam pressure coffee machine.

"What's yours?" asked the barman.

"Nada."

"Otro loco más," said the barman and turned away.

"A little cup," said the waiter.

The barman poured it for him.

"The light is very bright and pleasant but the bar is unpolished," the waiter said.

The barman looked at him but did not answer. It was too late at night for conversation.

"You want another copita?" the barman asked.

"No, thank you," said the waiter and went out. He disliked bars and bodegas. A clean, well-lighted café was a very different thing. Now, without thinking further, he would go home to his room. He would lie in the bed and finally, with daylight, he would go to sleep. After all, he said to himself, it is probably only insomnia. Many must have it.

Questions:

1. Point to sentences that establish the style of the story. What is distinctive in them? What repetitions of words or phrases seem particularly important?
2. Compare and contrast the younger waiter and the older waiter in their attitudes toward the old man? Whose attitude do you take to be closer to that of the author? Even though Hemingway does not state his own feelings, how does he make them clear to us?
3. Why does the older waiter so well understand the old man's need for a cafe? What does the cafe represent for the two of them?

John Collier (1901—1980)

The Chaser

Alan Austen, as nervous as a kitten, went up certain dark and creaky stairs in the neighborhood of Pell Street, and peered about for a long time on the dim landing before he found the name he wanted written obscurely on one of the doors.

He pushed open this door, as he had been told to do, and found himself in a tiny room, which contained no furniture but a plain kitchen table, a rocking-chair, and an ordinary chair. On one of the dirty buff-coloured walls were a couple of shelves, containing in all perhaps a dozen bottles and jars.

An old man sat in the rocking-chair, reading a newspaper. Alan, without a word, handed him the card he had been given. "Sit down, Mr. Austen," said the old man very politely. "I am glad to make your acquaintance."

"Is it true," asked Alan, "that you have a certain mixture that has—er—quite extraordinary effects?"

"My dear sir," replied the old man, "My stock in trade is not very 5
large—I don't deal in laxatives and teething mixtures—but such as it is, it is varied. I think nothing I sell has effects which could be precisely described as ordinary."

"Well, the fact is..." began Alan.

"Here, for example," interrupted the old man, reaching for a bottle from the shelf. "Here is a liquid as colourless as water, almost tasteless, quite imperceptible in coffee, wine, or any other beverage. It is also quite imperceptible to any known method of autopsy."

"Do you mean it is a poison?" cried Alan, very much horrified.

"Call it a glove-cleaner if you like," said the old man indifferently. "Maybe it will clean gloves. I have never tried. One might call it a life-cleaner. Lives need cleaning sometimes."

"I want nothing of that sort," said Alan.

"Probably it is just as well," said the old man. "Do you know the price of this? For one teaspoonful, which is sufficient, I ask five thousand dollars. Never less. Not a penny less."

"I hope all your mixtures are not as expensive," said Alan apprehensively.

"Oh dear, no," said the old man. "It would be no good charging that sort of price for a love potion, for example. Young people who need a love potion very seldom have five thousand dollars. Otherwise they would not need a love potion."

"I am glad to hear that," said Alan.

"I look at it like this," said the old man. "Please a customer with one article, and he will come back when he needs another. Even if it *is* more costly. He will save up for it, if necessary."

"So," said Alan, "you really do sell love potions?"

"If I did not sell love potions," said the old man, reaching for another bottle, "I should not have mentioned the other matter to you. It is only when one is in a position to oblige that one can afford to be so confidential."

"And these potions," said Alan. "They are not just—just—er—"

"Oh, no," said the old man. "Their effects are permanent, and extended far beyond the mere casual impulse. But they include it. Oh, yes, they include it. Bountifully, insistently. Everlastingly."

"Dear me!" said Alan, attempting a look of scientific detachment. "How very interesting!"

"But consider the spiritual side," said the old man.

"I do, indeed," said Alan.

"For indifference," said the old man, "they substitute devotion. For scorn, adoration. Give one tiny measure of this to the young lady—its flavour is imperceptible in orange juice, soup, or cocktails—and however gay and giddy she is, she will change altogether. She will want nothing but solitude and you."

"I can hardly believe it," said Alan. "She is so fond of parties."

"She will not like them any more," said the old man. "She will be afraid of the pretty girls you may meet."

"She will actually be jealous?" cried Alan in a rapture. "Of me?"

"Yes, she will want to be everything to you."

"She is, already. Only she doesn't care about it."

"She will, when she has taken this. She will care intensely. You will be her sole interest in life."

"Wonderful!" cried Alan.

"She will want to know all you do," said the old man. "All

that has happened to you during the day. Every word of it. She will want to know what you are thinking about, why you smile suddenly, why you are looking sad."

"That is love!" cried Alan.

"Yes," said the old man. "How carefully she will look after you! She will never allow you to be tired, to sit in a draught, to neglect your food. If you are an hour late, she will be terrified. She will think you are killed, or that some siren has caught you."

"I can hardly imagine Diana like that!" cried Alan, overwhelmed with joy.

"You will not have to use your imagination," said the old man. "And, by the way, since there are always sirens, if by any chance you *should*, later on, slip a little, you need not worry. She will forgive you, in the end. She will be terribly hurt, of course, but she will forgive you—in the end."

"That will not happen," said Alan fervently.

"Of course not," said the old man. "But, if it did, you need not worry. She would never divorce you. Oh, no! And, of course, she will never give you the least, the very least, grounds for—uneasiness."

"And how much," said Alan, "is this wonderful mixture?"

"It is not as dear," said the old man, "as the glove-cleaner, or life-cleaner, as I sometimes call it. No. That is five thousand dollars, never a penny less. One has to be older than you are, to indulge in that sort of thing. One has to save up for it."

"But the love potion?" said Alan.

"Oh, that," said the old man, opening the drawer in the kitchen table, and taking out a tiny, rather dirty-looking phial.

"That is just a dollar."

"I can't tell you how grateful I am," said Alan, watching him fill it.

"I like to oblige," said the old man. "Then customers come back, later in life, when they are better off, and want more expensive things. Here you are. You will find it very effective."

"Thank you again," said Alan. "Good-bye."

"Au revoir," said the old man.

Questions:

1. Are the two characters in this story static or dynamic? Round or flat? Representative or individual? To what extent do these choices help to focus the story and control the tone?
2. How is the setting of the story described? What is the old man's apartment like? How does this description contribute to the mood of the story and the characterization of the old man?
3. To what extent do the words of the story control the tone and attitude? What specific words help us form an attitude toward Alan Austen? Toward the old man?
4. To what extent is the story ironic? What do we and the old man know that Alan Austen, doesn't?
5. How is the title of the story ironic? What is a "chaser"? How are the old man's last words in the story ironic?

Chapter 6 Theme

Usually we feel that a story is about something, it has a point—a **theme**. The **theme** is a central or dominating idea in a work. In POETRY, FICTION, and DRAMA it is the abstract concept that is made concrete through its representation in person, action, and image in the work. No proper theme is simply a subject or an activity. Thus we should make a distinction between the **plot** and the **theme**: what happens is the **plot**; what the happenings add up to is the **theme**. The **theme** of a story is whatever general idea or insight the *entire* story reveals.

Yet, a word of caution is needed here. In literary fiction, a **theme** is seldom so obvious and so definite. What is the theme of "*Misery*"? One might formulate the theme thus:

> **Human beings must utter their grief, even if only to an animal.**

Another might formulate it thus:

> **Human beings are indifferent to the sufferings of others.**

Still another might offer this:

> **Deep sufferings are incommunicable, but the sufferer must try to find an outlet.**

Many other formulations are possible. Probably there is no "right" statement of the theme of "*Misery*" or of any other good story: a story is not simply an illustration of an abstract statement of theme. A story has a complex variety of details that modify any summary statement we may offer when we try to say what it is about. And what lives in our memory is not an abstract statement, such as "We should pay attention to the sufferings of others." What lives in us is an image that by every word in the story has convinced us that it is a representation of reality or of at least an aspect of reality.

Still, the writer is guided by a theme in the choice of details, i. e. in the variations and the development. However, these variations and development cannot be random, but must have a basis. We have already suggested that the episodes in "*Misery*"—the movement from the officer to the drunks and then to the house-porter and the other cabman—are not random, but somehow seem exactly "right," just as the remarks about the man and the horse both stretching their necks seem "right."

We can, then, talk about the theme of Hemingway's "*A Clean, Well-Lighted Place.*" When we come to the end of that finely wrought short story, it may be easy to sum up thc plot, but it is more difficult to sum up the story's main idea. Evidently, Hemingway relates events—how a young waiter gets rid of an old man and how an older waiter then goes to a coffee bar—but in themselves these events seem relatively slight, though the story as a whole seems full of meaning. For the meaning, we must look to other elements in the story besides what happens in it. And it is clear that Hemingway is most deeply interested in the thoughts and feelings of the older waiter, the character who has more and more to say as the story progresses, until at the end of the story is entirely confined to his thoughts and perceptions. Then what is meaningful in these thoughts and perceptions?

The older waiter understands the old man and sympathizes

with his need for a clean, well-lighted place.

If we say that, we are still talking about what happens in the story, though we have gone beyond merely recording its external events. But a theme is usually stated in *general* words. Then another might say:

Solitary people who cannot sleep need a cheerful, orderly place where they can drink with dignity.

That's a little better. We have indicated that Hemingway's story is about more than just an old man and two waiters. But what about the older waiter's meditation on *nada*, nothingness? Coming near the end of the story, it takes great emphasis; and probably no good statement of Hemingway's theme can leave it out. Still another might work out a statement:

Solitary people need a place of refuge from their terrible awareness that their lives (or perhaps, human lives) are essentially meaningless.

Neither this nor any other statement of the story's theme is unarguably right, but at least the sentence helps the reader to bring into focus one primary idea that Hemingway seems to be driving at.

Moral inferences may be drawn from the story, no doubt—for Hemingway is indirectly giving us advice for properly regarding and sympathizing with the lonely and the old. But the story doesn't set forth a lesson that we are supposed to put into practice. One could argue that "*A Clean, Well-Lighted Place*" contains *several* themes—and other statements could be made to take in Hemingway's view of love, of communication between people, and of dignity. Great short stories frequently have more than one theme.

But now, the point is that how we can formulate the theme of a literary work? Here we suggest that in the beginning, you look for whatever truth or insight you think the writer of a story reveals. Try to sum it up in a sentence, that is, make a sentence-statement of theme. By doing so, you will find yourself looking closely at the story, trying to define its principal meaning.

In making your sentence-statement of theme, you may find it helpful to consider these points:

1. Is the title informative? What does it mean or suggest? Did the meaning change after you read the story? Does the title help you to formulate a theme?

2. Does the main character in any way change in the story? Does this character arrive at any eventual realization or understanding?

3. Do certain passages—dialogue or description—seem to you to point especially toward the theme? Do you find certain repetitions of words or of incidents highly suggestive and helpful in directing your thoughts toward stating a theme?

4. Does the story contain any especially curious objects, significant animals? In literary stories, such symbols may point to central themes.

5. Is the meaning of the story embodied in the whole story, or does it seem stuck in, for example in certain passages of expressing opinions?

6. When you have worded your statement of theme, does your statement hold true for the story as a whole, or for just part of it?

7. When you have stated the theme of a story, would you say that the theme of that particular story reinforces values you hold, or does it to some degree challenge them?

William Carlos Williams (1883—1963)

The Use of Force

They were new patients to me, all I had was the name, Olson. Please come down as soon as you can, my daughter is very sick.

When I arrived I was met by the mother, a big startled looking woman, very clean and apologetic who merely said, Is this the doctor? and let me in. In the back, she added. You must excuse us, doctor, we have her in the kitchen where it is warm. It is very damp here sometimes.

The child was fully dressed and sitting on her father's lap near the kitchen table. He tried to get up, but I motioned for him not to bother, took off my overcoat and started to look things over. I could see that they were all very nervous, eyeing me up and down distrustfully. As often, in such cases, they weren't telling me more than they had to, it was up to me to tell them; that's why they were spending three dollars on me.

The child was fairly eating me up with her cold, steady eyes, and no expression to her face whatever. She did not move and seemed, inwardly, quiet; an unusually attractive little thing, and as strong as a heifer in appearance. But her face was flushed, she was breathing rapidly, and I realized that she had a high fever. She had magnificent blonde hair, in profusion. One of those picture children often reproduced in advertising leaflets and the photogravure sections of the Sunday papers.

She's had a fever for three days , began the father and we don't know what it comes from. My wife has given her things, you know, like people do, but it don't do no good. And there's been a lot of sickness around. So we tho't you'd better look her over and tell us what is the matter.

As doctors often do I took a trial shot at it as a point of departure. Has she had a sore throat?

Both parents answered me together, No... No, she says her throat don't hurt her.

Does your throat hurt you? added the mother to the child. But the little girl's expression didn't change nor did she move her eyes from my face.

Have you looked?

I tried to, said the mother, but I couldn't see.

As it happens we had been having a number of cases of diphtheria in the school to which this child went during that month and we were all, quite apparently, thinking of that, though no one had as yet spoken of the thing.

Well, I said, suppose we take a look at the throat first. I smiled in my best professional manner and asking for the child's first name I said, come on, Mathilda, open your mouth and let's take a look at your throat.

Nothing doing.

Aw, come on, I coaxed, just open your mouth wide and let me take a look. Look, I said opening both hands wide, I haven't anything in my hands. Just open up and let me see.

Such a nice man, put in the mother . Look how kind he is to you.

Come on, do what he tells you to. He won't hurt you.

At that I ground my teeth in disgust. If only they wouldn't use the word "hurt" I might be able to get somewhere. But I did not allow myself to be hurried or disturbed but speaking quietly and slowly I approached the child again.

As I moved my chair a little nearer suddenly with one cat-like movement both her hands clawed instinctively for my eyes and she almost reached them too. In fact she knocked my glasses flying and they fell, though unbroken, several feet away from me on the kitchen floor.

Both the mother and father almost turned themselves inside out in embarrassment and apology. You bad girl, said the mother, taking her and shaking her by one arm. Look what you've done. The nice man...

For heaven's sake, I broke in. Don't call me a nice man to her. I'm here to look at her throat on the chance that she might have diphtheria and possibly die of it. But that's nothing to her. Look here, I said to the child, we're going to look at your throat. You're old enough to understand what I'm saying. Will you open it now by yourself or shall we have to open it for you?

Not a move. Even her expression hadn't changed. Her breaths 20
however were coming faster and faster. Then the battle began. I had to do it. I had to have a throat culture for her own protection. But first I told the parents that it was entirely up to them. I explained the danger but said that I would not insist on a throat examination so long as they would take the responsibility.

If you don't do what the doctor says you'll have to go to the hospital, the mother admonished her severely.

Oh yeah? I had to smile to myself. After all, I had already fallen in love with the savage brat, the parents were contemptible to me. In the ensuing struggle they grew more and more abject, crushed, exhausted while she surely rose to magnificent heights of insane fury of effort bred of her terror of me.

The father tried his best, and he was a big man but the fact that she was his daughter, his shame at her behavior and his dread of hurting her made him release her just at the critical moment several times when I had almost achieved success, till I wanted to kill him. But his dread also that she might have diphtheria made him tell me to go on, go on though he himself was almost fainting, while the mother moved back and forth behind us raising and lowering her hands in an agony of apprehension.

Put her in front of you on your lap, I ordered, and hold both her wrists.

But as soon as he did the child let out a scream. Don't , you're hurting me. Let go of my hands. Let them go I tell you. Then she shrieked terrifyingly, hysterically. Stop it! Stop it! You're killing me!

Do you think she can stand it, doctor! said the mother.

You get out, said the husband to his wife. Do you want her to die of diphtheria?

Come on now, hold her, I said.

Then I grasped the child's head with my left hand and tried to get the wooden tongue depressor between her teeth. She fought, with clenched teeth, desperately! But now I also had grown furious—at a child. I tried to hold myself down but I couldn't. I know how to expose a throat for inspection. And I did my best.

When finally I got the wooden spatula behind the last teeth and just the point of it into the mouth cavity, she opened up for an instant but before I could see anything she came down again and gripping the wooden blade between her molars she reduced it to splinters before I could get it out again.

Aren't you ashamed, the mother yelled at her. Aren't you ashamed to act like that in front of the doctor?

Get me a smooth-handled spoon of some sort, I told the mother. We're going through with this. The child's mouth was already bleeding. Her tongue was cut and she was screaming in wild hysterical shrieks. Perhaps I should have desisted and come back in an hour or more. No doubt it would have been better. But I have seen at least two children lying dead in bed of neglect in such cases, and feeling that I must get a diagnosis now or never I went at it again. But the worst of it was that I too had got beyond reason. I could have torn the child apart in my own fury and enjoyed it. It was a pleasure to attack her. My face was burning with it.

The damned little brat must be protected against her own idiocy, one says to one's self at such times. Others must be protected against her. It is social necessity. And all these things are true. But a blind fury, a feeling of adult shame, bred of a longing for muscular release are the operatives. One goes on to the end.

In a final unreasoning assault I overpowered the child's neck and jaws. I forced the heavy silver spoon back of her teeth and down her throat till she gagged. And there it was—both tonsils covered with membrane. She had fought valiantly to keep me from knowing her secret. She had been hiding that sore throat for three days at least and lying to her parents in order to escape just such an outcome as this.

Now truly she *was* furious. She had been on the defensive before but now she attacked. Tried to get off her father's lap and fly at me while tears of defeat blinded her eyes.

Questions:

1. How would you characterize the little child and the doctor? Are they flat or round?
2. What is the story's theme? Do you think Williams is exploring the human nature?

Alice Walker (1944—)

Everyday Use

For your grandma

I will wait for her in the yard that Maggie and I made so clean and wavy yesterday afternoon. A yard like this is more comfortable than most people know. It is not just a yard. It is like an extended living room. When the hard clay is swept clean as a floor and the fine sand around the edges lined with tiny, irregular grooves anyone can come and sit and look up into the elm tree and wait for the breezes that never come inside the house.

Maggie will be nervous until after her sister goes: she will stand hopelessly in corners homely and ashamed of the burn scars down her arms and legs, eyeing her sister with a mixture of envy and awe. She thinks her sister has held life always in the palm of one hand, that "no" is a word the world never learned to say to her.

You've no doubt seen those TV shows where the child who has "made it" is confronted, as a surprise, by her own mother and father, tottering in weakly from backstage. (A pleasant surprise, of course: What would they do if parent and child came on the show only to curse out and insult each other?) On TV mother and child embrace and smile into each other's faces. Sometimes the mother and father weep, the child wraps them in her arms and leans across the table to tell how she would not have made it without their help. I have seen these programs.

Sometimes I dream a dream in which Dee and I are suddenly brought together on a TV program of this sort. Out of a dark and soft-seated limousine I am ushered into a bright room filled with many people. There I meet a smiling, gray, sporty man like Johnny Carson who shakes my hand and tells me what a fine girl I have. Then we are on the stage and Dee is embracing me with tears in her eyes. She pins on my dress a large orchid, even though she has told me once that she thinks orchids are tacky flowers.

In real life I am large, big-boned woman with rough, man- 5
working hands. In the winter I wear flannel nightgowns to bed and overalls during the day. I can kill and clean a hog as mercilessly as a man. My fat keeps me hot in zero weather. I can work outside all day, breaking ice to get water for washing. I can eat pork liver cooked over the open fire minutes after it comes steaming from the hog. One winter I knocked a bull calf straight in the brain between the eyes with a sledge hammer and had the meat hung up to chill before nightfall. But of course all this does not show on television. I

am the way my daughter would want me to be: a hundred pounds lighter, my skin like an uncooked barley pancake. My hair glistens in the hot bright lights. Johnny Carson has much to do to keep up with my quick and witty tongue.

But that is a mistake. I know even before I wake up. Who ever knew a Johnson with a quick tongue? Who can even imagine me looking a strange white man in the eye? It seems to me I have talked to them always with one foot raised in flight, with my head turned in whichever way is farthest from them. Dee, though. She would always look anyone in the eye. Hesitation was no part of her nature.

"How do I look, Mama?" Maggie says, showing just enough of her thin body enveloped in pink skirt and red blouse for me to know she's there, almost hidden by the door.

"Come out into the yard," I say.

Have you ever seen a lame animal, perhaps a dog run over by some careless person rich enough to own a car, sidle up to someone who is ignorant enough to be kind to him? That is the way my Maggie walks. She has been like this, chin on chest, eyes on ground, feet in shuffle, ever since the fire that burned the other house to the ground.

Dee is lighter than Maggie, with nicer hair and a fuller figure. 10
She's a woman now, though sometimes I forget. How long ago was it that the other house burned? Ten, twelve years? Sometimes I can still hear the flames and feel Maggie's arms sticking to me, her hair smoking and her dress falling off her in little black papery flakes. Her eyes seemed stretched open, blazed open by the flames reflected in them. And Dee. I see her standing off under the sweet

gum tree she used to dig gum out of; a look of concentration on her face as she watched the last dingy gray board of the house fall in toward the red-hot brick chimney. Why don't you do a dance around the ashes? I'd wanted to ask her. She had hated the house that much.

I used to think she hated Maggie, too. But that was before we raised the money, the church and me, to send her to Augusta to school. She used to read to us without pity; forcing words, lies, other folks' habits, whole lives upon us two, sitting trapped and ignorant underneath her voice. She washed us in a river of make-believe, burned us with a lot of knowledge we didn't necessarily need to know. Pressed us to her with the serious way she read, to shove us away at just the moment, like dimwits, we seemed about to understand.

Dee wanted nice things. A yellow organdy dress to wear to her graduation from high school; black pumps to match a green suit she'd made from an old suit somebody gave me. She was determined to stare down any disaster in her efforts. Her eyelids would not flicker for minutes at a time. Often I fought off the temptation to shake her. At sixteen she had a style of her own: and knew what style was.

I never had an education myself. After second grade the school was closed down. Don't ask me why: in 1927 colored asked fewer questions than they do now. Sometimes Maggie reads to me. She stumbles along good-naturedly but can't see well. She knows she is not bright. Like good looks and money, quickness passed her by. She will marry John Thomas (who has mossy teeth in an earnest face) and then I'll be free to sit here and I guess just sing church songs to myself. Although I never was a good singer. Never could carry a tune. I was always better at a man's job. I used to love to milk till I was hoofed in the side in '49. Cows are soothing and slow and don't bother you, unless you try to milk them the wrong way.

I have deliberately turned my back on the house. It is three rooms, just like the one that burned, except the roof is tin; they don't make shingle roofs any more. There are no real windows, just some holes cut in the sides, like the portholes in a ship, but not round and not square, with rawhide holding the shutters up on the outside. This house is in a pasture, too, like the other one. No doubt when Dee sees it she will want to tear it down. She wrote me once that no matter where we "choose" to live, she will manage to come see us. But she will never bring her friends. Maggie and I thought about this and Maggie asked me, "Mama, when did Dee ever *have* any friends?"

She had a few. Furtive boys in pink shirts hanging about on 15
washday after school. Nervous girls who never laughed. Impressed with her they worshiped the well-turned phrase, the cute shape, the scalding humor that erupted like bubble in lye. She read to them.

When she was courting Jimmy T she didn't have much time to pay to us, but turned all her faultfinding power on him. He *flew* to marry a cheap gal from a family of ignorant flashy people. She hardly had time to recompose herself.

When she comes I will meet—but there they are!

Maggie attempts to make a dash for the house, in her shuffling way, but I stay her with my hand. "Come back here," I say. And she stops and tries to dig a well in the sand with her toe.

It is hard to see them clearly through the strong sun. But even the first glimpse of leg out of the car tells me it is Dee. Her feet were always neatlooking, as if God himself had shaped them with a certain style. From the other side of the car comes a short, stocky man. Hair is all over his head a foot long and hanging from his chin like a kinky mule tail. I hear Maggie suck in her breath. "Uhnnnh," is what it sounds like. Like when you see the wriggling end of a snake just in front of your foot on the road. "Uhnnnh."

Dee next. A dress down to the ground, in this hot weather. A dress 20
so loud it hurts my eyes. There are yellows and oranges enough to throw back the light of the sun. I feel my whole face warming from the heat waves it throws out. Earrings, too, gold and hanging down to her shoulders. Bracelets dangling and making noises when she moves her arm up to shake the folds of the dress out of her armpits. The dress is loose and flows, and as she walks closer, I like it. I hear Maggie go "Uhnnnh" again. It is her sister's hair. It stands straight up like the wool on a sheep. It is black as night and around the edges are two long pigtails that rope about like small Jizards disappearing behind her ears.

"Wa-su-zo-Tean-o!" she says, coming on in that gliding way the dress makes her move. The short stocky fellow with the hair to his navel is all grinning and he follows up with "Asalamalakim, my mother and sister!" He moves to hug Maggie but she falls back, right up against the back of my chair. I feel her trembling there and when I look up I see the perspiration falling off her chin.

"Don't get up," says Dee. Since I am stout it takes something of a push. You can see me trying to move a second or two before I make it. She turns, showing white heels through her sandals, and goes back to the car. Out she peeks next with a Polaroid. She stoops down quickly and lines up picture after picture of me sitting there in front of the house with Maggie cowering behind me. She never takes a shot without making sure the house is included. When a cow comes nibbling around the edge of the yard she snaps it and me and Maggie *and* the house. Then she puts the Polaroid in the back seat of the car, and comes up and kisses me on the forehead.

Meanwhile Asalamalakim is going through the motions with Maggie's hand. Maggie's hand is as limp as a fish, and probably as cold, despite the sweat, and she keeps trying to pull it back. It looks like Asalamalakim wants to shake hands but wants to do it fancy. Or maybe he don't know how people shake hands. Anyhow, he soon gives up on Maggie.

"Well," I say. "Dee."

"No, Mama," she says. "Not 'Dee,' Wangero Leewanika Kemanjo!"

"What happened to 'Dee'?" I wanted to know.

"She's dead," Wangero said. "I couldn't bear it any longer being named after the people who oppress me."

"You know as well as me you was named after your aunt Dicie," I said. Dicie is my sister. She named Dee. We called her "Big Dee" after Dee was born.

"But who was *she* named after?" asked Wangero.

"I guess after Grandma Dee," I said.

"And who was she named after?" asked Wangero.

"Her mother," I said, and saw Wangero was getting tired.

"That's about as far back as I can trace it," I said. Though, in fact, I probably could have carried it back beyond the Civil War through the branches.

"Well," said Asalamalakim, "there you are."

"Uhnnnh," I heard Maggie say.

"There I was not," I said, "before 'Dicie' cropped up in our family, so why should I try to trace it that far back?"

He just stood there grinning, looking down on me like somebody inspecting a Model A car. Every once in a while he and Wangero sent eye signals over my head.

"How do you pronounce this name?" I asked.

"You don't have to call me by it if you don't want to," said Wangero.

"Why shouldn't I?" I asked. "If that's what you want us to call you, we'll call you."

"I know it might sound awkward at first," said Wangero.

"I'll get used to it," I said. "Ream it out again."

Well, soon we got the name out of the way. Asalamalakim had a name twice as long and three times as hard. After I tripped over it two or three times he told me just to call him Hakim-a-barber. I wanted to ask him was he a barber, but I didn't really think he was, so I didn't ask.

"You must belong to those beef-cattle peoples down the road," I said. They said "Asalamalakim" When they met you, too, but they didn't shake hands. Always too busy: feeding the cattle, fixing the fences, putting up saltlick shelters, throwing down hay. When the white folks poisoned some of the herd the men stayed up all night with rifles in their hands. I walked a mile and a half just to see the sight.

Hakim-a-barber said, "I accept some of their doctrines, but farming and raising cattle is not my style." (They didn't tell mc, and I didn't ask, whether Wangero [Dee] had really gone and married him.)

We sat down to eat and right away he said he didn't eat col- 45
lards and pork was unclean. Wangero, though, went on through the chitlins and corn bread, the greens and everything else. She talked a blue streak over the sweet potatoes. Everything delighted her. Even the fact that we still used the benches her daddy made for the table when we couldn't afford to buy chairs.

"Oh, Mama!" she cried. Then turned to Hakim-a-barber. "I never knew how lovely these benches are. You can feel the rump prints," she said, running her hands underneath her and along the bench. Then she gave a sigh and her hand closed over Grandma Dee's butter dish. "That's it!" she said. "I knew there was something I wanted to ask you if I could have." She jumped up from the table and went over in the corner where the churn stood, the milk in it clabber by now. She looked at the churn and looked at it.

"This churn top is what I need," she said. "Didn't Uncle Buddy whittle it out of a tree you all used to have?"

"Yes," I said.

"Uh, huh," she said happily. "And I want the dasher, too."

"Uncle Buddy whittle that, too?" asked the barber. 50

Dee (Wangero) looked up at me.

"Aunt Dee's first husband whittled the dash," said Maggie so low you almost couldn't hear her. "His name was Henry, but they called him Stash."

"Maggie's brain is like an elephant's," Wangero said, laughing. "I can use the churn top as a centerpiece for the alcove table," she said, sliding a plate over the churn, "and I'll think of something artistic to do with the dasher."

When she finished wrapping the dasher the handle stuck out. I took it for a moment in my hands. You didn't even have to look close to see where hands pushing the dasher up and down to make butter had left a kind of sink in the wood. In fact, there were a lot of small sinks; you could see where thumbs and fingers had sunk into the wood. It was beautiful light yellow wood, from a tree that grew in the yard where Big Dee and Stash had lived.

After dinner Dee (Wangero) went to the trunk at the foot of my bed and started rifling through it. Maggie hung back in the kitchen over the dishpan. Out came Wangero with two quilts. They had been pieced by Grandma Dee and then Big Dee and me had hung them on the quilt frames on the front porch and quilted them. One was in the Lone Star pattern. The other was Walk Around the Mountain. In both of them were scraps of dresses Grandma Dee had worn fifty and more years ago. Bits and pieces of Grandpa Jarrell's paisley shirts. And one teeny faded blue piece, about the piece of a penny matchbox, that was from Great Grandpa Ezra's uniform that the wore in the Civil War.

"Mama," Wangero said sweet as a bird. "Can I have these old quilts?"

I heard something fall in the kitchen, and a minute later the kitchen door slammed.

"Why don't you take one or two of the others?" I asked. "These old things was just done by me and Big Dee from some tops your grandma pieced before she died."

"No," said Wangero. "I don't want those. They are stitched around the borders by machine."

"That's make them last better," I said. 60

"That's not the point," said Wangero. "These are all pieces of dresses Grandma used to wear. She did all this stitching by hand. Imagine!" She held the quilts securely in her arms, stroking them.

"Some of the pieces, like those lavender ones, come from old clothes her mother handed down to her," I said, moving up to touch the quilts. Dee (Wangero) moved back just enough so that I couldn't reach the quilts. They already belonged to her.

"Imagine!" she breathed again, clutching them closely to her bosom.

"The truth is," I said, "I promised to give them quilts to Maggie, for when she marries John Thomas."

She gasped like a bee had stung her. 65

"Maggie can't appreciate these quilts!" she said. "She'd probably be backward enough to put them to everyday use."

"I reckon she would," I said. "God knows I been saving 'em for long enough with nobody using 'em. I hope she will!" I didn't want to bring up how I had offered Dee (Wangero) a quilt when she went away to college. Then she had told me they were old-fashioned, out of style.

"But they're *priceless*!" she was saying now, furiously; for she has a temper. "Maggie would put them on the bed and in five years they'd be in rags. Less than that!"

"She can always make some more," I said. "Maggie knows how to quilt."

Dee (Wangero) looked at me with hatred. "You just will not understand. The point is these quilts, *these* quilts!" 70

"Well," I said, stumped. "What would *you* do with them?"

"Hang them," she said. As if that was the only thing you *could* do with quilts.

Maggie by now was standing in the door. I could almost hear the sound her feet made as they scraped over each other.

"She can have them, Mama," she said, like somebody used to never winning anything, or having anything reserved for her. "I can 'member Grandma Dee without the quilts."

I looked at her hard. She had filled her bottom lip with checker- 75
berry snuff and it gave her face a kind of dopey, hangdog look. It was Grandma Dee and Big Dee who taught her how to quilt herself. She stood there with her scarred hands hidden in the folds of her skirt. She looked at her sister with something like fear but she wasn't mad at her. This was Maggie's portion. This was the way she knew God to work.

When I looked at her like that something hit me in the top of my head and ran down to the soles of my feet. Just like when I'm in church and the spirit of God touches me and I get happy and shout. I did something I never had done before: hugged Maggie to me, then dragged her on into the room, snatched the quilts out of Miss Wangero's hands and dumped them into Maggie's lap. Maggie just sat there on my bed with her mouth open.

"Take one or two of the others," I said to Dee.

But she turned without a word and went out to Hakim-a-barber.

"You just don't understand," she said, as Maggie and I came out to the car.

"What don't I understand?" I wanted to know. 80

"Your heritage," she said. And then she turned to Maggie,

kissed her, and said, "You ought to try to make something of yourself, too, Maggie. It's really a new day for us. But from the way you and Mama still live you'd never know it."

She put on some sunglasses that hid everything above the tip of her nose and her chin.

Maggie smiled; maybe at the sunglasses. But a real smile, not scared. After we watched the car dust settle I asked Maggie to bring me a dip of snuff. And then the two of us sat there just enjoying, until it was time to go in the house and go to bed.

Questions:

1. From whose point of view is "*Everyday Use*" told? What does the story gain from this point of view—instead of, say, from the point of view of Dee (Wangero)? How does the story bring out her judgements about her two daughters.
2. How are the two sisters different physically and mentally? How have their lives been different?
3. Why did Dee change her name to "Wangero?" How is the change important, and how is it reflected in her attitude toward the family artifacts in the narrator's house?
4. What levels of meaning do you find in the story's title? And how does it highlight the conflicting values in the story?
5. Contrast Dee's attitude toward her heritage with the attitudes of her mother and sister. How much truth is there in Dee's accusation that her mother and sister don't understand their heritage?

Chapter 7 Symbol

In literature, **a symbol** is a thing that stands for or suggests something else by reason of relationship, association, convention or accidental resemblance; especially, a visible sign of something invisible (for example, the lion is a symbol of courage and the cross is a symbol of Christianity). The symbol generally does not stand for the meaning, nor for anything absolutely definite; it evokes an object that suggests the meaning.

Consider, for example, Chopin's treatment of the season in which "*The Story of an Hour*" takes place. The story has to take place at *some* time, but Chopin does not simply say, "On a spring day," or an autumn day, and let things go at that. Instead, she tells us about the sky, the trees, the rain, the twittering sparrows. Yet, none of this material is strictly necessary to a story about a woman who has heard that her husband was killed in an accident, who grieves, then recovers, and then dies when he suddenly reappears.

Why, then, does Chopin give such emphasis to the season? Because, we think, she is using the season symbolically. In this story, the spring is not just a bit of detail added for realism. It is rich with suggestions of renewal, of the new life that Louise achieves for a moment. But here, a caution. We think that the spring in this story is symbolic, but this is not to say that whenever spring appears in a story, it always stands for renewal. Nor does it mean that since spring recurs, Louise will be reborn. In short, in this story Chopin uses the season to convey specific implications.

Symbol in fiction can be abstract terms like *love* or *truth*, but can also bc perceptible objects or worded descriptions that cause us to imagine them. In William Faulkner's "*A Rose for Emily*," Miss Emily's invisible watch ticking at the end of a golden chain not only indicates the passage of time, but suggests that time passes without even being noticed by the watch's owner, and the golden chain carries suggestions of wealth and authority. Besides, a *locale* can provide rich suggestions. Recall Ernest Hemingway's "*A Clean, Well-Lighted Place*," in which the cafe is not merely a cafe, but an island of refuge from night, chaos, loneliness, old age, and impending death. Even a *character* in a story is symbolic, as Faulkner's Miss Emily. Though Faulkner invests Miss Emily with life and vigor, he also clothes her in symbolic hints: she seems almost to personify the vanishing aristocracy of the antebellum South, still maintaining a black servant and being ruthlessly betrayed by a money-making Yankee.

Look at Hawthorne's "*Young Goodman Brown.*" "The figure of a man" whom Brown meets in the forest is simply a man, rather than the Devil. But that man holds a staff, "hich bore the likeness of a great black snake, so curiously wrought that it might almost be seen to twist and wriggle itself like a living serpent." If we are familiar with the story of Adam and Eve, in which Satan took the form of a serpent, it is hard not to think that Hawthorne is here implying that Brown's new acquaintance is Satan. And, to speak more broadly, as one reads the story one can hardly not set up opposing meanings or at least suggestions for the village (from which Brown sets out) and the forest (in which he enters). The village is associated with daylight, faith, and goodness; the forest with darkness, loss of faith, and evil.

Symbols generally fall into three classes. (1) ***Natural symbols*** present things not for themselves, but for the idea people commonly associate with them: a star for hope, a cloud for despair, night for death, a sunrise for a new beginning, rain usually for fertility or the renewal of life, a forest often for mental darkness or chaos, a mountain for stability, a valley for a place of security. (2) ***Conventional symbols*** present things for the meanings people within a particular group have agreed to give them: a national flag for the ideas of home or patriotism associated with it or a Christian cross for the association it evokes in people familiar with the appropriate religion. (3) ***Literary symbols*** sometimes build upon natural or conventional symbols, adding meanings appropriate primarily with the work at hand, but sometimes they also create meanings within a work for things that have no natural or conventional meaning outside it, as Melville does with his white whale, for instance. The great white whale of the book's title apparently means more than the literary dictionary-definition meaning of an aquatic mammal. He also suggests more than the devil, to whom some of the characters liken him. The great whale, as the story unfolds, comes to imply an amplitude of meaning: among them the forces of nature and the whole created universe.

Finally, symbol differs from allegory, a story in which persons, places, and things form a system of clearly labeled equivalents. Thus, in John Bunyan's "*The Pilgrim's Progress*," we meet characters with names such as Christian, Mr. Worldly

Wiseman, and the Giant Despair; we also encounter places such as Vanity Fair, City of Destruction, and finally (Christian's goal), the Celestial City. Bunyan tells us of a man named Christian, who, on the road to the Celestial City, comes to a place called Vanity Fair and encounters, among others, Giant Despair, Mr. World Wiseman, and Faithful. What all of these are equivalent to is clear from their names. It is also clear that Christian's journey stands for the trials of the soul in this world. There is, so to speak, a one-to-one relationship. For example, we asked what the road represents in "*The Pilgrim's Progress*," we can confidently say that it stands for the journey of life. Thus, "*The Pilgrim's Progress*" tells two stories, the surface story of a man making a trip, during which he meets various figures and visits various places, and a second story, understood through the first, of the trials that afflict the soul during its quest for salvation.

Langston Hughes (1902—1967)

On the Road

He was not interested in the snow. When he got off the freight, one early evening during the depression, Sargeant never even noticed the snow. But he must have felt it seeping down his neck, cold, wet, sopping in his shoes. But if you had asked him, he wouldn't have known it was snowing. Sargeant didn't see the snow, not even under the bright lights of the main street, falling white and flaky against the night. He was too hungry, too sleepy, too tired.

The Reverend Mr. Dorset, however, saw the snow when he switched on his porch light, opened the front door of his parsonage, and found standing there before him a big black man with snow on his face, a human piece of night with snow on his face—obviously unemployed.

Said the Reverend Mr. Dorset before Sargeant even realized he'd opened his mouth: "I'm sorry. No! Go right on down this street four blocks and turn to your left, walk up seven and you'll see the Relief Shelter. I'm sorry. No!" He shut the door. Sargeant wanted to tell the holy man that he had already been to the Relief Shelter, been to hundreds of relief shelters during the depression years, the beds were always gone and supper was over, the place was full, and they drew the color line anyhow. But the minister said, "No," and shut the door. Evidently he didn't want to hear about it. And he *had* a door to shut.

The big black man turned away. And even yet he didn't see the snow, walking right into it. Maybe he sensed it, cold, wet, sticking to his jaws, wet on his black hands, sopping in his shoes. He stopped and stood on the sidewalk hunched over —hungry, sleepy, cold—looking up and down. Then he looked right where he was—in front of a church. Of course! A church! Sure, right next to a parsonage, certainly a church.

It had *two* doors. 5

Broad white steps in the night all snowy white. Two high arched doors with slender stone pillars on either side. And way up, a round lacy window with a stone crucifix in the middle and Christ on the crucifix in stone. All this was pale in the street lights, solid and stony pale in the snow.

Sargeant blinked. When he looked up the snow fell into his eyes. For the first time that night he *saw* the snow. He shook his head. He shook the snow from his coat sleeves, felt hungry, felt lost, felt not lost, felt cold. He walked up the steps of the church. He knocked at the door. No answer. He tried the handle. Locked. He put his shoulder against the door and his long black body slanted like a ramrod. He pushed. With loud rhythmic grunts, like the grunts in a chain-gang song, he pushed against the door.

"I'm tired... Huh!... Hungry... Uh!... I'm sleepy... Huh! I'm cold... I got to sleep somewheres," Sargeant said. "This here is a church, ain't it? Well, uh!"

He pushed against the door.

Suddenly, with an undue cracking and screaking, the door began to give way to the tall black Negro who pushed ferociously against the door.

By now two or three white people had stopped in the street, and Sargeant was vaguely aware of some of them yelling at him concerning the door. Three or four more came running, yelling at him.

"Hey!" they said. "Hey!"

"Uh-huh," answered the big tall Negro, "I know it's a white folks' church, but I got to sleep somewhere." He gave another lunge at the door. "Huh!"

And the door broke open.

But just when the door gave way, two white cops arrived in a car, ran up the steps with their clubs and grabbed Sargeant. But Sargeant for once had no intention of being pulled or pushed away from the door.

Sargeant grabbed, but not for anything so weak as a broken door. He grabbed for one of the tall stone pillars beside the door, grabbed at and caught it. And held it. The cops pulled and Sargeant pulled. Most of the people in the street got behind the cops and helped them pull.

"A big black unemployed Negro holding onto our church!" thought the people. "The idea!"

The cops began to beat Sargeant over the head, and nobody protested. But he held on.

And then the church fell down.

Gradually, the big stone front of the church fell down, the walls and the rafters, the crucifix and the Christ. Then the whole thing fell down, covering the cops and the people with bricks and stones and debris. The whole church fell down in the snow.

Sargeant got out from under the church and went walking on up the street with the stone pillar on his shoulder. He was under the impression that he had buried the parsonage and the Reverend Mr. Dorset who said, "No!" So he laughed, and threw the pillar six blocks up the street and went on.

Sargeant thought he was alone, but listening to the crunch, crunch, crunch on the snow of his own footsteps, he heard other footsteps, too, doubling his own. He looked around and there was Christ walking beside him, the same Christ that had been on the cross on the church—still stone with a rough stone surface, walking along beside him just like he was broken off the cross when the church fell down.

"Well, I'll be dogged," said Sargeant. "This here's the first time I ever seed you off the cross."

"Yes," said Christ, crunching his feet in the snow. "You had to pull the church down to get me off the cross."

"You glad?" said Sargeant.

"I sure am." said Christ.

They both laughed.

"I'm a hell of a fellow, ain't I?" said Sargeant. "Done pulled the church down!"

"You did a good job," said Christ. "They have kept me nailed on a cross for nearly two thousand years."

"Whee-ee-e!" said Sargeant. "I know you are glad to get off."

"I sure am," said Christ.

They walked on in the snow. Sargeant looked at the man of stone.

"And you been up there two thousand years?"

"I sure have," Christ said.

"Well, if I had a little cash," said Sargeant , "I'd show you around a bit."

"I been around," said Christ.

"Yeah, but that was a long time ago."

"All the same," said Christ, "I've been around."

They walked on in the snow until they came to the railroad yards. Sargeant was tired, sweating and tired.

"Where you goin'?" Sargeant said, stopping by the tracks. He looked at Christ. Sargeant said. "I'm just a bum on the road. How about you? Where you goin'?"

"God knows," Christ said, "but I'm leavin' here."

They saw the red and green lights of the railroad yard half veiled by the snow that fell out of the night. Away down the track they saw a fire in a hobo jungle.

"I can go there and sleep," Sargeant said.

"You can?"

"Sure," said Sargeant. "That place ain't got no doors."

Outside the town, along the tracks, there were barren trees and bushes below the embankment, snow-gray in the dark. And down among the trees and bushes there were makeshift houses made out of boxes and tin and old pieces of wood and canvas. You couldn't see them in the dark, but you knew they were there if you'd ever been on the road, if you had ever lived with the homeless and hungry in a depression.

"I'm side-tracking," Sargeant said. "I'm tired."

"I'm gonna make it on to Kansas City," said Christ.

"O. K.," Sargeant said. "So long!"

He went down into the hobo jungle and found himself a place to sleep. He never did see Christ no more. About six A. M. a freight came by. Sargeant scrambled out of the jungle with a dozen or so more hoboes and ran along the track, grabbing at the freight. It was dawn, early dawn, cold and gray.

"Wonder where Christ is by now?" Sargeant thought. "He must-a gone on way on down the road. He didn't sleep in this jungle."

Sargeant grabbed the train and started to pull himself up into a moving coal car, over the edge of a wheeling coal car. But strangely enough, the car was full of cops. The nearest cop rapped

Sargeant soundly across the knuckles with his night stick. Wham! Rapped his big black hands for clinging to the top of the car. Wham! But Sargeant did not turn loose. He clung on and tried to pull himself into the car. He hollered at the top of his voice, "Damn it, lemme in this car!"

"Shut up," barked the cop. "You crazy coon!" He rapped Sargeant across the knuckles and punched him in the stomach. "You ain't out in no jungle now. This ain't no train. You in jail."

Wham! across his bare black fingers clinging to the bars of his cell. Wham! between the steel bars low down against his shins.

Suddenly Sargeant realized that he really was in jail. He wasn't on no train. The blood of the night before had dried on his face, his head hurt terribly, and a cop outside in the corridor was hitting him across the knuckles for holding onto the door, yelling and shaking the cell door.

"They must-a took me to jail for breaking down the door last night," Sargeant thought, "that church door."

Sargeant went over and sat on a wooden bench against the cold stone wall. He was emptier than ever. His clothes were wet, clammy cold wet, and shoes sloppy with snow water. It was just about dawn. There he was, locked up behind a cell door, nursing his bruised fingers.

The bruised fingers were his, but not the *door*.

Not the *club*, but the fingers.

"You wait," mumbled Sargeant, black against the jail wall. "I'm gonna break down this door, too."

"Shut up—or I'll paste you one," said the cop.

"I'm gonna break down this door," yelled Sargeant as he stood up in his cell.

Then he must have been talking to himself because he said, "I wonder where Christ's gone? I wonder if he's gone to Kansas City?"

Questions:

1. Are there any symbols in the story? If there are, what are they? And what are they symbolic of?
2. How does the setting contribute to the story as a whole? And how is the setting related to the story's theme?

William Faulkner (1897—1962)

A Rose for Emily

I

When Miss Emily Grierson died, our whole town went to her funeral: the men through a sort of respectful affection for a fallen monument, the women mostly out of curiosity to see the inside of her house, which no one save an old manservant—a combined gardener and cook—had seen in at least ten years.

It was a big, squarish frame house that had once been white, decorated with cupolas and spires and scrolled balconies in the heavily lightsome style of the seventies, set on what had once been our most select street. But garages and cotton gins had encroached and obliterated even the august names of that neighborhood; only Miss

Emily's house was left, lifting its stubborn and coquettish decay above the cotton wagons and the gasoline pumps—an eyesore among eyesores. And now Miss Emily had gone to join the representatives of those august names where they lay in the cedar-bemused cemetery among the ranked and anonymous graves of Union and Confederate soldiers who fell at the battle of Jefferson.

Alive, Miss Emily had been a tradition, a duty, and a care; a sort of hereditary obligation upon the town, dating from that day in 1894 when Colonel Sartoris, the mayor—he who fathered the edict that no Negro woman should appear on the streets without an apron—remitted her taxes, the dispensation dating from the death of her father on into perpetuity. Not that Miss Emily would have accepted charity. Colonel Sartoris invented an involved tale to the effect that Miss Emily's father had loaned money to the town, which the town, as a matter of business, preferred this way of repaying. Only a man of Colonel Sartoris' generation and thought could have invented it, and only a woman could have believed it.

When the next generation, with its more modern ideas, became mayors and aldermen, this arrangement created some little dissatisfaction. On the first of the year they mailed her a tax notice. February came, and there was no reply. They wrote her a formal letter, asking her to call at the sheriff's office at her convenience. A week later the mayor wrote her himself, offering to call or to send his car for her, and received in reply a note on paper of an archaic shape, in a thin, flowery calligraphy in faded ink, to the effect that she no longer went out at all. The tax notice was also enclosed, without comment.

They called a special meeting of the Board of Aldermen. A 5

deputation waited upon her, knocked at the door through which no visitor had passed since she ceased giving china-painting lessons eight or ten years earlier. They were admitted by the old Negro into a dim hall from which a stairway mounted into still more shadow. It smelled of dust and disuse—a close, dank smell. The Negro led them into the parlor. It was furnished in heavy, leather-covered furniture. When the Negro opened the blinds of one window, they could see that the leather was cracked; and when they sat down, a faint dust rose sluggishly about their thighs, spinning with slow motes in the single sunray. On a tarnished gilt easel before the fireplace stood a crayon portrait of Miss Emily's father.

They rose when she entered—a small, fat woman in black, with a thin gold chain descending to her waist and vanishing into her belt, leaning on an ebony cane with a tarnished gold head. Her skeleton was small and spare; perhaps that was why what would have been merely plumpness in another was obesity in her. She looked bloated, like a body long submerged in motionless water, and of that pallid hue. Her eyes, lost in the fatty ridges of her face, looked like two small pieces of coal pressed into a lump of dough as they moved from one face to another while the visitors stated their errand.

She did not ask them to sit. She just stood in the door and listened quietly until the spokesman came to a stumbling halt. Then they could hear the invisible watch ticking at the end of the gold chain.

Her voice was dry and cold. "I have no taxes in Jefferson. Colonel Sartoris explained it to me. Perhaps one of you can gain access to the city records and satisfy yourselves."

"But we have. We are the city authorities, Miss Emily. Didn't you get a notice from the sheriff, signed by him?"

"I received a paper, yes," Miss Emily said. "Perhaps he considers himself the sheriff.... I have no taxes in Jefferson."

"But there is nothing on the books to show that, you see. We must go by the—"

"See Colonel Sartoris. I have no taxes in Jefferson."

"But, Miss Emily—"

"See Colonel Sartoris." (Colonel Sartoris had been dead almost ten years.) "I have no taxes in Jefferson. Tobe!" The Negro appeared. "Show these gentlemen out."

II

So she vanquished them, horse and foot, just as she had vanquished their fathers thirty years before about the smell. That was two years after her father's death and a short time after her sweetheart—the one we believed would marry her—had deserted her. After her father's death she went out very little; after her sweetheart went away, people hardly saw her at all. A few of the ladies had the temerity to call, but were not received, and the only sign of life about the place was the Negro man—a young man then—going in and out with a market basket.

"Just as if a man—any man—could keep a kitchen properly," the ladies said; so they were not surprised when the smell developed. It was another link between the gross, teeming world and the high and mighty Griersons.

A neighbor, a woman, complained to the mayor, Judge Stevens, eighty years old.

"But what will you have me do about it, madam?" he said.

"Why, send her word to stop it," the woman said. "Isn't there a law?"

"I'm sure that won't be necessary," Judge Stevens said. It's probably just a snake or a rat that nigger of hers killed in the yard. I'll speak to him about it."

The next day he received two more complaints, one from a man who came in diffident deprecation. "We really must do something about it, Judge. I'd be the last one in the world to bother Miss Emily, but we've got to do something." That night the Board of Aldermen met—three graybeards and one younger man, a member of the rising generation.

"It's simple enough," he said. "Send her word to have her place cleaned up. Give her a certain time to do it in, and if she don't..."

"Dammit, sir," Judge Stevens said, "will you accuse a lady to her face of smelling bad?"

So the next night, after midnight, four men crossed Miss Emily's lawn and slunk about the house like burglars, sniffing along the base of the brickwork and at the cellar openings while one of them performed a regular sowing motion with his hand out of a sack slung from his shoulder. They broke open the cellar door and sprinkled lime there, and in all the outbuildings. As they recrossed the lawn, a window that had been dark was lighted and Miss Emily sat in it, the light behind her, and her upright torso motionless as that of an idol. They crept quietly across the lawn and into the shadow of the locusts that lined the street. After a week or two the smell went away.

That was when people had begun to feel really sorry for her. People in our town, remembering how old lady Wyatt, her great-aunt, had gone completely crazy at last, believed that the Griersons held themselves a little too high for what they really were. None of the young men were quite good enough for Miss Emily and such. We had long thought of them as a tableau, Miss Emily a slender figure in white in the background, her father a spraddled silhouette in the foreground, his back to her and clutching a horsewhip, the two of them framed by the back-flung front door. So when she got to be thirty and was still single, we were not pleased exactly, but vindicated; even with insanity in the family she wouldn't have turned down all of her chances if they had really materialized.

When her father died, it got about that the house was all that was left to her; and in a way, people were glad. At last they could pity Miss Emily. Being left alone, and a pauper, she had become humanized. Now she too would know the old thrill and the old despair of a penny more or less.

The day after his death all the ladies prepared to call at the house and offer condolence and aid, as is our custom. Miss Emily met them at the door, dressed as usual and with no trace of grief on her face. She told them that her father was not dead. She did that for three days, with the ministers calling on her, and the doctors, trying to persuade her to let them dispose of the body. Just as they were about to resort to law and force, she broke down, and they buried her father quickly.

We did not say she was crazy then. We believed she had to

do that. We remembered all the young men her father had driven away, and we knew that with nothing left, she would have to cling to that which had robbed her, as people will.

III

She was sick for a long time. When we saw her again, her hair was cut short, making her look like a girl, with a vague resemblance to those angels in colored church windows—sort of tragic and serene.

The town had just let the contracts for paving the sidewalks, and in the summer after her father's death they began the work. The construction company came with niggers and mules and machinery, and a foreman named Homer Barron, a Yankee—a big, dark, ready man, with a big voice and eyes lighter than his face. The little boys would follow in groups to hear him cuss the niggers, and the niggers singing in time to the rise and fall of picks. Pretty soon he knew everybody in town. Whenever you heard a lot of laughing anywhere about the square, Homer Barron would be in the center of the group. Presently we began to see him and Miss Emily on Sunday afternoons driving in the yellow-wheeled buggy and the matched team of bays from the livery stable.

At first we were glad that Miss Emily would have an interest, because the ladies all said, "Of course a Grierson would not think seriously of a Northerner, a day laborer." But there were still others, older people, who said that even grief could not cause a real lady to forget *noblesse oblige*[*]—without calling it *noblesse oblige*. They

---

* *French*: duty obligates, i. e., the duties, obligations, and honorable behavior expected from people of high rank.

just said, "Poor Emily. Her kinsfolk should come to her." She had some kin in Alabama; but years ago her father had fallen out with them over the estate of old lady Wyatt, the crazy woman, and there was no communication between the two families. They had not even been represented at the funeral.

And as soon as the old people said, "Poor Emily," the whispering began. "Do you suppose it's really so?" they said to one another. "Of course it is. What else could..." This behind their hands, rustling of craned silk and satin behind jalousies closed upon the sun of Sunday afternoon as the thin, swift clop-clop-clop of the matched team passed: "Poor Emily."

She carried her head high enough—even when we believed that she was fallen. It was as if she demanded more than ever the recognition of her dignity as the last Grierson; as if it had wanted that touch of earthliness to reaffirm her imperviousness. Like when she bought the rat poison, the arsenic. That was over a year after they had begun to say "Poor Emily," and while the two female cousins were visiting her.

"I want some poison," she said to the druggist. She was over thirty then, still a slight woman, though thinner than usual, with cold, haughty black eyes in a face the flesh of which was strained across the temples and about the eye-sockets as you imagine a lighthouse-keeper's face ought to look. "I want some poison," she said.

"Yes, Miss Emily. What kind? For rats and such? I'd recom—"

"I want the best you have. I don't care what kind."

The druggist named several. "They'll kill anything up to an elephant. But what you want is—"

"Arsenic," Miss Emily said. "Is that a good one?"

"Is... arsenic? Yes, ma'am. But what you want—"

"I want arsenic." 40

The druggist looked down at her. She looked back at him, erect, her face like a strained flag. "Why, of course," the druggist said. "If that's what you want. But the law requires you to tell what you are going to use it for."

Miss Emily just stared at him, her head tilted back in order to look him eye for eye, until he looked away and went and got the arsenic and wrapped it up. The Negro delivery boy brought her the package; the druggist didn't come back. When she opened the package at home there was written on the box, under the skull and bones: "For rats."

IV

So the next day we all said, "She will kill herself;" and we said it would be the best thing. When she had first begun to be seen with Homer Barron, we had said, "She will marry him." Then we said, "She will persuade him yet," because Homer himself had remarked—he liked men, and it was known that he drank with the younger men at the Elks' Club—that he was not a marrying man. Later we said, "Poor Emily" behind the jalousies as they passed on Sunday afternoon in the glittering buggy, Miss Emily with her head high and Homer Barron with his hat cocked and a cigar at his teeth, reins and whip in a yellow glove.

Then some of the ladies began to say that it was a disgrace to the town and a bad example to the young people. The men did not want to interfere, but at last the ladies forced the Baptist minister—Miss Emily's people were Episcopal—to call upon her. He would never divulge what happened during that interview, but he refused to go back again. The next Sunday they again drove about the streets, and the following day the minister's wife wrote to Miss Emily's relations in Alabama.

So she had blood-kin under her roof again and we sat back to watch developments. At first nothing happened. Then we were sure that they were to be married. We learned that Miss Emily had been to the jeweler's and ordered a man's toilet set in silver, with the letters H. B. on each piece. Two days later we learned that she had bought a complete outfit of men's clothing, including a nightshirt, and we said, "They are married." We were really glad. We were glad because the two female cousins were even more Grierson than Miss Emily had ever been.

So we were not surprised when Homer Barron—the streets had been finished some time since—was gone. We were a little disappointed that there was not a public blowing-off, but we believed that he had gone on to prepare for Miss Emily's coming, or to give her a chance to get rid of the cousins. (By that time it was a cabal, and we were all Miss Emily's allies to help circumvent the cousins.) Sure enough, after another week they departed. And, as we had expected all along, within three days Homer Barron was back in town. A neighbor saw the Negro man admit him at the kitchen door at dusk one evening.

And that was the last we saw of Homer Barron. And of Miss Emily for some time. The Negro man went in and out with the market basket, but the front door remained closed. Now and then we would see her at a window for a moment, as the men did that night when they sprinkled lime, but for almost six months she did not appear on the streets. Then we knew that this was to be expected too; as if that quality of her father which had thwarted her woman's life so many times had been too virulent and too furious to die.

When we next saw Miss Emily, she had grown fat and her hair was turning gray. During the next few years it grew grayer and grayer until it attained an even pepper-and-salt iron-gray, when it ceased turning. Up to the day of her death at seventy-four it was still that vigorous iron-gray, like the hair of an active man.

From that time on her front door remained closed, save for a period of six or seven years, when she was about forty, during which she gave lessons in china-painting. She fitted up a studio in one of the downstairs rooms, where the daughters and granddaughters of Colonie Sartoris' contemporaries were sent to her with the same regularity and in the same spirit that they were sent to church on Sundays with a twenty-five-cent piece for the collection plate. Meanwhile her taxes had been remitted.

Then the newer generation became the backbone and the spirit 50
of the town, and the painting pupils grew up and fell away and did not send their children to her with boxes of color and tedious brushes and pictures cut from the ladies' magazines. The front door closed upon the last one and remained closed for good. When the town got free postal delivery, Miss Emily alone refused to let them fasten the metal numbers above her door and attach a mailbox to it. She would not listen to them.

Daily, monthly, yearly we watched the Negro grow grayer and more stooped, going in and out with the market basket. Each December we sent her a tax notice, which would be returned by the post office a week later, unclaimed. Now and then we would see her in one of the downstairs windows—she had evidently shut up the top floor of the house—like the carven torso of an idol in a niche, looking or not looking at us, we could never tell which. Thus she passed from generation to generation—dear, inescapable, impervious, tranquil, and perverse.

And so she died. Fell ill in the house filled with dust and shadows, with only a doddering Negro man to wait on her. We did not even know she was sick; we had long since given up trying to get any information from the Negro. He talked to no one, probably not even to her, for his voice had grown harsh and rusty, as if from disuse.

She died in one of the downstairs rooms, in a heavy walnut bed with a curtain, her gray head propped on a pillow yellow and moldy with age and lack of sunlight.

V

The Negro met the first of the ladies at the front door and let them in, with their hushed, sibilant voices and their quick, curious glances, and then he disappeared. He walked right through the house and out the back and was not seen again.

The two female cousins came at once. They held the funeral on the second day, with the town coming to look at Miss Emily beneath a mass of bought flowers, with the crayon face of her father musing profoundly above the bier and the ladies sibilant and macabre; and the very old men—some in their brushed Confederate uniforms—on the porch and the lawn, talking of Miss Emily as if she had been a contemporary of theirs, believing that they had danced with her and courted her perhaps, confusing time with its mathematical progression, as the old do, to whom all the past is not a diminishing road but, instead, a huge meadow which no winter ever quite touches, divided from them now by the narrow bottle-neck of the most recent decade of years.

Already we knew that there was one room in that region above stairs which no one had seen in forty years, and which would have to be forced. They waited until Miss Emily was decently in the ground before they opened it.

The violence of breaking down the door seemed to fill this room with pervading dust. A thin, acrid pall as of the tomb seemed to lie everywhere upon this room decked and furnished as for a bridal: upon the valance curtains of faded rose color, upon the rose-shaded lights, upon the dressing table, upon the delicate array of crystal and the man's toilet things backed with tarnished silver, silver so tarnished that the monogram was obscured. Among them lay a collar and tie, as if they had just been removed, which lifted, left upon the surface a pale crescent in the dust. Upon a chair hung the suit, carefully folded; beneath it the two mute shoes and the discarded socks.

The man himself lay in the bed.

For a long while we just stood there, looking down at the profound and fleshless grin. The body had apparently once lain in the attitude of an embrace, but now the long sleep that outlasts love, that conquers even the grimace of love, had cuckolded him. What was left of him, rotted beneath what was left of the nightshirt, had become inextricable from the bed in which he lay; and upon him and upon the pillow beside him lay that even coating of the patient and biding dust.

Then we noticed that in the second pillow was the indentation 60
of a head. One of us lifted something from it, and leaning forward, that faint and invisible dust dry and acrid in the nostrils, we saw a long strand of iron-gray hair.

Questions:

1. What does the second paragraph contribute to the story?
2. What contrast does the narrator draw between changing reality and Emily's refusal or inability to recognize change?
3. How do the character and background of Emily Grierson differ from those of Homer Barron? What general observations about the society that Faulkner depicts can made from his portraits of these two characters?
4. What do you infer to be the author's attitude toward Emily Grierson? Is she simply a murderous madwoman?

Eudora Welty (1909—)

A Worn Path

It was December—a bright frozen day in the early morning. Far out in the country there was an old Negro woman with her head tied in a red rag, coming along a path through the pinewoods. Her name was Phoenix Jackson. She was very old and small and she walked slowly in the dark pine shadows, moving a little from side to side in her steps, with the balanced heaviness and lightness of a pendulum in a grandfather clock. She carried a thin, small cane, made from an umbrella, and with this she kept tapping the frozen earth in front of her. This made a grave and persistent noise in the still air, that seemed meditative like the chirping of a solitary little bird.

She wore a dark striped dress reaching down to her shoe tops, and an equally long apron of bleached sugar sacks, with a full pocket: all neat and tidy, but every time she took a step she might have fallen over her shoelaces, which dragged from her unlaced shoes. She looked straight ahead. Her eyes were blue with age. Her skin had a pattern all its own of numberless branching wrinkles and as though a whole little tree stood in the middle of her forehead, but a golden color ran underneath, and the two knobs of her cheeks were illumined by a yellow burning under the dark. Under the rag her hair came down on her neck in the frailest of ringlets, still black, and with an odor like copper.

Now and then there was a quivering in the thicket. Old Phoenix said, "Out of my way, all you foxes, owls, beetles, jack rabbits, coons and wild animals!... Keep out from under these feet, little bob-whites... Keep the big wild hogs out of my path. Don't let none of those come running my direction. I got a long way." Under her small black-freckled hand her cane, limber as a buggy whip, would switch at the brush as if to rouse up any hiding things.

On she went. The woods were deep and still. The sun made the pine needles almost too bright to look at, up where the wind rocked. The cones dropped as light as feathers. Down in the hollow was the mourning dove—it was not too late for him.

The path ran up a hill. "Seem like there is chains about my feet, 5 time, I get this far," she said, in the voice of argument old people keep to use with themselves. "Something always take a hold of me on this hill—pleads I should stay."

After she got to the top she turned and gave a full, severe look behind her where she had come. "Up through pines," she said at length. "Now down through oaks."

Her eyes opened their widest, and she started down gently. But before she got to the bottom of the hill a bush caught her dress.

Her fingers were busy and intent, but her skirts were full and long, so that before she could pull them free in one place they were caught in another. It was not possible to allow the dress to tear. "I in the thorny bush," she said. "Thorns, you doing your appointed work. Never want to let folks pass, no sir. Old eyes thought you was a pretty little *green* bush."

Finally, trembling all over, she stood free, and after a moment dared to stoop for her cane.

"Sun so high!" she cried, leaning back and looking, while the thick tears went over her eyes. "The time getting all gone here."

At the foot of this hill was a place where a log was laid across the creek.

"Now comes the trial," said Phoenix.

Putting her right foot out, she mounted the log and shut her eyes. Lifting her skirt, leveling her cane fiercely before her, like a festival figure in some parade, she began to march across. Then she opened her eyes and she was safe on the other side.

"I wasn't as old as I thought," she said.

But she sat down to rest. She spread her skirts on the bank around her and folded her hands over her knees. Up above her was a tree in a pearly cloud of mistletoe. She did not dare to close her eyes, and when a little boy brought her a plate with a slice of marble-cake on it she spoke to him. "That would be acceptable," she said. But when she went to take it there was just her own hand in the air.

So she left that tree, and had to go through a barbed-wire fence. There she had to creep and crawl, spreading her knees and stretching her fingers like a baby trying to climb the steps. But she talked loudly to herself: she could not let her dress be torn now, so late in the day, and she could not pay for having her arm or her leg sawed off if she got caught fast where she was.

At last she was safe through the fence and risen up out in the clearing. Big dead trees, like black men with one arm, were standing in the purple stalks of the withered cotton field. There sat a buzzard.

"Who you watching?"

In the furrow she made her way along.

"Glad this not the season for bulls," she said, looking sideways, 20
"and the good Lord made his snakes to curl up and sleep in the winter. A pleasure I don't see no two-headed snake coming around that tree, where it come once. It took a while to get by him, back in the summer.

She passed through the old cotton and went into a field of dead corn. It whispered and shook and was taller than her head. "Through the maze now," she said, for there was no path.

Then there was something tall, black, and skinny there, moving before her.

At first she took it for a man. It could have been a man

dancing in the field. But she stood still and listened, and it did not make a sound. It was as silent as a ghost.

"Ghost," she said sharply, "who be you the ghost of? For I have heard of nary death close by."

But there was no answer—only the ragged dancing in the wind.

She shut her eyes, reached out her hand, and touched a sleeve. She found a coat and inside that an emptiness, cold as ice.

"You scarecrow," she said. Her face lighted. "I ought to be shut up for good," she said with laughter. "My senses is gone. I too old. I the oldest people I ever know. Dance, old scarecrow," she said, "while I dancing with you."

She kicked her foot over the furrow, and with mouth drawn down, shook her head once or twice in a little strutting way. Some husks blew down and whirled in steamers about her skirts.

Then she went on, parting her way from side to side with the cane, through the whispering field. At last she came to the end, to a wagon track where the silver grass blew between the red ruts. The quail were walking around like pullets, seeming all dainty and unseen.

"Walk pretty," she said. "This is the easy place. This the easy going."

She followed the track, swaying through the quiet bare fields, through the little strings of trees silver in their dead leaves, past cabins silver from weather, with the doors and windows boarded shut, all like old women under a spell sitting there. "I walking in their sleep," she said, nodding her head vigorously.

In a ravine she went where a spring was silently flowing

through a hollow log. Old Phoenix bent and drank. "Sweet-gum makes the water sweet," she said, and drank more. "Nobody know who made this well, for it was here when I was born."

The track crossed a swampy part where the moss hung as white as lace from every limb. "Sleep on, alligators, and blow your bubbles." Then the track went into the road.

Deep, deep the road went down between the high green-colored banks. Over-head the live-oaks met, and it was as dark as a cave.

A black dog with a lolling tongue came up out of the weeds by 35
the ditch. She was meditating, and not ready, and when he came at her she only hit him a little with her cane. Over she went in the ditch, like a little puff of milkweed.

Down there, her sense drifted away. A dream visited her, and she reached her hand up, but nothing reached down and gave her a pull. So she lay there and presently went to talking. "Old woman," she said to herself, "that black dog come up out of the weeds to stall you off, and now there he sitting on his fine tail smiling at you."

A white man finally came along and found her—a hunter, a young man, with his dog on a chain.

"Well, Granny!" he laughed. "What are you doing there?"

"Lying on my back like a June-bug waiting to be turned over, mister," she said, reaching up her hand.

He lifted her up, gave her a swing in the air, and set her down. 40
"Anything broken, Granny?"

"No, sir, them old dead weeds is springy enough," said

Phoenix, when she had got her breath. "I thank you for your trouble."

"Where do you live, Granny?" he asked, while the two dogs were growling at each other.

"Away back yonder, sir, behind the ridge. You can't even see it from here."

"On your way home?"

"No sir, I goin to town."

"Why, that's too far! That's as far as I walk when I come out myself, and I get something for my trouble." He patted the stuffed bag he carried, and there hung down a little closed claw. It was one of the bob-whites, with its beak hooked bitterly to show it was dead. "Now you go on home, Granny!"

"I bound to go to town, mister," said Phoenix. "The time come around."

He gave another laugh, filling the whole landscape. "I know you old colored people! Wouldn't miss going to town to see Santa Claus!"

But something held old Phoenix very still. The deep lines in her face went into a fierce and different radiation. Without warning, she had seen with her own eyes a flashing nickel fall out of the man's pocket onto the ground.

"How old are you, Granny?" he was saying.

"There is no telling, mister," she said, "no telling."

Then she gave a little cry and clapped her hands and said, "Git no away from here, dog! Look! Look at that dog!" She laughed as if in admiration. "He ain't scared of nobody. He a big black dog." She whispered, "Sic him!"

"Watch me get rid of that cur," said the man. "Sic him, Pete! Sic him!"

Phoenix heard the dogs fighting, and heard the man running and throwing sticks. She even heard a gunshot. But she was slowly bending forward by that time, further and further forward, the lids stretched down over her eyes, as if she were doing this in her sleep. Her chin was lowered almost to her knees. The yellow palm of her hand came out from the fold of her apron. Her fingers slid down and along the ground under the piece of money with the grace and care they would have in lifting an egg from under a setting hen. Then she slowly straightened up, she stood erect, and the nickel was in her apron pocket. A bird flew by. Her lips moved. "God watching me the whole time. I come to stealing."

The man came back, and his own dog panted about them. "Well, 55
I scared him off that time," he said, and then he laughed and lifted his gun and pointed it at Phoenix.

She stood straight and faced him.

"Doesn't the gun scare you?" he said, still pointing it.

"No, sir, I seen plenty go off closer by, in my day, and for less than what I done," she said, holding utterly still.

He smiled, and shouldered the gun. "Well, Granny," he said, "you must be a hundred years old, and scared of nothing. I'd give you a dime if I had any money with me. But you take my advice and stay home, and nothing will happen to you."

"I bound to go on my way, mister," said Phoenix. She inclined 60
her head in the red rag. Then they went in different directions, but

she could hear the gun shooting again and again over the hill.

She walked on. The shadows hung from the oak trees to the road like curtains. Then she smelled wood-smoke, and smelled the river, and she saw a steeple and the cabins on their steep steps. Dozens of little black children whirled around her. There ahead was Natchez shining. Bells were ringing. She walked on.

In the paved city it was Christmas time. There were red and green electric lights strung and crisscrossed everywhere, and all turned on in the daytime. Old Phoenix would have been lost if she had not distrusted her eyesight and depended on her feet to know where to take her.

She paused quietly on the sidewalk where people were passing by. A lady came along in the crowd, carrying an armful of red-, green- and silver-wrapped presents; she gave off perfume like the red roses in hot summer, and Phoenix stopped her.

"Please, missy, will you lace up my shoe?" She held up her foot.

"What do you want, Grandma?"

"See my shoe," said Phoenix. "Do all right for out in the country, but wouldn't look right to go in a big building."

"Stand still then, Grandma," said the lady. She put her packages down on the sidewalk beside her and laced and tied both shoes tightly.

"Can't lace'em with a cane," said Phoenix. "Thank you, missy. I doesn't mind asking a nice lady to tie up my shoe, when I gets out on the street."

Moving slowly and from side to side, she went into the big building, and into a tower of steps, where she walked up and around and around until her feet knew to stop.

She entered a door, and there she saw nailed up on the wall the document that had been stamped with the gold seal and framed in the gold frame, which matched the dream that was hung up in her head.

"Here I be," she said. There was a fixed and ceremonial stiffness over her body.

"A charity case, I suppose," said an attendant who sat at the desk before her.

But Phoenix only looked above her head. There was sweat on her face, the wrinkles in her skin shone like a bright net.

"Speak up, Grandma," the woman said. "What's your name? We must have your history, you know. Have you been here before? What seems to be the trouble with you?"

Old Phoenix only gave a twitch to her face as if a fly were bothering her.

"Are you deaf ?" cried the attendant.

But then the nurse came in.

"Oh, that's just old Aunt Phoenix," she said. "She doesn't come for herself—she has a little grandson. She makes these trips just as regular as clockwork. She lives away back off the Old Natchez Trace." She bent down. "Well, Aunt Phoenix, why don't you just take a seat? We won't keep you standing after your long trip." She pointed.

The old woman sat down, bolt upright in the chair.

"Now, how is the boy?" asked the nurse.

Old Phoenix did not speak.

"I said, how is the boy?"

But Phoenix only waited and stared straight ahead, her face very solemn and withdrawn into rigidity.

"Is his throat any better?" asked the nurse. "Aunt Phoenix, don't you hear me? Is your grandson's throat any better since the last time you came for the medicine?"

With her hands on her knees, the old woman waited, silent, erect and motionless, just as if she were in armor.

"You mustn't take up our time this way, Aunt Phoenix," the nurse said. "Tell us quickly about your grandson, and get it over. He isn't dead, is he?"

At last there came a flicker and then a flame of comprehension across her face, and she spoke.

"My grandson. It was my memory had left me. There I sat and forgot why I made my long trip."

"Forgot?" the nurse frowned. "After you came so far?"

Then Phoenix was like an old woman begging a dignified forgiveness for waking up frightened in the night. "I never did go to school, I was too old at the Surrender," she said in a soft voice. "I'm an old woman without an education. It was my memory fail me. My little grandson, he is just the same, and I forgot it in the coming."

"Throat never heals, does it?" said the nurse, speaking in a loud, sure voice to old Phoenix. By now she had a card with something written on it , a little list. "Yes. Swallowed lye. When was it—January—two, three years ago—"

Phoenix spoke unasked now. "No, missy, he not dead, he

just the same. Every little while his throat begin to close up again, and he not able to swallow. He not get his breath. He not able to help himself. So the time come around, and I go on another trip for the soothing medicine."

"All right. The doctor said as long as you came to get it, you could have it," said the nurse. "But it's an obstinate case."

"My little grandson, he sit up there in the house all wrapped up, waiting by himself," Phoenix went on. "We is the only two left in the world. He suffer and it don't seem to put him back at all. He got a sweet look. He going to last. He wear a little patch quilt and peep out holding his mouth open like a little bird. I remember so plain now. I not going to forget him again, no, the whole enduring time. I could tell him from all the others in creation."

"All right." The nurse was trying to hush her now. She brought her a bottle of medicine. "Charity," she said, making a check mark in a book.

Old Phoenix held the bottle close to her eyes, and then carefully put it into her pocket.

"I thank you," she said.

"It's Christmas time, Grandma," said the attendant. "Could I give you a few pennies out of my purse?"

"Five pennies is a nickel," said Phoenix stiffly.

"Here's a nickel," said the attendant.

Phoenix rose carefully and held out her hand. She received the nickel and then fished the other nickel out of her pocket and laid it beside the new one. She stared at her palm closely, with her head on one side.

Then she gave a tap with her cane on the floor.

"This is what come to me to do," she said. "I going to the store and buy my child a little windmill they sells, made out of paper. He going to find it hard to believe there such a thing in the world. I'll march myself back where he waiting, holding it straight up in this hand."

She lifted her free hand, gave a little nod, turned around, and walked out of the doctor's office. Then her slow step began on the stairs, going down.

Questions:

1. From the description of her physical appearance, what do you conclude about Phoenix's economic condition? Is she accustomed to being alone?
2. Describe the plot of the story. With Phoenix as the protagonist, what are the antagonisms ranged against her? How might Phoenix be considered to be in the grip of large and indifferent social and political forces?
3. Describe the structure of the story according to exposition, complication, crisis, climax, and resolution. Does the actual structure correspond to this orderly arrangement? Wherein does it depart? Why?
4. A number of responses might be made to this story, among them admiration for Phoenix, pity for her and her grandson and for the downtrodden generally, anger at her impo-verished condition, and apprehension about her approaching senility. Do you share in any of these responses?

Poetry

Chapter 8 Reading a Poem

What Is Poetry?

Poetry may be roughly defined as a kind of writing that formulates a concentrated imaginative awareness of experience in language chosen and arranged to create a specific emotional response through its meaning, sound, and rhythm. Based on the definition, we can find that poetry deals with *emotions* as they are aroused by some scene or experience. The characteristic emotional content of poetry finds expression through a variety of techniques, from direct description to highly personalized symbolism. One of the most ancient and universal of these techniques is the use of metaphor and simile to alter and expand the reader's imaginative apprehension through implicit or explicit comparison. Poetry is *imaginative*. Poetry has *significance*; it adds to our store of knowledge or experience.

Another key to the content of poetry can be found in beauty. All poets agree to this element although by no means will all agree as to what is beautiful. But beauty, of some sort or degree, must be present. If it is a new, strange beauty of some familiar object, so much the better. The POET, like the artist and the musician, differs from most other people because of a sensitivity to beauty. "Poetry," says Shelly, "turns all things to loveliness; it exalts the beauty of that which is most beautiful, and it adds beauty to that which is most deformed."

Poetry may be distinguished from prose literature in terms of form by its compression, by its frequent use of the conventions of meter and rhyme, by its reliance upon the line as a formal unit, by its heightened vocabulary, and by its freedom of syntax. Since most poetry is relatively short, it is likely to be characterized by compactness of thought and expression, and intense UNITY, and some careful arrangement in climactic order. A vital element of great poetry is its *concreteness*. Poetry insists on the specific, the concrete, and the bodily.

The language of poetry may differ still further from that of prose. Since the function of poetry is to present IMAGES concretely, it is the responsibility of the poet to select language that succeeds in making those IMAGES concrete. The specific word, rich in connotative value and carrying implications of sound, color, and action—these are the special stock of the genuine POET. Modern poetry tends to dispense with the special vocabulary that was once thought of as the language of poetry.

How Do You Read a Poem?

Poetry appeals to the mind and arouses feelings. Poetry may state facts, but, more important, it makes imaginative statements that we may value even if its facts are incorrect. The work of a poem is to touch us, to stir us, to make us glad and possibly even to tell us something. But how to set about reading a poem? Here are a few suggestions.

To begin with, read the poem once straight through, with no particular expectations. Don't dwell on a troublesome word or difficult passage—just push on. Some of the difficulties may seem smaller when you read the poem for a second time.

On second reading, read for the exact sense of all the words; if there are words you don't understand, look them up in a dictionary. Dwell on any difficult parts as long as you need to.

When you read the poem silently to yourself, sound its words in your mind. Better still, read the poem aloud, or hear someone else read it. By so doing, you may discover meanings you didn't perceive in it before.

Finally, try to paraphrase the poem as a whole. In making a paraphrase, we generally work through a poem or a passage line by line.

Types of Poetry

1. Lyric Poetry

Lyric is a brief subjective poem strongly marked by imagination, melody and emotion, and creating a single unified impression. Lyrical poetry began in ancient Greece in connection with music, as poetry sung, for the most part, to the accompaniment of a musical instrument (in ancient times, usually a lyre). Lyrical poetry expresses the thoughts and feelings of the poet and is sometimes contrasted with narrative poetry and verse drama, which relate events in the form of a story. Elegies, odes, and sonnets are important types of lyric poetry.

Often a poet will write a lyric in the first person, as in William Butler Yeats's "*The Lake Isle of Innisfree*,"

The Lake Isle of Innisfree

I will arise and go now, and go to Innisfree,
And a small cabin build there, of clay and wattles made:
Nine bean-rows will I have there, a hive for the honey-bee,
And live alone in the bee-loud glade.
And I shall have some peace there, for peace comes dropping slow,
Dropping from the veils of the morning to where the cricket sings;
There midnight's all a glimmer, and noon a purple glow,
And evening full of the linnet's wings.

I will arise and go now, for always night and day
I hear lake water lapping with low sounds by the shore;
While I stand on the roadway, or on the pavements gray,
I hear it in the deep heart's core.

Piano

Softly, in the dusk, a woman is singing to me;
Taking me back down the vista of years, till I see
A child sitting under the piano, in the boom of the tingling strings

And pressing the small, poised feet of a mother who smiles as she sings.

In spite of myself, the insidious mastery of song
Betrays me back, till the heart of me weeps to belong
To the old Sunday evenings at home, with winter outside
And hymns in the cozy parlor, the tinkling piano our guide.

So now it is vain for the singer to burst into clamor
With the great black piano *appassionato*. The glamor
Of childish days is upon me, my manhood is cast
Down in the flood of remembrance, I weep like a child for the past.

——*D. H. Lawrence*

but not always. Instead, a lyric might describe an object or recall an experience without the speaker's ever bringing himself or herself into it. (For an example of such a lyric, see William Carlos Williams's "*The Red Wheelbarrow*.")

2. Narrative Poetry

A narrative poem is one that tells a story or presents a narrative, whether simple or complex, long or short. Epics, ballads and metrical romances are among the many kinds of narrative poems. Read Robert Frost's "*Out, Out—*"

3. Dramatic Poetry

A third kind of poetry is dramatic poetry which is written in the form of a speech of an individual character to an imaginary audience; it compresses into a single vivid scene a narrative sense of the speaker's history and psychological insight into his character. This kind of poetry, as the term suggests, employs dramatic form or some element of dramatic technique. The DRAMATIC MONOLOGUE is an example. A dramatic monologue is a monologue in verse in which a speaker addresses a silent listener, revealing, in DRAMATIC IRONY, things about himself or herself of which the speaker is unaware. If the listener replies, the poem becomes a dialogue in which the story unfolds in the conversation between two speakers. In addition to MONOLOGUE, the dramatic quality results also from the use of dialogues, the stressing of tense situation and emotional conflicts.

The term DRAMATIC MONOLOGUE is universally acknowledged to be chiefly associated with Robert Browning. In his "*My Last Duchess*," Robert Browning creates a Renaissance Italian Duke who, bargaining for a new duchess, reveals himself as a cold aesthete and materialist, who has murdered his innocent young "last duchess," quite evidently not the first. Read that poem carefully.

Langston Hughes (1902—1967)

Harlem

What happens to a dream deferred?
    Does it dry up
    like a raisin in the sun?
    Or fester like a sore—
    And then run?
    Does it stink like rotten meat?

Or crust and sugar over —
like a syrupy sweet?

Maybe it just sags
like a heavy load.

Or does it explode?

Questions:

1. In the light of the black experience with the "*American Dream*," what do you think is meant by the phrase "dreamed deferred"?
2. Explain the similes in lines 3, 4, 6, 8, and 10. Why are these apt comparisons? What sorts of human actions are implied in these figures?
3. What is the meaning of the metaphor in line 11? Why do you think Hughes shifted from similes to a metaphor in this line?

Robert Frost (1874—1963)

"Out, Out—"

The buzz-saw snarled and rattled in the yard
And made dust and dropped stove-length sticks of wood,
Sweet-scented stuff when the breeze drew across it.
And from there those that lifted eyes could count
Five mountain ranges one behind the other
Under the sunset far into Vermont.

And the saw snarled and rattled, snarled and rattled,
As it ran light, or had to bear a load.
And nothing happened: day was all but done.
Call it a day, I wish they might have said
To please the boy by giving him the half hour
That a boy counts so much when saved from work.
His sister stood beside them in her apron
To tell them "Supper." At the word, the saw,
As if to prove saws knew what supper meant,
Leaped out at the boy's hand, or seemed to leap—
He must have given the hand. However it was,
Neither refused the meeting. But the hand!
The boy's first outcry was a rueful laugh,
As he swung toward them holding up the hand
Half in appeal, but half as if to keep
The life from spilling. Then the boy saw all—
Since he was old enough to know, big boy
Doing a man's work, though a child at heart—
He saw all spoiled. "Don't let him cut my hand off—
The doctor, when he comes. Don't let him, sister!"
So. But the hand was gone already.
The doctor put him in the dark of ether.
He lay and puffed his lips out with his breath.
And then—the watcher at his pulse took fright.
No one believed. They listened at his heart.
Little—less—nothing! —and that ended it.
No more to build on there. And they, since they
Were not the one dead, turned to their affairs.

※The title of this poem echoes the words of Shakespeare's Macbeth on receiving news that his queen is dead: "Out, out, brief candle! / Life's but a walking shadow, a poor player/ That struts and frets his hour upon the stage/ And then is heard no more. It is a tale/ Told by an idiot, full of sound and fury, / Signifying nothing." (*Macbeth* V.)

Questions:

1. How does this poem differ from a newspaper account that might have dealt with the same incident?
2. What do you think of the people who surround the boy? To whom does "they" refer? The boy's family? The doctor and hospital attendants? Casual onlookers? Do they seem to you concerned and compassionate, cruel, indifferent, or what?
3. Does the ending of this poem seem to you callous or merely realistic? Would a more tearful and sentimental ending have made the poem better or worse?

Robert Browning (1812—1889)

My Last Duchess

Ferrara *

That's my last Duchess painted on the wall,
Looking as if she were alive. I call
That piece a wonder, now; Frà Pandolf's hands
Worked busily a day, and there she stands.
Will't please you sit and look at her? I said
"Frà Pandolf" ** by design, for never read
Strangers like you that pictured countenance,
The depth and passion of its earnest glance,
But to myself they turned (since none puts by
The curtain I have drawn for you, but I)
And seemed as they would ask me, if they durst,
How such a glance came there; so, not the first
Are you to turn and ask thus. Sir, 'twas not
Her husband's presence only, called that spot
Of joy into the Duchess' cheek; perhaps
Frà Pandolf chanced to say "Her mantle laps
Over my Lady's wrist too much," or, "Paint

---

* *Ferrara*: a city in northern Italy, is the scene. Browning may have modeled his speaker after Alonzo, Duke of Ferrara (1533—1598).

** 6 *Frà Pandof*: an imaginary painter.

Must never hope to reproduce the faint
Half-flush that dies along her throat."Such stuff
Was courtesy, she thought, and cause enough
For calling up that spot of joy. She had
A heart—how shall I say? —too soon made glad,
Too easily impressed; she liked whate'er
She looked on, and her looks went everywhere.
Sir, 'twas all one! My favor at her breast,
The dropping of the daylight in the west,
The bough of cherries some officious fool
Broke in the orchard for her, the white mule
She rode with round the terrace—all and each
Would draw from her alike the approving speech,
Or blush, at least. She thanked men—good! but thanked
Somehow—I know not how—as if she ranked
My gift of a nine-hundred-years-old name
With anybody's gift. Who'd stoop to blame
This sort of trifling? Even had you skill
In speech—(which I have not)—to make your will
Quite clear to such an one, and say, "Just this
Or that in you disgusts me; here you miss.
Or there exceed the mark"—and if she let
Herself be lessoned so, nor plainly set
Her wits to yours, forsooth, and made excuse,
—E'en then would be some stooping; and I choose
Never to stoop. Oh, Sir, she smiled, no doubt,
Whene'er I passed her; but who passed without
Much the same smile? This grew; I gave commands;

Then all smiles stopped together. There she stands
As if alive. Will't please you rise? We'll meet
The company below, then. I repeat,
The Count your master's known munificence
Is ample warrant that no just pretense
Of mine for dowry will be disallowed;
Though his fair daughter's self, as I avowed
At starting, is my object. Nay, we'll go
Together down, Sir. Notice Neptune*, though,
Taming a sea-horse, thought a rarity,
Which Claus of Innsbruck** cast in bronze for me!

Questions:

1. Ferrara is in Italy. The time is during the Renaissance, probably the sixteenth century. To whom is the Duke speaking? What is the occasion? Are the Duke's remarks about his last Duchess a digression, or do they have some relation to the business at hand?
2. Characterize the Duke as fully as you can. How does your characterization differ from the Duke's opinion of himself? What kind of irony is this?
3. Why was the Duke dissatisfied with his last Duchess? What opinion do you get of the Duchess's personality, and how does it differ from the Duke opinion?
4. What happened to the Duchess? Should we have been told?

---

* 54 *Nepture*: Roman god of the sea.

** 56 *Claus of Innsbruck*: a fictitious sculptor.

5. What kind of person do you finally decide the speaker is? Why?

Li-young Lee (1957—)

I Ask My Mother to Sing

She begins, and my grandmother joins her.
Mother and daughter sing like young girls.
If my father were alive, he would play
his accordion and sway like a boat.

I've never been in Peking, or the Summer Palace,
nor stood on the great Stone Boat to watch
the rain begin on Kuen Ming Lake, the picnickers
running away in the grass.

But I love to hear it sung.
how the waterlilies fill with rain until
they overturn, spilling water into water,
then rock back, and fill with more.

Both women have begun to cry.
But neither stops her song.

Questions:

1. Why might the speaker ask the women to sing?
2. Why do the women cry? Why do they continue to sing?

Chapter 9 The Speaking Tone of Voice

Tone has been used in modern CRITICISM, following I. A. Richards's example, as a term designating the attitudes towards the subject and toward the audience implied in a literary work.

Like tone of voice, **tone** in literature often conveys an attitude toward the person addressed. Like the manner of a person, the manner of a poem may be friendly or hostile toward its reader. Again like tone of voice, the tone of a poem may tell us how the speaker feels about himself or herself: cocksure or humble, sad or glad.

But usually when we ask, "what is the tone of a poem?" we mean, "what attitude does the poet take toward a theme or a subject?" In reading a poem, although we can neither see a face nor hear a voice, we can infer the poet's attitude from other evidence. Is the poet being formal, informal, affectionate, hostile, earnest, playful, ironic or sarcastic? Clearly, tone in this sense contributes in a major way to the effect and the effectiveness of a literary work.

Strictly speaking, tone isn't an attitude; it is whatever in the poem makes an attitude clear to us: the choice of certain words instead of others, the picking out of certain details. To perceive the tone of a poem, we need to read the poem carefully, paying attention to whatever suggestions we find in it. Let's take for example Theodore Roethke's "*My Papa's Waltz.*"

My Papa's Waltz

The whiskey on your breath
Could make a small boy dizzy;
But I hung on like death:
Such waltzing was not easy.

We romped until the pans
Slid from the kitchen shelf;
My mother's countenance
Could not unfrown itself.

The hand that held my wrist
Was battered on one knuckle;
At every step you missed
My right ear scraped a buckle.

You beat time on my head
With a palm caked hard by dirt,
Then waltzed me off to bed
Still clinging to your shirt.

What is the tone of this poem? Most readers find the speaker's attitude toward his father affectionate and take this recollection of childhood to be a happy one. This is supported by the rollicking rhythms of the poem, the playfulness of a rime like *dizzy* and *easy*, the joyful suggestions of the words *waltz*, *waltzing*, and *romped*, the comic scene with kitchen pans falling and the father happily using his son's head for a drum. But some reader, because of concentrating on certain other details, thinks that the speaker takes a resentful attitude toward his father, a drunken brute with dirty hands and a whiskey breath who carelessly hurt the child's ear and manhandled him. That misunderstanding of the tone of the poem results from the reader's understanding of and concentration on certain details instead of others. He fails to feel the suggestions in the last line, with the boy *still clinging* with persistent love.

In reading a poem, the first and most important question to ask yourself is this: *Who is speaking?* Consider, for example, the following poem by Emily Dickinson.

I'm Nobody! Who Are You?

I'm Nobody! Who are you?
Are you—Nobody—too?
Then there's a pair of us!
Don't tell! they'd banish us—you know!

How dreary—to be—Somebody!
How public—like a Frog—
To tell your name—the livelong June—
To an admiring Bog!

Let's consider the sort of person we hear in "I'm Nobody! Who are you?" The voice in line 1 is rather like that of a child playing a game with a friend. In lines 2 and 3 the speaker sees the reader as a fellow spirit ("Are you—Nobody—too?") and invites the reader to join her ("Then there's a pair of us!") in forming a sort of conspiracy of silence against outsiders ("Don't tell!"). In "they'd banish us," however, we hear a word that a child would not be likely to use, and we probably feel that the speaker is a playful adult, who here is speaking to an intimate friend. And since we hear this voice, we are or we become the friend.

In the second stanza, the speaker puts aside the childlike manner. In "How dreary," the first words of the second stanza, we hear a sophisticated voice. The last two lines do at least two things: They amusingly explain to the speaker's new friend (the reader) in what way a Somebody is public (it proclaims its presence all day), and they also indicate the absurdity of the Somebody-Frog's behavior (the audience is "an admiring Bog"). By the end of the poem we are quite convinced that it is better to be a Nobody (like Dickinson's speaker and the reader) than a Somebody (a loudmouth, like a croaking frog).

In the following poem you will hear at least three voices—the voice of the person who begins the poem by telling us about a dead man ("Nobody heard him, the dead man"), the voice of the dead man ("I was much further out than you thought/ And not waving but drowning"), and the collective voice of the dead man's friends ("Poor chap, he always loved larking").

Not Waving but Drowning

Nobody heard him, the dead man,
But still he lay moaning:

I was much further out than you thought
And not waving but drowning.

Poor chap, he always loved larking
And now he's dead.
It must have been too cold for him his heart gave way,
They said.

Oh, no, no, no, it was too cold always
(Still the dead one lay moaning.)
I was much too far out all my life
And not waving but drowning.

——***Stevin Smith***

As discussed above, when we read a poem, the first thing we should do is to know whose "voice" speaks to us. "The poet's voice" is one possible answer; and in the case of many a poem, that answer may be right. And yet, we are liable to take it for granted that when the poet says "I", he or she is making a personal statement. But reflect: do all poems have to be personal? Definitely not. In many other poems, the speaker is obviously a persona, a "mask." Such a persona exists in Huck Finn, in which the use of Huck Finn gave Mark Twain as a mask through whom he could speak things he dared not utter in his own person. The *persona* is almost invariably distinct from the author; it is the voice chosen by the author for a particular artistic purpose. The speaker in a poem doesn't even have to be human; some good poems have been uttered by inanimate things, such as clouds, flowers, and etc.

Let's consider the following poem spoken not by a poet, but by a persona—a tree.

The Pruned Tree

As a torn paper might seal up its side,
Or a streak of water stitch itself to silk
And disappear, my wound has been my healing,
And I am made more beautiful by losses.
See the flat water in the distance nodding
Approval, the light that fell in love with statues,
Seeing me alive, turn its motion toward me.
Shorn, I rejoice in what was taken from me.

What can the moonlight do with my new shape
But trace and retrace its miracle of order?
I stand, waiting for the strange reaction
Of insects who knew me in my larger self,
Unkempt, in a naturalness I did not love.
Even the dog's voice rings with a new echo,
And all the little leaves I shed are singing,
Singing to the moon of shapely newness.

Somewhere what I lost I hope is springing
To life again. The roofs, astonished by me,
Are taking new bearings in the night, the owl
Is crying for a further wisdom, the lilac
Putting forth its strongest scent to find me.

Butterflies, like sails in grooves, are winging
Out of the water to wash me.
Now, I am stirring like a seed in China.

——*Howard Moss*

Questions on the poem:

1. The literal subject of the poem is how a tree can grow stronger and more beautiful by having its branches pruned. Is the poem about anything else less obvious?
2. What is the tree's attitude toward its "wound"?
3. Why would a poet want to write a poem in the voice of a tree? Is anything gained by using a non-human voice?

Countee Cullen (1903—1946)

For a Lady I Know

She even thinks that up in heaven
  Her class lies late and snores,
While poor black cherubs rise at seven
  To do celestial chores.

Questions:

1. What is Cullen's message?
2. How would you characterize the tone of this poem? Wrathful? Amused? Playful? Serious?

Mitsuye Yamada

For a Lady I Know

To the Lady

The one in San Francisco who asked:
Why did the Japanese Americans let
the government put them in
those camps without protest?

Come to think of it I
  should've run off to Canada
  should've hijacked a plane to Algeria
  should've pulled myself up from my
  bra straps
  and kicked'm in the groin
  should've bombed a bank
  should've tried self-immolation
  should've holed myself up in a
  woodframe house
  and let you watch me
  burn up on the six o'clock news
  should've run howling down the street
  naked and assaulted you at breakfast

by AP wirephoto
should've screamed bloody murder
Like Kitty Genovese *

Then
YOU would've
come to my aid in shining armor
laid yourself across the railroad track
marched on Washington
tatooed a Star of David on your arm
written six million enraged
letters to Congress

But we didn't draw the line
anywhere
law and order Executive Order 9066**
social order moral order internal order

YOU let'm
I let'm
All are punished.

---

* 21 *Kitty Genovese*: in 1964 Kitty Genovese of Kew Gardens, New York, was stabbed to death when she left her car and walked toward her home. Thirty-eight persons heard her screams, but no one came to her assistance.

** 32 *Executive Order* 9066: an authorization, signed in 1941 by President Franklin D. Roosevelt, allowing military authorities to relocate Japanese and Japanese-Americans who resided on the Pacific Coast of the United States.

Questions:

1. What is the gist of what Yamada is saying?
2. What do you think of the tone of the poem?

Lyn Lifshin (1944—)

My Mother and the Bed

No, not that way she'd
Say when I was 7, pulling
The bottom sheet smooth,
You've got to saying
Hospital corners

I wet the bed much later
Than I should, until
Just writing this I
Hadn't thought of
The connection

My mother would never
Sleep on sheets someone
Else had I never
Saw any stains on hers
Tho her bedroom was

A maze of powder hair
Pins black dresses

Sometimes she brings her
Own sheets to my house,
Carries toilet seat covers

Did anybody sleep
In my she always asks
Her sheets her hair
She says the rooms here
Smell funny

We drive at 3 a. m.
Slowly into Boston and
Strip what looks like
Two clean beds as the
Sky gets light I

Smooth on the form
Fitted flower bottom,
She redoes it
She thinks of my life
As a bed only she
Can make right

Questions:

1. What do you make of the extra spaces—for instance, the space between "to" and "saying" in line 4?
2. Would you agree that the poem is humorous and, on the whole, genial? Or do you think that bitterness overshadows the humor?

Walter De La Mare (1873—1956)

An Epitaph

Here lies a most beautiful lady:
Light of step and heart was she;
I think she was the most beautiful lady
That ever was in the West Country.

But beauty vanishes; beauty passes;
However rare—rare it be;
And when I crumble, who will remember
This lady of the West Country?

Questions:

1. Who is the speaker of the poem?
2. Do you think that the last two lines introduce a new idea, or do they deepen the implications of the earlier lines?

Chapter 10 Figures of Speech

Figures of speech refer to the various forms of expression used to convey meaning or heighten effect, often by comparing or identifying one thing with another that has a meaning or connotation familiar to the reader or listener. Figures of speech are of two major kinds: *rhetorical figures*, which are departures from customary or standard uses of language to achieve special effects without a change in the radical meaning of the words; and *tropes*, which involve a change in meaning, such as metaphor, simile, and irony.

In their broader sense, figures of speech are generally classified in five major categories: (1) figures of resemblance or relationship (e. g., simile, metaphor, parallelism); (2) figures of emphasis or understatement (e. g., hyperbole, litotes, rhetorical question, antithesis, climax, paradox, oxymoron, and irony); (3) figures of sound (e. g., alliteration, repetition, anaphora and onomatopoeia); (4) verbal games and gymnastics (e. g., pun and anagram); and (5) errors (e. g., malapropism, periphrasis, and spoonerism).

Metaphor and Simile

Metaphor is a figure of speech in which a word or phrase deno-ting one kind of object or action is used in place of another to suggest a likeness or analogy between them. I. A. Richards's distinction between the TENOR and the VEHICLE of a metaphor has been widely accepted and is very useful. The TENOR is the idea being expressed or the subject of the comparison; the VEHICLE is the IMAGE by which this idea is conveyed or the subject communi-cated. When Shakespeare writes:

> That time of year thou mayst in me behold
> When yellow leaves, or none, or few, do hang
> Upon those boughs which shake against the cold,
> Bare ruined choirs where late the sweet birds sang.

the TENOR is the loneliness and old age, the VEHICLE is the season of late fall or a tree in late fall, conveyed through a group of IMAGES unusually rich in implications. A metaphor is an implied comparison. If Shakespeare had written "I am like a tree losing its leaves," he would have stated the comparison and made a SIMILE.

In a **simile**, items from different classes are explicitly compared by a connective such as *like*, *as*, or *than* or by a verb such as *appears*, *seems*, or *resembles*. If the objects compared are from the same class, e. g., "Your fingers are like mine," no simile is present, it is a literal observation. But to say, "Your fingers are like sausages" is to use a simile. A simile is an explicit comparison. Consider Robert Burns's "*A Red, Red Rose.*"

A Red, Red Rose

O, my luve is like a red, red rose,
  That's newly sprung in June.
O, my luve is like the melodie,
  That's sweetly played in tune.

As fair art thou, my bonnie lass,
So deep in luve am I,
And I will luve thee still, my dear,
Till a' the seas gang dry.

Till a' the seas gang dry, my dear,
And the rocks melt wi' the sun!
And I will luve thee still, my dear,
While the sands o' life shall run.

And fare thee weel, my only luve,
And fare thee weel awhile!
And I will come again, my luve,
Though it were ten thousand mile!

The opening comparison in the poem ("my luve is like a red, red rose") brings before our eyes the lady's beauty in a way that the reasonable assertion "She is beautiful" does not. By comparing the woman to a rose, the poet invites us to see the woman through a special sort of lens: she is fragrant; her lips (and perhaps her cheeks) are like a rose in texture and color; she will not keep her beauty long.

Metonymy and Synecdoche

These two types of metaphor deserve special attention. In **metonymy**, the name of a thing is substituted for that of another closely related to it. "The White House," for example, is used to stand for the US President; "the crown," an object closely associated with kingship thus is made to stand for "king." In the following passage James Shirley names certain objects (scepter and crown; scythe and spade), using them to replace social classes (royalty; agricultural labor) to which they are related.

> Scepter and crown must tumble down
> And in the dust be equal made
> With the poor crooked scythe and spade.

In **synecdoche**, the whole is replaced by the part, or the part by the whole. In order to be clear, a good synecdoche must be based on an *important* part of the whole and not a minor part and, usually, the part selected to stand for the whole must be one directly associated with the subject under discussion. Thus, under the first restriction we say "threads" and "wheels" for "clothes" and "cars," and under the second we use "hands" for people who are at work at manual labor.

Another kind of metonymy is the **transferred epithet**: a device of emphasis in which the poet attributes some characteristics of a thing to another thing closely associated with it. When we read Thomas Gray's line "drowsy tinklings lull the distant folds," we know that sheep's bells *do not drowse*, but *sheep do*.

The same device turns up in such common terms as "foreign policy" and "abnormal psychology": the policy itself is not foreign but rather *domestic*— one state's policy with respect to foreign states; the psychology itself is not abnormal but rather normal—the psychological study of abnormality.

Other Figures of Speech

Personification

Personification is a figure of speech in which human characteristics are attributed to an abstract quality, animal, or inanimate object. Samuel Johnson opens his "*Vanity of Human Wishes*" (1749) with the lines:

> Let Observation with extensive view,
> Survey mankind, from China to Peru;
> Remark each anxious toil, each eager strife,
> And watch the busy scenes of crowded life;
> Then say how Hope and Fear, Desire and Hate,
> O'erspread with snares the clouded maze of Fate.

Here Johnson and his readers would picture a huge being named Observation, who would have a view extensive enough for its detailed survey, after which it could describe how four devious persons named Hope, Fear, Desire, and Hate spread their characteristic snares over the paths, covered with fog in a maze in a garden owned by a person named Fate.

Apostrophe

Hand in hand with personification often goes **apostrophe**: an address to an imaginary or absent person, a thing, or a personified abstraction. The form is frequently used in patriotic oratory, the speaker addressing some glorious leader of the past and invoking his or her aid in the present, as in Wordsworth's lines:

> Milton! thou shouldst be living at this hour:
> England hath need of thee....

Overstatement (or Hyperbole)

Overstatement or **hyperbole** is a figure of speech that is an intentional exaggeration for emphasis or comic effect. This form is common in love poetry—an example is the following passage from William Shakespeare's "*The Merchant of Venice*":

> Why, if two gods should play some heavenly match
> And on the wager lay two earthly women,
> And Portia one, there must be something else
> Pawned with the other, for the poor rule world
> Hath not her fellow.

The following lines are taken from Scanberg's "*Yankee Doodle.*" Read them and try to find what is (or are) exaggerated:

> Fath'r and I went down to camp,
> Along with Captain Good'in,
> And there we saw the men and boys
> As thick as hasty puddin'.
> ...
> And there was Captain Washington
> Upon a slapping stallion,

A giving order to his men;
I guess there was a million.

The opposite of overstatement is **understatement** or **meiosis**, which is the technique of making big things seem trifles by substituting a lighter word for emphasis or comic effect, as when in "*Romeo and Juliet*" Mercutio, knowing himself mortally wounded, replies to Benvolio's belief that the wound can't be that bad, "Ay, ay, a scratch, a scratch... 'tis not so deep as a well, nor so wide as a church door; but'tis enough, 'twill serve."

Paradox and Oxymoron

Paradox is an apparently untrue or self-contradictory statement or circumstance that proves true upon reflection or when examined in another light. The purpose of a paradox is to arrest attention and provoke fresh thought. Examples include Shakespeare's "When my love swears that she is made of truth / I do believe her, though I know she lies," Wordsworth's "The child is father of the man," and George Orwell's "All animals are equal, but some animals are more equal than others."

Paradox has a function in poetry, however, that goes beyond wit or attention-getting. Modern critics have sometimes stressed paradox as fundamental to literature, just as life itself may be seen as replete with paradoxes.

When a paradox is compressed into two words, as in "loud silence," "lonely crowd," or "living death," it is called **oxymoron**. "*Oxymoron*" itself is an oxymoron, from the Greek meaning "sharp-dull." One of the most famous examples of the use of oxymorons is the following speech by Romeo from William Shakespeare's "*Romeo and Juliet*":

Why then, O brawling love! O loving hate!
O anything, of nothing first create!
O heavy lightness! serious vanity!
Mis-shapen chaos of well-seeming forms!
Feather of lead, bright smoke, cold fire, sick health!
Still-waking sleep, that is not what it is!
This love feel I, that feel no love in this.

Pun

Pun is a figure of speech involving a play on words, usually humorous, but sometimes with serious intent. In one form of punning, a word is repeated, with a shift in meaning: "To England will I steal, and there I'll steal" (*Henry V* by William Shakespeare). In another form, a word is used to suggest a second word s pelled differently, but sounding the same, as in John Donne's "*A Hymn to God the Father*," where *son* equals *sun* and *done* is pronounced the same as the poet's name:

I have a sin of fear, that when I have spun
My last thread, I shall perish on the shore;
Swear by Thy self, that at my death Thy Son
Shall shine as he shines now and heretofore;
And, having done that, Thou hast done,
  I fear no more.

What conclusions, then, can we draw about figurative language? First, figurative language forces the reader to attend to the *connotations* (suggestions, associations) rather than to the *denotations* (dictionary definitions) of one of the terms.

Second, although figurative language is said to differ from ordinary discourse, it is found in ordinary discourse as well as in literature. "It rained cats and dogs," "I am as busy as a bee," "War is hell," and other tired figures are part of our daily utterances.

Third, good figurative language is usually (1) concrete (lending precision and vividness), (2) condensed (seen by attempting to paraphrase some of the figures), and (3) interesting (making us open our eyes wider and take notice).

Finally, the point must be made that although figurative language is one of the poet's chief tools, a poem does not have to contain figures.

Here is a poem by William Carlos Williams. Does it contain any figures of speech?

The Red Wheelbarrow

so much depends
upon

a red wheel
barrow

glazed with rain
water

beside the white
chickens.

Sylvia Plath (1932—1963)

Metaphors

I'm a riddle in nine syllables,
An elephant, a ponderous house,
A melon strolling on two tendrils.
O red fruit, ivory, fine timbers!
This loaf's big with its yeasty rising.
Money's new-minted in this fat purse.
I'm a means, a stage, a cow in calf.
I've eaten a bag of green apples.
Boarded the train there's no getting off.

Questions:

1. The speaker calls herself a "riddle in nine syllables." What is the answer to the riddle? In what sense is the poem also a riddle? How are the answers to both riddles related?
2. This poem is a riddle to be solved by identifying the literal terms of its metaphors. After you have identified the speaker ("riddles," "elephant," "house," "melon," "stage," "cow"), identify the literal meanings of the related metaphors ("syllables," "tendrils," "fruit," "ivory," "timbers," "loaf," "yeasty rising," "money," "purse," "train"). How is line 8 to be interpreted?

3. Which of the metaphors do you find amusing, shocking, or demeaning? What do these suggest about the speaker's attitude towards herself?
4. How does the form of the poem relate to its content?

Alfred, *Lord Tennyson* (1809—1892)

The Eagle

Fragment
He clasps the crag with crooked hands;
Close to the sun in lonely lands,
Ringed with the azure world, he stands.
The wrinkled sea beneath him crawls;
He watches from his mountain walls,
And like a thunderbolt he falls.

Questions:

1. What is peculiarly effective about the expressions "crooked hands," "close to the sun," "ringed with the azure world," "wrinkled," "crawls," and "like a thunderbolt"?
2. Notice the formal pattern of the poem, particularly the contrast of "he stands" in the first stanza and "he falls" in the second. Is there any other contrast between the two stanzas?

William Wordsworth (1770—1850)

London, **1802**

Milton! thou should'st be living at this hour:
England hath need of thee: she is a fen
Of stagnant waters: altar, sword, and pen,
Fireside, the heroic wealth of hall and bower,
Have forfeited their ancient English dower
Of inward happiness. We are selfish men;
Oh! raise us up, return to us again;
And give us manners, virtue, freedom, power.
Thy soul was like a star, and dwelt apart:
Thou hadst a voice whose sound was like the sea:
Pure as the naked heavens, majestic, free,
So didst thou travel on life's common way,
In cheerful godliness; and yet thy heart
The lowliest duties on herself did lay.

Questions:

1. What is the effect of Wordsworth's apostrophe to Milton?
2. In lines 3 and 4, the device of metonymy is used. What do these details represent?
3. Consider the use of overstatement, or hyperbole, from lines 2-6 and in lines 9-14. What effect does Wordsworth achieve by using the device so extensively? What does he mean by the metonymic references to *soul* (line 9) and *heart* (line 13)?

James Stephens (1862—1950)

The Wind

The wind stood up and gave a shout.
He whistled on his fingers and

Kicked the withered leaves about
And thumped the branches with his hand

And said he'd kill and kill and kill,
And so he will and so he will.

N. Scott Momaday (1934—)

Simile

What did we say to each other
that now we are as the deer
who walk in single file
with heads high
with ears forward
with eyes watchful
with hooves always placed on firm ground
in whose limbs there is latent flight.

Questions:

1. The poet never tells us what was said. Does this omission keep us from understanding the comparison?
2. The comparison is extended with each detail adding some new twist. Explain the implications of the last line.

Margaret Atwood (1939—)

You Fit Into Me

you fit into me
like a hook into an eye

a fish hook
an open eye

Questions:

1. How does the simile contribute to the poem?
2. What is the paradoxical meaning of this poem?

William Shakespeare (1564—1616)

Shall I Compare Thee to a Summer's Day?

Shall I compare thee to a summer's day?
Thou art more lovely and more temperate.
Rough winds do shake the darling buds of May,

And summer's lease hath all too short a date.
Sometime too hot the eye of heaven shines,
And often is his gold complexion dimmed;
And every fair* from fair sometimes declines,
By chance, or nature's changing course, untrimmed.
But thy eternal summer shall not fade,
Nor lose possession of that fair thou ow'st**;
Nor shall death brag thou wand'rest in his shade,
When in eternal lines to time thou grow'st.
  So long as men can breathe or eyes can see,
  So long lives this, and this gives life to thee.

Howard Moss (1922—1987)

Shall I Compare Thee to a Summer's Day?

Who says you're like one of the dog days?
You're nicer. And better.
Even in May, the weather can be gray,
And a summer sub-let doesn't last forever.
Sometimes the sun's too hot;
Sometimes it is not.
Who can stay young forever?
People break their necks or just drop dead!

---

* 7 *fair*: one
** 10 *ow'st*: have

But you? Never!
If there's just one condensed reader left
Who can figure out the abridged alphabet,
  After you're dead and gone,
  In this poem you'll live on!

Questions:

1. Identify the figurative language in the two poems.
2. Compare and contrast the two poems. Which one is more memorable? Why?
3. Can you explain Shakespeare's play on the word *untri-mmed* (line 8)? What are its possible interpretations?

Chapter 11 Imagery and Symbolism

The term **imagery**, used widely in contemporary criticism, has a great variety of meanings. In its literal sense it means the collection of IMAGES within a literary work. Though the term *image* suggests a thing seen, when speaking of images in poetry we generally mean a word or sequence of words that refers to any sensory expe-rience. The images, taken individually, are representative of things accessible to the five senses: sight, hearing, touch, taste, and smell. Thus, the water imagery of a work may be a sight (visual imagery, suggesting a picture); it may be a sound (auditory imagery, representing the sounds of a running brook); it may also be a touch (tactile imagery, if wetness or temperature is brought to mind); or even a taste or smell(gustatory or olfactory imagery, if the water is given a taste or smell).

Imagery is fundamental to literature in the primary sense that art is an imitation of nature, and an emphasis on imagery is one of the characteristics that distinguishes *imaginative writing* from *expository writing*, although that, too, may employ imagery in significant ways. Of course, this primary relation to sense impressions does not mean that the images of literature are limited to the immediate sensory experience of the writer. It is not necessary to have a swan in view in order to create the image of a swan in a poem. In this sense, the imagination is free to create images that cannot be directly experienced except through literature.

Images may be either "tied" or "free." A "tied" image is one so employed that its meaning and associational value are the same or nearly the same for all readers; and a "free" image is one not so fixed by context that its possible meanings or associational values are limited; it is, therefore, capable of having various meanings or values for various people.

Images may also be either literal or figurative. A literal image is one that involves no necessary change or extension in the obvious meaning of the words; and a figurative image is one that involves a "turn" on the literal meaning of the words. An example of a collection of literal images may be seen in Coleridge's "Kubla Khan":

> In Xanadu did Kubla Khan
> A stately pleasure-dome decree:
> Where Alph, the sacred river, ran
> Through caverns measureless to man
> Down to a sunless sea.

These images apparently represent a literal scene. But the following lines by Wordsworth show both kinds of images, literal and figurative:

> It is a beauteous evening, calm and free;
> The holy time is quiet as a Nun
> Breathless with adoration; the broad sun
> Is sinking down in its tranquillity.

The two middle lines are highly figurative, whereas the first and fourth lines are broadly literal, although there are figurative "turns" present by implication in "free" and "tranquillity."

Images standing for single things in nature tend to represent the world in simple, primary terms. When an image is made to stand for two things, as when a rose represents itself and also the color in a young woman's cheeks, the image turns into a metaphor, simile or other forms of figurative language. When an image is used so as to suggest complex or multiple meanings, as when a rose represents itself, young women generally, and also beauty and fragility or the transience of beauty, it becomes a symbol. The following poem by William Blake uses the symbol of the rose, but uses it in a non-traditional way.

The Sick Rose

O rose, thou are sick!
The invisible worm
That flies in the night
In the howling storm

Has found out thy bed
Of crimson joy
And his dark secret love
Does thy life destroy.

One might argue that the worm is "invisible" merely because it is hidden within the rose, but an "invisible worm/That flies in the night" is more than a long, slender, soft-bodied creeping animal; and a rose that has, or is, a "bed/ Of crimson joy" is more than a gardener's rose.

Blake's worm and rose suggest things beyond themselves. Many western readers hold that the worm is male, the rose female, and that the poem is about the violation of virginity. Some other readers say that the poem is about the destruction of beauty: woman's beauty, rooted in joy, is destroyed by a power that feeds on her. But these interpretations are not fully satisfying: the poem presents a worm and a rose, and yet it is not merely about a worm and a rose. These objects stimulate our thoughts about something else, but the something else is elusive, not the same thing as in Burns's "*A Red, Red Rose*".

A symbol, then, is an image so loaded with significance that it is not simply literal, and it does not simply stand for something else; it is both itself *and* something else that it richly suggests. Blake's poem is about a blighted rose and at the same time about much more. To know more about SYMBOL, read Chapter 7.

Ezra Pound (1885—1972)

In a Station of the Metro

The apparition of these faces in the crowd;
Petals on a wet, black bough.

Questions:

1. Does the image of the petals on a wet, black bough evoke

cheer or sadness? If the petals were "blooming" on a tree in the sunlight in spring, would the image be more pleasant?

2. What is the meaning of the image suggested by "apparition"? Does it suggest a positive or negative view of human life?

T. S. Eliot (1888—1965)

The Winter Evening Settles Down

The winter evening settles down
With smell of steaks in passageways.
Six o'clock.
The burnt-out ends of smoky days.
And now a gusty shower wraps
The grimy scraps
Of withered leaves about your feet
And newspapers from vacant lots;
The showers beat
On broken blinds and chimney-pots,
And at the corner of the street
A lonely cab-horse steams and stamps.
And then the lighting of the lamps.

Questions:

1. What mood is evoked by the images in Eliot's poem?
2. What kind of city neighborhood has the poet chosen to describe?

Wallace Stevens (1879—1955)

The Emperor of Ice-Cream

Call the roller of big cigars,
The muscular one, and bid him whip
In kitchen cups concupiscent curds.
Let the wenches dawdle in such dress
As they are used to wear, and let the boys
Bring flowers in last month's newspapers.
Let be be finale of seem.
The only emperor is the emperor of ice-cream.

Take from the dresser of deal*,
Lacking the three glass knobs, that sheet
On which she embroidered fantails once

And spread it so as to cover her face.
If her horny feet protrude, they come
To show how cold she is, and dumb.
Let the lamp affix its beam.
The only emperor is the emperor of ice-cream.

---

* 9 *deal*: fir or pine wood

Questions:

1. What associations does the word "emperor" have for you? The word "ice-cream"? What, then, do you make of "the emperor of ice-cream"?
2. This poem describes the preparations for a wake, and in line 15 it insists on facing the reality of death. In this context, then, what do you make of the last line of each stanza?

Robert Frost (1874—1963)

The Road Not Taken

Two roads diverged in a yellow wood,
And sorry I could not travel both
And be one traveler, long I stood
And looked down one as far as I could
To where it bent in the undergrowth;

Then took the other, as just as fair,
And having perhaps the better claim,
Because it was grassy and wanted wear;
Though as for that the passing there
Had worn them really about the same,

And both that morning equally lay
In leaves no step had trodden black.
Oh, I kept the first for another day!
Yet knowing how way leads on to way,

I doubted if I should ever come back.

I shall be telling this with a sigh
Somewhere ages and ages hence:
Two roads diverged in a wood, and I—
I took the one less traveled by,
And that has made all the difference.

Questions:

1. What symbolism do you find in this poem, if any? Back up your claim with evidence.
2. What do you think is the theme of this poem?
3. Does the speaker really take "the one less traveled by"?

T. S. Eliot (1888—1965)

The Boston Evening Transcript

The readers of the *Boston Evening Transcript*
Sway in the wind like a field of ripe corn.
When evening quickens faintly in the street,
Wakening the appetites of life in some
And to others bringing the *Boston Evening Transcript*,
I mount the steps and ring the bell, turning
Wearily, as one would turn to nod good-bye to La Rochefoucauld,
If the street were time and he at the end of the street,

And I say, "Cousin Harriet, here is the *Boston Evening Transcript.*"

Questions:

1. Do you happen to think that Eliot uses the newspaper as a symbol? If so, what is that symbolic of?
2. Why does Eliot want to communicate his meaning through symbols instead of statements?

Sharon Olds (1942—)

Rites of Passage

As the guests arrive at my son's party
They gather in the living room—
short men, men in first grade
with smooth jaws and chins.
Hands in pockets, they stand around
jostling, jockeying for place, small fights
breaking out and calming. One says to another
How old are you? Six. I'm seven. So?
They eye each other, seeing themselves
tiny in the other's pupils. They clear their
throats a lot, a room of small bankers,
they fold their arms and frown. *I could beat you*
up, a seven says to a six,
the dark cake, round and heavy as a
turret, behind them on the table. My son,
freckles like specks of nutmeg on his cheeks,

chest narrow as the balsa keel of a
model boat, long hands
cool and thin as the day they guided him
out of me, speaks up as a host
for the sake of the group.
We could easily kill a two-year-old,
he says in his clear voice. The other
men agree, they clear their throats
like Generals, they relax and get down to
playing war, celebrating my son's life.

Questions:

1. The speaker provides the details about the boys. What do the details reveal about them?
2. Some readers find the ironies in this poem to be somewhat comical, while others conclude that the poem as a whole is meant to be upsetting, even frightening. How would you describe the kinds of irony that Olds uses here?
3. Does the mother sentimentalize her own son by seeing him as better than the other boys?

William Blake (1775—1827)

The Tyger

Tyger! Tyger! burning bright
In the forests of the night,
What immortal hand or eye

Could frame thy fearful symmetry?

In what distant deeps or skies
Burnt the fire of thine eyes?
On what wings dare he aspire?
What the hand, dare seize the fire?

And what shoulder, & what art,
Could twist the sinews of thy heart?
And when thy heart began to beat,
What dread hand? & what dread feet?

What the hammer? what the chain?
In what furnace was thy brains?
What the anvil? what dread grasp
Dare its deadly terrors clasp?

When the stars threw down their spears
And water'd heaven with their tears,
Did he smile his work to see?
Did he who made the Lamb make thee?

Tyger! Tyger! burning bright
In the forests of the night,
What immortal hand or eye
Dare frame thy fearful symmetry?

Questions:

1. What do the associations of the image of "burning" suggest? And what does the image of night suggest?
2. Describe the images of lines 4 – 20. What ideas is Blake's speaker representing by these images?
3. Line 20 is a question about the image of a creator. What is implied in the question concerning the mixture of good and evil in the world?

Chapter 12 Irony

There is a kind of discourse which need not use similes, metaphors, apostrophes, personification, or symbols. Without using these figures, speakers may say things that are not to be taken literally. They may employ **irony**.

In general, **irony** is the perception of a clash or discrepancy between appearance and reality, between *seems* and *is*, between *ought* and *is*. If speakers say things that are not to be taken literally, the writer has adopted an *ironic point of view*—the speaker says one thing and we sense that the writer is in fact saying something else. For example, the word love means hate here as in "I just love to stay home and do my exercises on a Saturday night!"

Irony often occurs in stories. When we read Hemingway's "*A Clean, Well-Lighted Place*" surely we feel that most of the time the older waiter speaks for the author. Though the waiter gives us a respectful, compassionate view of a lonely old man, and we don't doubt that the view is Hemingway's, yet, in the closing lines of the story we are reminded that author and waiter are not identical. Musing on the sleepless night ahead of him, the waiter tries to shrug off his problem—"After all, it is probably only insomnia"—but the reader, who recalls the waiter's bleak view of *nada*, nothingness, knows that it certainly isn't mere insomnia that keeps him awake but a dread of solitude and death.

A poem is often made complicated and more interesting by the use of irony. In verbal irony, as the term is now used, what is *stated* in some degree negated by what is *suggested*. We had best be alert for irony, for if we miss it, our interpretations of a poem may go wild. Read Robert Creeley's "*Oh, no.*"

If you wander far enough
you will come to it
and when you get there
they will give you a place to sit

for yourself only, in a nice chair,
and all your friends will be there
with smiles on their faces
and they will likewise all have places.

This poem is rich in verbal irony. The title helps point out that between the speaker's words and attitude lie deep differences. In line 2, what is *it*? Old age? The wandering suggests a conventional me-taphor for the journey of life. Or is *it* literally a rest home for old people? We can't be sure, but the speaker's attitude toward this final sitting place is definite. It is a place for the selfish, as we infer from the phrase "for yourself only." And "smiles on their faces" may hint that the smiles are unchanging and forced. Note the difference between saying "They had smiles on their faces" and "They smiled": the latter suggests that the smiles came from within. The word "nice" is to be regarded with distrust. If we see through this speaker, we realize that, while pretending to be sweet-talking us into a seat, actually he is revealing the horror of a little hell. And the title is the poet's reaction to it: "Oh no! Not that!"

In dramatic irony, the audience's or reader's knowledge of events or individuals surpasses that of the characters. The words and actions of the characters therefore take on a different meaning for the audience or reader than they have for the play's characters. The irony may be produced when a character reacts in an inappropriate or foolish way or when a character lacks self-awareness and thus acts under false assumptions. So understood, dramatic irony is responsible for much of the interest in fiction and drama and in works of tragedy in particular, because the reader or spectator enjoys being in on the secret. For example, in Shakespeare's "*Hamlet*" (in Act I), Hamlet tells his father's ghost that he will sweep to his revenge with wings as swift as meditation or the thoughts of love, his words gather more and more dramatic irony as he dawdles on and on through most of the play. Dramatic irony can also be seen in O Henry's short story "*The Gift of the Magi*" in which James and Della, a young couple who, despite their poverty, individually resolve to give each other an elegant gift on Christmas Eve. Della sells her beautiful long hair in order to buy a platinum fob chain for Jim's antique gold watch. Meanwhile, Jim pawns his treasured watch to purchase jeweled tortoise-shell combs for Della's precious tresses. The tale concludes with the exchange of gifts and the couple's recognition of the irony of their sacrifices.

In addition to verbal irony and dramatic irony, there is situational irony—events turning to the opposite of what is expected or what should be (also called circumstantial irony and the irony of fate or, in some circumstances, cosmic irony). Situational irony is the very essence of both comedy and tragedy. The young lovers run into the worst possible luck, until everything clears up happily. The most noble spirits go to their death, while the featherheads survive.

Irony also blends with **sarcasm**, with which it is frequently confused. Sarcasm has a cutting edge. It derives from Greek *sarkazein*, "to tear the flesh." The tearing may be ironic, but it may also be straight malice, a remark intended to hurt where it hurts most. "You're a great guy; a real friend," said to a friend who won't lend you ten *yuan* is sarcastic. "Well, little man, what now?" is straight sarcasm when a dwarf interrupts the class; it is ironic sarcasm when a two-meterer bursts in.

Daniel Halpern (1945—)

How to Eat Alone

While it's still light out
set the table for one;
a red linen tablecloth,
one white plate, a bowl
for the salad
and the proper silverware.
Take out a three-pound leg of lamb,
rub it with salt, pepper and cumin,
then push in two cloves
of garlic splinters.
Place it in a 325-degree oven
and set the timer for an hour.

Put freshly cut vegetables
into a pot with some herbs
and the crudest olive oil
you can find.
Heat on a low flame.
Clean the salad.
Be sure the dressing is made
with fresh dill, mustard
and the juice of hard lemons.
Open a bottle of good late harvest zinfandel
and let it breathe on the table.
Pour yourself a glass
of cold California chardonnay
and go to your study and read.
As the story unfolds
you will smell the lamb
and the vegetables.
This is the best part of the evening:
the food cooking, the armchair,
the book and bright flavor
of the chilled wine.
When the timer goes off
toss the salad
and prepare the vegetables
and the lamb. Bring them out
to the table. Light the candles
and pour the red wine
into your glass.

Before you begin to eat,
raise your glass in honor
of yourself.
The company is the best you'll ever have.

Questions:

1. Note the reference to "you" in line 16. Who is this "you"? Is it the reader?
2. Why is Halpern so specific in giving directions for "how to eat alone"?
3. Is the final line surprising? Is it meant to be ironic or simply true?

Edna St. Vincent Millay (1892—1950)

Love Is Not All: It Is Not Meat Nor Drink

Love is not all: it is not meat nor drink
Nor slumber nor a roof against the rain;
Nor yet a floating spar to men that sink
And rise and sink and rise and sink again;
Love can not fill the thickened lung with breath.
Nor clean the blood, nor set the fractured bone;
Yet many a man is making friends with death
Even as I speak, for lack of love alone.
It well may be that in a difficult hour,
Pinned down by pain and moaning for release,
Or nagged by want past resolution's power,

I might be driven to sell your love for peace,
Or trade the memory of this night for food.
It well may be. I do not think I would.

Questions:

1. Who is the speaker? And who is the audience?
2. What are the speaker's assertions about love?

W. H. Auden (1907—1973)

The Unknown Citizen

(To JS/07/M/378
This is Marble Monument
Is Erected by the State)

He was found by the Bureau of Statistics to be
One against whom there was no official complaint,
And all the reports on his conduct agree
That, in the modern sense of an old-fashioned word, he was a saint,
For in everything he did he served the Greater Community.
Except for the War till the day he retired
He worked in a factory and never got fired,
But satisfied his employers, Fudge Motors Inc.
Yet he wasn't a scab or odd in his views,
For his Union reports that he paid his dues,
(Our report on his Union shows it was sound)

And our Social Psychology workers found
That he was popular with his mates and liked a drink.
The Press are convinced that he bought a paper every day
And that his reactions to advertisements were normal in every way.
Policies taken out in his name prove that he was fully insured,
And his Health-card shows he was once in hospital but left it cured.
Both Producers Research and High-Grade Living declare
He was fully sensible to the advantages of the Installment Plan
And had everything necessary to the Modern Man,
A phonograph, a radio, a car and a frigidaire.
Our researchers into Public Opinion are content
That he held the proper opinions for the time of year;
When there was peace, he was for peace; when there was war, he went.
He was married and added five children to the population,
Which our Eugenist says was the right number for a parent of his generation,
And our teachers report that he never interfered with their education.
Was he free? Was he happy? The question is absurd:
Had anything been wrong, we should certainly have heard.

Questions:

1. How does the epitaph at the beginning of the poem help establish the voice by which the rest of the poem is spoken?
2. What ironic discrepancies do you find between the speaker's

attitude toward the subject and that of the poet himself? By what is the poet's attitude made clear?

3. What tendencies in the modern civilization does Auden satirize?

Chapter 13 Sound

Sound as Meaning

The sounds of consonants and vowels can contribute greatly to a poem's effect. When, in a poem, the sound of words working together with meaning pleases mind and ear, the effect is euphony (pleasing, harmonious, or acoustic effect produced by words so formed and combined as to please the ear), as in Tennyson's frequented quoted lines from "*The Princess*" :

> Myriads of rivulets hurrying through the lawn,
> The moan of doves in immemorial elms,
> And murmuring of innumerable bees.

Euphony results from smooth-flowing meter or sentence rhythm as well as attractive sounds, with emphasis on vowels and on liquid consonants and semivowels(l, m, n, r, w, y). In general, vowels are considered more euphonious than consonants and back vowels(u:, u, ʌ, ə:) more euphonious than front vowels (e, i, ei, i:).

Its opposite is **cacophony**, harsh or discordant sound; more spe-cifically, harshness in the sound of words or phrases. Cacophony is usually produced by combinations of words that require a staccato, explosive delivery. In this case, the harsher sounds of stops (b, d, g, k, p, t) and fricatives (f, s, v, z) help achieve that effect. Used skillfully, intentional cacophony can vitalize the content of imagery. Three lines from Walt Whitman's "*The Dalliance of the Eagles*" illustrate cacophony:

> The clinching interlocking claws, a living, fierce,
> gyrating wheel,
> Four beating wings, two beaks, a swirling mass tight
> grappling,
> In tumbling turning clustering loops, straight
> downward falling.

Sound does carry meaning. That is, either a pleasant sound or a harsh sound is chosen for the sake of meaning. The sound of *s*, for example, can suggest the swishing of water as in Surrey's line "Calm is the sea, the waves and work less and less." The consonant sound *sl* often begins a word that conveys ideas of wetness and smoothness—*slick*, *slimy*, *slippery*, and *slush*. And then, is sound always identical with meaning? Definitely not. In the three lines from Tennyson, for instance, the cooing of doves is not *exactly a moan*. The words *slave* and *slow* have nothing to do with wetness and smoothness.

Relating sound more closely to meaning, the device called onomatopeia is an attempt to represent a thing or action by a vocal imitation of the sound associated with it (such as buzz, hiss, crash, crack, bang, ding-dong, pitter-patter, etc.). This occurs frequently in poetry, where a line of verse can express a characteristic of the thing being portrayed. The following lines from "*The Brook*" by Alfred, Lord Tennyson are an example:

I chatter over stony ways,
In little sharps and trebles,
I bubble into eddying bays,
I babble on the pebbles.

Alliteration, Assonance and Consonance

Alliteration is often defined as the repetition of initial identical consonant sounds or any vowel sounds in successive or closely asso-ciated syllables, especially stressed syllables. A good example of consonantal alliteration is Coleridge's lines:

The fair breeze blew, the white foam flew,
The furrow followed free.

Alliteration is found in many common phrases, such as "pretty as a picture" and "dead as a doornail." In its simplest form, it reinforces one or two consonantal sounds, as in this line from William Shakespeare's "*Sonnet* XII":

When I do count the clock that tells the time

or as in Coleridge's lines above reinforcing the image of the sea waves.

Note, however, we recognize alliteration by sound, not by spelling: *Know* and *nail* alliterate, but *know* and *key* do not.

As a poetic device, alliteration is often discussed with **assonance** and **consonance**. In prosody, assonance is defined as the repetition of stressed vowel sounds within words with different end consonants as in the phrase "quite like." In this sense, assonance is to be distinguished from regular rhyme, in which initial consonants differ but both vowel and end-consonant sounds are identical, as in the phrase "quite right." To make it clear, *lake* and fate demonstrate rhyme; *lake* and *fate* assonance.

As a poetic device, internal assonance is usually combined with alliteration to enrich the texture of the poetic line. Sometimes two or more vowel sounds are repeated, as in the opening lines of Percy Bysshe Shelley's "*The Indian Serenade*":

> *I* ar*i*se from dr*ea*ms of th*ee*
> in the first sw*ee*t sl*ee*p of n*i*ght.

Assonance is common substitution for end rhyme (the rhyming words occurring at the ends of the lines). Such substitution of assonance for end rhyme is found more frequently in modern poetry. Their use of assonance instead of end rhyme was often adopted by such poets as W. H. Auden, Stephen Spender, and Dylan Thomas. As an enriching ornament within the line, assonance is of great use to the poets. It is extensively used for musical effect. And it also slows the reader down and focuses attention.

One more poetic device relating to alliteration and assonance is **consonance**, the repetition of identical consonant sounds and differing vowel sounds in words in proximity (*fail* and *feel*; *rough* and *roof*). Sometimes consonance is more loosely defined merely as the repetition of a consonant (*fail* and *peel*). Frequently found within a line of poetry, consonance also substitutes at times for end rhyme as in Emily Dickinson's "*I Like to See It Lap the Miles*":

I like to see it lap the Miles—
And lick the Valleys up—
And stop to feed itself at Tanks—
And then—prodigious step

Around a Pile of mountains—
And supercilious peer
In Shanties—by the sides of Roads—
And then a Quarry pare

To fit its Ribs
And crawl between
Complaining all the while
In horrid-hooting stanza—
Then chase itself down Hill—

And neigh like Boanerges *
Then—punctual as a Star
Stop—docile and omnipotent
At its own stable door—

Rhyme

A **rhyme** (or **rime**) occurs when two or more words or phrases contain an identical or similar vowel-sound, usually stressed, and the consonant sounds that follow the vowel sound are

* 14 *Boanerges*: a name said to mean "Sons of Thunder"

identical and preceded by different consonants. That is, *fan* and *ran* constitute true rhymes because the vowel and succeeding consonant sounds ("*an*") are the same but the preceding consonants are different. Rhyme, in this case, is related to assonance and alliteration, but it is unlike them in construction and in being commonly used at stipulated intervals, whereas assonance and alliteration are likely to range with relative freedom through various positions.

The types of rhyme are classified according to three schemes: (1) the sound of syllables involved, (2) the number of syllables involved, and (3) the position of the rhymed syllables in the line.

On the basis of sound, we have: 1) **exact** (full, true, perfect, complete, whole) **rhymes**, repeating end sounds precisely (*foe* and *toe*; *meet* and *fleet*, *buffer* and *rougher*); 2) **slant** (half, approximate, imperfect, near, off, oblique) **rhyme**, providing an approximation of the sound (*cat* and *cot*, *hope* and *cup*; *defeated* and *impeded*); 3) **identical rhyme**, repeating the entire sound, including the initial consonant, sometimes by repeating the same word in a rhyme position and sometimes by repeating the sound with two senses (*two* and *too*); and 4) **eye rhymes**, looking alike, but sounding different as in

> If this be error, and upon me *proved*,
> I never writ, nor no man ever *loved*.

On the basis of the number of syllables presenting similarity of sound, we have: 1) **masculine rhyme**, where the correspondence of sound is restricted to the final stressed syllable (*stark* and *mark*, *support* and *retort*) ; 2) **feminine rhyme** (or double rhyme), where stressed rhyming syllables are followed by identical unstressed syllables (*revival* and *arrival*; *flatter* and *batter*, *fountain* and *mountain*) ; and 3) **triple rhyme**, where the rhyming stressed syllable is followed by two identical unstressed syllables (*machinery* and *scenery*, *tenderly* and *slenderly*, *glorious* and *victorious*). Although triple rhyme has been used for serious work, it is usually used to help achieve a humorous or satirical effect.

Rhymes may also be classified by position. Most rhyme is **end rhyme** (or **terminal rhyme**), which occurs at the end of a line of poetry. **Initial rhyme** (or **beginning rhyme**) comes at the beginning, and is sometimes combined with end rhyme, as in these lines from Sidney Lanier's "*Symphony*":

> *Vainly* might Plato's brain *revolve it.*
> *Plainly* the heart of a child could *solve it.*

Internal rhyme (sometimes called leonine rhyme) occurs within one line or in successive middles, as in "And wears man's smudge and shares man's smell..." **Crossed rhyme** (or interlaced rhyme) combines internal and end rhyme in an interlaced pattern, giving a long-line couplet the sound of a short-line quatrain, as in Swinburne's "*Hymn to Proserpine*":

> Laurel is green for a *season*, and love is sweet for a *day*,
> But love grows bitter with *treason*, and laurel outlives not *May*.

Rhyme is more than a mere ornament or device of *versification*, for it performs valuable functions. The ear of the reader recognizes a sound already echoing in the consciousness, and the accord the two similar sounds set up is likely to bring the reader a sensuous gratification. The recurrence of rhyme at regular intervals helps to establish the form of the stanza. Rhyme serves to unify and distinguish divisions of a poem, since it is likely that the rhyme sounds followed in one stanza will be changed when the next stanza is started. The fact that these qualities, as well as others, reside in rhyme will be summed up as four essential functions: pleasurable, mnemonic, structural, and rhetorical.

Galway Kinnell (1927—)

Blackberry Eating

I love to go out in late September
among the fat, overripe, icy, black blackberries
to eat blackberries for breakfast,
the stalks very prickly, a penalty
they earn for knowing the black art
of blackberry-making; and as I stand among them
lifting the stalks to my mouth, the ripest berries
fall almost unbidden to my tongue,
as words sometimes do, certain peculiar words
like *strengths* or *squinched*,
many-lettered, one-syllabled lumps,
which I squeeze, squinch open, and splurge well
in the silent, startled, icy, black language

of blackberry-eating in late September.

Questions:

1. Read aloud the poem. What sense can you get from the sounds? Any fun?
2. In lines 7—10, what does Kinnell compare eating blackberries to?

T. S. Eliot (1888—1965)

Virginia

Red river, red river,
Slow flow heat is silence
No will is still as a river
Still. Will heat move
Only through the mocking-bird
Heard once? Still hills
Wait. Gates wait. Purple trees,
White trees, wait, wait,
Delay, decay. Living, living,
Never moving. Ever moving
Iron thoughts came with me
And go with me:
Red river, river, river.

Questions:

1. Analyze the poem for language with ear-appeal. What are the poem's sound features?

2. How is the poem's sound connected with its meaning?

A. E. Housman (1859—1936)

Eight O'Clock

He stood, and heard the steeple
  Sprinkle the quarters on the morning town.
One, two, three, four, to market-place and people
  It tossed them down.

Strapped, noosed, nighing his hour,
  He stood and counted them and cursed his luck;
And then the clock collected in the tower
  Its strength, and struck.

Questions:

1. Why does the protagonist in this brief drama curse his luck? What is his situation?
2. For so short a poem, "Eight O'Clock" carries a great weight of alliteration? What effect is created by all this heavy emphasis?

Robert Frost (1874—1963)

Desert Places

Snow falling and night falling fast, oh, fast

In a field I looked into going past,
And the ground almost covered smooth in snow,
But a few weeds and stubble showing last.

The woods around it have it—it is theirs.
All animals are smothered in their lairs,
I am too absent-spirited to count;
The loneliness includes me unawares.

And lonely as it is, that loneliness
Will be more lonely ere it will be less—
A blanker whiteness of benighted snow
With no expression, mothing to express.

They cannot scare me with their empty spaces
Between stars—on stars where no human races is.
I have it in me so much nearer home
To scare myself with my own desert places.

Questions:

1. What are these desert places that the speaker finds in himself?
2. Notice how many times, within lines 8—10, Frost says *lonely* (or *loneliness*). What other words in the poem contain similar sounds that reinforce these words?
3. In the closing stanza, the feminine rimes *spaces*, *race is*, and *places* might well occur in light or comic verse. Does "*Desert Places*" leave you laughing?

Chapter 14 Rhythm

The technical vocabulary of prosody (the study of the principles of verse structure, including meter, rhyme, stress and stanzaic patterns) is large. An understanding of these terms is helpful to one to discuss some aspects of poetry more efficiently. Here the terms **rhythm**, **meter** and **foot** are to be discussed.

When we speak of the **rhythm** of a poem we mean the recurrence of specific sounds or kinds of sounds or the recurrence of str-essed and unstressed syllables. In English poetry, the rhythmic pattern is most often established by a combination of *stress* (accent) and number of syllables. This pattern of a fairly regular number of syllables with a relatively fixed sequence of stressed and unstressed syllables leads itself to certain kinds of basic rhythmic analysis in English verse structures.

Most English poetry has a pattern of *stressed* (*accented*) sou-nds, and this pattern is the meter, the rhythm established by the regular or almost regular occurrence of similar units of sound pattern.

In a line of poetry, the foot is the basic unit of measurement. On rare occasions it is a single stressed syllable, but generally a foot consists of two or three syllables, one of which is stressed. (Stress is indicated by—, and lack of stress by ◡.) The repetition of feet, then, produces a pattern of stresses throughout the poem.

Two cautions:

1. A poem will seldom contain only one kind of foot throughout; significant variations usually occur, but one kind of foot is dominant.
2. In reading a poem one pays attention to the sense as well as to the metrical pattern. By paying attention to the sense, one often finds that the stress falls on a word that according to the metrical pattern would be unstressed. Or a word that according to the pattern would be stressed may be seen to be unstressed. The most common feet in English poetry are the four listed below:

Iamb (**iambic**): one unstressed syllable followed by one stressed syllable (◡—). The iamb is the most common in English poetry. The following example, taken from Tennyson's "*The Eagle*," has four iambic feet (but with two inverted feet):

— ◡ ◡ — ◡ — ◡ —
Close to | the sun | in lone- | ly lands, |

— ◡ ◡ — ◡ — ◡ —
Ringed with | the az- | ure world | he stands. |

Anapest (**anapestic**): two unstressed syllables followed by one stressed (◡ ◡—). The following lines from Shelley's "*The Cloud*" are anapestic:

◡ ◡ — ◡ ◡ — ◡ ◡ —
Like a child | from the womb, | like a ghost |
◡ ◡ —
from the tomb, |
◡ ◡ — ◡ ◡ — ◡ ◡ —
I a rise | and unbuild | it again. |

These two are also called rising meter, which goes from light to heavy.

Trochee (**trochaic**): one strcssed syllable followed by one unstressed, as in Longfellow's "*A Psalm of Life*":

— ◡ | — ◡ | — ◡ | — ◡
Tell me | not in | mourn ful | numb er s |

Trochaics are generally unpopular with poets for sustained writing, but for lyrics the trochee has been popular. Long rhymed trochaic poems are extremely rare, since all the *rhymes* would have to be *feminine*, and such rhymes are relatively few and can be monotonous.

Dactyl (**dactylic**): one stressed syllable followed by two unstressed, as in Longfellow's "*Evangeline*":

— ◡ ◡ | — ◡ ◡ | — ◡ ◡ | — ◡ ◡
This is the | for est prim- | ev al. The | murmur ing

— ◡ ◡ | — ◡
| pines and the | hemlocks |

— ◡ ◡ | —
Bearded with | moss....

This trisyllabic foot, in general, like the anapest, is common in light verse or verse suggesting joy.

The above two are also called falling meter, which goes from heavy to light.

In addition to the four mentioned already, there are **spondee** (**spondaic**), a foot composed of two stressed syllable and pyrrhic, a foot of two unstressed syllables, which is unusual in English poetry.

A metrical line consists of one or more feet and is named for the number of feet in it. The following names are used:

monometer:	one foot	pentameter:	five feet
dimeter:	two feet	hexameter:	six feet
trimeter:	three feet	heptameter:	seven feet
tetrameter:	four feet	octameter:	eight feet

Meter produces rhythm, recurrences at equal intervals, but rhythm is usually applied to large units than feet. Often it depends most obviously on pauses. If a line ends in a full pause—usually indicated by some mark of punctuation—we call it end-stopped. A line that does not end in punctuation and that therefore is read with only a slight pause after it is called a run-on line. Because a run-on line gives us only part of a phrase, clause, or sentence, we have to read on to the line or lines following, in order to complete a thought. Most of the lines from Robert Browning's "*My Last Duchess*" are run-on lines.

To sum up: rhythm is recurrence. In poems, it is made of stresses and pauses. The poet can produce it by making the intervals between stresses fixed or varied; by indicating pauses within lines; by end-stopping lines or running them over. Rhythm in itself cannot convey meaning. And yet if a poet's words have meaning, their rhy-thm must be one with it.

Let us take John Keats's "*The Eve of St. Agnes*" for example and describe it in terms of *stresses*, *feet*, *meter* and *rhythm*:

◡ — ◡ — ◡ — ◡ — ◡ —
And still | she slept | an az | ure-lid | ded sleep |

◡ — ◡ — ◡ — ◡ — ◡ —
In blanch | ed lin | en, smooth | and lav | enaered, |

◡ — ◡ — ◡ — ◡ — ◡ —
While he | from forth | the clos | et brought | a heap |

◡ — ◡ — ◡ — ◡ — ◡ —
Of can | died ap | ple, quince, | and plum, | and gourd; |

◡ — ◡ — ◡ — ◡ — ◡ —
With jel | lies sooth | er than | the cream | y curd, |

◡ — ◡ — ◡ — ◡ — ◡ —
And lu | cent syr | ops, tinct | with cin | na mon; |

— ◡ ◡ — ◡ — ◡ — ◡ —
Manna | ana dates, | in ar | go sy | transferred |

◡ — ◡ — ◡ — ◡ — ◡ —
From Fez; | and spic | ed dain | ties, ev | ery one |

◡ — ◡ — ◡ — ◡ — ◡ — ◡ —
From silk | en Sam | ar cand | to ce | dared Leb | a non. |

Such a mechanical marking of *stresses* and division into *feet* discloses that the rhythm of the stanza is predominantly composed of one unstressed syllable followed by a stressed, called an iambic foot, as explained previously. Next we discover that characteristically there are five of these feet to the line; such a line is called pentameter. We are now, as the result of our scanning, prepared to state that the rhythm and meter of the poem can be summed up as iambic pentameter. As our example stanza is scanned, there are only two obvious exceptions to this pattern: 1) the first foot of the seventh line consists of a stressed syllable preceding an unstressed (and is thus a trochee), and 2) the ninth line consists of six feet instead of five (and is thus a hexameter). So, finally, we have found that this stanza consists of eight iambic pentameter lines with a ninth that is hexameter—a pattern called the Spenserian stanza, whose rhyme scheme is *ababbcbcc.* (As for this, see more in the next chapter.)

Thomas Hardy (1840—1928)

The Man He Killed

"Had he and I but met
By some old ancient inn,
We should have sat us down to wet
Right many a nipperkin!"

"But ranged as infantry,
And staring face to face,
I shot at him as he at me,
And killed him in his place."

"I shot him dead because—
Because he was my foe.
Just so: my foe of course he was;
That's clear enough; although"

"He thought he'd' list, perhaps,
Off-hand like—just as I—
Was out of work—had sold his traps—
No other reason why."

"Yes; quaint and curious war is!
You shoot a fellow down
You'd treat if met where any bar is,
Or help to half-a-crown."

Questions:

1. What situation and event is the speaker recalling and relating?
2. What is the speaker's attitude toward his "foe" and toward what he has done?

Robert Frost (1874—1963)

Stopping by Woods on a Snowy Evening

Whose woods these are I think I know.
His house is in the village though;
He will not see me stopping here
To watch his woods fill up with snow.

My little horse must think it queer
To stop without a farmhouse near
Between the woods and frozen lake
The darkest evening of the year.

He gives his harness bells a shake
To ask if there is some mistake.
The only other sound's the sweep

Of easy wind and downy flake.

The woods are lovely, dark and deep,
But I have promises to keep,
And miles to go before I sleep,
And miles to go before I sleep.

Questions:

1. Why do you suppose that the speaker wants to watch the "woods fill up with snow"?
2. The last stanza offers two alternative attitudes and courses of action. What are they? Which does the speaker choose?

Chapter 15 Stanzaic Forms

Lines of poetry are commonly arranged in a rhythmical unit called a stanza. A **stanza** is sometimes called a verse paragraph. More strictly, a stanza is a grouping of a prescribed number of lines in a given *meter*, usually with a particular *rhyme scheme*, repeated as a unit of structure. As structural units, stanzas stand apart like rooms in the house of the poem, each worthy of separate consideration, but each bound structurally to the whole. In discussing stanzas, rhymes are indicated by identical letters. Thus *a b a b* indicates that the first and third lines rhyme with each other, while the second and fourth lines are linked by a different rhyme. Common stanzaic forms in English poetry are the following:

Couplet: a stanza of two lines with similar end-rhymes. Formally, the couplet is a two-line stanza with both grammatical structure and idea complete within itself. A couplet in which the sense is relatively independent is a closed couplet. It is "closed" in the sense that its meaning is complete within the two lines and does not depend on what precedes or follows for its grammatical structure or thought. Almost all instances in English are *iambic tetrameter* or *pentameter*, as in these closed couplets by William Blake and Alexander Pope:

> A dog starved at his Master's Gate
> Predicts the ruin of the State.

A little learning is a dang'rous Thing;
Drink deep, or taste not the Pierian Spring.

A couplet that cannot stand alone, or in which the sense of the second line runs on to the next couplet for completion, is an open couplet.

Couplets are most frequently used as units of composition in long poems; but since they lend themselves to pithy, epigrammatic statements, they are often composed as independent poems or function as parts of other verse forms. William Shakespeare always concluded his sonnets with a couplet.

Heroic couplet: a rhyming couplet of iambic pentameter, with a fairly heavy pause at the end of the first line and a still heavier one at the end of the second. Commonly, there is a *parallel* or an *antithesis* (contrast) within a line or between the two lines, as in Denham's famous apostrophe to the Thames from "*Cooper's Hill*":

O could I flow like thee, and make thy stream
My great example, as it is my theme:
Tho'deep, yet clear; tho'gentle, yet not dull;
Strong without rage; without o'verflowing full.

Another example is from Pope's "*Eloisa to Abelard*":

Then share thy pain, allow that sad relief;
Ah, more than share it, give me all thy grief.

It is called "heroic" because in England in the eighteenth

century, it was much used for heroic (epic) poems.

Triplet (or Tercet): a unit or group of three lines of verse, usually containing rhyme, as in Herrick's "*Upon Julia's Clothes*," and Shakespeare's "*The Phoenix and the Turtle*":

Whenas in silks my Julia goes
Then, then (methinks) how sweetly flows
That liquefaction of her clothes.

Death is now the phoenix'nest
And the turtle's loyal breast
To eternity doth rest, ...

Quatrain: a stanza of four lines, rhymed or unrhymed. The possible rhyme schemes vary from an unrhymed quatrain to almost any arrangement of one-rhyme, two-rhyme, or three-rhyme lines. Perhaps the most common form is the *abab* sequence; other popular rhyme patterns are *aabb*; *abba*; *aabc*; *abcb*.

Sonnet: a fixed verse form of Italian origin consisting of 14 lines that are characteristically in iambic pentameter. The sonnet is unique among poetic forms in western literature in that it has retained its appeal for major poets for more than six centuries. There are two principal sonnet forms: the Italian or Petrarchan sonnet, named for the Italian poet Francesco Petrarch (1304—1374) and the English or Shakespearean sonnet.

The Petrarchan sonnet typically treats its theme in two parts. The first eight lines, the *octave*, state a problem, ask a question, or express an emotional tension. The last six lines the *sestet*, resolve the problem, answer the question, or relieve the tension. The *octave is rhymed abba abba*. The rhyme scheme of the *sestet* varies; it may be *cde cde*, *cdc cdc*, *or cd cd cd*, or in some variant pattern, but with no closing couplet.

The Shakespearean sonnet is usually arranged into three quatrains and a couplet, rhyming *abab cdcd efef gg*. A Shakespearean sonnet frequently introduces a subject in the first quatrains, expands it in the second, and once more in the third, and concludes in the couplet.

Named variations on the sonnet include the Spenerian and Miltonic. **A Spenserian sonnet** (or link sonnet) employs three quatrains linked by rhyme, followed by a couplet: *abab bcbc cdcd ee*. **A Miltonic sonnet** is simply an Italian sonnet that eliminates the pause between octave and sestet. Other variations include blendings of the two forms.

Dylan Thomas (1914—1953)

Do Not Go Gentle Into That Good Night

Do not go gentle into that good night,
Old age should burn and rave at close of day;
Rage, rage against the dying of the light.

Though wise men at their end know dark is right,
Because their words had forked no lightning they
Do not go gentle into that good night.

Good men, the last wave by, crying how bright
Their frail deeds might have danced in a green bay,
Rage, rage against the dying of the light.

Wild men who caught and sang the sun in flight,
And learn, too late, they grieved it on its way,
Do not go gentle into that good night.

Grave men, near death, who see with blinding sight
Blind eyes could blaze like meteors and be gay,
Rage, rage against the dying of the light.
And you, my father, there on the sad height,
Curse, bless, me now with your fierce tears, I pray.
Do not go gentle into that good night.
Rage, rage against the dying of the light.

Questions:

1. What can you surmise about the speaker? And the listener?
2. What four different kinds of men does the speaker discuss in lines 4–15?
3. What puns and connotative words can you find in this poem? Consider the *good* of "good night" and the word *grave* (line 13).
4. What does the speaker want the listener to do? What is the poem's theme?

Michael Drayton (1563—1631)

Since There Is No Help, Come Let Us Kiss and Part

Since there's no help, come let us kiss and part;
Nay, I have done, you get no more of me,
And I am glad, yea, glad with all my heart
That thus so cleanly I myself can free;
Shake hands for ever, cancel all our vows,
And when we meet at any time again,
Be it not seen in either of our brows
That we one jot of former love retain.
Now at the last gasp of Love's latest breath,
When, his pulse failing, Passion speechless lies,
When Faith is kneeling by his bed of death,
And Innocence is closing up his eyes,
  Now if thou wouldst, when all have given him over,
  From death to life thou-mightst him yet recover.

Elizabeth Barrett Browning (1806—1861)

Grief

I tell you, hopeless grief is passionless;
  That only men incredulous of despair,
  Half-taught in anguish, through the midnight air

Beat upward to God's throne in loud access
Of shrieking and reproach. Full desertness
  In souls, as countries, lieth silent-bare
  Under the blanching, vertical eye-glare
Of the absolute Heavens. Deep-hearted man, express
Grief for the Dead in silence like to death:
  Most like a monumental statue set
In everlasting watch and moveless woe
Till itself crumble to the dust beneath.
  Touch it: the marble eyelids are not wet—
If it could weep, it could arise and go.

Questions:

1. Both of the above poems are made up of 14 lines. What difference can you find between them as far as the rhyme schemes are concerned?
2. How would you find the division in thought in each of the poems?
3. What is the relationship of the last two lines to the rest of the sonnet?

Edward Arlington Robinson (1869—1935)

Richard Cory

Whenever Richard Cory went down town,
We people on the pavement looked at him:
He was a gentleman from sole to crown,

Clean favored, and imperially slim.

And he was always quietly arrayed,
And he was always human when he talked;
But still he fluttered pulses when he said,
"Good morning," and he glittered when he walked.

And he was rich—yes, richer than a king—
And admirably schooled in every grace:
In fine, we thought that he was everything
To make us wish that we were in his place.

So on we worked, and waited for the light,
And went without the meat, and cursed the bread;
And Richard Cory, one calm summer night,
Went home and put a bullet through his head.

Questions:

1. What is the effect of using "down town," "pavement," "meat," and "bread" in connection with the people who admire Richard Cory?
2. What are the connotations and implications of the name *Richard Cory*? Of the word *gentleman*?
3. What ideas about the human condition does this poem explore?

Chapter 16 Open Form

A poem in open form, generally speaking, has neither a rhyme scheme nor a basic meter informing the whole of it. A good deal of English poetry is unrhymed, much of it in **free verse**: a kind of verse based on the irregular rhythmic cadence of the recurrence, with va-riations, of phrases, images, and syntactical patterns rather than the conventional use of meter. *Rhyme* may or may not be present in free verse, but when it is, it is used with great freedom. In conventional verse, the unit is the *foot*, or the line; in free verse the units are larger, being words, phrases, sentences and sometimes paragraphs. Such poetry may seem formless; Robert Frost, who strongly preferred regular meter and rhyme, said that he would not consider writing free verse any more than he would consider playing tennis without a net. But free verse does have a form or a pattern, often largely based on repetition and parallel grammatical structure. The term is loosely applied to the poetry of Walt Whitman, whose "*When I Heard the Learn'd Astronomer*" is a typical example:

> When I heard the learn'd astronomer,
> When the proofs, the figures, were ranged in columns
>   before me,
> When I was shown the charts and diagrams, to add, to
>   divide, and measure them,

When I sitting heard the astronomer where he lectured with much applause in the lecture-room,
How soon unaccountable I became tired and sick,
Till rising and gliding out I wander'd off by myself.
In the mystical moist night-air, and from time to time,
Look'd up in perfect silence at the stars.

What can be said about the rhythmic structure of this poem? Rhymes are absent, and the lines vary greatly in the number of syllables, ranging from 9 (the first line) to 23 (the fourth line), but when we read the poem we sense a rhythmic structure. The first four lines obviously hang together, each beginning with "when"; indeed, three of these lines begin with "When I." We may notice, too, that each of these four lines has more syllables than its predecessor (the numbers are 9, 14, 18, and 23); this increase in length, like the initial repetition, is a kind of pattern. But then, with the fifth line, which speaks of fatigue and surfeit, there is a shrinkage to 14 syllables, offering an enormous relief from the previous swollen line with its 23 syllables.

The second half of the poem also has a pattern, and this pattern is more or less the reverse of the first half of the poem. We may notice too that the last line (in which the poet, now released from the oppressive lecture hall, is in communion with nature) is very close to an iambic pentameter line; that is, the poem concludes with a metrical form said to be the most natural in English. The effect of naturalness or ease in this final line, moreover, is increased by the absence of repetitions (e. g., not only of "When I," but even of such syntactic repetitions as "charts and diagrams," "tired and sick," "rising and gliding") that characterize most of the previous lines. This final effect of naturalness is part of a carefully constructed pattern in which rhythmic structure is part of meaning.

Another kind of unrhymed poetry is **blank verse**, unrhymed iambic pentameter. This form, generally accepted as that best adapted to dramatic verse in English, is commonly used for long poems whether dramatic or narrative. The freedom gained through lack of rhyme is offset by the demands for variety, which may be obtained by the skillful poet through a number of means: the shifting of pause, from place to place within the line; the shifting of the stress among syllables; the use of the run-on line, which permits thought-grouping in large or small blocks; variation in tonal qualities by changing the level of diction from passage to passage; and, finally the adaptation of the form to reflect differences in the speech of characters and in emotional expression.

Some poems, to be sure, seem more widely open in form than others. A poet, for instance, may employ rhyme, but have the rhymes recur at various intervals; or perhaps rhyme lines of various length. Many poets have even written prose poems, works in prose form that have some of the technical or literary qualities of poems, such as regular rhythm, definitely patterned structure, or emotional or imaginative heightening. But the poet prints words in a block like a prose paragraph. Read Carolyn Forche's "*The Colonel*":

> What you have heard is true. I was in his house. His wife carried a tray of coffee and sugar. His daughter filed her nails, his son went out for the night. There were daily papers, pet dogs, a pistol on the cushion beside him. The moon swung

bare on its black cord over the house. On the television was a cop show. It was in English. Broken bottles were embedded in the walls around the house to scoop the kneecaps from a man' legs or cut his hands to lace. On the windows there were gratings like those in liquor stores. We had dinner, rack of lamb, good wine, a gold bell was on the table for calling the maid. The maid brought green mangoes, salt, a type of bread. I was asked how I enjoyed the country. There was a brief commercial in Spanish. He is wife took everything away. There was some talk then of how difficult it had become to govern. The parrot said hello on the terrace. The colonel told it to shut up, and pushed himself from the table. My friend said to me with his eyes: say nothing. The colonel returned with a sack used to bring groceries home. He spilled many human ears on the table. They were like dried peach halves. There is no other way to say this. He took one of them in his hands, shook it in our faces, dropped it into a water glass. It came alive there. I am tired of fooling around he said. As for the rights of anyone, tell your people they can go fuck themselves. He swept the ears to the floor with his arm and held the last of his wine in the air. Something for your poetry, no? he said. Some of the ears on the floor caught this scrap of his voice. Some of the ears on the floor were pressed to the ground.

May 1978

Stephen Crane (1871—1900)

The Heart

In the desert
I saw a creature, naked, bestial,
Who, squatting upon the ground,
Held his heart in his hands,
And ate of it.

I said, "Is it good, friend?"
"It is bitter—bitter," he answered;
"But I like it
Because it is bitter,
And because it is my heart."

Questions:

1. What is Crane attempting to say in the poem?
2. Is Crane exploring human nature? If so, what is it?

Wallace Stevens (1879—1955)

Thirteen Ways of Looking at a Blackbird

I

Among twenty snowy mountains,

The only moving thing
Was the eye of the blackbird.

II

I was of three minds,
Like a tree
In which there are three blackbirds.

III

The blackbird whirled in the autumn winds.
It was a small part of the pantomime.

IV

A man and a woman
Are one.
A man and a woman and a blackbird
Are one.

V

I do not know which to prefer,
The beauty of inflections
Or the beauty of innuendoes,
The blackbird whistling
Or just after.

VI

Icicles filled the long window
With barbaric glass.

The shadow of the blackbird
Crossed it, to and fro.
The mood
Traced in the shadow
An indecipherable cause.

VII

O thin men of Haddam,
Why do you imagine golden birds?
Do you not see how the blackbird
Walks around the feet
Of the women about you?

VIII

I know noble accents
And lucid, inescapable rhythms;
But I know, too,
That the blackbird is involved
In what I know.

IX

When the blackbird flew out of sight,
It marked the edge
Of one of many circles.

X

At the sight of blackbirds
Flying in a green light,

Even the bawds of euphony
Would cry out sharply.

XI

He rode over Connecticut
In a glass coach.
Once, a fear pierced him,
In that he mistook
The shadow of his equipage
For blackbirds.

XII

The river is moving.
The blackbird must be flying.

XIII

It was evening all afternoon.
It was snowing
And it was going to snow.
The blackbird sat
In the cedar-limbs.

Questions:

1. What do the landscapes of winter contribute to the poem's effectiveness?
2. What role does imagery play in Steven's statements of his ideas?
3. Consider any one of the thirteen parts. What patterns of sound

and rhythm do you find in it? What kind of structure does it have?

4. Does the poem seem an arbitrary combination of thirteen separate poems?

Drama

Chapter 17 The Elements of Drama

The word drama is derived from the Greek word *dran*, which means "to do" or "to act." Although "drama" is often used as a synonym for "play," the word drama can also refer to a group of plays, such as Elizabethan drama, or to all plays collectively.

Types of Drama

Aristotle divided all drama into tragedy and comedy. Tragedy **involves** the downfall of a hero or heroine; it begins in prosperity and ends in adversity. **Comedy** describes the reformation of a group of people or a society; it begins in adversity and resolves in prosperity. To a much fuller definition of tragedy and comedy, see the next two chapters.

Pure forms of tragedy and comedy have rarely appeared in modern drama; most British and American plays offer some mixture of the two forms. That is, tragedies may include witty and humorous scenes, and comedies often deal with serious and threatening problems. When the patterns and emotions are mixed, the play is called a **tragicomedy**, a term commonly used to refer to plays that offer a mixture of tragic and comic effects. In many ways, tragicomedy is the dominant form of twentieth-century drama.

Other forms of drama that have to do with tragedy and comedy include **farce**, **melodrama**, and **social drama**. Farce is a wildly comic play that uses highly improbable situations, stereotyped characters, extravagant exaggeration, and violent horseplay, frequently with satiric intent. Charlie Chaplin's film comedy *Modern Times* is a good example of farce. Melodrama, originated from early nineteenth century France, is a debased form of tragedy with a happy ending. Featuring stock characters such as the noble hero, the long-suffering heroine, and the cold-blooded, hard-hearted villain, the drama emphasizes sensational incident at the expense of character development. By the early twentieth century motion pictures had become the most popular vehicle for melodramas; later television also became a popular medium for the form. Social drama, sometimes called *problem plays*, evolved in the nineteenth century and dominated the stage through the early part of the twentieth century. This type of drama stresses the social world, with emphasis on the individual's place in the society of his or her time. Examples of social drama are Susan Glaspell's *Trifles* and Arther Miller's *Death of a Salesman.*

One further distinction will be helpful in the exploration of drama. Full-length plays are dramas that usually contain three or five separate acts (as in *Hamlet*). Such plays provide for complete and in-depth development of character, conflict, and idea. Shorter dramas, however, do not permit extensive development because they are by definition more limited and confined. One-act plays, (such as *Before Breakfast*) flows smoothly from episode to episode without a break. If we consider parallels with fiction, the full-length play is analogous to the novel, while the one-act play is like the short story.

Given all these terms and types, we should keep in mind that classification is not the goal of reading plays. It is less important to identify *A* as a comedy or *B* as a melodramatic tragedy than it is to feel and understand the experiences and ideas that each play offers us.

The Basic Elements of Dramatic Literature

Aristotle identifies six components of drama: plot, character, language, spectacle, thought, and song. Although modern drama cannot be judged exclusively on the basis of those six aspects, yet his list illustrates the continuity of dramatic elements and techniques.

Plot, Action, and Conflict

Handbooks on the drama often suggest that a plot (arrangement of happenings or a planned sequence of interrelated actions) should have a rising action, a climax, and a falling action. This sort of plot can be diagrammed as a pyramid, the tension rising through complications, or crisis, to a climax, at which point the fate of the protagonist (chief character) is firmly established; the climax is the apex, and the tension slackens as we witness the denouement (unknotting). Such a *plot structure*, according to the German critic Gustav Freytag, can be further illustrated as follows:

1. Exposition or Introduction
2. Complication and Development

3. Climax or Crisis
4. Falling Action, Catastrophe
5. Resolution or Denouement

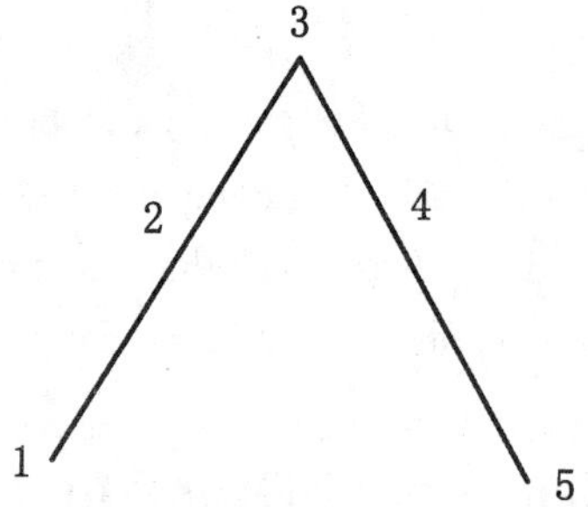

In the stage of the exposition, we receive essential background information; we meet the characters; we are introduced to what happened before the curtain rose and even the conflicts. In *Hamlet*, fot example, the conversations of Barnardo, Marcellus, and Horatio provide critical information.

In the second stage, the complication, the conflicts grow heated and the plot becomes more involved. Complication leads into climax, the turning point of the play, the moment when tension reaches its greatest height. In the third stage the hero or heroine often faces a crucial decision or chooses a course of action that determines the outcome of the play. In *Trifles*, for instance, the climax occurs when Mrs. Peters finds herself torn between her desire to save Minnie and her duty to the law.

The pyramid begins its downward slope in stage four, the catastrophe. The catastrophe (not to be confused without modern use of the term to mean "disaster") refers to the moment of revelation when all the pieces fall into place. It is often caused by the discovery of certain information that has been unknown to most of the characters up to that instant. During the final stage, the resolution, conflicts are resolved. (knots are untied.)

But it must be remembered that this five-stage structure is only generally applicable, fot not all plays follow the pattern precisely as outlined. The pattern is merely a model to explain plot.

Character

Many of the types of characters that populate prose fiction are also found in drama. In drama as in fiction, for instance, we find both round characters and flat characters. The round characters are fully developed and usually undergo some change in the course of the play; flat characters, on the other hand, tend to be undeveloped and unchanging. Characters in full-length plays are usually round while those in one-act plays tend to be flat. Characters in drama can also be considered either static—that is, fixed and unchanging—or dynamic—that is, growing and developing. Flat characters are usually static; round characters are often dynamic.

Because drama depends on conflict as fully as does prose fiction, we also find protagonists and antagonists in plays. The protagonist is usually the character we identify with and cheer on; the antagonist opposes the protagonist and is often the villain of the piece. In O'Neill's *Before Breakfast*, for example, Alfred Rowland is the protagonist and his wife the antagonist; their relationship forms the central conflict of the play.

Dramatic characters may be realistic, nonrealistic, symbolic and stereotyped. Realistic characters are normally accurate imitations of individualized men and women; they are provided with backgrounds, personalities, desires, motivations, and thoughts. Nonrealistic characters are usually not provided with such individualizing touches; they are often undeveloped. Symbolic characters represent an idea, a way of life, moral values, or some other abstraction. Stereotyped characters represent generalized racial or social traits repeated as typical from work to work, with no individualizing traits.

The major difference between characters in prose fiction and characters in drama lies in the way they are unfolded. Playwrights do not have the freedom to tell us directly about a character, as fiction writers do. We learn about characters in play by paying attention to their words and actions, by listening to what other characters say about them, and by watching what other characters do to them. Finally, we arrive at our own judgement or understanding of characters.

Point of View

Point of view in drama is strikingly different from that in prose fiction. Playwrights usually employ the dramatic point of view in which we receive only the information communicated by the characters. The method is characterized by complete objectivity in description of characters and scenes and in reporting of action and speech. The playwright does not overly guide us toward any conclusions. Thus, we draw conclusions from all the details presented in the play.

Setting

Setting in drama serves to place the action in a specific time and place and to help create the appropriate mood. The setting is usually the first thing we see on the stage. In *Trifles*, for example, the first thing we see is a Nebraska farm kitchen, complete with stove, sink, and unwashed dishes. Besides employing settings to establish a specific time and place, playwrights also use settings to convey information about characters. In *Before Breakfast*, fot instance, O'Neill uses the single stage setting to tell the reader a great deal about the characters and their lives. The Rowland's apartment in Greenwich Village, a part of New York City that was a traditional gathering place for artists, writers and actors, defines their status, their relationship, and their way of Liffe.

Diction, Style and Language

Words give plays their emotional impact and meaning. Most of what we learn about characters, relationships and conflict in drama is conveyed through language. The language must be appropriate for the play in which it is spoken; it must fit the time, the place, and the characters. This sense of appropriateness is called decorum.

The words and rhetorical devices spoken in a play delineate character, emotion, and theme, much as they do in prose fiction. Dramatists can employ words that have wide-ranging connotations, as with the words *trifle* and *knot* in Glaspell's play *Trifles*. Dramatists also employ accents, dialects, idiom, jargon, or cliches to define character. In short, playwrights have access to every stylistic and rhetorical device of language in their creation of character, conflict, emotion, and ideas.

Tone

Tone in drama, as in prose fiction, signifies the way moods and attitudes are created and conveyed. Tonc in plays may be conveyed directly to the spectator through voice and movement. Tone may create an atmosphere or mood that dominates a play. In the opening scene of *Hamlet*, for instance, Shakespeare uses tempo, diction and tone to build the dominant mood; it is dark, close to midnight, and Francisco carries a torch:

Barnardo: Who's there?

Francisco: Nay, answer me. Stand and unfold yourself.

Barnardo: Long live the king!

Francisco: Barnardo?

Barnardo: He.

Notice the short lines, the questions, and the choppy and rapid exchange. The tone of the dialogue is anxious and questioning. The exchange thus suggests nervousness, tension, and insecurity.

In dealing with tone, one should be careful to distinguish between the tone of an individual character and the playwright's tone that shapes our total response to the play. In *Trifles*, for example, the tones of some speeches are noted as *resentful*, *apologetic* or *mild*. The play as a whole, however, is predominantly bitter and ironic.

One of the most common methods employed by playwrights to control the tone of a play is dramatic irony—the audience knows more than the characters in a play. In *Trifles*, one of the characters mockingly dismisses a woman's behavior by noting that "women are used to worrying about such trifles". The line acquires vast dramatic irony as we watch the women in the play achieve understanding through careful attention to "trifles" that the men ignore.

Subject and Theme

Playwrights often write plays with specific ideas about the human condition in mind. The aspects of humanity a playwright explores constitute the subject of a play. Plays may thus be about love, hatred, war, death, ambition or anything else that is part of the human condition. The ideas that the play dramatizes about its subject make up the play's theme or meaning. Thus, a play might explore the idea that love will always find a way or that marriage can be destructive, that pride always leads to disaster, or that grief can be conquered through strength and a commitment to life. Theme is the end result of all the other elements of drama and one of the things we are left to think about after we have read a play. Since theme is created and conveyed through all the other elements of drama, great efforts are sometimes required to identify it.

Susan Glaspell (1882—1948)

Trifles

CAST OF CHARACTERS

George Henderson, *county attorney*

Henry Peters, *sheriff*

Lewis Hale, *a neighboring farmer*

Mrs. Peters

Mrs. Hale

SCENE. *The kitchen in the now abandoned farmhouse of JOHN WRIGHT, a gloomy kitchen, and left without having been put in order—unwashed pans under the sink, a loaf of bread outside the bread-box, a dish-towel on the table—other signs of incompleted work. At the rear the outer door opens and the SHERIFF comes in followed by the COUNTY ATTORNEY and HALE. The SHERIFF and HALE are men in middle life, the COUNTY ATTORNEY is a young man; all are much bundled up and go at once to the stove. They are followed by the two women—the SHERIFF'S wife first; she is a slight wiry woman, a thin nervous face. MRS. HALE is larger and would ordinarily be called more comfortable looking, but she is disturbed now and looks fearfully about as she enters. The women have come in slowly, and stand close together near the door.*

COUNTY ATTORNEY. [*Rubbing his hands.*] This feels good. Come up to the fire, ladies.

MRS. PETERS. [*After taking a step forward.*] I'm not cold.

SHERIFF. [*Unbuttoning his overcoat and stepping away from the stove as if to mark the beginning of official business.*] Now, Mr. Hale, before we move things about, you explain to Mr. Henderson just what you saw when you came here yesterday morning.

COUNTY ATTORNEY. By the way, has anything been moved? Are things just as you left them yesterday?

SHERIFF. [*Looking about.*] It's just the same. When it dropped below zero last night I thought I'd better send Frank out this morning to make a fire for us—no use getting pneumonia with a big case on, but I told him not to touch anything except the stove—and you know Frank.

COUNTY ATTORNEY. Somebody should have been left here yesterday.

SHERIFF. Oh—yesterday. When I had to send Frank to Morris Center for that man who went crazy—I want you to know I had my hands full yesterday. I knew you could get back from Omaha by today and as long as I went over everything here myself—

COUNTY ATTORNEY. Well, Mr. Hale, tell just what happened when you came here yesterday morning.

HALE. Harry and I had started to town with a load of potatoes. We came along the road from my place and as I got here I said, "I'm going to see if I can't get John Wright to go in with me on a party telephone." I spoke to Wright about it once before and he put me off, saying folks talked too much anyway, and all he asked was peace and quiet—I guess you know about how much he talked himself; but I thought maybe if I went to the house and talked about it before his wife, though I said to Harry that I didn't know as what his wife wanted made much difference to John—

COUNTY ATTORNEY. Let's talk about that later, Mr. Hale. I do want to talk about that, but tell now just what happened when you got to the house.

HALE. I didn't hear or see anything; I knocked at the door, and still it was all quiet inside. I knew they must be up, it was past eight o'clock. So I knocked again, and I thought I heard somebody say, "Come in." I wasn't sure, I'm not sure yet, but I opened the door—this door [*Indicating the door by which the two women are still standing.*] and there in that rocker—[*Pointing to it.*] sat Mrs. Wright. [*They all look at the rocker.*]

COUNTY ATTORNEY. What—was she doing?

HALE. She was rockin' back and forth. She had her apron in her hand and was kind of—pleating it.

COUNTY ATTORNEY. And how did she—look?

HALE. Well, she looked queer.

COUNTY ATTORNEY. How do you mean—queer?

HALE. Well, as if she didn't know what she was going to do next. And kind of done up.

COUNTY ATTORNEY. How did she seem to feel about your coming?

HALE. Why, I don't think she minded—one way or other. She didn't pay much attention. I said, "How do, Mrs. Wright, it's cold, ain't it?" And she said, "Is it?"—and went on kind of pleating at her apron. Well, I was surprised; she didn't ask me to come up to the stove, or to set down, but just sat there, not even looking at me, so I said, "I want to see John." And then she—laughed. I guess you would call it a laugh. I thought of Harry and the team outside, so I said a little sharp: "Can't I see John?" "No," she says, kind o'dull like. "Ain't he home?" says I. "Yes," says she, "he's home." "Then why can't I see him?" I asked her, out of patience. "'Cause he's dead," says she. "*Dead?*" says I. She just nodded her head, not getting a bit excited, but rockin'back and forth. "Why—where is he?" says I, not knowing what to say. She just pointed upstairs—like that. [*Himself pointing to the room above.*] I got up, with the idea of going up there. I walked from there to here—then I says, "Why, what did he die of?" "He died of a rope round his neck," says she, and just went on pleatin' at her apron. Well, I went out and called Harry. I thought I might—need help. We went upstairs and there he was lyin'—

COUNTY ATTORNEY. I think I'd rather have you go into that upstairs, where you can point it all out. Just go on now with the rest of the story.

HALE. Well, my first thought was to get that rope off. It looked... [*Stops, his face twitches.*]... but Harry, he went up to him, and he said, "No, he's dead all right, and we'd better not touch anything." So we went back downstairs. She was still sitting that same way. "Has anybody been notified?" I asked. "No," says she, unconcerned. "Who did this, Mrs. Wright?" said Harry. He said it businesslike—and she stopped pleation' of her apron. "I don't know," she says. "You don't *know*?" says Harry. "No," says she. "Weren't you sleepin' in the bed with him?" says Harry. "Yes," says she, "but I was on the inside." "Somebody slipped a rope round his neck and strangled him and you didn't wake up?" says Harry. "I didn't wake up," she said after him. We must' a looked as if we didn't see how that could be, for after a minute she said, "I sleep sound." Harry was going to ask her more questions but I said maybe we ought to let her tell her story first to the coroner, or the sheriff, so Harry went fast as he could to Rivers' place, where there's a telephone.

COUNTY ATTORNEY. And what did Mrs. Wright do when she knew that you had gone for the coroner?

HALE. She moved from that chair to this one over here [*Pointing to a small chair in the corner.*] and just sat there with her hands held together and looking down. I got a feeling that I ought to make some conversation, so I said I had come in to see if John wanted to put in a telephone, and at that she started to laugh, and then she stopped and looked at me—scared. [*The COUNTY ATTORNEY, who has had his notebook out, makes a note.*] I dunno, maybe it wasn't scared. I wouldn't like to say it was. Soon Harry got back, and then Dr. Lloyd came, and you, Mr. Peters, and so I guess that's all I know that you don't.

COUNTY ATTORNEY. [*Looking around.*] I guess we'll go upstairs first—and then out to the barn and around there. [*To the SHERIFF.*] You're convinced that there was nothing important here—nothing that would point to any motive.

SHERIFF. Nothing here but kitchen things.

[*The COUNTY ATTORNEY, after again looking around the kitchen, opens the door of a cupboard closet. He gets up on a chair and looks on a shelf. Pulls his hand aways, sticky.*]

COUNTY ATTORNEY. Here's a nice mess.

[*The women draw nearer.*]

MRS. PETERS. [*To the other woman.*] Oh, her fruit; it did freeze. [*To the LAWYER.*] She worried about that when it turned so cold. She said the fire'd go out and her jars would break.

SHERIFF. Well, can you beat the women! Held for murder and worryin' about her preserves.

COUNTY ATTORNEY. I guess before we're through she may have something more serious than preserves to worry about.

HALE. Well, women are used to worrying over trifles.

[*The two women move a little closer together.*]

COUNTY ATTORNEY. [*With the gallantry of a young politician.*] And yet, for all their worries, what would we do without the ladies? [*The women do not unbend. He goes to the sink, takes a dipperful of water from the pail and pouring it into a basin, washes his hands. Starts to wipe them on the roller-towel, turns it for a cleaner place.*] Dirty towels! [*Kicks his foot against the pans under the sink.*] Not much of a housekeeper, would you say, ladies?

MRS. HALE. [*Stiffly.*] There's a great deal of work to be done on a farm.

COUNTY ATTORNEY. To be sure. And yet [*with a little bow to her.*] I know there are some Dickson county farmhouses which do not have such roller towels.

[*He gives it a pull to expose its full length again.*]

MRS. HALE. Those towels get dirty awful quick. Men's hands aren't always as clean as they might be.

COUNTY ATTORNEY. Ah, loyal to your sex, I see. But you and Mrs. Wright were neighbors. I suppose you were friends, too.

MRS. HALE. [*Shaking her head.*] I've not seen much of her of late years. I've not been in this house—it's more than a year.

COUNTY ATTORNEY. And why was that? You didn't like her?

MRS. HALE. I liked her all well enough. Farmers' wives have their hands full, Mr. Henderson. And then—

COUNTY ATTORNEY. Yes—?

MRS. HALE. [*Looking about.*] It never seemed a very cheerful place.

COUNTY ATTORNEY. No—it's not cheerful. I shouldn't say she had the homemaking instinct.

MRS. HALE. Well, I don't know as Wright had, either.

COUNTY ATTORNEY. You mean that they didn't get on very well?

MRS. HALE. No, I don't mean anything. But I don't think a place'd be any cheerfuller for John Wright's being in it.

COUNTY ATTORNEY. I'd like to talk more of that a little later. I want to get the lay of things upstairs now.

[*He goes to the left, where three steps lead to a stair door.*]

SHERIFF. I suppose anything Mrs. Peters does'll be all right. She was to take in some clothes for her, you know, and a few little things. We left in such a hurry yesterday.

COUNTY ATTORNEY. Yes, but I would like to see what you take, Mrs. Peters, and keep an eye out for anything that might be of use to us.

MRS. PETERS. Yes, Mr. Henderson.

[*The women listen to the men's steps on the stairs, then look about the kitchen.*]

MRS. HALE. I'd hate to have men coming into my kitchen, snooping around and criticising.

[*She arranges the pans under sink which the LAWYER had shoved out of place.*]

MRS. PETERS. Of course it's no more than their duty.

MRS. HALE. Duty's all right, but I guess that deputy sheriff that came out to make the fire might have got a little of this on. [*Gives the roller towel a pull.*] Wish I'd thought of that sooner. Seems mean to talk about her for not having things slicked up when she had to come away in such a hurry.

MRS. PETERS. [*Who has gone to a small table in the left rear corner of the room, and lifted one end of a towel that covers a pan.*] She had bread set.

[*Stands still.*]

MRS. HALE. [*Eyes fixed on a loaf of bread beside the breadbox, which is on a low shelf at the other side of the room. Moves slowly toward it.*] She was going to put this in there. [*Picks up loaf, then abruptly drops it. In a manner of returning to familiar things.*] It's a shame about her fruit. I wonder if it's all gone. [*Gets up on the chair and looks.*] I think there's some here that's all right, Mrs. Peters. Yes—here; [*Holding it toward the window.*] this is cherries, too. [*Looking again.*] I declare I believe that's the only one. [*Gets down, bottle in her hand. Goes to the sink and wipes it off on the outside.*] She'll feel awful bad after all her hard work in the hot weather. I remember the afternoon I put up my cherries last summer.

[*She puts the bottle on the big kitchen table, center of the room. With a sigh, is about to sit down in the rocking-chair. Before she is seated realizes what chair it is; with a slow look at it, steps back. The chair which she has touched rocks back and forth.*]

MRS. PETERS. Well, I must get those things from the front room closet. [*She goes to the door at the right, but after looking into the other room, steps back.*] You coming with me, Mrs. Hale? You could help me carry them.

[*They go in the other room; reappear, MRS. PETERS carrying a dress and skirt, MRS. HALE following with a pair of shoes.*]

MRS. PETERS. My, it's cold in there.

[*She puts the clothes on the big table and hurries to the stove.*]

MRS. HALE. [*Examining the skirt.*] Wright was close. I think maybe that's why she kept so much to herself. She didn't even belong to the Ladies Aid. I suppose she felt she couldn't do her part, and then you don't enjoy things when you feel shabby. She used to wear pretty clothes and be lively, when she was Minnie Foster, one of the town girls singing in the choir. But that—oh, that was thirty years ago. This all you was to take in?

MRS. PETERS. She said she wanted an apron. Funny thing to want, for there isn't much to get you dirty in jail, goodness knows. But I suppose just to make her feel more natural. She said they was in the top drawer in this cupboard. Yes, here. And then her little shawl that always hung behind the door. [*Opens stair door and looks.*] Yes, here it is.

[*Quickly shuts door leading upstairs.*]

MRS. HALE. [*Abruptly moving toward her.*] Mrs. Peters?

MRS. PETERS. Yes, Mrs. Hale?

MRS. HALE. Do you think she did it?

MRS. PETERS. [*In a frightened voice.*] Oh, I don't know.

MRS. HALE. Well, I don't think she did. Asking for an apron and her little shawl. Worrying about her fruit.

MRS. PETERS. [*Starts to speak, glances up, where footsteps are heard in the room above. In a low voice.*] Mr. Peters says it looks bad for her. Mr. Henderson is awful sarcastic in a speech and he'll make fun of her sayin' she didn't wake up.

MRS. HALE. Well, I guess John Wright didn't wake when

they was slipping that rope under his neck.

MRS. PETERS. No, it's strange. It must have been done awful crafty and still. They say it was such a—funny way to kill a man, rigging it all up like that.

MRS. HALE. That's just what Mr. Hale said. There was a gun in the house. He says that's what he can't understand.

MRS. PETERS. Mr. Henderson said coming out that what was needed for the case was a motive; something to show anger, or—sudden feeling.

MRS. HALE. [*Who is standing by the table.*] Well, I don't see any signs of anger around here. [*She puts her hand on the dish towel which lies on the table, stands looking down at table, one half of which is clean, the other half messy.*] It's wiped to here. [*Makes a move as if to finish work, then turns and looks at a loaf of bread outside the breadbox. Drops towel. In that voice of coming back to familiar things.*] Wonder how they are finding things upstairs. I hope she had it a little more red-up* up there. You know, it seems kind of *sneaking*. Locking her up in town and then coming out here and trying to get her own house to turn against her!

MRS. PETERS. But Mrs. Hale, the law is the law.

MRS. HALE. I s'pose 'tis. [*Unbuttoning her coat.*] Better loosen up your things, Mrs. Peters. You won't feel them when you go out.

[*MRS. PETERS takes off her fur tippet***, goes to hang it on hook at back of room, stands looking at the under part of the small corner table.*]

MRS. PETERS. She was piecing a quilt.

---

* *red-up*: neat, arranged in order.

** *tippet*: scarflike garment of fur or wool for the neck and shoulders.

[*She brings the large sewing basket and they look at the bright pieces.*]

MRS. HALE. It's log cabin pattern. Pretty, isn't it? I wonder if she was goin' to quilt it or just knot it?

[*Footsteps have been heard coming down the stairs. The SHERIFF enters followed by HALE and the COUNTY ATTORNEY.*]

SHERIFF. They wonder if she was going to quilt it or just knot it!

[*The men laugh; the women look abashed.*]

COUNTY ATTORNEY. [*Rubbing his hands over the stove.*] Frank's fire didn't do much up there, did it? Well, let's go out to the barn and get that cleared up.

[*The men go outside.*]

MRS. HALE. [*Resentfully.*] I don't know as there's anything so strange, our takin' up our time with little things while we're waiting for them to get the evidence. [*She sits down at the big table smoothing out a block with decision.*] I don't see as it's anything to laugh about.

MRS. PETERS. [*Apologetically.*] Of course they've got awful important things on their minds.

[*Pulls up a chair and joins Mrs. HALE at the table.*]

MRS. HALE. [*Examining another block.*] MRS. Peters, look at this one. Here, this is the one she was working on, and look at the sewing! All the rest of it has been so nice and even. And look at this! It's all over the place! Why, it looks as if she didn't know what she was about!

[*After she has said this they look at each other, then start to glance back at the door. After an instant MRS. HALE has pulled at a knot and ripped the sewing.*]

MRS. PETERS. Oh, what are you doing, Mrs. Hale?

MRS. HALE. [*Mildly.*] Just pulling out a stitch or two that's not sewed very good. [*Threading a needle.*] Bad sewing always made me fidgety.

MRS. PETERS. [*Nervously.*] I don't think we ought to touch things.

MRS. HALE. I'll just finish up this end. [*Suddenly stopping and leaning forward.*] Mrs. Peters?

MRS. PETERS. Yes, Mrs. Hale?

MRS. HALE. What do you suppose she was so nervous about?

MRS. PETERS. Oh—I don't know. I don't know as she was nervous. I sometimes sew awful queer when I'm just tired. [*MRS. HALE starts to say something, looks at MRS. PETERS, then goes on sewing.*] Well I must get these things wrapped up. They may be through sooner than we think. [*Putting apron and other things together.*] I wonder where I can find a piece of paper, and string.

MRS. HALE. In that cupboard, maybe.

MRS. PETERS. [*Looking in cupboard.*] Why, here's a bird-cage. [*Holds it up.*] Did she have a bird, Mrs. Hale?

MRS. HALE. Why, I don't know whether she did or not—I've not been here for so long. There was a man around last year selling canaries cheap, but I don't know as she took one; maybe she did. She used to sing real pretty herself.

MRS. PETERS. [*Glancing around.*] Seems funny to think of a bird here. But she must have had one, or why would she have a cage? I wonder what happened to it.

MRS. HALE. I s'pose maybe the cat got it.

MRS. PETERS. No, she didn't have a cat. She's got that feeling some people have about cats—being afraid of them. My cat got in her room and she was real upset and asked me to take it out.

MRS. HALE. My sister Bessie was like that. Queer, ain't it?

MRS. PETERS. [*Examining the cage.*] Why, look at this door. It's broke. One hinge is pulled apart.

MRS. HALE. [*Looking too.*] Looks as if someone must have been rough with it.

MRS. PETERS. Why, yes.

[*She brings the cage forward and puts it on the table.*]

MRS. HALE. I wish if they're going to find any evidence they'd be about it. I don't like this place.

MRS. PETERS. But I'm awful glad you came with me, Mrs. Hale. It would be lonesome for me sitting here alone.

MRS. HALE. It would, wouldn't it? [*Dropping her sewing.*] But I tell you what I do wish, Mrs. Peters. I wish I had come over sometimes when *she* was here. I—[*Looking around the room.*]—wish I had.

MRS. PETERS. But of course you were awful busy, Mrs. Hale—your house and your children.

MRS. HALE. I could've come. I stayed away because it weren't cheerful—and that's why I ought to have come. I—I've never liked this place. Maybe because it's down in a hollow and you don't see the road. I dunno what it is, but it's a lonesome place and always was. I wish I had come over to see Minnie Foster sometimes. I can see now —

[*Shakes her head.*]

MRS. PETERS. Well, you mustn't reproach yourself, Mrs. Hale. Somehow we just don't see how it is with other folks until—something comes up.

MRS. HALE. Not having children makes less work—but it makes a quiet house, and Wright out to work all day, and no company when he did come in. Did you know John Wright, Mrs. Peters?

MRS. PETERS. Not to know him; I've seen him in town. They say he was a good man.

MRS. HALE. Yes—good; he didn't drink, and kept his word as well as most, I guess, and paid his debts. But he was a hard man, Mrs. Peters. Just to pass the time of day with him—[*Shivers.*] Like a raw wind that gets to the bone. [*Pauses, her eye falling on the cage.*] I should think she would'a wanted a bird. But what do you suppose went with it?

MRS. PETERS. I don't know, unless it got sick and died.

[*She reaches over and swings the broken door, swings it again, both women watch it.*]

MRS. HALE. You weren't raised round here, were you? [*MRS. PETERS shakes her head.*] You didn't know—her?

MRS. PETERS. Not till they brought her yesterday.

MRS. HALE, She—come to think of it, she was kind of like a bird herself—real sweet and pretty, but kind of timid and—fluttery. How—she—did—change. [*Silence; then as if struck by a happy thought and relieved to get back to everyday things.*] Tell you what, Mrs. Peters, why don't you take the quilt in with you? It might take up her mind.

MRS. PETERS. Why, I think that's a real nice idea, Mrs. Hale. There couldn't possibly be any objection to it, could there? Now, just what would I take? I wonder if her patches are in here—and her things.

[*They look in the sewing basket.*]

MRS. HALE. Here's some red. I expect this has got sewing things in it. [*Brings out a fancy box.*] What a pretty box. Looks like something somebody would give you. Maybe her scissors are in here. [*Opens box. Suddenly puts her hand to her nose.*] Why—[*MRS. PETERS bends nearer, then turns her face away.*] There's something wrapped up in this piece of silk.

MRS. PETERS. Why, this isn't her scissors.

MRS. HALE. [*Lifting the silk.*] Oh, Mrs. Peters—its—

[*MRS. PETERS bends closer.*]

MRS. PETERS. It's the bird.

MRS. HALE. [*Jumping up.*] But, Mrs. Peters—look at it! Its neck! Look at its neck! It's all—other side *to.*

MRS. PETERS. Somebody—wrung—its—neck.

[*Their eyes meet. A look of growing comprehension, of horror. Steps are heard outside. MRS. HALE slips box under quilt pieces, and sinks into her chair. Enter SHERIFF and COUNTY ATTORNEY. MRS. PETERS rises.*]

COUNTY ATTORNEY [*As one turning from serious things to little pleasantries.*] Well, ladies, have you decided whether she was going to quilt it or knot it?

MRS. PETERS. We think she was going to—knot it.

COUNTY ATTORNEY. Well, that's interesting, I'm sure. [*Seeing the bird-cage.*] Has the bird flown?

MRS. HALE. [*Putting more quilt pieces over the box.*] We think the—cat got it.

COUNTY ATTORNEY. [*Preoccupied.*] Is there a cat?

[*MRS. HALE glances in a quick covert way at MRS. PETERS.*]

MRS. PETERS. Well, not *now*. They're superstitious, you know. They leave.

COUNTY ATTORNEY. [*TO SHERIFF PETERS, continuing an interrupted conversation.*] No sign at all of anyone having come from the outside. Their own rope. Now let's go up again and go over it piece by piece. [*They start upstairs.*] It would have to have been someone who knew just the—

[*MRS. PETERS sits down. The two women sit there not looking at one another, but as if peering into something and at the same time holding back. When they talk now it is in the manner of feeling their way over strange ground, as if afraid of what they are saying, but as if they cannot help saying it.*]

MRS. HALE. She liked the bird. She was going to bury it in that pretty box.

MRS. PETERS. [*In a whisper.*] When I was a girl—my kitten—there was a boy took a hatchet, and before my eyes—and before I could get there—[*Covers her face an instant.*] If they hadn't held me back I would have—[*Catches herself, looks upstairs where steps are heard, falters weakly*]—hurt him.

MRS. HALE. [*With a slow look around her.*] I wonder how it would seem never to have had any children around. [*Pause.*] No, Wright wouldn't like the bird—a thing that sang. She used to sing. He killed that, too.

MRS. PETERS. [*Moving uneasily.*] We don't know who killed the bird.

MRS. HALE. I knew John Wright.

MRS. PETERS. It was an awful thing was done in this house that night, Mrs. Hale. Killing a man while he slept, slipping a rope around his neck that choked the life out of him.

MRS. HALE. His neck. Choked the life out of him.

[*Her hand goes out and rests on the bird-cage.*]

MRS. PETERS. [*With rising voice.*] We don't know who killed him. We don't know.

MRS. HALE. [*Her own feeling not interrupted.*] If there'd been years and years of nothing, then a bird to sing to you, it would be awful—still, after the bird was still.

MRS. PETERS. [*Something within her speaking.*] I know what

stillness is. When we homesteaded in Dakota, and my first baby died—after he was two years old, and me with no other then—

MRS. HALE. [*Moving.*] How soon do you suppose they'll be through, looking for the evidence?

MRS. PETERS. I know what stillness is. [*Pulling herself back.*] The law has got to punish crime, Mrs. Hale.

MRS. HALE. [*Not as if answering that.*] I wish you'd seen Minnie Foster when she wore a white dress with blue ribbons and stood up there in the choir and sang. [*A look around the room.*] Oh, I *wish* I'd come over here once in a while! That was a crime! That was a crime! Who's going to punish that?

MRS. PETERS. [*Looking upstairs.*] We mustn't—take on.

MRS. HALE. I might have known she needed help! I know how things can be—for women. I tell you, it's queer, Mrs. Peters. We live close together and we live far apart. We all go through the same things—it's all just a different kind of the same thing. [*Brushes her eyes, noticing the bottle of fruit, reaches out for it.*] If I were you I wouldn't tell her her fruit was gone. Tell her it *ain't*. Tell her it's all right. Take this in to prove it to her. She—she may never know whether it was broke or not.

MRS. PETERS. [*Takes the bottle, looks about for something to wrap it in; takes petticoat from the clothes brought from the other room, very nervously begins winding this around the bottle. In a false voice.*] My, it's a good thing the men couldn't hear us. Wouldn't they just laugh! Getting all stirred up over a little thing like a—dead canary. As if that could have anything to do with—with—wouldn't they *laugh*!

[*The men are heard coming down stairs.*]

MRS. HALE. [*Under her breath.*] Maybe they would—maybe they wouldn't.

COUNTY ATTORNEY. No, Peters, it's all perfectly clear except a reason for doing it. But you know juries when it comes to women. If there was some definite thing. Something to show—something to make a story about—a thing that would connect up with this strange way of doing it—

[*The women's eyes meet for an instant. Enter HALE from outer door.*]

HALE. Well, I've got the team around. Pretty cold out there.

COUNTY ATTORNEY. I'm going to stay here a while by myself. [*To the SHERIFF.*] You can send Frank out for me, can't you? I want to go over everything. I'm not satisfied that we can't do better.

SHERIFF. Do you want to see what Mrs. Peters is going to take in?

[*The COUNTY ATTORNEY goes to the table, picks up the apron, laughs.*]

COUNTY ATTORNEY. Oh, I guess they're not very dangerous things the ladies have picked out. [*Moves a few things about, disturbing the quilt pieces which cover the box. Steps back.*] No, Mrs. Peters doesn't need supervising. For that matter, a Sheriff's wife is married to the law. Ever think of it that way, Mrs. Peters?

MRS. PETERS. Not—just that way.

SHERIFF. [*Chuckling.*] Married to the law. [*Moves toward the other room.*] I just want you to come here in a minute, George. We ought to take a look at these windows.

COUNTY ATTORNEY. [*Scoffingly.*] Oh, windows!

SHERIFF. We'll be right out, Mr. Hale.

[*HALE goes outside. The SHERIFF follows the COUNTY ATTORNEY into the other room. Then MRS. HALE rises, hands tight together, looking intensely at MRS. PETERS, whose eyes make a slow turn, finally meeting MRS. HALE's. A moment MRS. HALE holds her, then her own eyes point the way to where the box is concealed. Suddenly MRS. PETERS throws back quilt pieces and tries to put the box in the bag she is wearing. It is too big. She opens box, starts to take bird out, cannot touch it, goes to pieces, stands there helpless. Sound of a knob turning in the other room. MRS. HALE snatches the box and puts it in the pocket of her big coat. Enter COUNTY ATTORNEY and SHERIFF.*]

COUNTY ATTORNEY. [*Facetiously.*] Well, Henry, at least we found out that she was not going to quilt it. She was going to—what is it you call it, ladies?

MRS. HALE. [*Her hand against her pocket.*] We call it—knot it, Mr. Henderson.

CURTAIN

Questions:

1. How does the setting described in the first stage direction alert you that something has gone wrong at the Wright farm and how does it help us to understand Mrs. Wright's deed?
2. How does the first entrance of the characters begin to establish a distinction between the men and women in the play? What attitudes toward women do the Sheriff and the County Attorney

express? How do Mrs. Hale and Mrs. Peters react to these sentiments?

3. What is the crisis of the play and where does it occur?
4. To what does the title of this play refer? To what extent is the word ironic? How does this irony help shape the play's meaning?
5. What is the central conflict? How and when is it resolved? How does the resolution help establish the play's themes?

Eugene O'Neill (1888—1953)

Before Breakfast

CHARACTERS

Mrs. Rowland, *The Wife*

Mr. Alfred Rowland, *The Husband*

SCENE. *A small room serving both as kitchen and dining room in a flat on Christopher Street, New York City. In the rear, to the right, a door leading to the outer hallway. On the left of the doorway, a sink, and a two-burner gas stove. Over the stove, and extending to the left wall, a wooden closet for dishes, etc. On the left, two windows looking out on a fire escape where several potted plants are dying of neglect. Before the windows, a table covered with oilcloth. Two cane-bottomed chairs are placed by the table. Another stands against the wall to the right of door in the rear. In the right wall, rear, a doorway leading into a bedroom. Farther forward, different articles of a man's and a woman's clothing are hung on pegs. A clothes line is strung from the left corner, rear, to the right wall, forward.*

It is about eight-thirty in the morning of a fine, sunshiny day in the early fall.

Mrs. Rowland enters from the bedroom, yawning, her hands still busy putting the finishing touches on a slovenly toilet by sticking hairpins into her hair which is bunched up in a drab-colored mass on top of her round head. She is of medium height and inclined to a shapeless stoutness, accentuated by her formless blue dress, shabby and worn. Her face is characterless, with small regular features and eyes of a nondescript blue. There is a pinched expression about her eyes and nose and her weak, spiteful mouth. She is in her early twenties but looks much older.

She comes to the middle of the room and yawns, stretching her arms to their full length. Her drowsy eyes stare about the room with the irritated look of one to whom a long sleep has not been a long rest. She goes wearily to the clothes hanging on the right and takes an apron from a hook. She ties it about her waist, giving vent to an exasperated "damn" when the knot fails to obey her clumsy fingers. Finally gets it tied and goes slowly to the gas stove and lights one burner. She fills the coffee pot at the sink and sets it over the flame. Then slumps down into a chair by the table and puts a hand over her forehead as if she were suffering from headache. Suddenly her face brightens as though she had remembered something, and she casts a quick glance at the dish closet; then looks sharply at the bedroom door and listens intently for a moment or so.

MRS. ROWLAND. [*In a low voice.*] Alfred! Alfred! [*There is no answer from the next room and she continues suspiciously in a louder tone.*] You needn't pretend you're asleep. [*There is no reply to this from the bedroom, and reassured, she gets up from her chair and tiptoes cautiously to the dish closet. She slowly opens one door, taking great care to make no noise, and slides out, from their hiding place behind the dishes, a bottle of Gordon gin and a glass. In doing so she disturbs the top dish, which rattles a little. At this sound she starts guiltily and looks with sulky defiance at the doorway to the next room.*]

[*Her voice trembling.*] Alfred!

[*After a pause, during which she listens for any sound, she takes the glass and pours out a large drink and gulps it down; then hastily returns the bottle and glass to their hiding place. She closes the closet door with the same care as she had opened it, and heaving a great sign of relief, sinks down into her chair again. The large dose of alcohol she has taken has an almost immediate effect. Her features become more animated, she seems to gather energy, and she looks at the bedroom door with a hard, vindictive smile on her lips. Her eyes glance quickly about the room and are fixed on a man's coat and vest which hang from a hook at right. She moves stealthily over to the open doorway and stands there, out of sight of anyone inside, listening for any movement.*]

[*Calling in a half-whisper.*] Alfred!

[*Again there is no reply. With a swift movement she takes the coat and vest from the hook and returns with them to her chair. She sits down and takes the various articles out of each pocket but quickly puts them back again. At last, in the inside pocket of the vest, she finds a letter.*]

[*Looking at the handwriting—slowly to herself.*] Hmm! I knew it.

[*She opens the letter and reads it. At first her expression is one of hatred and rage, but as she goes on to the end it changes to one of triumphant malignity. She remains in deep thought for a moment, staring before her, the letter in her hands, a cruel smile on her lips. Then she puts the letter back in the pocket of the vest, and still careful not to awaken the sleeper, hangs the clothes up again on the same hook, and goes to the bedroom door and looks in.*]

[*In a loud, shrill voice.*] Alfred! [*Still louder.*] Alfred! [*There is a muffled, yawning groan from the next room.*] Don't you think it's about time you got up? Do you want to stay in bed all day? [*Turning around and coming back to her chair.*] Not that I've got any doubts about your being lazy enough to stay in bed forever. [*She sits down and looks out of the window, irritably.*] Goodness knows what time it is. We haven't even got any way of telling the time since you pawned your watch like a fool. The last valuable thing we had, and you knew it. It's been nothing but pawn, pawn, pawn, with you—anything to put off getting a job, anything to get out of going to work like a man. [*She taps the floor with her foot nervously, biting her lips.*]

[*After a short pause.*] Alfred! Get up, do you hear me? I want to make that bed before I go out. I'm sick of having this place in a continual muss on your account. [*With a certain vindictive satisfaction.*] Not that we'll be here long unless you manage to get some money some place. Heaven knows I do my part—and more—going out to sew every day while you play the gentleman and loaf around bar rooms with that good-for-nothing lot of artists from the Square.

[*A short pause during which she plays nervously with a cup and saucer on the table.*]

And where are you going to get money, I'd like to know? The rent's due this week and you know what the landlord is. He won't let us stay a minute over our time. You say you *can't* get a job. That's a lie and you know it. You never even look for one. All you do is moon around all day writing silly poetry and stories that no one will buy—and no wonder they won't. I notice I can always get a position, such as it is; and it's only that which keeps us from starving to death.

[*Gets up and goes over to the stove—looks into the coffee pot to see if the water is boiling; then comes back and sits down again.*]

You'll have to get money today some place. I can't do it all, and I won't do it all. You've got to come to your senses. You've got to beg, borrow, or steal it somewheres. [*With a contemptuous laugh.*] But where, I'd like to know? You're too proud to beg, and you've borrowed the limit, and you haven't the nerve to steal. [*After a pause—getting up angrily.*] Aren't you up yet, for heaven's sake? It's just like you to go to sleep again, or pretend to. [*She goes to the bedroom door and looks in.*] Oh, you are up. Well, it's about time. You needn't look at me like that. Your airs don't fool me a bit any more. I know you too well—better than you think I do—you and your goings-on. [*Turning away from the door—meaningly.*] I know a lot of things, my dear. Never mind what I know, now. I'll tell you before I go, you needn't worry. [*She comes to the middle of the room and stands there, frowning.*]

[*Irritably.*] Hmm! I suppose I might as well get breakfast ready—not that there's anything much to get. [*Questioningly.*] Unless you have some money? [*She pauses for an answer from the next room which does not come.*] Foolish question! [*She gives a short, hard laugh.*] I ought to know you better than that by this time. When you left here in such a huff last night I knew what would happen. You can't be trusted for a second. A nice condition you came home in! The fight we had was only an excuse for you to make a beast of yourself. What was the use pawning your watch if all you wanted with the money was to waste it in buying drink?

[*Goes over to the dish closet and takes out plates, cups, etc., while she is talking.*]

Hurry up! It don't take long to get breakfast these days, thanks to you. All we got this morning is bread and butter and coffee; and you wouldn't even have that if it wasn't for me sewing my fingers off. [*She slams the loaf of bread on the table with a bang.*]

The bread's stale. I hope you'll like it. *You* don't deserve any better, but I don't see why *I* should suffer.

[*Going over to the stove.*] The coffee'll be ready in a minute, and you needn't expect me to wait for you.

[*Suddenly with great anger.*] What on earth are you doing all this time? [*She goes over to the door and looks in.*] Well, you're *almost* dressed at any rate. I expected to find you back in bed. That'd be just like you. How awful you look this morning! For heaven's sake, shave! You're disgusting! You look like a tramp. No wonder no one will give you a job. I don't blame them—when you don't even look halfway decent. [*She goes to the stove.*] There's plenty of hot water right here. You've got no excuse. [*Gets a bowl and pours some of the water from the coffee pot into it.*] Here.

[*He reaches his hand into the room for it. It is a sensitive hand with slender fingers. It trembles and some of the water spills on the floor.*]

[*Tauntingly*] Look at your hand tremble! You'd better give up drinking. You can't stand it. It's just your kind that get the D. T.'s. *That would be* the last straw! [*Looking down at the floor.*]

Look at the mess you've made of this floor—cigarette butts and ashes all over the place. Why can't you put them on a plate? No, you wouldn't be considerate enough to do that. You never think of me. You don't have to sweep the room and that's all you care about.

[*Takes the broom and commences to sweep viciously, raising a cloud of dust. From the inner room comes the sound of a razor being stropped.*]

[*Sweeping.*] Hurry up! It must be nearly time for me to go. If I'm late I'm liable to lose my position, and then I couldn't support you any longer. [*As an afterthought she adds sarcastically.*] And then you'd have to go to work or something dreadful like that. [*Sweeping under the table.*] What I want to know is whether you're going to look for a job today or not. You know your family won't help us any more. They've had enough of you, too. [*After a moment's silent sweeping.*] I'm about sick of all this life. I have a good notion to go home, if I wasn't too proud to let them know what a failure you've been—you, the millionaire Rowland's only son, the Harvard graduate, the poet, the catch of the town—Huh! [*With bitterness.*] There wouldn't be many of them now envy my catch if they knew the truth. What has our marriage been, I'd like to know? Even before your *millionaire* father died owing every one in the world money, you certainly never wasted any of your time on your wife. I suppose you thought I'd ought to be glad you were *honorable* enough to marry me—after getting me into trouble. You were ashamed of me with your fine friends because my father's only a grocer, that's what you were. At least he's honest, which is more than any one could say about yours. [*She is sweeping steadily toward the door. Leans on her broom for a moment.*]

You hoped every one would think you'd been forced to marry me, and pity you, didn't you? You didn't hesitate much about telling me you loved me, and making me believe your lies, before it happened, did you? You made me think you didn't want your father to buy me off as he tried to do. I know better now. I haven't lived with you all this time for nothing. [*Somberly*] It's lucky the poor thing was born dead, after all. What a father you'd have been!

[*Is silent, brooding moodily for a moment—then she continues with a sort of savage joy.*]

But I'm not the only one who's got you to thank for being unhappy. There's one other, at least, and *she* can't hope to marry you now. [*She puts her head into the next room.*] How about Helen? [*She starts back from the doorway, half frightened.*]

Don't look at me that way! Yes, I read her letter. What about it? I got a right to. I'm your wife. And I know all there is to know, so don't lie. You needn't stare at me so. You can't bully me with your superior airs any longer. Only for me you'd be going without breakfast this very morning. [*She sets the broom back in the corner—whiningly.*] You never did have any gratitude for what I've done. [*She comes to the stove and puts the coffee into the pot.*] The coffee's ready. I'm not going to wait for you. [*She sits down in her chair again.*]

[*After a pause—puts her hand to her head—fretfully.*] My head aches so this morning. It's a shame I've got to go to work in a stuffy room all day in my condition. And I wouldn't if you were half a man. By rights I ought to be lying on my back instead of you. You know how sick I've been this last year; and yet you object when I take a little something to keep up my spirits. You even didn't want me to take that tonic I got at the drug store. [*With a hard laugh.*] I know you'd be glad to have me dead and out of your way; then you'd be free to run after all these silly girls that think you're such a wonderful, misunderstood person—this Helen and the others. [*There is a sharp exclamation of pain from the next room.*]

[*With satisfaction.*] There! I knew you'd cut yourself. It'll be a lesson to you. You know you oughtn't to be running around nights drinking with your nerves in such an awful shape. [*She goes to the door and looks in.*]

What makes you so pale? What are you staring at yourself in the mirror that way for? For goodness sake, wipe that blood off your face! [*With a shudder.*] It's horrible. [*In relieved tones.*] There, that's better. I never could stand the sight of blood. [*She shrinks back from the door a little.*] You better give up trying and go to a barber shop. Your hand shakes dreadfully. Why do you stare at me like that? [*She turns away from the door.*] Are you still mad at me about that letter? [*Defiantly.*] Well, I had the right to read it. I'm your wife. [*She comes to the chair and sits down again. After a pause.*]

I knew all the time you were running around with someone. Your lame excuses about spending the time at the library didn't fool me. Who is this Helen, anyway? One of those artists? Or does she write poetry, too? Her letter sounds that way. I'll bet she told you your things were the best ever, and you believed her, like a fool. Is she young and pretty? I was young and pretty, too, when you fooled me with your fine, poetic talk; but life with you would soon wear anyone down. What I've been through!

[*Goes over and takes the coffee off the stove.*] Breakfast is ready. [*With a contemptuous glance.*] Breakfast! [*Pours out a cup of coffee for herself and puts the pot on the table.*] Your coffee'll be cold. What are you doing—still shaving, for heaven's sake? You'd better give it up. One of these mornings you'll give yourself a serious cut. [*She cuts off bread and butters it. During the following speeches she eats and sips her coffee.*]

I'll have to run as soon as I've finished eating. One of us has got to work. [*Angrily.*] Are you going to look for a job today or aren't you? I should think some of your fine friends would help you, if they really think you're so much. But I guess they just like to hear you talk. [*Sits in silence for a moment.*]

I'm sorry for this Helen, whoever she is. Haven't you got any feelings for other people? What will her family say? I see she mentions them in her letter. What is she going to do—have the child—or go to one of those doctors? That's a nice thing, I must say. Where can she get the money? Is she rich? [*She waits for some answers to this volley of questions.*]

Hmm! You won't tell me anything about her, will you? Much I care. Come to think of it, I'm not so sorry for her after all. She knew what she was doing. She isn't any schoolgirl, like I was, from the looks of her letter. Does she know you're married? Of course, she must. All your friends know about your unhappy marriage. I know they pity you, but they don't know my side of it. They'd talk different if they did.

[*Too busy eating to go on for a second or so.*]

This Helen must be a fine one, if she knew you were married. What does she expect, then? That I'll divorce you and let her marry you? Does she think I'm crazy enough for that—after all you've made me go through? I guess not! And you can't get a divorce from me and you know it. No one can say *I've* ever done anything wrong. [*Drinks the last of her cup of coffee.*]

She deserves to suffer, that's all I can say. I'll tell you what I think; I think your Helen is no better than a common street-walker, that's what I think. [*There is a stifled groan of pain from the next room.*]

Did you cut yourself again? Serves you right. [*Gets up and takes off her apron.*] Well, I've got to run along. [*Peevishly*] This is a fine life for me to be leading! I won't stand for your loafing any longer. [*Something catches her ear and she pauses and listens intently.*] There! You've overturned the water all over everything. Don't say you haven't. I can hear it dripping on the floor. [*A vague expression of fear comes over her face.*] Alfred! Why don't you answer me?

[*She moves slowly toward the room. There is the noise of a chair being overturned and something crashes heavily to the floor. She stands, trembling with fright.*]

Alfred! Alfred! Answer me! What is it you knocked over? Are you still drunk? [*Unable to stand the tension a second longer she rushes to the door of the bedroom.*]

Alfred!

[*She stands in the doorway looking down at the floor of the inner room, transfixed with horror. Then she shrieks wildly and runs to the other door, unlocks it and frenziedly pulls it open, and runs shrieking madly into the outer hallway.*]

[*The curtain falls*]

Questions:

1. What does the setting tell you about the Rowlands?
2. How does Mrs. Rowland treat Alfred? What tone does she use in speaking to him? What does she complain about? What does she accuse Alfred of being and doing?
3. What is Mrs. Rowland's attitude toward Helen? How does she treat her husband's feelings for Helen? What does this suggest about the Rowlands' marriage?
4. Where is the crisis of the play? Which character comes to a crisis? What actions and descriptions indicate that the character and play have reached a crisis?
5. Mrs. Rowland precipitates the catastrophe of this play with her discussion of Alfred's affair with Helen. What do we learn about Helen? What pushes Alfred over the edge? What is the catastrophe?
6. Why is Alfred Rowland kept off stage (except for his hand) and given no dialogue? How does this affect the play?
7. Alfred Rowland is presented from his wife's point of view. How accurate is this portrait? Is Alfred the man that his wife describes?

Chapter 18 Tragedy

Tragedy is a drama of a serious and dignified character that typically describes the development of a conflict between the protagonist and a superior force (such as destiny, circumstance, or society) and reaches a sorrowful or disastrous couclusion.

The origins of the tragic form are Greek. The materials of Greek tragedy were drawn from familiar myths of gods and mortals found in the works of Homer and elsewhere. Prompted by circumstance or ignorance, the tragic protagonist is confronted in the end by an inexorable fate that ensures an unhappy outcome.

By the time of Aristotle in the fourth century B. C., tragedy as a form had developed its own characteristics. In his *Poetics*, Aristotle states that tragedy is "an imitation of an action that is serious, complete, and of a certain magnitude;... in the form of a drama, not of narrative; through pity and fear effecting the proper purgation of these emotions." (S. H. Butcher, 1932) An analysis of the separate parts of Aristotle's definition of tragedy will help you to be a successful reader. "Serious" indicates that the subject matter must be elevated and that the characters must be important and worth considering. By "complete" Aristotle means that the story must have a beginning, a middle and an end that make a logical, causal, and artistic whole.

The tragedy must be "in the form of a drama" rather than a narrative. That is, the plot must be acted out rather than told. By "action," Aristotle means the complete process of working out a single motivation from its beginning in activity to its conclusion in the recognition of a truth. In Hamlet, for example, the action grows out of Hamlet's resolution to purify Denmark by avenging the murder of his father. In the course of dramatizing the complete working out of an original motive, the action of a tragedy moves from purpose, through emotion, and finally to recognition.

Perhaps the most interesting part of Aristotle's description of tragedy is his assertion that tragic drama arouses fear and pity in the spectators and leads to a purgation of these emotions. The pity and fear that the play evokes in us allow us to experience these emotions vicariously in an extreme form. At the end of the tragedy, these emotions have been purged from our psyche, and thus, we are refreshed. The purgation of fear and pity may also be explained more fully with reference to the dramatic structure (see Chapter 17). Looking at that structure, we see that fear and anxiety are touched most heavily during the tension and uncertainty, leading up to the climax, and pity and regret are the major emotions after the climax during the "falling action."

Language and Tone in Tragedy

Just as character and action are important, so also are language and tone. Greek tragedy was always written in verse; Roman tragedy is poetic; English Renaissance and Restoration tragedy is written mostly in blank verse and heroic couplets. (This does not mean that all tragedy before the nineteenth century is written completely in verse.) Just as tragic protagonists are important and elevated, so also is the language that they speak. Yet, in the twentieth century, tragedy has become a great deal less poetic and elevated, and working-class protagonists have been included. The shift to the common man and woman as the tragic protagonist has led to a concurrent shift from poetry to colloquial and conversational dialogue. The characters in Miller's *Death of a Salesman*, for example, speak idiomatic American English of the 1940's. In a word, modern tragedies have loosened the structure of tragic plots and lowered the level of language.

The tone of tragedy is frequently ironic. One of the most important is dramatic irony. In Arther Miller's *Death of a Salesman*, Willy Loman (that is, "low man") gains his heroic aura only through being a representative of a specific social development, the emphasis on hustling and hard-selling capitalism which at one time formed a prominent part of what is called the American dream. Loman's isolation in itself is simply ironic: it is the collapse of the dream he embodies that is tragic.

John Millington Synge (1871—1909)

Riders to the Sea *

Characters

Maurya, an old woman

---

* *Riders to the sea*: The title alludes to a well-known Bible story. After Moses opens a corridor in the sea for the children of Israel to pass through, he obeys the Lord and lets the waters "come again upon the Egyptians, upon their chariots, and upon their horsemen". Then he and the Israelites "sing unto the Lord, for he has triumphed gloriously: the horse and his rider hath he thrown into the sea" (Exodus 14: 21-31, 15: 1-5).

Barley, her son
Cathleen, her daughter
Nora, a younger daughter
Men and Women

Scene. *An Island off the West of Ireland.*

Cottage kitchen, with nets, oil-skins, spinning-wheel, some new boards standing by the wall, etc. Cathleen, a girl of about twenty, finishes kneading cake, and puts it down in the pot-oven by the fire; then wipes her hands, and begins to spin at the wheel. Nora, a young girl, outs her head in at the door.

Nora (*in a low voice*): Where is she?

Cathleen: She's lying down, God help her, and may be sleeping, if she's able.

Nora comes in softly, and takes a bundle from under her shawl.

Cathleen (*spinning the wheel rapidly*): What is it you have?

Nora: The young priest is after bringing them.* It's a shirt and a plain stocking were got off a drowned man in Donegal.

Cathleen stops her wheel with a sudden movement, and leans out to listen.

Nora: We're to find out if it's Michael's they are, some time herself will be down looking by the sea.

Cathleen: How would they be Michael's, Nora? How would he go the length of that way to the far north?

Nora: The young priest says he's known the like of it. "If it's

---

* *is after bringing them*: has just brought them.

Michael's they are," says he, "you can tell yourself he's got a clean burial by the grace of God, and if they're not his, let no one say a word about them, for she'll be getting her death," says he, "with crying and lamenting".

The door which Nora half-closed is blown open by a gust of wind.

Cathleen (*looking out anxiously*): Did you ask him would he stop Bartley going this day with the horses to the Galway fair?

Nora: "I won't stop him," says he, "but let you not be afraid. Herself does be saying prayers half through the night, and the Almighty God won't leave her destitute," says he, "with no son living."

Cathleen: Is the sea bad by the white rocks, Nora?

Nora: Middling bad, God help us. There's a great roaring in the west, and it's worse it'll be getting when the tide's turned to the wind.

She goes over to the table with the bundle.

Shall I open it now?

Cathleen: Maybe she'd wake up on us, and come in before we'd done. (*Coming to the table.*) It's a long time we'll be, and the two of us crying.

Nora(*goes to the inner door and listens*): She's moving about on the bed. She'll be coming in a minute.

Cathleen: Give me the ladder, and I'll put them up in the turf-loft, the way she won't know of them at all, and maybe when the tide turns she'll be going down to see would he be floating from the east.

They put the ladder against the gable of the chimney; Cathleen goes up a few steps and hides the bundle in the turf-loft. Maurya comes from the inner room.

Maurya (*looking up at Cathleen and speaking querulously*): Isn't it turf enough you have for this day and evening?

Cathleen: There's a cake baking at the fire for a short space (*throwing down the turf*) and Bartley will want it when the tide turns if he goes to Connemara.

Nora picks up the turf and puts it round the pot-oven.

Maurya (*sitting down on a stool at the fire*): He won't go this day with the wind rising from the south and west. He won't go this day, for the young priest will stop him surely.

Nora: He'll not stop him, mother, and I heard Eamon Simon and Stephen Pheety and Colum Shawn saying he would go.

Maurya: Where is he itself?

Nora: He went down to see would there be another boat sailing in the week, and I'm thinking it won't be long till he's here now, for the tide's turning at the green head, and the hooker's * tacking from the east.

Cathleen: I hear some one passing the big stones.

Nora (*looking out*): He's coming now, and he in a hurry.

Bartley (*comes in and looks round the room. Speaking sadly and*

---

* *hooker*: a one-masted fishing boat.

quietly): Where is the bit of new rope, Cathleen, was bought in Connemara?

Cathleen(*coming down*): Give it to him, Nora; it's on a nail by the white boards. I hung it up this morning, for the pig with the black feet was eating it.

Nora(*giving him a rope*): Is that it, Bartley?

Maurya: You'd do right to leave that rope, Bartley, hanging by the boards. (*Bartley takes the rope.*) It will be wanting in this place. I'm telling you, if Michael is washed up tomorrow morning, or the next morning, or any morning in the week, for it's a deep grave we'll make him by the grace of God.

Bartley(*beginning to work with the rope*): I've no halter the way I can ride down on the mare, and I must go now quickly. This is the one boat going for two weeks or beyond it, and the fair will be a good fair for horses I heard them saying below.

Maurya: It's a hard thing they'll be saying below if the body is washed up, and there's no man in it to make the coffin, and I after giving a big price for the finest white boards you'd find in Connemara.

She looks round at the boards.

Bartley: How would it be washed up, and we after looking each day for nine days, and a strong wind blowing a while back from the west and south?

Maurya: If it wasn't found itself, that wind is raising the sea, and there was a star up against the moon, and it rising in the night. If it was a hundred horses, or a thousand horses you had itself, what is the price of a thousand horses against a son where there is one son only?

Bartley(*working at the halter*, *to Cathleen*): Let you go down each day, and see the sheep aren't jumping in on the rye, and if the jobber comes you can sell the pig with the black feet if there is a good price going.

Maurya: How would the like of her get a good price for a pig?

Bartley(*to Cathleen*): If the west wind holds with the last bit of the moon let you and Nora get up weed enough for another cock for the kelp*. It's hard set we'll be from this day with no one in it but one man to work.

Maurya: It's hard set we'll be surely the day you're drownd'd with the rest. What way will I live and the girls with me, and I an old woman looking for the grave?

Bartley lays down the halter, takes off his old coat, and puts on a newer one of the same flannel.

Bartley(*to Nora*): Is she coming to the pier?

Nora(*looking out*): She's passing the green head and letting fall her sails.

Bartley (*getting his purse and tobacco*): I'll have half an hour to go down, and you'll see me coming again in two days, or in three days, or maybe in four days if the wind is bad.

---

* *another cock for the kelp*: another pile of seaweed. The islanders harvest the weed to fertilize their sparse, rocky soil.

Maurya (*turning round to the fire, and putting her shawl over her head*): Isn't it a hard and cruel man won't hear a word from an old woman, and she holding him from the sea?

Cathleen: It's the life of a young man to be going on the sea, and who would listen to an old woman with one thing and she saying it over?

Bartley (*taking the halter*): I must go now quickly. I'll ride down on the red mare, and the gray pony'll run behind me.... The blessing of God on you.

He goes out.

Maurya (*crying out as he is in the door*): He's gone now, God spare us, and we'll not see him again. He's gone now, and when the black night is falling I'll have no son left me in the world.

Cathleen: Why wouldn't you give him your blessing and he looking round in the door? Isn't it sorrow enough is on every one in this house without your sending him out with an unlucky word behind him, and a hard word in his ear?

Maurya takes up the tongs and begins raking the fire aimlessly without looking round.

Nora (*turning towards her*): You're taking away the turf from the cake.

Cathleen (*crying out*): The Son of God forgive us, Nora, we're after forgetting his bit of bread.

She comes over to the fire.

Nora: And it's destroyed he'll be going till dark night, and he after eating nothing since the sun went up.

Cathleen(*turning the cake out of the oven*) : It's destroyed he'll be, surely. There's no sense left on any person in a house where an old woman will be talking for ever.

Maurya sways herself on her stool.

Cathleen(*cutting off some of the bread and rolling it in a cloth*; *to Maurya*) : Let you go down now to the spring well and give him this and he passing. You'll see him then and the dark word will be broken, and you can say "God speed you," the way he'll be easy in his mind.

Maurya(*taking the bread*) : Will I be in it as soon as himself?

Cathleen: If you go now quickly.

Maurya(*standing up unsteadily*) : It's hard set I am to walk.

Cathleen(*looking at her anxiously*) : Give her the stick, Nora, or maybe she'll slip on the big stones.

Nora: What stick?

Cathleen: The stick Michael brought from Connemara.

Maurya(*taking a stick Nora gives her*) : In the big world the old people do be leaving things after them for their sons and children, but in this place it is the young men do be leaving things behind for them that do be old.

She goes out slowly. Nora goes over to the ladder.

Cathleen: Wait, Nora, maybe she'd turn back quickly. She's that sorry, God help her, you wouldn't know the thing she'd do.

Nora: Is she gone around by the bush?

Cathleen (*looking out*): She's gone now. Throw it down quickly, for the Lord knows when she'll be out of it again.

Nora (*getting the bundle from the loft*): The young priest said he'd be passing tomorrow, and we might go down and speak to him below if it's Michael's they are surely.

Cathleen (*taking the bundle*): Did he say what way they were found?

Nora (*coming down*): "There were two men," says he, "and they rowing round with poteen before the cocks crowed*, and the oar of one of them caught the body, and they passing the black cliffs of the north."

Cathleen (*trying to open the bundle*): Give me a knife, Nora, the strings perished with the salt water, and there's a black knot on it you wouldn't loosen in a week.

Nora (*giving her a knife*): I've heard tell it was a long way to Donegal.

Cathleen (*cutting the string*): It is surely. There was a man in here a while ago—the man sold us that knife—and he said if you set off walking from the rock beyond, it would be seven days you'd be in Donegal.

Nora: And what time would a man take, and he floating?

---

* *rowing round with poteen*... crowed: transporting moonshine whiskey under cover of darkness.

Cathleen opens the bundle and takes out a bit of a stocking. They look at them eagerly.

Cathleen (*in a low voice*): The Lord spare us, Nora! isn't it a queer hard thing to say if it's his they are surely?

Nora: I'll get his shirt off the hook the way we can put the one flannel on the other. (*She looks through some clothes hanging in the corner.*) It's not with them, Cathleen, and where will it be?

Cathleen: I'm thinking Bartley put it on him in the morning, for his own shirt was heavy with the salt in it. (*Pointing to the corner.*) There's a bit of a sleeve was of the same stuff. Give me that and it will do.

Nora brings it to her and they compare the flannel.

Cathleen: It's the same stuff, Nora; but if it is itself aren't there great rolls of it in the shops of Galway, and isn't it many another man may have a shirt of it as well as Michael himself?

Nora (*who has taken up the stocking and counted the stitches, crying out*): It's Michael, Cathleen, it's Michael; God spare his soul, and what will herself say when she hears this story, and Bartley on the sea?

Cathleen (*taking the stocking*): It's a plain stocking.

Nora: It's the second one of the third pair I knitted, and I put up three score stitches, and I dropped four of them.

Cathleen (*counts the stitches*): It's that number is in it. (*Crying out.*)

Ah, Nora, isn't it a bitter thing to think of him floating that way to the far north, and no one to keen* him but the black hags that do be flying on the sea?

Nora(*swinging herself round, and throwing out her arms on the clothes*): And isn't it a pitiful thing when there is nothing left of a man who was a great rower and fisher, but a bit of an old shirt and a plain stocking?

Cathleen(*after an instant*): Tell me is herself coming, Nora? I hear a little sound on the path.

Nora(*looking out*): She is, Cathleen. She's coming up to the door.

Cathleen: Put these things away before she'll come in. Maybe it's easier she'll be after giving her blessing to Bartley, and we won't let on we've heard anything the time he's on the sea.

Nora(*helping Cathleen to close the bundle*): We'll put them here in the corner.

They put them into a hole in the chimney corner. Cathleen goes back to the spinning-wheel.

Nora: Will she see it was crying I was?

Cathleen: Keep your back to the door the way the light'll not be on you.

Nora sits down at the chimney corner, with her back to the door. Maurya

* *keen*: weep and wail.

comes in very slowly, without looking at the girls, and goes over to her stool at the other side of the fire. The cloth with the bread is still in her hand. The girls look at each other, and Nora points to the bundle of bread.

Cathleen (*after spinning for a moment*): You didn't give him his bit of bread?

Maurya begins to keen softly, without turning round.

Cathleen: Did you see him riding down?

Maurya goes on keening.

Cathleen (*a little impatiently*): God forgive you; isn't it a better thing to raise your voice and tell what you seen, than to be making lamentation for a thing that's done? Did you see Bartley, I'm saying to you.

Maurya (*with a weak voice*): My heart's broken from this day.

Cathleen (*as before*): Did you see Bartley?

Maurya: I seen the fearfulest thing.

Cathleen (*leaves her wheel and looks out*): God forgive you; he's riding the mare now over the green head, and the gray pony behind him.

Maurya (*starts, so that her shawl falls back from her head and shows her white tossed hair. With a frightened voice*): The gray pony behind him.

Cathleen (*coming to the fire*): What is it ails you, at all?

Maurya (*speaking very slowly*): I've seen the fearfulest thing any person has seen, since the day Bride Dara seen the dead man with the child in his arms.

Cathleen and Nora: Uah. *

They crouch down in front of the old woman at the fire.

Nora: Tell us what it is you seen.

Maurya: I went down to the spring well, and I stood there saying a prayer to myself. Then Bartley came along, and he riding on the red mare with the gray pony behind him. (*She puts up her hands, as if to hide something from her eyes.*) The Son of God spare us, Nora!

Cathleen: What is it you seen?

Maurya: I seen Michael himself.

Cathleen (*speaking softly*): You did not Mother; it wasn't Michael you seen, for his body is after being found in the far north, and he's got a clean burial by the grace of God.

Maurya (*a little defiantly*): I'm after seeing him this day, and he riding and galloping. Bartley came first on the red mare; and I tried to say "God speed you," but something choked the words in my throat. He went by quickly; and "the blessing of God on you," says he, and I could say nothing. I looked up then, and I crying, at the gray pony, and there was Michael upon it—with fine clothes on him,

---

* *Uah*: exclamation of horror and surprise.

and new shoes on his feet.

Cathleen (*begins to keen*): It's destroyed we are from this day. It's destroyed, surely.

Nora: Didn't the young priest say the Almighty God wouldn't leave her destitute with no son living?

Maurya (*in a low voice, but clearly*): It's little the like of him knows of the sea... Bartley will be lost now, and let you call in Eamon and make me a good coffin out of the white boards, for I won't live after them. I've had a husband, and a husband's father and six sons in this house—six fine men, though it was a hard birth I had with every one of them and they coming to the world—and some of them were found and some of them were not found, but they're gone now the lot of them... There were Stephen, and Shawn, were lost in the great wind, and found after in the Bay of Gregory of the Golden Mouth, and carried up the two of them on the one plank, and in by that door.

She pauses for a moment, the girls start as if they heard something through the door that is half open behind them.

Nora (*in a whisper*): Did you hear that, Cathleen? Did you hear a noise in the north-east?

Cathleen (*in a whisper*): There's some one after crying out by the seashore.

Maurya (*continues without hearing anything*): There was Sheamus and his father, and his own father again, were lost in a dark night, and not a stick or sign was seen of them when the sun went up. There was Patch after was drowned out of a curagh* that turned over. I was sitting here with Bartley, and he a baby, lying on my two knees, and I seen two women, and three women, and four women coming in, and they crossing themselves, and not saying a word. I looked out then, and there were men coming after them, and they holding a thing in the half of a red sail, and water dripping out of it—it was a dry day, Nora—and leaving a track to the door.

She pauses again with her hand stretched out towards the door. It opens softly and old women begin to come in, crossing themselves on the threshold, and kneeling down in front of the stage with red petticoats over their heads.

Maurya (*half in a dream, to Cathleen*): Is it Patch, or Michael, or what is it at all?

Cathleen: Michael is after being found in the far north, and when he is found there how could he be here in this place?

Maurya: There does be a power of young men floating round in the sea, and what way would they know if it was Michael they had, or another man like him, for when a man is nine days in the sea, and the wind blowing, it's hard set his own mother would be to say what man was it.

---

* *curagh*: a canvas-bottomed boat.

Cathleen: It's Michael, God spare him, for they're after sending us a bit of his clothes from the far north.

She reaches out and hands Maurya the clothes that belonged to Michael. Maurya stands up slowly and takes them in her hand. Nora looks out.

Nora: They're carrying a thing among them and there's water dripping out of it and leaving a track by the big stones.

Cathleen (*in a whisper to the women who have come in*): Is it Bartley it is?

One of the Women: It is surely, God rest his soul.

Two younger women come in and pull out the table. Then men carry in the body of Bartley, laid on a plank, with a bit of sail over it, and lay it on the table.

Cathleen (*to the women, as they are doing so*): What way was he drowned?

One of the Women: The gray pony knocked him into the sea, and he was washed out where there is a great surf on the white rocks.

Maurya has gone over and knelt down at the head of the table. The women are keening softly and swaying themselves with a slow movement. Cathleen and Nora kneel at the other end of the table. The men kneel near the door.

Maurya (*raising her head and speaking as if she did not see the people around her*): They're all gone now, and there isn't anything more the sea can do to me...I'll have no call now to be up crying and praying when the wind breaks from the south and you can hear the surf is in the east, and the surf is in the west, making a great stir with the two noises, and they hitting one on the other. I'll have no call now to be going down and getting Holy Water in the dark nights after Samhain,* and I won't care what way the sea is when the other women will be keening. (*To Nora.*) Give me the Holy Water, Nora, there's a small cup still on the dresser.

Nora gives it to her.

Maurya (*drops Michael's clothes across Bartley's feet, and sprinkles the Holy Water over him.*): It isn't that I haven't prayed for you, Bartley, to the Almighty God. It isn't that I haven't said prayers in the dark night till you wouldn't know what I'ld be saying; but it's a great rest I'll have now, and it's time surely. It's a great rest I'll have now, and great sleeping in the long nights after Samhain, if it's only a bit of wet flour we do have to eat, and maybe a fish that would be stinking.

She kneels down again, crossing herself, and saying prayers under her breath.

---

* *Samhain*: All Saints' Day.

Cathleen (*to an old man*) : Maybe yourself and Eamon would make a coffin when the sun rises. We have fine white boards herself bought, God help her, thinking Michael would be found, and I have a new cake you can eat while you'll be working.

The Old Man (*looking at the boards*) : Are there nails with them?

Cathleen : There are not, Colum; we didn't think of the nails.

Another Man : It's a great wonder she wouldn't think of the nails, and all the coffins she's been made already.

Cathleen : It's getting old she is, and broken.

Maurya stands up again very slowly and spreads out the pieces of Michael's clothes beside the body, sprinkling them with the last of the Holy Water.

Nora (*in a whisper to Cathleen*) : She's quiet now and easy; but the day Michael was drowned you could hear her crying out from this to the spring well. It's fonder she was of Michael, and would any one have thought that?

Cathleen (*slowly and clearly*) : An old woman will be soon tired with anything she will do, and isn't it nine days herself is after crying and keening, and making great sorrow in the house?

Maurya (*puts the empty cup mouth downwards on the table, and lays her hands together on Bartley's feet*) : They're all together this time, and the end is come. May the Almighty God have mercy on Bartley's soul, and on Michael's soul, and on the souls of Sheamus and Patch, and Stephen and Shawn (*bending her head*); and may He have mercy on my soul, Nora, and on the soul of every one is left living in the world.

She pauses, and the keen rises a little more loudly from the women, then sinks away.

Maurya(*continuing*): Michael has a clean burial in the far north, by the grace of the Almighty God. Bartley will have a fine coffin out of the white boards, and a deep grave surely. What more can we want than that? No man at all can be living for ever, and we must be satisfied.

She kneels down again and the curtain falls slowly.

Questions:

1. What is the situation at the start of "*Riders to the Sea*"? What motivates Cathleen and Nora to hide Michael's clothes from their mother?
2. What motivates the priest not to interfere with Bartley's plan to take the horses to the Galway fair?
3. How does Bartley die? At what moment is his death foreshadowed?
4. Does "*Riders to the Sea*" have any protagonist? If so, what character has this central role?

Chapter 19 Comedy

Types of Comedy

Compared with tragedy, **comedy** is a lighter form of drama that aims primarily to amuse and that ends happily. Comedy is often divided into two varieties—"high" and "low." **High comedy** relies more on wit and wordplay than on physical action for its humor. Its appeal is predominantly intellectual. Thus, jokes about physical appearances would, for example, be avoided. One technique it employs to appeal to a sophisticated, verbal audience is the use of a brief and witty statement that expresses some truth, as in Oscar Wilde's plays *The Importance of Being Earnest* (1895) and *Lady Windermere's Fan* (1892): "I can resist everything except temptation"; "Experience is the name everyone gives to their mistakes"; "There is only one thing worse than being talked about, and that is not being talked about."

The opposite of high comedy, **low comedy** has been called "elemental comedy", in that it is lacking in seriousness of purpose or subtlety of manner and has little intellectual appeal. Some typical features of low comedy are: quarreling, fighting, noisy singing, boasting, clownishness, drunkenness, coarse jesting, scolding and shrewishness. Low comedy places greater emphasis on physical action, sight gags and bawdy jokes and its comic effects do not require much intellect to appreciate.

Consideration of the form as it actually exists suggests that what might be regarded as different kinds of comedy derive fundamentally from differences in the attitude of authors towards their subjects. When an author's intention is to ridicule, satirical comedy emerges. Satirical comedy is designed to correct social and individual behavior by ridiculing human vices and follies. Moliere and George Bernard Shaw, for instance, have written satirical comedy to expose and thus correct the follies of their ages.

Progress from troubles to the triumph of love in a happy outcome produces romantic comedy. Romantic comedy aims to entertain and amuse rather than to ridicule and reform. Usually the audience is encouraged to sympathize with the young lovers. Shakespeare perfected the type in the play *The Merchant of Venice*. Characteristics commonly found include: love as chief motive; an idealized heroine; love subjected to great difficulties; easy reconciliations; happy ending.

Satire of social convention and within social convention creates the comedy of manners. Such plays are designed to satirize the manners and fashions of a particular social class. One of the greatest exponents of the comedy of manners was Moliere, who satirized the hypocrisy and pretension of seventeenth-century French society.

Other types of modern and contemporary comedy include ironic comedy, realistic comedy, and comedy of the absurd. All of these have in common a movement away from the happy endings of traditional comedy. Often, the initial problem—either a realistic an absurdist dilemma—remains unsolved at the close of the play. Such comedies, which began to appear in the late nineteenth century, are frequently designed to illustrate the complexities or absurdities of modern life.

In view of the various kinds of comedies discussed above, you should keep in mind that comedies are rarely pure forms of one type. High comedies can include crude physical humor, especially with characters from the lower class; low comedies may contain some wit and elegance. Satirical comedies can also deal with the successful efforts of young lovers, and romantic comedies often mock the vices and follies of eccentric characters.

The Pattern of Comedy

Comedies begin in adversity; during their exposition, we usually learn that something is wrong. These initial problems can involve thwarted love, eccentric behavior, corruption in society, or a combination of ingredients. As the play moves from exposition to complication, these problems usually get much worse. In comedy, complication is often fueled by confusion, misunderstanding and errors in judgement.

The climax of a comedy occurs when these confusions reach a peak, choices must be made, and solutions must be found. The catastrophe is frequently a sudden revelation of truth in which some key fact, identity or event is explained to the characters and the audience at the same time. Inmost comedies, the events of the catastrophe resolve the initial problems and allow for the comic resolution of the play, setting things right: new families are formed through marriages, and a healthy social order is established.

Language in Comedy

As in other types of drama and literature, language is

employed in comedy to delineate and define character, to establish tone and mood, and to express ideas and feelings. In comedies, however, language is also one of the most important vehicles for creating humor. Some comedies are characterized by elegant and witty language, others by bawdy jokes, puns, and inarticulate utterances. Those characters who are skillful with language can use a witty phrase like a knife to satirize their friends and foes, while those who are unskilled with language bungle through a speech with their misuse of words and inadvertent puns. Both types of characters are amusing.

Wendy Wasserstein (1950—)

The Man in a Case

LIST OF CHARACTERS
BYELINKOV
VARINKA

SCENE: *A small garden in the village of Mironitsk, in* 1898
(*Byelinkov is pacing. Enter Varinka out of breath.*)
BYELINKOV. You are ten minutes late.
VARINKA. The most amazing thing happened on my way over here. You know the woman who runs the grocery store down the road. She wears a black wig during the week, and a blond wig on Saturday nights. And she has the daughter who married an engineer in Moscow who is doing very well thank you and is living, God bless them,

in a three-room apartment. But he really is the most boring man in the world. All he talks about is his future and his station in life. Well, she heard we were to be married and she gave me this basket of apricots to give to you.

BYELINKOV. That is a most amazing thing!

VARINKA. She said to me, Varinka, you are marrying the most honorable man in the entire village. In this village he is the only man fit to speak with my son-in-law.

BYELINKOV. I don't care for apricots. They give me hives.

VARINKA. I can return them. I'm sure if I told her they give you hives she would give me a basket of raisins or a cake.

BYELINKOV. I don't know this woman or her pompous son-in-law. Why would she give me her cakes?

VARINKA. She adores you!

BYELINKOV. She is emotionally loose.

VARINKA. She adores you by reputation. Everyone adores you by reputation. I tell everyone I am to marry Byelinkov, the finest teacher in the country.

BYELINKOV. You tell them this?

VARINKA. If they don't tell me first.

BYELINKOV. Pride can be an imperfect value.

VARINKA. It isn't pride. It is the truth. You are a great man!

BYELINKOV. I am the master of Greek and Latin at a local school at the end of the village of Mironitski.

(*Varinka kisses him.*)

VARINKA. And I am to be the master of Greek and Latin's

wife!

BYELINKOV. Being married requires a great deal of responsibility. I hope I am able to provide you with all that a married man must properly provide a wife.

VARINKA. We will be very happy.

BYELINKOV. Happiness is for children. We are entering into a social contract, an amicable agreement to provide us with a secure and satisfying future.

VARINKA. You are so sweet! You are the sweetest man in the world!

BYELINKOV. I'm a man set in his ways who saw a chance to provide himself with a small challenge.

VARINKA. Look at you! Look at you! Your sweet round spectacles, your dear collar always starched, always raised, your perfectly pressed pants always creasing at right angles perpendicular to the floor, and my most favorite part, the sweet little galoshes, rain or shine, just in case. My Byelinkov, never taken by surprise. Except by me.

BYELINKOV. You speak about me as if I were your pet.

VARINKA. You are my pet! My little school mouse.

BYELINKOV. A mouse?

VARINKA. My sweetest dancing bear with galoshes, my little stale babka. *

BYELINKOV. A stale babka?

---

* *babka*: cake with almonds and raisins.

VARINKA. I am not Pushkin.*

BYELINKOV (*laughs.*) That depends what you think of Pushkin.

VARINKA. You're smiling. I knew I could make you smile today.

BYELINKOV. I am a responsible man. Every day I have for breakfast black bread, fruit, hot tea, and every day I smile three times. I am halfway into my translation of the *Aeneid*** from classical Greek hexameter into Russian alexandrines. In twenty years I have never been late to school. I am a responsible man, but no dancing bear.

VARINKA. Dance with me.

BYELINKOV. Now? It is nearly four weeks before the wedding!

VARINKA. It's a beautiful afternoon. We are in your garden. The roses are in full bloom.

BYELINKOV. The roses have beetles.

VARINKA. Dance with me!

BYELINKOV. You are a demanding woman.

VARINKA. You chose me. And right. And left. And turn. And right. And left.

BYELINKOV. And turn. Give me your hand. You dance like a school mouse. It's a beautiful afternoon! We are in my garden. The roses are in full bloom! And turn. And turn. (*Twirls Varinka around.*)

---

* *Pushkin*: Alexander Pushkin (1799—1837), Russian poet.

** *Aeneid*: Latin epic poem by the Roman poet Virgil (70—19B.C.).

VARINKA. I am the luckiest woman!

(*Byelinkov stops dancing.*)

Why are you stopping?

BYELINKOV. To place a lilac in your hair. Every year on this day I will place a lilac in your hair.

VARINKA. Will you remember?

BYELINKOV. I will write it down. (*Takes a notebook from his pocket.*) Dear Byelinkov, don't forget the day a young lady, your bride, entered your garden, your peace, and danced on the roses. On that day every year you are to place a lilac in her hair.

VARINKA. I love you.

BYELINKOV. It is convenient we met.

VARINKA. I love you.

BYELINKOV. You are a girl.

VARINKA. I am thirty.

BYELINKOV. But you think like a girl. That is an attractive attribute.

VARINKA. Do you love me?

BYELINKOV. We've never spoken about housekeeping.

VARINKA. I am an excellent housekeeper. I kept house for my family on the farm in Gadyatchsky. I can make a beetroot soup with tomatoes and aubergines which is so nice. Awfully awfully nice.

BYELINKOV. You are fond of expletives.

VARINKA. My beet soup, sir, is excellent!

BYELINKOV. Please don't be cross. I too am an excellent housekeeper. I have a place for everything in the house. A shelf for each pot, a cubby for every spoon, a folder for favorite recipes. I have cooked for myself for twenty years. Though my beet soup is not outstanding, it is sufficient.

VARINKA. I'm sure it's very good.

BYELINKOV. No. It is awfully, awfully not. What I am outstanding in, however, what gives me greatest pleasure, is preserving those things which are left over. I wrap each tomato slice I haven't used in a wet cloth and place it in the coolest corner of the house. I have had my shoes for seven years because I wrap them in the galoshes you are so fond of. And every night before I go to sleep I wrap my bed in quilts and curtains so I never catch a draft.

VARINKA. You sleep with curtains on your bed?

BYELINKOV. I like to keep warm.

VARINKA. I will make you a new quilt.

BYELINKOV. No. No new quilt. That would be hazardous.

VARINKA. It is hazardous to sleep under curtains.

BYELINKOV. Varinka, I don't like change very much. If one works out the arithmetic, the final fraction of improvement is at best less than an eighth of value over the total damage caused by disruption. I never thought of marrying till I saw your eyes dancing among the familiar faces at the headmaster's tea. I assumed I would grow old preserved like those which are left over, wrapped suitably in my case of curtains and quilts.

VARINKA. Byelinkov, I want us to have dinners with friends and summer country visits. I want people to say, "Have you spent time with Varinka and Byelinkov? He is so happy now that they are married. She is just what he needed."

BYELINKOV. You have already brought me some happiness. But I never was a sad man. Don't ever think I thought I was a sad man.

VARINKA. My sweetest darling, you can be whatever you want! If you are sad, they'll say she talks all the time, and he is softspoken and kind.

BYELINKOV. And if I am difficult?

VARINKA. Oh, they'll say he is difficult because he is highly intelligent. All great men are difficult. Look at Lermontov, Tchaikovsky, Peter the Great.

BYELINKOV. Ivan the Terrible. *

VARINKA. Yes, him too.

BYELINKOV. Why are you marrying me? I am none of these things.

VARINKA. To me you are.

BYELINKOV. You have imagined this. You have constructed an elaborate romance for yourself. Perhaps you are the great one. You are the one with the great imagination.

---

* *Lermontov... Ivan the Terrible*: Mikhail Lermontov (1814—1841), poet and novelist; Peter Ilich Tchaikovsky (1840—1893), composer; Peter the Great (1672—1725) and Ivan the Terrible (1530—1584), czars credited with making Russia a great European power.

VARINKA. Byelinkov, I am a pretty girl of thirty. You're right, I am not a woman. I have not made myself into a woman because I do not deserve that honor. Until I came to this town to visit my brother I lived on my family's farm. As the years passed I became younger and younger in fear that I would never marry. And it wasn't that I wasn't pretty enough or sweet enough, it was just that no man ever looked at me and saw a wife. I was not the woman who would be there when he came home. Until I met you I thought I would lie all my life and say I never married because I never met a man I loved. I will love you, Byelinkov. And I will help you to love me. We deserve the life everyone else has. We deserve not to be different.

BYELINKOV. Yes. We are the same as everyone else.

VARINKA. Tell me you love me.

BYELINKOV. I love you.

VARINKA (*takes his hands.*) We will be very happy. I am very strong. (*Pauses.*) It is time for tea.

BYELINKOV. It is too early for tea. Tea is at half past the hour.

VARINKA. Do you have heavy cream? It will be awfully nice with apricots.

BYELINKOV. Heavy cream is too rich for teatime.

VARINKA. But today is special. Today you placed a lilac in my hair. Write in your note pad. Every year we will celebrate with apricots and heavy cream. I will go to my brother's house and get some.

BYELINKOV. But your brother's house is a mile from here.

VARINKA. Today it is much shorter. Today my brother gave me his bicycle to ride. I will be back very soon.

BYELINKOV. You rode to my house by bicycle! Did anyone see you!

VARINKA. Of course. I had such fun. I told you I saw the grocery store lady with the son-in-law who is doing very well thank you in Moscow, and the headmaster's wife.

BYELINKOV. You saw the headmaster's wife!

VARINKA. She smiled at me.

BYELINKOV. Did she laugh or smile?

VARINKA. She laughed a little. She said, "My dear, you are very progressive to ride a bicycle." She said you and your fiancé Byelinkov must ride together sometime. I wonder if he'll take off his galoshes when he rides a bicycle.

BYELINKOV. She said that?

VARINKA. She adores you, We had a good giggle.

BYELINKOV. A woman can be arrested for riding a bicycle. That is not progressive, it is a premeditated revolutionary act. Your brother must be awfully, awfully careful on behalf of your behavior. He has been careless—oh so careless—in giving you the bicycle.

VARINKA. Dearest Byelinkov, you are wrapping yourself under curtains and quilts! I made friends on the bicycle.

BYELINKOV. You saw more than the headmaster's wife and the idiot grocery woman.

VARINKA. She is not an idiot.

BYELINKOV. She is a potato-vending, sausage-armed fool!

VARINKA. Shhh! My school mouse. Shhh!

BYELINKOV. What other friends did you make on this bicycle?

VARINKA. I saw students from my brother's classes. They waved and shouted, "Anthropos in love! Anthropos in love!!"

BYELINKOV. Where is that bicycle?

VARINKA. I left it outside the gate. Where are you going?

BYELINKOV (*muttering as he exits.*) Anthropos in love, anthropos in love.

VARINKA. They were cheering me on. Careful, you'll trample the roses.

BYELINKOV (*returning with the bicycle.*) Anthropos is the Greek singular for man. Anthropos in love translates as the Greek and Latin master in love. Of course they cheered you. Their instructor, who teaches them the discipline and contained beauty of the classics, is in love with a sprite on a bicycle. It is a good giggle, isn't it? A very good giggle! I am returning this bicycle to your brother.

VARINKA. But it is teatime.

BYELINKOV. Today we will not have tea.

VARINKA. But you will have to walk back a mile.

BYELINKOV. I have my galoshes on. (*Gets on the bicycle.*) Varinka, we deserve not to be different. (*Begins to pedal. The bicycle doesn't move.*)

VARINKA. Put the kickstand up.

BYELINKOV. I beg your pardon.

VARINKA (*giggling.*) Byelinkov, to make the bicycle move,

you must put the kickstand up.

(*Byelinkov puts it up and awkwardly falls off the bicycle as it moves.*)

(*Laughing.*) Ha ha ha. My little school mouse. You look so funny! You are the sweetest dearest man in the world. Ha ha ha!

(*Pause.*)

BYELINKOV. Please help me up. I'm afraid my galosh is caught.

VARINKA (*trying not to laugh.*) Your galosh is caught! (*Explodes in laughter again.*) Oh, you are so funny! I do love you so. (*Helps Byelinkov up.*) You were right, my pet, as always. We don't need heavy cream for tea. The fraction of improvement isn't worth the damage caused by the disruption.

BYELINKOV. Varinka, it is still too early for tea. I must complete two stanzas of my translation before late afternoon. That is my regular schedule.

VARINKA. Then I will watch while you work.

BYELINKOV. No. You had a good giggle. That is enough.

VARINKA. Then while you work I will work too. I will make lists of guests for our wedding.

BYELINKOV. I can concentrate only when I am alone in my house. Please take your bicycle home to your brother.

VARINKA. But I don't want to leave you. You look so sad.

BYELINKOV. I never was a sad man. Don't ever think I was a sad man.

VARINKA. Byelinkov, it's a beautiful day, we are in your garden. The roses are in bloom.

BYELINKOV. Allow me to help you on to your bicycle. (*Takes Varinka's hand as she gets on the bike.*)

VARINKA. You are such a gentleman. We will be very happy.

BYELINKOV. You are very strong. Good day, Varinka.

(*Varinka pedals off. Byelinkov, alone in the garden, takes out his pad and rips up the note about the lilac, strews it over the garden, then carefully picks up each piece of paper and places them all in a small envelope as lights fade to black.*)

Questions:

1. What scene in the play do you think is funny? And why is it funny? Can you formulate a theory of comedy based on this episode?
2. At the end of the play Byelinkov tears up the note but then collects the pieces. What do you interpret these actions to mean?

Critical Approaches to Literature

Formalist (or New) Criticism

Formalism was first a Russian school of literary criticism that flourished from 1914 to 1928. It began in two groups: OPOYAZ (an acronym for Russian words meaning "Society for the Study of Poetic Language"), founded in 1914 at St. Petersburg and led by the linguistic critic Victor Shklovsky; and the Moscow Linguistic Circle, founded in 1915. Both groups made use of the linguistic techniques of Ferdinand de Saussure. Although they based their approach largely on Symbolist notions concerning the autonomy of the text and the discontinuity between literary and other uses of language, the **Formalists** sought to make their analyses more objective and scientific than those of **Symbolist** criticism.

Formalism was a powerful influence in the former Soviet Union until 1929, when it was condemned for its lack of political perspective. Later, largely through the work of the structuralist linguist, Roman Jakobson, it became highly influential in the West, notably in Anglo-American **New Criticism**.

New Criticism developed in England and the United States after World War I. In a strict sense, the term is applied to the criticism written by John Crowe Ransom, Allen Tate, R. P. Blackmur, Robert Penn Warren and Cleanth Brooks, and it is derived from Ransom's **The New Criticism**, published in 1941, which discusses a movement in America in the 1930s that paralleled movements in England led by critics like T.S. Eliot, I.A. Richards, and William Empson. Generally the term is applied, however, to the whole body of criticism that concentrates on the work of art as an object in itself; finds in it a special kind of language opposed to, (or at least different from) the language of science or philosophy; and examines it through a process of close analysis. In other words, **The New Criticism** focused intensively upon the language, imagery, and emotional or intellectual tensions in particular works in an attempt to explain their total formal aesthetic organization. New Critics insisted on the *intrinsic* value of a work of art and focused attention on the work alone as an independent unit of meaning, with no regard for its writer and the writer's background—that is, independent of biology, psychology, sociology, and history.

Formalist criticism, also called **the New Criticism**, begins with a personal response to the literary work, but it goes on to try to account for the response by closely examining the work. It assumes that the author shaped the poem, play, or story so fully that the work guides the reader's response. For the formalist critic, the final work contains a stable meaning that all competent readers can perceive.

A key method that formalists use to explore the intense

relationships within a poem is **close reading**, a careful step-by-step **analysis (the examination of the relations of parts) and explication** (the unfolding of meaning, line by line or even word by word). The purpose of close reading is to understand how various elements in a literary text work together to shape its effects on the reader. Since formalists believe that the various stylistic and the thematic elements of literary work influence each other, these critics insist that form and content cannot be meaningfully separated. The complete interdependence of form and content is what makes a text literary.

To repeat: **Formalist** criticism assumes that a work of art is stable. An artist constructs a coherent, comprehensible work, thus conveying to a reader an emotion or an idea.

Formalist criticism began to achieve prominence in the late 1920s and was the dominant form from the late 1930s until about 1970, and even today it is widely considered the best way for a student to begin to study a work of literature.

Marxist (or Sociological) Criticism

Marxist criticism sees history primarily as a struggle between socioeconomic classes, and it sees literature as the product of economic forces of the period.

For Marxist critics, economics is the "base" or "infrastructure"; on this base rests a "superstructure" of ideology (law, politics, philosophy, religion, and arts, including literature), reflecting the interests of the dominant class. Thus, literature is a material product, produced — like bread or battleships—in order to be consumed in a given society. Like every other product, literature is the product of work, and it *does* work. A bourgeois society, for example, will produce literature that in one way or another celebrates bourgeois values, such as individualism.

Marxist criticism examines literature in the cultural, economic and political context in which it is written or received. Art is not created in a vacuum. It is the work not simply of a person, but of an author fixed in time and space. Marxist criticism explores the relationships between the artist and society. Sometimes it looks at the sociological status of the author to evaluate how the profession of the writer affected what was written. Marxist criticism also analyzes the social context of literary works—what cultural, economic or political values a particular text implicitly or explicitly promotes. Finally, Marxist criticism examines the role the audience has in shaping literature.

Marxist criticism, like the work of the Hungarian philosopher George Lukacs, often explores the ideological content of literature. According to Lukacs, it is the view of the world, the ideology underlying a writer's work that counts. And it is the writer's attempt to reproduce this view of the world which constitutes his intention. Whereas a formalist critic would maintain that form and content are inextricably blended, Lukacs believed that content determines form and that therefore, all art is political. Consequently, Marxist criticism is frequently evaluative and judges some literary work better than others on an ideological basis; this tendency can lead to reductive judgement, as when Russian critics rated Jack London a novelist superior to William Faulkner, Ernest Hemingway, because he illustrated the principles of class struggle most clearly. In the heyday of Marxism in the United States, during the depression of the 1930s, it was also common for such Marxist critics as Granville Hicks to assert that the novel must show the class struggle.

Another important Marxist critic and perhaps one of the most influential among the critical world is Terry Eagleton, who observed that:

> *Literature may be an artefact, a product of social consciousness, a world vision; but it is also an industry. Books are not just structures of meaning, they are also commodities produced by publishers and sold on the market at a profit. Drama is not just a collection of literary texts; it is a capitalist business which employs certain men (authors, directors and actors) to produce a commodity to be consumed by an audience at a profit. Critics are not just analysts of texts; they are also (usually) academics hired by the state to prepare students*

ideologically for their functions within capitalist society. Writers are not just transposers of trans-individual mental structures, they are also workers hired by publishing houses to produce commodities which will sell.

Marxist critics take seriously Marx's famous comment that "the philosophers have only *interpreted* the world in various ways; the point is to *change* it". The critic's job is to change the world, by revealing the economic basis of arts.

Structuralism

Structuralism was an European critical movement of the mid-20th century. It was based on the linguistic theories of Swiss-born linguist Ferdinand de Saussure, which held that language is a self-contained system of signs, and the cultural theories of social anthropologist Claude Levi-Strauss, which held that cultures, like languages, could be viewed as systems of signs and could be analyzed in terms of the structural relations among their elements. Literary structuralism views literary texts as systems of interlocking signs and seeks to make explicit in a semiscientific way the "grammar" (the rules and codes or system of organization) that governs the form and content of all literature. Michel Foucault, Roman Jakobson, Jo-nathan Culler, and Roland Barthes are among the more prominent structuralists.

Structuralism arises from the revolutionary linguistic theories of Ferdinand de Saussure. Saussure divided language into individual utterances (parole) and the larger systems of rules and relationships that give them meaning (langue). Saussure also changed how we think about words. Language, Saussure argued, is made up of signs. Signs combine symbols (what Saussure calls *signifiers*) with concepts (*signifieds*) to stand for—or *signify*—something. In language the signifier is a word's sounds or letters; the signified is its meaning. For Saussure, signs don't actually represent reality since a word's sounds or letters are arbitrary. A sign's meaning comes from its position in the language system it belongs to. So meaning is always relational to other signs within a language or another signifying system.

In 1945 French anthropologist Claude Levi-Strauss began applying language theory to nonlinguistic studies. If anything with meaning is a sign, he reasoned, any social system is a sort of language. So why not use linguistic techniques to analyze everything, including kinship patterns, myths, eating rules, clothing, gender and other cultural practices.

Noting Saussure's principle that meaning depends on differences between signs, Levi-Strauss was particularly interested in binary oppositions. Levi-Strauss identified *binary oppositions* in every aspect of human culture: nature/culture, raw/cooked, male/female, clothed/naked, knowledge/ignorance, life/death, and so on. For Levi-Strauss the human mind naturally operates using such opposition. The binary oppositions in the story's structure reveal its meaning.

Structuralists also examine the codes and conventions that determine meaning and interpretation. The idea of codes comes from Roman Jakobson's famous communication model. Jakobson identifies six essential elements in communication. Most simply, a *sender* directs a *message* to a *receiver* through a *contact* (voice, telephone, printed page, facial expression) and within a *context* (the physical and psychological environment). All this is framed within certain *codes*, or culturally shared patterns of meaning. Any society involves many codes. For example, we find codes for different professions, regions, religions and so on. The legal profession has its own codes designating what constitutes guilt. A member of the clergy, a thief with a hungry family, or a parent might define guilt very differently. Further, each individual knows many different codes. We think in very different patterns in a college class than we are playing basketball or on a date. Therefore both writers and readers need to know some codes in order to create or interpret a text competently.

Connections between linguistics and literature are obvious. But we should keep in mind that structuralist literary critics have little interest in interpreting particular works. Instead, they seek to discover the structure or codes that allow texts to have meaning. In this sense, analyzing literature reminds us that we must interpret everything and that we do so according to various codes. Yet, structuralists approach literary texts in a variety of ways.

In many ways literary applications of structuralism begin with structural linguist Roman Jakobson, who analyzes a text's "literariness"—what makes a verbal message a work of art. Some structuralists reduce the texts they study into the smallest structures possible and then investigate the relations among the parts. Some structuralist critics study structural patterns in individual texts and examine binary oppositions: relationship between *rich* and *poor*, *presence* and *absence*, *old* and *young*. Many other structuralists, like Robert Scholes, focus on the codes shared by author and audience and triggered by texts. Where there are texts, there are rules governing text production and interpretation. Understanding texts means identifying codes behind them. The text itself, to these critics, can only rework cultural and literary codes already in place. To use one of Barthes's favorite phrase, in a sense every text is "always already written" before the author begins it. Another important branch of structuralism shifts attention from the text to its readers. For Jonathan Culler, structures and codes are not really in texts but in writers and readers. Just as linguists investigate language competence, Culler does the same thing with readers' literary competence. Culler wants to know what constitutes literary competence within a culture.

If we observe structuralism carefully, we may find that formalism and structuralism do share traits on the one hand, but differ in crucial ways on the other. Both approaches examine texts without reference to author or history. Both investigate how textual elements relate to create some sort of whole. Yet, differences between them seem to be obvious. Formalism seeks to *interpret* texts, while structuralism studies *how* interpretation and meaning are possible. Formalism pursues thematic unity; structuralism relationships. Moreover, formalists generally believe that language—especially literary language—reveals truth. Structuralists deny the possibility of referential truth; for them "truth" depends entirely on the systems that create meaning.

Post-structuralism

Post-structuralism is a movement in literary criticism conceived in France in the late 1960s. Based on the linguistic theories of Ferdinand de Saussure and the deconstructionist theories of Jacques Derrida in particular, post-structuralism is centered around the idea that language is based on differences and therefore is inherently unreliable and cannot possess absolute meaning in itself. In opposition to formalist critics, who see a literary work as an independent whole containing a fixed meaning, post-structuralists believe that all meaning resides in *intertextuality*, the work's connections with a vast context of writings or the relationship of the text to past and future texts. What language expresses is already absent; the present is already past when expressed. In writing, the object is even farther absent, as the word *differs* from what it signifies and *defers* meaning as the utterance lags behind the thought.

Post-structuralism challenges the New Criticism, which seeks a truth fixed within the "verbal icon," the text, in W. K. Wimsatt's term. Post-structuralism invites interpretations through the spaces left by the way words operate. No text (including the text of the world), according to post-structuralists, can be understood directly, but only through language. Consequently, truth always hides behind signs, whether these occur in language itself; in the conflict between unconscious desire and socially charged ego; in the clash between ideology, power, and individuality; or in signs themselves.

Emphasis shifts from text to reader. The New Criticism deletes the authors and their intentions, concentrating on the text. Post-structuralism deletes the author and demotes the text, since the loopholes in language itself throw the certainty of both into question. Post-structuralism concentrates on the reader, who is free, according to Roland Barthes, to play with the text's possibilities, producing new texts for subsequent play. Reading and writing are the same kind of enterprise, and all writing is text.

Both literature and philosophy, says Derrida, can only pretend toward truth. Paul de Man agrees, seeing the same, not separate. Literature and philosophy both wrongly assume a fixed presence of reality. Derrida points to the inevitable *absence* of reality in language, and in the perceiver's mind. All the reader has is a *trace* of object, or thought, even as the reader tries to find words to express it. Thus reality itself becomes a text, and every text depends on a *pretext.* For literature, reality has vanished. Meaning depends on *intertextuality*, as the reader utters new texts in response to old, new pages moving on from their predecessors. Because different readers bring different things, meaning is thus ever-changing. In this view, no text is self-sufficient, and no writer fully controls the meaning of the text. Because we are talking about connections of which the writer is unaware, and because "meaning" is in part the creation of the reader, the author is by no means an authority. Literary critic Julia Kristeva in the 1960s introduced the term to express the idea that every new literary text is an intersection of texts—that it has absorbed and transformed previous works and that it will be absorbed and transformed by future texts. To put it short, a text's quality is interdependent with all previous and future discourse.

In all, like the practitioners of reader-response, feminist, Marxist, and psychoanalytic criticism, post-structuralists do not support the traditional Western insistence on a single correct reading of a text. Writers associated with the movement include Roland Barthes, Jacques Lacan, Julia Kristeva, and Michel Foucault.

Deconstructionist Criticism

Deconstruction is a method of literary criticism which assumes that language refers only to itself rather than to an extratextual reality and which asserts multiple conflicting interpretations of a text and bases such interpretations on the philosophical, political or social implications of the use of language in the text rather than on the author's intention.

Deconstruction was initiated by French critic Jacques Derrida, who in a series of books published beginning in the late 1960s, launched a major critique of traditional Western metaphysics. Derrida's deconstructive strategies, which expand on Ferdinand de Saussure's insistence on the arbitrariness of the verbal sign, have subsequently established themselves as an important part of postmodernism, especially in poststructural literary theory and text analysis.

Deconstruction begins with the assumptions that the world is unknowable and that language is unstable, elusive and unfaithful. Consequently, literary texts, which are made up of words, have no fixed, single meaning. Since they believe that literature cannot definitely express its subject matter, deconstructionists tend to shift their attention away from *what* is being said to *how* language is being used in a text.

Like formalist critics, deconstructionists try to find the meaning of a text by close reading. But while a formalist usually tries to demonstrate how the diverse elements of a text cohere with meaning and often holds that a competent author constructs a coherent work with a stable meaning and that competent readers can perceive this meaning, deconstructionists seek to show that a literary work (usually called "a text" or "a discourse") inevitably is self-contradictory and approach attempts to show how the text "deconstructs", that is, how it can be broken down into mutually irreconcilable positions. Deconstructionists reject the notion that the critic should endorse the myth of authorial control over language. Deconstructionist critics like Roland Barthes and Michel Foucault have therefore called for "the death of the author", that is, the rejection of the assumption that the author can fully control the meaning of a text. They have also announced the death of literature as a special category of writing. In their view, poems and novels are merely words on a page; all texts are created equal—equally untrustworthy.

Deconstructionists focus on how language is used to achieve power. Since they believe, in the words of critic David Lehman, that "there are no truths, only rival interpretations", deconstructionists try to understand how some "interpretations" come to be regarded as truth. Deconstruction ultimately questions the possibility of arriving at absolute truth, challenges Western modes of thought, and exchanges interpretation and closure for "textuality" and "play". In essence, deconstruction refuses to let us feel satisfied with easy, totaling perceptions and interpretations.

Deconstruction may strike you as a negative, even destructive, critical approach, and yet by patient analysis, deconstructive critics often reveal fascinating aspects of the most familiar literary texts and expose the hidden limits of our interpretive systems—textual and otherwise.

Psychoanalytic Criticism

Modern psychology has had a tremendous effect on both literature and literary criticism. Sigmund Freud's psychoanalytic theories changed our notions of human behavior by exploring new or controversial areas like wish-fulfillment, sexuality, the unconsciousness, and repression. **Psychoanalytic criticism** usually examines the author's writings in the framework of Freudian psychology. A central doctrine of Sigmund Freud is the Oedipus complex, the view that all males unconsciously wish to displace their fathers and to sleep with their mothers. According to Freud, hatred for the father and love of the mother, normally repressed, may appear disguised versions of repressed wishes. Thus one might interpret William Faulkner's "A Rose for Emily" as such an example: Emily's father always repressed her sexual desire to marry. Although she cannot literally resist her father's oppression while she is alive, she does so after he dies. Nevertheless, she has internalized her father's sexual repression. In fulfilling her sexual desire by sleeping with a man, she represses that desire by sleeping with a dead man. A theme of this short story may be that sexual desire must be repressed, but that it will still erupt in extraordinary ways. This eruption is referred to as the "return of the repressed."

One way of understanding psychoanalytic approaches to literature is to say that there are two major schools of thought: the American and the French. The American school of criticism leans toward accepting and applying Freudian concepts to literary texts. Between 1910s and 1930s psychoanalytic critics and Freud in particular, researched the author's childhood and read the text, its characters and symbols to understand the author's psyche. In addition to psychoanalyzing authors, they also analyzed the neuroses of fictional characters. Later in the 1950s and 1960s, some American psychoanalytic critics moved from psychoanalyzing authors and characters to studying the dynamics between the reader and the text. Norman Holland has spent his career evolving his own brand of psychoanalytic criticism. He assumes that each reader has a "characteristic way of dealing with the demands of outer and inner reality." That is, each individual has an essential core self with an "identity theme" that never changes. Holland believes that readers use texts to deal with their own psychological issues and to help them achieve successful solutions within their identity themes. By accepting Freud's theory of two human instincts: the death instinct, or the desire to die, and the sexual instinct, or the desire to live, Peter Brooks believes that these instincts explain fictional narratives. That is, novels "drive toward the end" (the death instinct), yet they also resist ending (the sexual instinct). If the sex instinct underlies narrative, then this calls for an "erotics of reading," or the study of how reading always involves desire. Harold Bloom, another influential American psychoanalytic critic, explains literary history by applying the Freudian Oedipal complex to literature, for Bloom conceives of the artist as a son in a struggle with his poetic father. Since the son has not yet achieved fame the way the precursor has, he wants to become the precursor. He must kill the father and his influence. Although his precursor is already dead, yet he has a powerful influence on society and on the son in particular, the son kills the father in his imagination (the literary work). Bloom, based on Freudian principles, suggests that the son kills the father and his influence through "misreading." "Misreading" occurs when the son internalizes but rewrites the precursor. Thus, "misreading" signals the son's independence from the precursor.

The French school of psychoanalytic criticism not only has changed how we think about literature, writing, reading, and language, but also alters our understanding of the sciences and philosophy. Unlike American school of criticism, the French drastically revises Freud. Jacques Lacan is the foremost French psychoanalytic theorist, but his theory is difficult. Lacan's major revision of Freud is his belief that *language* forms our identity. Lacan maps out three domains, the Real, the Imaginary and the Symbolic, all of which anticipate, participate in, or are mediated by language. The Real, according to Lacan, is the actual world and everything in it, all of which remain unknowable to the individual. Individuals in the Imaginary and Symbolic stages try to master the Real, but they cannot directly experience it. The Imaginary is the world of images, fantasy, wish fulfillment; it appears to be a utopian state of oneness with the mother. And the Symbolic is the realm in which the child learns to use language and becomes subject to the father's rule. Lacan's concept of language is crucial to his belief that individuals are fragmented. Lacan believes that "the speaker is subjected to language rather than master of it." Lacan asserts that language, which we think accurately communicates and orders our understanding, actually only obstructs it. Thus, when the child acquires language, it is also barred because its unconscious urges are repressed from the conscious.

To sum up: Psychological criticism is a diverse category, but it often employs three approaches. First, it investigates the creative process of the artist, that is, how does the nature of literary genius related to normal mental functions? The second major study is of a particular artist, employing psychology to understand the subject's motivations and behavior. The third common area of psychological criticism is the analysis of fictional characters. Freud's studies of Oedipus is the prototype for this approach that tries to bring modern insights about human behavior into the study of how fictional people act.

Reader-response Criticism

Reader-response criticism is a critical method that examines the reader and the act of reading rather than the text being read. The reader-response approach evolved out of phenomenological and interpretive analyses and is closely related to reception theory; it analyzes the reader's role in the production of meaning when engaged with a written text. Reader-response critics examine, for example, the inferences the reader must supply, the set of assumptions the reader must make, the gaps the reader must fill, the set of schemata the reader must actualize in order to make sense of the text, and the ideologies that determine all of the above.

Reader-response criticism emphasizes the idea that various readers respond in various ways and therefore the "meaning" of a work is not merely something put into the work by the writer; rather, the "meaning" is an interpretation created or constructed or produced by the reader as well as the writer. Stanley Fish, an exponent of reader-response theory, in *Is There a Text in This Class?* (1980), puts it this way: "Interpretation is not the art of construing but of constructing. Interpreters do not decode poems; they make them."

If we try to relate these ideas more specifically to comments about literature, we might ask: If "meaning" is the production or creation not simply of the writer but also of the perceiver, does it follow that there is no such thing as a "correct" interpretation of the meaning of a work of literature? Answers to this question differ. At one extreme, the reader is said to construct or reconstruct the text under the firm guidance of the author. That is, the author shapes or constructs the text so powerfully that the reader is virtually compelled to perceive or reconstruct it the way the author wants it to be perceived. (We can call this view *the objective view*, since it holds that readers look objectively at the work and see what the author put into it.) At the other extreme, the reader constructs the meaning according to his or her own personality, that is, according to the reader's psychological identity. (We can call this view *the subjective view*, since it holds that readers project their feelings into what they perceive.)

Against the objective view one can argue thus: No author can fully control a reader's response to every detail of the text. No matter how carefully constructed the text is, it leaves something to the reader's imagination. Besides, there are always *gaps* and *indeterminacies*, to use the words of Wolfgang Iser, a reader-response critic, between the reader and the text. Readers always go beyond the text, drawing inferences, and evaluating the text in terms of their own experience.

In an extreme form the subjective view denies that authors can make us perceive the meanings that they try to put into their works. This position suggests that every reader has a different idea of what a work means, an idea that reflects the reader's own ideas.

As has been mentioned above, reader-response criticism evolves out of phenomenology which makes three assertions: (1) Meaning exists in the perceiver's mind, not in the outside world; (2) We don't simply receive perceptions passively. Our consciousness actually helps form what we perceive; (3) We don't just see surfaces of things; we can perceive their "essences"—what is permanent, what gives them their unique, individual being. The most influential representative of phenomenologist literary critics, Belgian critic Georges Poulet applies these three principles to literary texts. (1) Since work only exists in consciousness, Poulet "brackets out" everything external to its existence in the minds of writer and reader. (2) The author's consciousness "intends" the novel's "world". (3) As readers we can perceive through the text the "essence" of the author's world. Wolfgang Iser shares Poulet's phenomenologist belief that literary texts do not correspond to any objective reality outside themselves. For Iser, reader and text converge to produce meaning. As we read, we encounter "gaps", holes in the text which must be filled for the text to be complete and whole. Only the reader can bridge the gaps by filling in the missing parts in her own way. The reader must thus "write" part of the text. By doing so, the reader "makes concrete" or "realizes" the text in an act of cocreation.

Not surprisingly, one branch of reader-response criticism considers the individual psychology of readers. American Freudian critic Norman Holland believes that literary meaning is entirely subjective. Holland argues that each individual reads texts according to his own personal *identity theme*, originally imprinted on his personality by his "mother figure" and complete by adulthood. When we read literary texts, we approach them through our own identity themes. According to Holland, as we read, we use the literary work to symbolize and finally to replicate ourselves. We typically follow three strategies in doing this: (1) We discover in the work the very things we desire or fear most in our own lives. And we interpret the text using the same strategies and defenses we use for coping with the world. (2) Next, we develop pleasurable fantasies about what we read. We may identify with certain characters' personalities, roles, or actions, for example. (3) Finally, because raw fantasies usually awaken guilt and anxiety, we transform them into socially or aesthetically acceptable forms. Holland believes we use all three strategies whenever we interpret a literary work. This approach closes the gap between reader and text.

American David Bleich's *subjective criticism* also asserts that texts have no meaning apart from readers. Bleich argues that we distinguish between three kinds of things: objects, symbols, and people. A text is an object only in its physical sense: as black marks on pages between covers. It has no *objective* meaning. But it does have meaning as a *symbol*, which is entirely a mental creation. An object can become a symbol only in the mind of a perceiver.

To sum up, reader-response critics believe that no text provides self-contained meaning; literary texts do not exist independently of readers' interpretations. Rather than declare one interpretation correct and the other mistaken, reader-response criticism recognizes the inevitable plurality of readings. It explores how the different individuals see the same text differently and emphasizes hoe religious, cultural and social values affect meanings; it also overlaps with gender criticism in exploring how men and women read the same text with different assumptions.

Feminist (Gender) Criticism

Feminist literary theory originated largely in the women's liberation movement that followed World War II. Two of the earliest documents of feminist theory are Simone de Beauvoir's *The Second Sex* (1949) and Kate Miller's *Sexual Politics* (1970). Feminist criticism established several aims, one of which is to critique the established "canon" of Western literature and to expose the standards on which it is based as patriarchal. Feminist critics believe that culture has been so completely dominated by men that literature is full of unexamined "male-produced" assumptions. For feminists, women have been subordinated in societal institutions and all societies are based on gender ideologies that favor men. The male is thought to be superior by nature, and the female inferior.

Some feminist critics aim to recover forgotten and neglected texts by women in order to reevaluate them. Elaine Showalter created the term "gynocritics" to describe such analyses. Part of the purpose of gynocritics has been what is called the "recuperation" of female-authored texts. To recuperate texts means to add to the canon of "approved," highly regarded, and regularly studied works texts that have previously been lost or ignored. By so doing, these critics want to show contemporary readers how courageous these early women authors were, given the constraints upon them.

Some feminist critics tend to establish a woman's canon on the basis of the study of woman-centered writing. They might ask why there are so few female-authored texts in the "Great Books" lists and what the standards used to decide whether or not a text belongs in the canon. Women have had fewer opportunities than men to become writers of fiction, poetry, and drama—for one thing, they have been less well educated in the things that the male patriarchy valued—but even when they *have* managed to write, men sometimes have neglected their work simply because it had been by a woman. Feminists have further argued that certain forms of writing have been especially the province of women—for instance, journals, diaries, and letters; and predictably, these forms have not been given adequate space in the traditional, male-oriented canon.

Feminist critics rightly point out that men have established the conventions of literature and that men have established the canon—that is, the body of literature that is said to be worth reading.

These feminists suggest that women should resist the meanings that male authors—or female authors who have inherited patriarchal values—bury in their books. In resisting the obvious meanings, women may discover more significant meanings. In her book *The Resisting reader* (1978), Fetterly argues that Faulkner's "*A Rose for Emily*" is a story "not of a conflict between the South and the North or between the old order and the new;...it is a story of a woman victimized and betrayed by the system of sexual politics." (34-35)

Feminist critics also explore the cultural construction of gender and identity. Until the mid-1980s Anglo-American and French feminism were dominant theoretical forms of literary feminist scholarship. In general, most American and French feminists agree that women are constructed rather than born, but they disagree on what that means. American feminists tend to be more interested in literary analysis than critical theory, and they are more likely to analyze realist texts, while French feminists have tended to be more interested in theory, psychoanalysis, and linguistics than in analysis of literary works. While American feminists tend to believe that despite cultural constraints, there is an autonomous female consciousness which cannot be influenced by patriarchy and attempt to restore women to literary history, French feminists suggest that women are imprisoned in language and it is difficult to override the sexism inherent in language. Take the terms *governor/governess* and *master/mistress* for example. The first word in the set is used for a male and has connotations of great power and institutional authority. The second word in the set is subordinate in its designation of the inferior role. Thus French feminists find that because women are erased in patriarchal culture and language they cannot "exist" in patriarchal culture or language, and French feminists do not attempt to restore women authors to literary history. However, French feminists believe that women can overturn patriarchy by disrupting language itself.

As can be seen from the above, feminist critics are extremely varied in their approaches. Among the writers who have had a great impact on feminist critical discourse are Ellen Moers, Carolyn Heilbrum, Sandra Gilbert, Susan Gubar, Annette Kolodny, Adrienne Rich, Elaine Showalter, Nina Byym, Alice Jardine, Catherine Sti-mpson, Gayatri Spivak, Helene Cixous, Luce Irigaray, and Julia Kristeva.

Mythic and Archetypal Criticism

Mythic and archetypal criticism examines two closely related elements of literature: myths (sacred stories that explain the meaning and origin of the world and the things in it) and archetypes (symbols found repeatedly in myths and in later literature).

Mythic criticism examines the nature and function of mythology, especially in traditional cultures in which myth represents a prelogical way of understanding the world. In addition, mythic criticism looks for the mythic elements—particular images and stories and particular ways of looking at the world—in all literature.

Myths may be defined as stories of ostensibly historical events that serve to unfold part of a worldview of a people or a practice, belief, or natural phenomenon. According to many scholars, myths are the most true of stories, because they are largely stories about origins, including the origin of the cosmos and all that it includes. Consequently, myths give meaning to the world, to human life, and to things in the world by explaining how all these have come into being. Furthermore, because they deal with sacred events and also with sacred beings—with gods, myths are sacred, exemplary and significant, thus supplying models for human behavior and giving meaning and value to life.

Among the first modern thinkers to take a more respectful view of myth was Friedrick Nietzsche, who argued that modern culture had lost touch with the nourishing power of myth. Myth, which Nietzsche called "a concentrated image of the world," channels artistic imagination and gives a culture a "fixed and consecrated place of origin." Sigmund Freud also contributed to the development of modern mythic criticism. For example, Freud's emphasis on the subrational element in human nature has made it easier to view the fantastic and sometimes barbarous world of myth as a genuine revelation of truth about human experience. Myth also plays an important role in one of Freud's best-known theories, the Oedipus complex. This theory derives its name from Freud's view that Oedipus myth is a key to male psychic development.

Though Nietzsche and Freud made important contributions, the emphasis on myth as a tool of literary criticism resulted largely from the rise of anthropology in the late nineteenth and twentieth centuries. Mythic criticism was effectively founded with the publication of the multivolume work *The Golden Bough* (1890—1915) by British anthropologist and folklorist J. G. Frazer. Among those influenced by Frazer were a group of anthropologists such as Gilbert Murray, Jane Harrison, F. M. Cornford, and others, who came to be known as the "Cambridge School." Among those influenced by the scholarly interest in myth were the great Modernist writers such as T. S. Eliot, Ezra Pound, James Joyce and Thomas Mann, among others. The difficulty of reading Modernist works comes in part from the frequency and obscurity of the allusions to myth. Two of the best-known works from these authors are Joyce's novel *Ulysses*, patterned after the *Odyssey*, and Eliot's poem *The Waste Land*, which uses the Grail legend and vegetation myths, along with a multitude of other literary and historical sources.

Archetypal criticism is concerned with the discovery and analysis of the original pattern or model for themes, motifs, and characters in poetry and prose. Archetypal criticism starts with the assumptions that certain images and patterns in literature are universal—that is, they occur over and over again in many times and pla-ces—and that by identifying these archetypes a critic can discover important aspects of a work's meaning and effects. According to Jung, these archetypes belong to the "collective unconscious" that all human beings share—hence, their universality. We inherit the collective unconscious genetically. The collective unconscious is made up of "primordil images" or "archetypes," which form "the common heritage of mankind." This approach to literature is based on the idea that narratives are structured in accordance with an underlying archetypal model: the specific plot and characters are important insofar as they allude to a traditional plot or figure or to patterns that have recurred with wide implications in human history. An archetypal critic, for example, on examining Katherine Anne Porter's story "Flowering Judas," would note that it echoes and ironically inverts the traditional Christian legend of Judas Iscariot.

Mythic and archetypal criticism became especially popular during the 1950s and 1960s. The most important myth-archetype critic of this period was Canadian critic Northrop Frye. Frye adopted ideas from Freud, Jung and others to develop his own intricate view of culture and literature. Frye begins with the assumption that we must study literature not by exposing ourselves to it directly, but by approaching it with a conceptual framework. In the highly structured framework for understanding literature Frye proposes, myth and archetype play important roles.

In Frye's view, the literature of a culture resembles that culture's mythology because it occupies the same verbal structure established by myth. Thus, "literature is a reconstructed mythology, with its structural principles derived from those of myth". Realistic literature thus resembles myth because it uses the same structural elements, but it differs from myth in content: the specific details in myth are "displaced" by more believable details.

As we have seen, Jung considers archetypes to be universal possibilities of ideas or expressions that we inherit from our ancestors. Frye considers them to be literary conventions that derive from primitive myth.

Scholars generally agree that the great strength of mythic and archetypal criticism is that it unites many different ways of looking at literature. Because mythic and archetypal criticism deals with images, characters, and narrative patterns, it has affinities with formalism. Mythic and archetypal criticism takes account of a work's author, audience, and social milieu, thus having affinities with sociological and historical criticism. Especially where influenced by Jung, mythic and archetypal approaches also have affinities with psychological criticism. Myth and archetype explain not only the social functions of literature, but also its effects on the individual psyche. Mythic and archetypal criticism thus has connections with many other critical approaches, and it can claim to avoid many of their deficiencies.

Glossary of Literary Terms

Fictional Terms

Antagonist Any force in a story that is in conflict with the ***protagonist***. An antagonist may be another person, an aspect of the physical or social environment, or a destructive element in the protagonist's own nature.

Artistic unity That condition of a successful literary work whereby all its elements work together for the achievements of its central purpose. In an artistically unified work nothing is included that is irrelevant to the central purpose, nothing is omitted that is essential to it, and the parts are arranged in the most effective order for the achievement of that purpose.

Chance The occurrence of an event that has no apparent cause in antecedent events or in predisposition of character.

Character (1) Any of the persons involved in a story. (2) The distinguishing moral qualities and personal traits of a ***character.***

Flat character A ***character*** (sense 1) whose ***character*** (sense 2) is summed up in one or two traits.

Round character A ***character*** (sense 1) whose ***character*** (sense 2) is complex and many sided.

Stock character A stereotyped character: one whose nature is familiar to us from prototypes in previous fiction.

Static character A character who is the same sort of person at the end of a story as he was at the beginning.

Dynamic (or developing) character A ***character*** (sense 1) who during the course of a story undergoes a permanent change in some aspect of his ***character*** (sense 2) or outlook.

Climax The turning point or the moment of highest tension in a plot.

Coincidence The chance concurrence of two events having a peculiar correspondence between them.

Commercial fiction Fiction written to meet the taste of a wide popular audience and relying usually on tested formulas for satisfying such taste.

Conflict A clash of actions, desires, ideas, or goals in the plot of a story. Conflict may exist between the main character and some other person or persons (man against man), between the main character and some external force—physical nature, society, or "fate" (man against environment), or between the main character and some destructive element in his own nature (man against himself).

Denouement That portion of a plot that reveals the final outcome of its conflicts or the solution of its mysteries.

Developing character See ***Character.***

Dilemma A situation in which a character must choose between two courses of action, both undesirable.

Dramatic irony See ***Irony.***

Dramatic point of view See ***Point of view.***

Dramatization The presentation of character or of emotion through the speech or action of characters rather than through exposition, analysis, or description by the author. See ***Indirect presentation.***

Dynamic character See ***Character.***

Editorializing Writing that departs from the narrative or dramatic mode and instructs the reader how to think or feel about the events of a story or the behavior of a character.

Escape literature Literature written purely for entertainment, with little or no attempt to provide insights into the true nature of human life or behavior.

Falling action That segment of the plot that comes between the climax and the conclusion.

Fantasy A kind of fiction that pictures creatures or events beyond the boundaries of known reality.

First person point of view See ***Point of view.***

Flat character See ***Character.***

Happy ending An ending in which events turn out well for a sympathetic protagonist.

Indeterminate ending An ending in which the central problem or conflict is left unresolved.

Indirect presentation of character That method of characterization in which the author shows us a character in action, compelling us to infer what he is like from what he says or does.

Interpretive literature Literature that attempts to provide valid insights into the nature of human life or behavior.

Irony A situation, or a use of language, involving some kind of incongruity or discrepancy. In general, three kinds of irony are distinguished.

Verbal irony A figure of speech in which what is said is the opposite of what is meant.

Dramatic irony An incongruity or discrepancy between what a character says and what the reader knows to be true (or between what a character perceives and what the author intends the reader to perceive.)

Irony of situation A situation in which there is an incongruity between appearance and reality, or between expectation and fulfillment, or between the actual situation and what would seem appropriate.

Limited omniscient point of view See ***Point of view.***

Moral A rule of conduct or maxim for living expressed or implied as the "point" of a literary work. Compare Theme.

Motivation The incentives or goals that, in combination with the inherent natures of characters, cause them to behave as they do. In poor fiction actions may be unmotivated, insufficiently motivated, or implausibly motivated.

Mystery An unusual set of circumstances for which the reader craves an explanation, used to create suspense.

Objective point of view See ***Point of view***.

Omniscient point of view See ***Point of view***.

Plot The sequence of incidents or events of which a story is composed.

Poeticizing Writing that uses immoderately heightened or distended language to sway the reader's feelings.

Point of view The angle of vision from which a story is told. The four basic points of view are as follows:

Omniscient point of view The author tells the story, using the third person; he knows all and is free to tell us anything, including what the characters are thinking or feeling and why they act as they do.

Limited omniscient point of view The author tells the story, using the third person, but limits himself to a complete knowledge of one character in the story and tells us only what one character thinks, feels, sees, or hears.

First person point of view The story is told by one of its characters, using the first person.

Objective (or Dramatic) point of view The author tells the story, using the third person, but limits himself to reporting what his characters say or do; he does not interpret their behavior or tell us their private thoughts or feelings.

Protagonist The central character in a story.

Quality fiction Fiction that rejects tested formulas in a attempt to give a fresh interpretation of life.

Rising action That development of plot in a story that precedes and leads up to the climax.

Round character See ***Character.***

Sentimentality Unmerited or contrived tender feeling; that quality in a story that elicits or seeks to elicits tears through an oversimplification or falsification of reality.

Setting The context in time and place in which the action of a story occurs.

Static character See ***Character.***

Stock character See ***Character.***

Surprise An unexpected turn in the development of a plot.

Surprise ending A completely unexpected revelation or turn of plot at the conclusion of a story.

Suspense That quality in a story that makes the reader eager to discover what happens next and how it will end.

Symbol Something that means more than what it is; an object, person, situation, or action that in addition to its literal meaning suggests other meanings as well.

Theme The central idea or unifying generalization implied or stated by a literary work.

Unhappy ending An ending that turns out unhappily for a sympathetic protagonist.

Verbal irony See ***Irony.***

Poetic Terms

Accent The same as stress. A syllable given more prominence in pronunciation than its neighbors is said to be more accented.

Allegory A narrative or description having a second meaning beneath the surface one.

Alliteration The repetition at close intervals of the initial consonant sounds of accented syllables or important words (for example, *m*ap-*m*oon, *k*ill-*c*ode, *pr*each-ap*pr*ove). Important words and accented syllables beginning with vowels may also be said to alliterate with each other inasmuch as they all have the same lack of an initial consonant sound.

Allusion A reference, explicit or implicit, to something in previous literature or history.

Anapest A metrical foot consisting of two unaccented syllables followed by one accented syllable (un-der-stand).

Anapestic meter A meter in which a majority of the feet are anapests.

Apostrophe A figure of speech in which someone absent or dead or something nonhuman is addressed as if it were alive and present and could reply.

Approximate rime (also known as ***imperfect rime***, ***near rime***, ***slant rime***, or ***oblique rime***). A term used for the words in a riming pattern that have some kind of sound correspondence but are not perfect rimes. See rime. Approximate rimes occur occasionally in patterns where most of the rimes are perfect, and sometimes are used systematically in place of perfect rime.

Assonance The repetition at close intervals of the vowel sounds of accented syllables or important words (for example, h*a*t-r*a*n-*a*mber, v*ei*n-m*a*de).

Ballad A fairly short narrative poem written in a songlike stanza form. Also see ***Folk ballad***.

Blank verse Unrimed iambic pentameter.

Cacophony A harsh, discordant, unpleasant-sounding choice and arrangement of sounds.

Caesura See ***Grammatical pause*** and ***Rhetorical pause***.

Connotation What a word suggests beyond its basic definition, a word's overtones of meaning.

Consonance The repetition at close intervals of the final consonant sounds of accented syllables or important words (for example, boo*k*-pla*qu*e-thi*ck*er).

Continuous form That form of a poem in which the lines follow each other without formal grouping, the only breaks being dictated by units of meaning.

Couplet Two successive lines, usually in the same meter, linked by rime.

Dactyl A metrical foot consisting of one accented syllable followed by two unaccented syllables (for example, mer-i i -i y).

Dactylic meter A meter in which a majority of the feet are dactyls. (But see ***Triple meter***.)

Denotation The basic definition or dictionary meaning of a word.

Didactic poetry Poetry having as a primary purpose to teach or preach.

Dimeter A metrical line consisting two feet.

Dipodic foot The basic foot of ***dipodic verse***, consisting (when complete) of an unaccented syllable, a lightly accented syllable, an unaccented syllable, and a heavily accented syllable, in that succession. However, dipodic verse accommodates a tremendous amount of variety.

Dipodic verse A meter in which there is a perceptible alteration between light and heavy stresses. See ***Dipodic foot***.

Double rime A rime in which the repeated vowel is in the second last syllable of the words involved (for example, politely-rightly-spritely); one form of feminine rime.

Dramatic framework The situation, whether actual or fictional, realistic or fanciful, in which an author places his or her characters in order to express the theme.

Dramatic irony See ***Irony***.

Duple meter A meter in which a majority of the feet contain two syllables. Iambic and trochaic are both duple meters.

Elegy A poem, usually formal, sustained, and meditative, expressing sorrow or lamentation over the death of someone loved or esteemed by the poet.

End rime Rimes that occur at the ends of lines.

End-stopped line A line that ends with a natural speech pause, usually marked by punctuation.

English (or ***Shakespearean***) ***sonnet*** A sonnet riming *ababcdcdefefgg*. Its content or structure ideally parallels the rime scheme, falling into three coordinate quatrains and a concluding couplet; but it is often structured, like the Italian sonnet, into octave and sestet, the principal break in thought coming at the end of the eighth line.

Euphony A smooth, pleasant-sounding choice and arrangement of sounds.

Expected rhythm The metrical expectation set up by the basic meter of a poem.

Extended figure (also known as ***sustained figure***) A figure of speech (usually metaphor, simile, personification, or apostrophe) sustained or developed through a considerable number of lines or through a whole poem.

Feminine rime A rime in which the repeated accented vowel is in either the second or third last syllable of the words involved (for example, ceiling-appealing; hurrying-scurrying).

Figurative language Language employing figures of speech; language that cannot be taken literally or only literally.

Figures of speech Broadly, any way of saying something other than the ordinary way; more narrowly a way of saying one thing and meaning another.

Fixed form Any form of poem in which the length and pattern are prescribed by previous usage or tradition, such as ***sonnet***, ***limerick***, ***villanelle***, ***haiku***, ***sestina***, and so on.

Folk ballad A narrative poem designed to be sung, composed by an anonymous author, and transmitted orally for years or generations before being written down. It has usually undergone modification through the process of oral transmission.

Foot The basic unit used in the scansion or measurement of verse. A foot usually contains one accented syllable and one or two unaccented syllables, but the ***monosyllabic foot***, the ***spondaic foot*** (***spondee***), and the ***dipodic foot*** are all modifications of this principle.

Form The external pattern or shape of a poem, describable without reference to its content, as ***continuous form***, ***stanzaic form***, ***fixed form*** (and their varieties), ***free verse***, and ***syllabicverse***. See ***Structure***.

Free verse Non-metrical verse. Poetry written in free verse is arranged in lines, may be more or less rhythmical, but has no fixed metrical pattern or expectation.

Grammatical pause (also known as ***caesura***) A pause introduced into the reading of a line by a mark of punctuation. Grammatical pauses do not affect scansion.

Haiku A three-line poem, Japanese in origin, narrowly conceived of as a fixed form in which the lines contain respectively 5, 7, and 5 syllables (in American practice this requirement is frequently dispensed with). Haiku are generally concerned with some aspect of nature and present a single image or two juxtaposed images without comment, relying on suggestion rather than on explicit statement to communicate their meaning.

Heard rhyme The actual rhythm of a metrical poem as we hear it when it is read naturally. The heard rhythm mostly conforms to but sometimes departs from or modifies the ***expected rhythm***.

Heptameter A metrical line containing seven feet.

Hexameter A metrical line containing six feet.

Hyperbole See ***Overstatement***.

Iamb A metrical foot consisting of one unaccented syllable followed by one accented syllable (for example,
◡ —
r e -hea-rse).

Iambic meter A meter in which the majority of feet are iambs. The most common English meter.

Iambic-anapestic meter A meter which freely mixes iambs and anapests, and in which it might be difficult to determine which foot prevails without actually counting.

Imagery The representation through language of sense experience.

Internal rime A rime in which one or both of the rime-words occur within the line.

Irony A situation, or use of language, involving some kind of incongruity or discrepancy. Three kinds of irony are distinguished in this book:

Verbal irony A figure of speech in which what is meant is the opposite of what is said.

Dramatic irony A device by which the author implies a different meaning from that intended by the speaker (or by a speaker) in a literary work.

Situational irony (or ***irony of situation***) A situation in which there is an incongruity between actual circumstances and those that would seem appropriate or between what is anticipated and what actually come to pass.

Italian (or ***Petrarchan***) ***sonnet*** A sonnet of an octave riming *abbaabba* and of a sestet using any arrangement of two or three additional rimes, such as *cdcdcd* or *cdecde*.

Limerick A fixed form consisting of five lines of anapestic meter, the first two trimeter, the next two dimeter, the last line trimeter, riming *aabba*; used exclusively for humorous or nonsense verse.

Masculine rime (also known as ***single rime***) A rime in which the repeated accented vowel sound is in the final syllable of the words involved (for example, dance-pants, scald-recalled).

Metaphor A figure of speech in which an implicit comparison is made between two things essentially unlike. It may take one of four forms: (1) that in which the literal term and the figurative term are both *named*; (2) that in which the literal term is *named*and the figurative term *implied*; (3) that in which the literal term is *implied* and the figurative term *named*; (4) that in which both the literal and the figurative terms are *implied*.

Meter Regularized rhythm; an arrangement of language in which the accents occur at apparently equal intervals in time.

Metonymy A figure of speech in which some significant aspect or detail of an experience is used to represent the whole experience. In this book the term ***metonymy*** is used for what are sometimes distinguished as two separate figures: ***synecdoche*** (the use of the part for the whole) and ***metonymy*** (the use of something closely related for the thing actually meant).

Metrical pause A pause that supplies the place of an expected accented syllable. Unlike ***grammatical*** and ***rhetorical pauses***, metrical pauses affect scansion.

Monometer A metrical line containing one foot.

Monosyllabic foot A foot consisting of a single accented syllable (for example, shine).

Octameter A metrical line containing eight feet.

Octave (1) An eight-line stanza. (2) The first eight lines of a sonnet, especially one structured in the manner of an Italian sonnet.

Onomatopoeia The use of words that supposedly mimic their meaning in their sound (for example, boom, click, plop).

Onomatopoetic language Language employing ***onomatopoeia***.

Overstatement (or ***hyperbole***) A figure of speech in which exaggeration is used in the service of truth.

Oxymoron A compact paradox, one in which two successive words apparently contradict each other.

Paradox A statement or situation containing apparently contradictory or incompatible elements.

Paradoxical statement (or ***verbal paradox***) A figure of speech in which an apparently self contradictory statement is nevertheless found to be true.

Paraphrase A restatement of the content of a poem designed to make its prose meaning as clear as possible.

Pentameter A metrical line containing five feet.

Personification A figure of speech in which human attributes are given to an animal, an object, or a concept.

Petrarchan sonnet See ***Italian sonnet***.

Prose Non-metrical language; the opposite of verse.

Prose meaning That part of a poem's total meaning that can be separated out and expressed through paraphrase.

Prose poem Usually a short composition having the intentions of poetry but written in prose rather than verse.

Quatrain (1) A four-line stanza. (2) A four-line division of a sonnet marked off by its rime scheme.

Refrain A repeated word, phrase, line, or group of lines, normally at some fixed position in a poem written in stanzaic form.

Rhetorical pause (also known as ***caesura***) A natural pause, unmarked by punctuation, introduced into the reading of a line by its phrasing or syntax. Rhetorical pauses do not affect scansion.

Rhetorical poetry Poetry using artificially eloquent language, that is, language too high-flown for its occasion and unfaithful to the full complexity of human experience.

Rhythm Any wavelike recurrence of motion or sound.

Rime (or ***rhyme***) The repetition of the accented vowel sound and all succeeding sounds in importantly positioned words (for example, old-cold, vane-reign, court-report, order recorder). The above definition applies to***perfect rime***and assumes that the accented vowel sounds involved are preceded by differing consonant sounds. If the preceding consonant sound is the same (for example, manse-romance, style-stile), or if there is no preceding consonant sound in either word (for example, aisle-isle, alter-altar), or if the same word is repeated in the riming position (for example, hill-hill), the words are called ***identical rimes***. Both ***perfect rimes*** and ***identical rimes*** are to be distinguished from ***approximate rimes***.

Rime scheme Any fixed pattern of rimes characterizing a whole poem or its stanzas.

Run-on line A line which has no natural speech pause as its end, allowing the sense to flow uninterruptedly into the succeeding line.

Sarcasm Bitter or cutting speech; speech intended by its speaker to give pain to the person addressed.

Satire A kind of literature that ridicules human folly or vice with the purpose of bringing about reform or of keeping others from falling into similar folly or vice.

Scansion The process of measuring verse, that is, of making accented and unaccented syllables, dividing the lines into feet, identifying the metrical pattern, and noting significant variations from that pattern.

Sentimental poetry Poetry aimed primarily at stimulating the emotions rather than at communicating experience honestly and freshly.

Sestet (1) A six-line stanza. (2) The last six lines of a sonnet structured on the Italian model.

Sestina A complex fixed form of six six-line stanzas plus an ***envoi***(or ***envoy***), using the same six end-words throughout but repeated in a different order in each stanza.

Shakespearean sonnet See ***English sonnet***.

Simile A figure of speech in which an explicit comparison is made between two things essentially unlike. The comparison is made explicit by the use of some such word or phrase as *like*, *as*, *than*, *similar to*, *resembles*, or *seems*.

Single rime See ***Masculine rime***.

Situational irony See ***Irony***.

Sonnet A fixed form of fourteen lines, normally iambic pentameter, with a rime scheme conforming to or approximating one of two main types—the ***Italian*** or the ***English***.

Spondee A metrical foot consisting of two syllables equally or almost equally accented (for example, true-blue).

Stanza A group of lines whose metrical pattern (and usually its rime scheme as well) is repeated throughout a poem.

Stanzaic form The form taken by a poem when it is written in a series of units having the same number of lines and usually other characteristics in common, such as metrical pattern or rime scheme.

Stress In this book, the same as ***Accent***.

Structure The internal organization of a poem's content. See ***Form***.

Sustained figure See ***Extended figure***.

Syllabic verse Verse measured by the number of syllables rather than the number of feet per line. Also see ***Haiku***.

Symbol A figure of speech in which something (object, person, situation, or action) means more than what it is. A symbol, in other words, may be read both literally and metaphorically.

Synecdoche A figure of speech in which a part is used for the whole. In this book it is subsumed under the term ***Metonymy***.

Tetrameter A metrical line containing four feet.

Theme The central idea of a literary work.

Tone The writer's or speaker's attitude toward his subject, his audience, or himself; the emotional coloring, or emotional meaning, of a work.

Total meaning The total experience communicated by a poem. It includes all those dimensions of experience by which a poem communicates—sensuous, emotional, imaginative, and intellectual—and it can be communicated in no other words than those of the poem itself.

Trimeter A metrical line containing three feet.

Triple meter A meter in which a majority of the feet contain three syllables. (Actually, if more than 25 percent of the feet in a poem are triple, its effect is more triple than duple, and it ought perhaps to be referred to as triple meter.) Anapestic and dactylic are both triple meter.

Triple rime A rime in which the repeated accented vowel sound is in the third last syllable of the words involved (for example, gainfully-disdainfully); one form of ***feminine rime***.

Trochaic meter A meter in which the majority of feet are trochees.

Trochee A metrical foot consisting of one accented syllable followed by one unaccented syllable (for example, bār-tĕr).

Understatement A figure of speech that consists of saying less than one means, or of saying what one means with less force than the occasion warrants.

Verbal irony See ***Irony***.

Verse Metrical language; the opposite of ***prose***.

Dramatic Terms

Absurd*, *Drama of the A type of drama, allied to comedy, radically non-realistic in both content and presentation, that emphasizes the absurdity, emptiness, or meaninglessness of life.

Aside A brief speech in which a character turns from the person he is addressing to speak directly to the audience; a dramatic device for letting the audience know what he is really thinking or feeling as opposed to what he pretends to think or feel.

Catharsis A term used by Aristotle to describe some of emotional release experienced by the audience at the end of a successive tragedy.

Chorus A group of actors speaking or chanting in unison, often while going through the steps of an elaborate formalized dance; a characteristic device of Greek drama for conveying communal or group emotion.

Comedy A type of drama, opposed to tragedy, having usually a happy ending, and emphasizing human limitation rather than human greatness.

Scornful comedy A type of comedy whose main purpose is to expose and ridicule human folly, vanity, or hypocrisy.

Romantic comedy A type of comedy whose likable and sensible main characters are placed in difficulties from which they are rescued at the end of the play, either attaining their ends or having their good fortunes restored.

Dramatic convention Any dramatic device which, though it departs from reality, is implicitly accepted by author and audience as a means of representing reality.

Farce A type of drama related to comedy but emphasizing improbable situations, violent conflicts, physical action, and coarse wit over characterization or articulated plot.

Melodrama A type of drama related to tragedy but featuring sensational incidents, emphasizing plot at the expense of characterization, relying on cruder conflicts (virtuous protagonist versus villainous antagonist), and having a happy ending in which good triumphs over evil.

Narrator In drama a character, found in some plays, who, speaking directly to the audience, introduces the action and provides a string of commentary between the dramatic scenes. He may or may not be a major character in the action itself.

Nonrealistic drama. Drama that, in content, presentation, or both, departs markedly from fidelity to the outward appearances of life.

Playwright A maker of plays.

Realistic drama Drama that attempts, in content and in presentation, to preserve the illusion of actual, everyday life.

Romantic comedy See ***Comedy***.

Scornful comedy See ***Comedy***.

Soliloquy A speech in which a character, alone on the stage, addresses himself; a soliloquy is a "thinking out loud," a dramatic means of letting an audience know a character's thoughts and feelings.

Tragedy A type of drama, opposed to comedy, in which the protagonist, a person of unusual moral or intellectual stature or outstanding abilities, suffers a fortune because of some error of judgement, excessive virtue, or flaw in his nature.

Bibliography

Bach, B. C., & Browning Gordon. *Fiction for Composition.* Scott, Foresman and Company, Glenview, Illinois, 1968

Barnet, S., Berman, M., Burto, W. & Cain, W. E. *Literature: Thinking, Reading & Writing Critically.* Second Edition, Addison Wesley Longman, Inc., 1997

Birkerts, Sven. *Instructor's Manual for Literature: The Evolving Canon.* Simon & Schuster, Inc., Needham Heights, Massachusetts, 1993

Cowles, David(ed.). *The Critical Experience: Literary Reading, Writing, and Criticism.* Kendall/Hunt Publishing Company, Iowa, 1994

Eaves, Morris, & Fischer, Michael, (ed.). *Romanticism and Contemporary Criticism.* Cornell University Press, Ithaca, New York, 1986

Encyclopedia of Literature. Merriam-Webster, Incorporated, Publishers, Springfield, Massachusetts, 1995

Frye, N., Baker, S., & Perkins G. *The Harper Handbook to Literature.* Harper & Row Publishers, Inc., New York, 1985

Holman, C. H., & Harmon, W. *A Handbook to Literature.* Fifth Edition, Macmillan Publishing Company, New York, 1986

Instructor's Resource Manual for Bowman/Daily/Hunt/Smith. *The Riverside Anthology of Literature.* Third Edition, Houghton

Mifflin Company, 1997

Kennedy, X. J., & Gioia, Dana. *Literature: An Introduction to Fiction, Poetry, and Drama*. Sixth Edition, Harper Collins College Publishers, 1995

Longman Dictionary of Contemporary English. Third Edition, Longman Group Ltd.,1995

Marsh, Nicholas. *How to Begin Studying English Literature*. Macmillan Education Ltd., 1987

Moore, Lisa, (ed.). *Instructor's Manual*to *Accompany Barnet/* Berman/Burto/Cain *Introduction to Literature*. Ele-venth Edition, Longman Publishers USA, a Division of Addison Wesley Longman, Inc., 1997

Rees, R. J. *English Literature: An Introduction for Foreign Readers*. The Macmillan Press Ltd.,1984

Roberts, E. V., & Jacobs, H. E. *Literature: An Introduction to Reading and Writing*. Second Edition, Prentice-Hall, Inc., Englewood Cliffs, New Jersey, 1989

The New American Desk Encyclopedia. Third Edition, Concord Reference Books, Inc.,1993

王先霈,王又平.文学批评术语词典.上海:上海文艺出版社,1999

赵毅衡.新批评——一种独特的形式主义文论.北京:中国社会科学出版社,1986

钱青.美国文学名著精选(下册).北京:商务印书馆,1995

魏伯·司各特,蓝仁哲译.西方文艺批评的五种模式.重庆:重庆出版社,1983